PRESUMPTION

OF GUILT

PRESUMPTION OF GUILT

RICHARD GARNER

UMBRIA PRESS

Published by Umbria Press
London SW15 5DP
www.umbriapress.co.uk

Printed and bound in Poland by Totem
www.totem.com

ISBN 978 1 910074 32 9

CHAPTER ONE

Rick Harper slowly took a handkerchief from out of his pocket. He dabbed his face with it removing the spit from where it had landed on his cheek. He sighed. He had thought it was all over by now – but there seemed to be people who still had memories of that crime four years ago. He had not recognised the woman who had spat at him but her words would remain with him for some time to come. "You ought to have been put inside for what you did – and they should have thrown away the key," she had said and had then spat at him with as much force as she could muster.

A staff member at the supermarket had run over to him. "Are you all right, sir?" he had inquired. Rick finished mopping his cheek. "Yes," he said, "don't worry."

"We'll call the police.". Two security staff surrounded the woman in an attempt to ensure she did not leave.

"No," said Rick. "No need."

"But it's an assault, sir, "the supermarket employee insisted.

"I'm sure she feels it was justified," said Rick putting the handkerchief away again.

The man looked puzzled by his response. "We have a firm policy," he began.

"I wouldn't be pressing charges if you called the police," he said. "In fact, I wouldn't be helping their investigation in any way." At that, he turned to leave the supermarket. As he approached the exit, a young lad who had witnessed the incident stared at him. "What are you looking at?" Rick asked aggressively. The lad shrugged his shoulders and Rick went outside. Once in the high street, he leaned against the wall and thought about the events of the past few minutes – the memories it had stirred.

It had been four years ago – that fateful night. In between, he had been away to university, the events of that night had delayed his start to the course but the university had been sympathetic once it appeared he had been cleared of any involvement with the case. They had allowed him to delay his course by a year – hence the fact that he had only just completed it and come back to live with his parents in the town where the crime had taken place. Indeed, it was his first visit to the supermarket since he had gone away to university. It spoke volumes about what he could expect if he stayed in the neighbourhood, he thought to himself.

He had first known about the events of that night when the police had arrived at his parents' home in Hertford the following day. A neighbour of the Welsh family had told them he had been loitering in The Close, where Jenny Welsh had lived, late that previous evening – and they had come round to question him. Ironically, just as they made their way up the driveway to his home, the telephone rang. It was Ed – a friend of his who had been at the dance the previous evening. "Have you heard?" he asked when Rick picked up the receiver.

"Heard what?"

"Jennifer Welsh is dead. She's been murdered."

"No," he said in disbelief.

"Lesley Peters, too."

At that moment, the doorbell rang. He could see through the window that it was two men – ridiculously well dressed for a Sunday afternoon, in his view. "I'm going to have to go," he said. "I think the police have arrived. I'll call you back." He put the receiver down and went to the door.

"Mr Harper? Mr Richard Harper?" said one of them.

"Yes."

"I'm Detective Chief Inspector Brett – and this is Sergeant Hales." They both produced their warrant cards. "Could we come in?" the man named Brett asked.

At that moment his mother poked her head round the living room door. "Who is it, dear?"

"It's all right, mother. I can deal with it. It's the police."

"The police?" She sounded surprised. "What do they want?"

"They want to ask me some questions. Apparently, Jennifer Welsh is dead." It was not the reaction of a guilty man, he reflected on recalling the words. "Do come in," he said to the two policemen. "We can go in here." He pointed to the dining room which led off from the hallway.

Once inside the room, Brett indicated that he and Hales would prefer to remain standing. Rick decided not to sit down, either. "How did you know she was dead?" asked Brett.

"A friend just told me. I didn't have time to go into details before you arrived."

Brett nodded. "Perhaps you'd like to now," he said.

"What?"

"Go into details."

"I don't have any."

"I think you do," said Brett. "You were at her house last night."

"I wasn't."

"You were seen hanging around outside."

"Oh, that."

"That."

"Wait a minute," said Rick. "Am I a suspect, then?"

"Everyone's a suspect until they're ruled out," said Brett.

"Shouldn't you be cautioning me, then?"

"Do you think we should?" asked Brett. "I don't think we've got to that stage yet. We're just asking questions – questions we would ask anybody. So what did you mean when you said 'oh, that'?"

Rick nodded. "I suppose I'd better explain that to you. We were leaving a dance in town – me and my friend, Tim Rathbone. Jennifer and her friend, Lesley Peters, were leaving at the same time. Jennifer invited us round for drinks. She said her parents were away and we could have the run of the place. Lesley was staying with her for the weekend."

"So did you go? I would have done. Two lovely girls on their own – and no parents in sight."

"I'll admit I was tempted," he said. "They went on ahead – and I had a chat with my friend, Tim. He didn't seem very keen so I decided to drop the idea I said goodbye to him when we reached his road and I set off for my home, which was a little further on. Suddenly, I changed my mind and decided I would take Jennifer up on her offer so I made a detour to The Close – where she lived. Once I got there, though, I couldn't remember her house number so – rather than knock people up in the middle of the night to ask where she lived – I decided to go home."

"Didn't you have a mobile so you could ring her? I thought all teenagers had one."

"I did but the battery was flat." Brett looked at him as if he didn't believe him. "It's true," he said.

"So you never went inside the house?"

"No," said Rick. "You must know that. You must have finger-printed the place."

"Our investigations at the house are still continuing," said Brett. He thought for a moment. "Tell me," he said. "Did you dance with Jennifer much that evening?"

"No," said Rick. "I was on the door. I'd helped organise the dance with the band – Jay and the Sundowners. I didn't really have time for dancing."

"So you felt you were owed some good times when the dance was over."

"If I did, I didn't get them, inspector," he said. "Now, if you have no further questions?" He walked to the door and held it open for them.

"We are finished – for now," said Brett.

"Pardon me if I say I hope we don't meet again," he said as Brett and Hales filed past him.

He opened the front door for them and watched as they walked down the pathway.

Brett turned to Hales when they reached his car. "I'd like to knock that arrogant little sod off his perch," he said. "He never asked about Jennifer – how badly was she hurt, did she suffer yet 24 hours ago you can bet your bottom dollar he was contemplating going to bed with her."

Over the next few months, Brett had made several attempts to knock that "arrogant little sod" off his perch – but to no avail. Rick brought his mind back to the present after recalling the conversation with Brett and Hales – or Brett rather; Hales had never opened his mouth as far as he could remember. Rick had taken an instant dislike to Brett – whom, he was to sum up to acquaintances, was a signed up member of the 'guilty until proven innocent'

8

brigade. He was to get to know him quite well over the next few months – being hauled into the police station for questioning at least three times, once even under police caution. Then, suddenly, it had stopped. After the third encounter, he had never heard from them again. There was no attempt to tell him that he had been ruled out of their enquiries or that he was no longer a suspect – just a gradual realisation that he was no longer top of their wanted list. The trouble was that word had already got out around the neighbourhood that he was – and nobody had let it be known to the community that he was no longer the prime suspect.

He thought to himself. He now had a first-class degree in English from a middle-ranking university and wanted to try his hand at publishing. He needed to earn enough money to set himself up in his own house or flat. Okay, his parents would probably help him out but he did not want to be beholden to them. One thing was clear. He could not stay where he was. He didn't want to undergo more encounters like the one he had had in the supermarket that day.

He strolled along the High Street to where he had parked his car. His eye alighted on an office doorway – the main tenants appeared to be a firm of solicitors but there were several buzzers denoting multiple tenancy. Over one buzzer was the words "Philip Rivers' private detective agency". He rang the buzzer. There was no reply. It was a Saturday morning, after all. Maybe the office was only open Monday to Friday. There was a number to ring. He took a note of it and – when he had returned to his car – got his mobile out of his pocket and rang it. It was on answerphone but it did give details of a mobile number to ring in emergencies. He took a note of it, resolving to ring it later in the day. It was no emergency, after all. It was four years after the murders had taken place.

He felt pleased with himself for spotting the detective agency. It was almost as if fate had drawn him to it. There was another way to stop himself becoming a target for – as he saw them – ill-informed gossips. That was to find the real murderer himself – perhaps through this private detective agency.

• • • • •

"More champagne?" Nikki asked Debra as she noticed her glass was empty.

"No," said Debra, "it makes me squiffy." She covered her glass with her hand.

"Yes, but this is a celebration," said Nikki. "We've finally got a house with a garden." Nikki had already indulged in three glasses of champagne as she and Rivers celebrated moving into their new home in Hertford. It had been a long time since their planned move from their flat in Finchley. Indeed, for a while, it had looked as if the modest income Rivers earned from his detective agency would not be enough to purchase a house with a garden in the location they had so wanted to move to. It was only when Nikki, Rivers' wife, had secured a new job as events' organiser with a major fashion firm that their financial situation had become rosy enough to make the purchase.

Meanwhile, in the garden, Rivers was deep in conversation with his journalist friend, Mark Elliott, "Will you be developing green fingers now you've got all this to attend to?" said Mark pointing out how large the garden seemed to his erstwhile neighbour in the block of flats in Finchley where Rivers had lived.

"No, I don't think so," said Rivers wistfully. "I think I'll leave that up to Nikki. She was the main motivator behind our move here."

Mark nodded. He could understand that. He knew from years of association with Rivers that the private detective was not the house-proud type. He was also the sort of a person who – when asked what type of car he had – would reply: "A red one." When asked about where he lived, he would probably reply: "in Hertford." He would then struggle to remember whether it had two or three bedrooms. Nikki, on the other hand, would remember every single detail of both the house and the garden.

"What about you, Mark? Do you ever think of moving?"

"Prunella does." Prunella was his wife and – to be truthful – their roles in their relationship were similar to those of Nikki and Rivers. As they spoke, Nikki passed by, champagne bottle in hand. "More fizz?" she asked. Mark eagerly held out his glass. "I think I'll get a beer," said Rivers.

"Honestly," said Nikki. "I think Philip would have been

happier if we'd held this housewarming party in the Dog and Partridge." It was their local pub where the landlord brewed his own ale on the premises.

"That's a good idea," said Rivers. Nikki looked at him askance. "Only joking," he said. She smiled.

"Half joking," said Mark relishing the thought of a pint of the landlord's finest ale.

The conversation was interrupted by the ringing of the doorbell. Nikki went to answer. "Francesca," she said as she recognised her new guest. "So glad you could come."

"It is Saturday," said Francesca who was accompanied by Rivers' assistant, the black former Bahamian boatman, Jo. "They do let the police go to sleep or even enjoy themselves on a Saturday."

"Not much crime about, then?" said Rivers greeting his new guest with a kiss. "I suppose I should be worried about that now I've moved the office to Hertford as well."

"Don't worry, something will turn up."

At this stage Debra, whom Rivers had taken on as his receptionist, came over to join them. "Hello, stranger," she said to Jo. Rivers looked puzzled – the two of them were supposed to be living in the same flat.

Jo looked embarrassed. "Sorry," he said. "I've been spending more time at Francesca's," he said to Rivers by way of explanation.

"Is that something else we should also be celebrating?" Rivers asked.

"Not yet," said Jo enigmatically.

It was at that moment that Rivers' mobile rang. He took it out of his pocket and looked at the number. He didn't recognise it. "I think I ought to take this," he said – moving away from the rest of his guests, "Yes?" he asked.

"Is that Mr Rivers?" said the voice on the other end of the line.

"Yes, it is."

"You don't know me – but I've got some work that I want to put your way."

"Good," said Rivers. He was not so busy that he could afford to turn anything down. "It's a bit difficult to talk at the moment."

"I want you to clear me of murder."

"Murder?" He was aware that Francesca's ears pricked up. She was standing only a few feet away from him. She was a police officer.

"Yes," said the voice.

"Have you been charged with it – the murder, I mean?"

"Only by the gossips in the community where I live – and they seem to have found me guilty."

"I see."

"Look, if you're busy, maybe I could come to your office on Monday morning and we could discuss it then?"

"If you're sure it can wait." Rivers was worried that his caller might be put off by a perceived lack of enthusiasm.

"It's waited four years. I guess two more days won't matter."

"Let me assure you I would really like to take your case on," said Rivers.

"Until Monday, then?"

"Yes," said Rivers, "but – before you ring off – what's your name?"

"Rick Harper."

"And who are you supposed to have killed?"

"Jennifer Welsh and Lesley Peters." The caller paused for a moment. "Until Monday, then?" he repeated.

"Yes."

"And thank you for agreeing to take the case on." With that, he was gone but Rivers felt sure he would turn up on Monday morning.

"Who was that?" said Francesca sidling up to Rivers,

"A man by the name of Rick Harper who wants me to clear him of murder. Ever heard of him?"

Francesca racked her brains. "No, I don't think I have. Who's he supposed to have murdered?"

"Two women – Jennifer Welsh and Lesley Peters, I think it was."

"Their names ring a bell," said Francesca, "Two teenage girls, killed a while ago."

"Four years ago, according to our Mr Harper."

"Quite possibly," said Francesca. "Before my time here. The case was never solved, as far as I can remember. It remains on the

12

back burner until new evidence comes up. It's not under active investigation, I gather."

"Well, it will be under investigation soon – by me," said Rivers.

• • ● • •

"Who could that be?" said Arthur Welsh in an irritated fashion when the doorbell rang late that Saturday afternoon.

"Only one way to find," said his wife, Sylvia. She got up from her seat and made her way over to the door. She knew that, if left to his own devices, Arthur would probably never have answered the ring. He was like that nowadays. He would just slump in front of the TV early in the morning and stay there for the most of the day – only breaking his vigil by walking to the newsagents mid-morning to get a paper. He had been crushed by the death of his daughter. There was no other way of describing it, she thought. He had retired from work – sold the business on. He had been an undertaker and Jennifer's was the last funeral he had organised. He had had no enthusiasm to carry on after that. Despite his profession, he had a reputation of being a jovial guy – quite the life and soul of the party at get-togethers. There was now no sign of that. Come to think of it, Sylvia could not remember the last time he had cracked a joke. It was hard on her, yes, but harder still on their other daughter, Anne. Jennifer had taken after her father – she was the life and soul of the party, too.

Anne was the more studious type. Indeed, she had been rewarded for her studying by gaining a place at Cambridge to read history. Four years on from her sister's death, she had just gained a first-class honours degree. Her father had smiled when he heard of her achievement but it had been up to her mother to arrange a celebration meal and – predictably – Arthur had felt too ill to attend.

All these thoughts were spinning round in her head as she went to answer the door that afternoon. The caller was Barbara Hardy, her next door neighbour – a widow who now lived on her own following the death of her husband.

"I've seen him," she said. "He's back – bold as brass."

"Who?" asked Sylvia genuinely amazed.

"Let me in and I'll tell you," she said. With that she marched past Sylvia at the door and made her way into the living room to sit opposite Arthur. Despite his depressive demeanour, he was enough of a gentleman to get up and greet her before resuming his seat.

"Barbara," he said, "what brings you over?" Any excuse to talk to somebody, I'll be bound, he thought to himself.

"I've seen him," she said again.

"She keeps saying that," said Sylvia joining them, "but so far hasn't elaborated on who it is."

"Rick Harper, of course." she said. "He was in the supermarket this lunchtime – large as life and bold as brass."

"What did he do?" asked Sylvia,

"Well, he was there. Isn't that enough? It means he's back. I told him 'you ought to be locked up for what you did'."

Arthur said nothing. He stared in front of him and just shook his head. "We can't lock him up for just going to the supermarket," said Sylvia,

"No, but they ought to at least re-open the case," said Barbara. "I've a good mind to go round to his parents and tell them they shouldn't have allowed him back."

It was at that moment that the front door opened and Anne entered the room. She could see the three of them sitting grim-faced on the sofa. "What's happened?" she asked.

"Rick Harper's back," said Sylvia. "Barbara seems to think we should take some kind of vigilante action and run him out of town."

"It's no more than he deserves," said her neighbour.

"He hasn't been charged with anything," said Anne. "He may not have done anything."

"Do you think they'd have spent so much time questioning him if they didn't think he was guilty?"

"Thinking it and proving it are two different things," said Anne.

"I don't think there's anyone else around here – apart from you – who doesn't think he's guilty," said Barbara.

"Maybe I'm the only one of us who knows him," said Anne.

Arthur waved his hand at her as if to command her to stop speaking. He cleared his throat. "Maybe some good can come of this," he said. Sylvia looked at him closely. It was the most animated she had seen him for a long time. "We can take advantage of his return to put the police on the spot and ask them what they intend doing about the case," he said. "Maybe we can get it reopened."

They sat in silence for a moment – Barbara obviously thinking that Arthur's solution was not drastic enough and Sylvia dreading what effect a reopening of the case would have on her husband. Anne, for her part, seemed largely unperturbed by the prospect of the investigation into her sister's death being stepped up again.

"I'll go down to the police station on Monday morning and see what we can do," Arthur resolved. Sylvia smiled. It promised to be the most active day of his life for quite a while, she reckoned.

• • • • •

Barbara Hardy had not been the only person in the supermarket that morning to notice Rick Harper's presence. Over in a different isle, George Brett had been shopping by himself – buying himself a modest dinner for one when he saw a woman spitting at the man who had once been his prime suspect for the murders of Jennifer Welsh and Lesley Peters.

He recognised Rick Harper immediately. He recognised Barbara Hardy, too. She had been one of the residents of The Close who had given evidence that they had seen Rick Harper loitering outside the Welsh household on the night of the murders. Brett had decided not to intervene. He was no longer in the police force – he had been forced to retire a year ago on grounds of stress. It was caused by an accumulation of events. He had suffered an assault in arresting a suspect. Then there was the car crash as a result of chasing another suspect. Being unable to solve the Welsh/Peters murders probably hadn't helped either. He had thought he was immune to such feelings but gradually a sense of panic had set in and he found himself unable to go out on operations. Within months, he had negotiated an ill-health retirement pension which had left him comfortably off but with little to do to while away his time. His health had deteriorated to the point where he could only walk with the aid of a stick. He was contemplating having to leave his first floor flat and look around for a retirement home in the neighbourhood.

He collected his thoughts as he saw Rick Harper – to his mind – strutting out of the supermarket. That was the trouble with Rick, too arrogant for his good, he recalled. The deaths of Jennifer Welsh and Lesley Peters were the low point of his police career. The only outstanding murder case he had ever been involved with and it seemed as if no-one had taken on responsibility for investigating it once he had been invalided out of the service. He resolved to do something about it and drove to the police station (he could still drive and was the owner of an automatic car) – where he was greeted by the desk sergeant.

"George," he said. "George Brett. What a sight for sore eyes."

Brett smiled. It was the kind of greeting he was used to. No-one ever remarked on how well he looked (he didn't.) Neither did anyone enquire into what was wrong with him.

"I've come to speak to someone in CID. Anyone in?"

"Just the rota detective constable. I'll buzz up for him if you like."

"Nobody left from my time, then?"

"I'm afraid not, George." The desk sergeant did as he had said and within a couple of minutes Detective Constable Gary Clarke came out to greet George. "I'll get you both cups of tea," said the desk sergeant. Gary looked at him in an annoyed fashion – which seemed to suggest he didn't want to spend longer in George's company than he had to. "Humour him," the desk sergeant whispered as he passed Gary to make the teas. "He's had forty years' service in the police force." Gary grimaced but indicated to the desk sergeant he would grant Brett a hearing.

"George Brett, ex-detective chief inspector at this station," said Brett offering his hand to Gary – who accepted the handshake.

"What can I do for you?" Gary asked.

"I don't know," confessed Brett. "It's about a murder I was investigating. Still unsolved I gather. The Jennifer Welsh case." It was funny, he thought to himself, it was always referred to as the Jennifer Welsh case – almost as if Lesley Peters had not existed. He had been as guilty as anyone of adopting that line, he reflected. It was just that there had been plenty of theories as to why someone would have wanted to do away with a good-time girl like Jennifer but people were wracking their brains as to why Lesley should have been a target. He looked at Gary Clarke to see if there was any glint of recognition in his eyes.

"Ah, yes," said Gary. "I have heard of it. It's the one big outstanding murder case in this area, I believe?"

"Small thanks to me," said Brett. "I was the investigating officer until I was forced to retire on ill health grounds."

"Yes?"

"I'm not enjoying retirement," he confessed. "I keep on thinking that there must have been things I could have done to help us solve the murder."

"I'm sorry if it's causing you trouble," said Gary, "but I really don't think there's anything I could do about that."

"You could devote some time to the case," said George. "Maybe you could catch the killer."

"How?" asked Gary.

"He's back in town. He's been away for four years but I saw him in the supermarket today."

"That would be….?" asked Gary.

"Rick Harper," said Brett. "Arrogant sod."

"How do you know he's the killer?"

"I feel it in my bones."

"Oh, great, we'll present that as our evidence to the judge, shall we? I'm sorry, but I don't think that's grounds for us reopening the investigation."

"As far as I was aware, it was never closed," said Brett.

"You know what I mean," said Gary. "It's all about priorities." He paused for a moment. "Look," he said. "I'll tell you what I'll do. I'll have a word with Detective Chief Inspector Manners when I see her on Monday morning and see what she has to say – but I don't think I can go further than that."

Brett sighed. "All right," he said reluctantly. "I wish I was a younger man," he said suddenly.

"Well, we could all wish that," said Gary. "Why?"

"Well, I would be able to do a spot of investigating myself."

Gary looked him up and down and focussed on his frail physique, "If I were you, I wouldn't try that," he said. "Leave it to Francesca."

"Francesca?"

"Detective Chief Inspector Manners."

"God," said Brett mumbling disapprovingly, "They've replaced me with a Francesca, have they?" With that, he shuffled off.

• • ● • •

"I think you'll like it here," said Rivers as he introduced Debra to their new offices in Hertford. "Solicitors downstairs if you get into trouble."

"I'm not likely to."

Rivers mentally chided himself for his choice of words. It was difficult to remember Debra had learning difficulties and took every comment at face value – she gave such an outward indication of coping with everything that came her way. "No, I know," he said. "I just meant if there ever was any time that you – or I – or Jo needed any legal help, they would be on hand."

"Sorry," said Debra.

"Don't apologise," said Rivers. He strolled over to the window. "Take away pizza on hand just across the street," he said. "Two Italian restaurants and one that specialises in fish. What more could we want – other than clients?" Debra smiled. "Reception area here," he said pointing to a desk and chair by the door. "Couple of offices off the main reception area – one for me and one for Jo – by the way where is he?"

"He stayed at Francesca's last night."

"That seems to be becoming quite a regular occurrence," said Rivers. "Are you happy with that?"

Debra looked at him quizzically. "It's nothing to do with me," she said. "It's up to him where he stays."

"I meant are you coping on your own?" Debra nodded but Rivers felt it was a topic to which he may well have to return in future. He and Nikki had taken Debra in when her closest friend and flatmate had been murdered several months ago. To give themselves more space and prepare for their move to Hertford, they had been delighted when Jo volunteered to share a flat with her – so that she was not been living on her own since the death of her flatmate. Rivers did not want to bring that up and bring back unhappy memories. He looked at Debra closely again. She showed no outward signs of any emotional difficulties and seemed to enjoy the receptionist's job he had given her.

"Well, I'd better get things ready for work," said Debra. She brought a shopping bag out from under the desk. "I just got these," she said. There was a diary and a pen and three mugs – one for each of the three people who were working there.

Rivers smiled. "There's a computer shop over the road," he said. "I suggest we go over there and get you a laptop later on this morning. I'll bring mine in from home. In the meantime, I'll just go and have a look round my office."

"It won't take you long," said Debra. She sat down on the chair behind the receptionist's desk. It swivelled. For a few moments she had fun gently rocking from side to side – but then the buzzer sounded. It took Debra by surprise. "Rivers detective agency," she said.

"I have an appointment with Mr Rivers," said a voice from the other end of the intercom.

"Come on up," said Debra pressing the buzzer to allow the caller to enter. "First floor."

Within seconds, Rick Harper had come through the door. "Right," he said on arrival, "where's the head honcho?"

"I don't think we have one of those," said Debra. "If it's the toilet you want it's between the first and second floors."

"No, I meant the head honcho – main man."

"I think I may be what you're looking for," said Rivers. "Not everybody is familiar with your jargon. I take it you wanted to see Mr Rivers – and that's me. And you are?"

"Rick Harper." He held out his hand to the private detective who accepted the handshake.

"And you want me to prove you're not a murderer?"

"That's about the size of it."

"Perhaps you might better be able to convince me to do that if you dropped the colourful language – and just concentrated on telling me the facts of the case."

"I'm sorry," said Rick. "I was nervous. I over compensated for it."

"Apology accepted. Now remember: I don't bite and neither does Debra who is busy making you a cup of tea. It's all we've got. I left the coffee at home and we haven't stocked up the office yet. We've only just moved here. Got the signs up last week and opened for business today. We have a track record of investigations, though. I've had an office in Finchley for several years but you're our first client here. Sit down. We do have chairs – as you can see."

Rick sat down. "Where do you want me to start?" he asked. Before he could, though, Debra arrived with the tea. She placed some sugar in a bowl on the table by the cups. "Thanks," said Rick.

"Why do you think you need to be cleared of murder? I looked up the Jennifer Welsh murder. Nobody's been charged. Nobody's even been questioned for the past three years or so, it seems."

"I was the main suspect in the eyes of the police," he said. "I was even interviewed under caution. I've been away for nearly four years – at university – and I've only just come back."

"Yes?"

"Somebody spat at me in the supermarket yesterday – and told me I should be locked up for what I'd done. It was my first outing in the high street since I moved back to live with my parents. It makes me worried about what will happen next. Could someone even be violent towards me?"

"Maybe it wasn't such a smart idea to move back to live with your parents. Maybe you should have moved to somewhere else and turned over a new leaf?"

"Turned over a new leaf? I haven't done anything wrong. I should be allowed to walk the streets around here free from harassment – just like anybody else."

"Sorry. Wrong phrase. But you get my drift."

"I do. Look, Mr Rivers, do you want this case or not? If you think I've brought it all on myself, then maybe you're not the right person to investigate this."

"Why do you think you became the main murder suspect?" asked Rivers.

"That's easy. I was seen wandering round outside Jennifer's home late that evening. I admitted to the police that I had been invited round by her – her parents were away. I thought it could be fun but then I couldn't remember her house number. It was too late to go knocking up other people to find it out, so I just went home."

"How did the two girls die?"

"Jennifer was punched and strangled. Lesley, the other girl in the house, was beaten to death. The police thought Jennifer was the target. They think Lesley just stumbled on the killer leaving the house – and that's why he killed her."

"He?"

Rick shrugged his shoulders. "I don't know," he said, "but it's most likely. It would have needed some force to kill Jennifer."

"The police never found any evidence that you had been in the house, did they?"

"No."

"So I repeat – why did the police make you the main suspect?"

"They had no evidence to link anyone else with the house that night." Rick then began to look a little sheepish. "Besides, I think I came across as a bit bumptious to the detective who was investigating the case."

Saints preserve me, thought Rivers. I can't think how that could have happened. He smiled. "That's as maybe," he said, "but I think it's the absence of any other suspects that's a bit worrying."

"I think there were," Rick began hesitantly.

"Then enlighten me."

"I don't know who they were but – put it this way – Jennifer had a reputation as a good time girl. When I was asked round that evening because her parents were out, I knew exactly what she meant and what would happen. I'd had a one night stand with her once before."

"Did you admit this to the police?"

"No, of course not. What do you take me for?"

A bit bumptious, thought Rivers. He declined to give voice to his thoughts, though. "So there were other men who thought they might stand a good chance of having it off with her, were there?" he asked.

"There were and there were probably previous boyfriends who wouldn't have liked the idea of her going with me."

"But you don't know who they were?"

"No," said Rick

Rivers paused for thought. "What was Lesley supposed to be doing while you were with Jennifer?" he asked.

"I was with a friend. Tim Rathbone. He was invited round too. We both discussed it after Jennifer and Lesley had left for Jennifer's home. Tim didn't fancy it."

"Did he know Jennifer's address?"

Rick seemed surprised by the question. "I don't know," he said. "He could have done."

"Do you think he could have had a change of heart and gone round later?"

"I shouldn't have thought so," said Rick. "He was a bit straight laced. Wasn't into that kind of thing."

Rivers was tempted to utter the saying "it's the quiet ones you've got to watch" but declined. After all, Rick had got into trouble for being loud and bumptious. It would have sounded like everyone was under suspicion. Which of course they were at this stage of Rivers' investigation. "I shall have to have a word with him," said Rivers.

"I'd better warn him."

"No, it's better that I catch him off guard."

"But he's a friend – not a ...." His voice tailed off.

"Suspect?" suggested Rivers. "Everyone is until I rule them out."

"This whole thing is going to be raked up again, isn't it?" said Rick adopting a concerned air.

"Of course it is," said Rivers, "if you want to be cleared in the eyes of the public of any involvement in the girls' murder."

Rick nodded. "I guess I'll just have to brace myself for that," he said.

"You will," said Rivers. "One more thing – did anyone else hear you receiving the invitation from Jennifer?"

"No, I don't think so. It was made as we were leaving the dance hall. There may have been one or two people milling around but I couldn't remember who after all this time."

"Shame," said Rivers. "Now, what I want you to do is to go away and think of all the people you knew at the dance – and their relationship with Jennifer if possible. Have a think about it today and write their names down and come back to me with it tomorrow."

"Okay," said Rick. He got up as if to go.

"By the way – my fee is £500 a week plus expenses." Rick nodded. "And just one more thing. You didn't kill her, did you?" he asked almost innocently.

A look of anger came over Rick's face. "Of course not," he said. "Why would I have come to you and asked you to reopen the case if I was guilty?"

Because you're bumptious and arrogant, according to the police, thought Rivers. You think you could blag your way out of it. He declined to give voice to the thoughts that had come to him. "No," he said, "of course you wouldn't."

• • ● • •

"Well," said Francesca as she arrived in her bedroom carrying two cups of tea. "You still here?"

Jo pretended to look around him. "Looks as if I am," he said.

She glanced at her watch. "You're also a bit late for work," she said. "First day in the new office. Bad impression."

"If I'm late, you are," said Jo defiantly.

"I'm going to be working late tonight. I've got to prepare for a court appearance. Gary Clarke is holding the fort."

"Oh, dear," said Jo. "I'd better get in. You'll need a private detective agency to cover for the police force."

"Gary's not that bad," said Francesca. "He's learning fast." She was wearing a sleek silk bathrobe which she had put on to go and make the tea. The kitchen was visible from the street. Hence the donning of the attire.

23

"Take that off and come back to bed," said Jo.

"No, Jo," she said. "A quick cup of tea and then we'd better get moving." She handed him the tea and then kissed him firmly on the mouth. "So, this is now going to be a regular occurrence, is it?"

"I'd like to think so," said Jo.

"I've been thinking," said Francesca. "We ought to be having a conversation about putting this on a more permanent footing. I don't want us to just drift into living together. I want it to be a proper commitment."

"So do I," said Jo.

"What about Debra?" asked Francesca.

"What about Debra?"

"Well, is she still frail after the death of her lodger?"

"I don't think so," said Jo. "Anyway, she's coped really well in the last few weeks when I've been over here."

"Good," said Francesca. "I do think we should explain the situation to her – and not just leave her to guess that you've moved over here. I think, though, you should continue paying the rent over there until she gets another lodger. She won't be able to afford it by herself." She began dressing as she talked to Jo and soon looked immaculate in a brown trouser suit and silver satin shirt. Jo, for his part, still sipped his tea while lying on the bed.

"I'll have a word with her tonight."

"I won't ask you for any contribution to here until you've sorted out the flat," Francesca added.

"Contribution to here?" Jo echoed nervously.

"Surely you didn't think you could just move in and not pay towards the mortgage or anything?"

"I think if you stopped after the words 'didn't think' that would be an accurate description of what's happened," said Jo, "but you're right. I'm sure we can sort things out amicably." He gave her another kiss – to which she responded amicably. Then she pushed him away. "I'm off to work," she said.

With that, she left her house. It was bigger than the flat Jo had been sharing with Debra. It had a garden which Francesca would admit to not tending properly. She and Jo had been "seeing each other" as her parents' generation would have described it for about six months. She had initially been reluctant to get involved with him because of a let-down in a previous relationship. Her partner had cheated on her. She was self-sufficient, had a good career and really liked Jo and looked forward to sharing small things with him like taking responsibility for the garden and cooking for each other. She hoped Jo had thought as deeply about their relationship as she had.

By the time these thoughts had entered her head she was in the car park at the police station. Gary Clarke was already at his desk when she reached the office.

"Good morning," said Gary.

Francesca nodded. "You've been on all weekend – anything happened?"

"Mostly quiet. Somebody's attacked one of the allotments near Hartham Common. Seems like a feud between two allotment holders – one's vegetables were straying on to the other's territory."

Francesca smiled. "I think I can leave you to deal with that," she said. "The word 'sorry' may solve that situation."

"You haven't met the allotment holders," said Gary. "There was another thing."

Francesca could tell from the sound of his voice that it was a subject he felt was a little delicate to broach with her. "Go on," she said in order to encourage him.

"Well, I had your predecessor in here on Saturday afternoon," he said. "George Brett."

"Oh, how's he?"

It wasn't the response Gary had expected and he found it difficult to answer. "Not too good – to be honest," he said. "He went on about a murder that he'd failed to solve."

"The Jennifer Welsh case?"

"Yes. How did you guess?"

"It's the only major crime in this area that's still outstanding – and I knew he was in charge of the investigation. The general consensus was that he didn't cover himself with glory over it. Rory Gleeson – the Chief Constable – said as much when he gave me a briefing on outstanding cases when I took on this job."

"He thinks we should reopen the case. Claims he can't rest easy at nights while the killer hasn't been nailed."

"It's a difficult thing to come to terms with," agreed Francesca. "Two innocent young girls slaughtered on your watch and nothing to show for weeks – maybe months – of painstaking investigation. As to reopening the case, the file has never been closed. There just haven't been any leads to investigate."

"He thinks there is one."

"Oh?"

"Rick Harper, his prime suspect, has come back to live in the area."

"And?"

"Er, that's it."

"But he's perfectly entitled to. He's done nothing wrong in the eyes of the law."

"He was attacked in the supermarket on Saturday."

"Attacked?"

"Well, somebody spat at him."

"So should we be protecting him?"

"I don't think that was what George Brett was asking for. I think he wanted us to haul him in for questioning."

"I'm sure you're right," said Francesca, "but then we're not here to do George Brett's bidding. I think we should keep an eye on the situation. Maybe have a word with Rick Harper and see if he wants protection." She thought for a moment. "Interestingly enough, I was at a party over the weekend."

"Aren't you the lucky one?" interjected Gary.

Francesca chose to ignore what he had said. "At Philip Rivers' place," she said. "He took a call while I was there from Rick Harper – asking him to investigate the murders and clear his name."

"I'm not sure George Brett would be happy with that, either."

"No, but Philip Rivers is thorough. If he finds his enquiries are leading him to believe that Rick Harper is guilty, he won't mince his words. He'll say so." She was deep in thought again, Gary noticed. "You know, that could be the best solution. The Chief Constable, I reckon, will be reluctant for us to spend time on this case while there are other pressing commitments and leads.

Philip, though, will have all the time in the world. He may well carry out a more thorough investigation than Brett did."

• • ● • •

Tim Rathbone seemed genuinely shocked when he opened the door and saw Rick Harper standing on the doormat. "Rick, I didn't know you were back from Uni," he said.

"You must be about the only person that doesn't," he said. "Word seems to have spread round like wildfire. Can I come in?"

"Well." He glanced around himself nervously. "I suppose that's all right," he said eventually. It was not exactly the kind of response you would expect from a friend, thought Rick.

"What's the matter, Tim? What are you worried about?"

"Well, I was thinking for a moment that I don't think my parents would welcome seeing you around again. They think you nearly got me in trouble – saddled me with coping with a murder investigation. They're out, though. Mum's not likely to be back until six. Dad's working and he never returns till 7.30 at the earliest."

"That's a fascinating insight into the habits of the Rathbone family," said Rick sarcastically. "I wouldn't have thought, though, that I need that long winded explanation to a simple request to come inside and have a chat with an old friend."

"Trouble is it's not simple, is it?" said Tim. "The only thing we've got in common now is our involvement in the Welsh/Peters murders."

"Which neither of us committed." Tim remained silent after this comment which prompted Rick to add: "Did we?"

"No," said Tim. "I suppose not."

"Well, if that's the best I'm going to get from you. I came to tell you I'm reopening the investigation."

"You're reopening the investigation? What do you mean?"

"I want to clear my name. I'm sick of people like you acting as if you're walking on hot bricks when I come to visit you."

"How can you reopen the investigation? Surely it's a police matter?"

"And they've long since drawn a discreet veil over the murders. No, I've hired a private detective to reopen the investigation. As I said, I want my name cleared."

"You may regret doing that."

"How? How could things be worse than they are now? People feeling free to attack me in a supermarket. I don't know what may be around the corner."

"Suppose he comes up with evidence that you were involved with the killing."

"Well, he's not going to because I wasn't. Besides, I'm paying his wages. It's not in his interests to say that I'm the guilty party."

"So he's corrupt, is he?"

"What do you mean?"

"Part of his remit is that you're not to be found guilty at the end of the day?"

"Well, no, it's not like that." Rick heaved a huge sigh. "Look, I only came round out of a spirit of friendship to warn you that the case was going to be reopened. I'm beginning to wish I hadn't bothered."

"I'm sorry," said Tim.

"Don't worry. Forget it. I'll go." He paused, though, before exiting. "Maybe the reason you don't like the idea of me reopening the case is that you've got something to hide. Maybe you were like me and you had second thoughts about going round to Jennifer's house that evening. Something happened and one of the girls – perhaps Lesley, she was the one earmarked for you – ended up dead. She was too nice. She couldn't go through sleeping with you and you lost your temper. Then you had to cover your tracks."

"Does that sound like me?" said Tim.

"No, but does it sound like me to have killed Jennifer?"

"You know what she was like. She may have taunted you with past lovers."

Rick ignored what Tim had just said. "I'd better go," he said. He got up but spoke before heading for the door. "You know, it's sad," he said. "People of our age – when we meet up after a time lapse ask each other about how was Uni, do you have any new girlfriends, what plans do you have for the future. We just accuse each other of murder." With that, he flounced out of his former friend's house.

• • • • •

"There's an Arthur Welsh for you downstairs in the front office," said Gary on answering the phone in the detectives' office.

"Did he ask to speak to me?" asked Francesca.

"No," said Gary, "he asked to speak to the person in charge of the investigation into his daughter's murder. I think it would be diplomatic if you agreed to see him."

Francesca nodded. "You're right," she said. "I'll take him into one of the interview rooms downstairs."

Gary agreed and told the desk sergeant on the other end of the line that Francesca would be coming down to see him. "Mr Welsh?" she asked on seeing an elderly man sitting in the reception area. "I'm Detective Chief Inspector Francesca Manners. Can I help you?"

"Are you in charge of the investigation into my daughter's death?"

"Yes," she said. "Would you like to come into one of our interview rooms so we can talk about it?" He nodded. She gave a glance towards the desk sergeant before ushering Arthur Welsh into the room. He interpreted it correctly and turned to one of the constables behind him. Soon the constable appeared with cups of tea for Francesca and Arthur Welsh.

"What progress have you made?" Mr Welsh asked Francesca once they were sitting down.

She should have expected that one, she thought. The plain truth, though, was that she hadn't. "The investigation is still active," she said, "but I have to admit that not of lot of information has come forward recently."

"By recently do you mean in the past four years? Be honest with me."

"I've only been here for the past twelve months and nothing has emerged during that time."

"So you've given up on the case?"

"That's not what I said," said Francesca. "We never say never."

"I've come to ask you to reopen the enquiry – give it more priority. You know Rick Harper has returned to live here. It's causing disquiet in the community."

"Is it causing you disquiet?"

"Do you mean do I think Rick Harper is guilty and therefore I couldn't bear to see him again?" Francesca nodded. "Your predecessor," Mr Welsh continued, "told me he was certain that Rick Harper did it but he just couldn't get the evidence together."

"He shouldn't have done that."

"Well, I'm glad that someone was prepared to be straight with me."

"Detectives shouldn't name a suspect to a victim until they're certain that suspect is going to be charged. It can open the doors to vigilantes."

"You think I might have gone and killed him?" Arthur Welsh was in his sixties and quite frail. Okay, he was more vulnerable than he was at the time of the killing and his health had deteriorated but a brawl between him and Rick Harper could only ever have had one outcome.

"It could be someone you talked to and passed on the information to," said Francesca. "I'm not saying it did happen. In fact, it obviously didn't but it wouldn't have been a good precedent to set. May I ask you? Do you think Rick Harper killed your daughter?"

"That's what I have been told by the police."

"But there was no evidence to connect him with Jennifer's – your – house."

"I know," said Mr Walsh quietly. "There was no evidence to connect anyone else either. Whoever did it skilfully removed all evidence of their presence."

"Whoever did it?"

"I haven't ruled out the possibility it could have been someone else."

"Good," said Francesca, "then I may have some good news for you. Someone is launching a new investigation into the murders."

"Someone?"

"A private investigator named Philip Rivers."

"Why?"

"Because someone is paying him to do it."

"Who?"

Francesca paused to clear her throat. "Rick Harper," she said. "He's anxious to clear his name, he says. Let me assure you this investigation will be no whitewash. Philip Rivers is a strong enough man to tell Rick Harper he suspects he's guilty if the evidence points that way. We will also be monitoring the investigation closely. Any new leads will be followed up."

"Well," said Mr Welsh. "I suppose that's better than nothing."

"It's early days," said Francesca. "We can't promise you that anything will emerge – but at least it does bring a fresh eye on to the proceedings."

She got up and shepherded Arthur Welsh to the exit. He seemed reluctant to go. "Thank you, inspector," he said shaking her hand.

"Can I ask you one thing? Why didn't your wife or daughter accompany you here this afternoon? I notice you're a bit frail. They could have given you a lift."

"They didn't think anything good would come of it. They think I'm obsessed. They're trying to get on with their lives."

"And you?" He ignored that question and made his way slowly out of the police station. Francesca watched him go before turning to return to her office. "That's one very sad man," she said to the desk sergeant as she passed him. Once back in her office, she noticed Gary Clarke hastily putting the telephone down as she entered. "What's going on?" she asked.

Gary decided to confess. "Sorry, private call in work time," he said. "I won't make a habit of it."

"What was it about?"

"I'm trying to find a flat in Hertford. I'm still living in the police section house."

"You poor thing," said Francesca, "I might"– she bit her lip. She was going to mention that there was a spare room in Debra's flat now Jo was leaving – but Debra and Gary had history.

Debra had been rather brutally questioned by Gary in a previous investigation. She thought they had cleared the air but reckoned it would be better to check it out with Debra first.

"You might what?" asked Gary.

"I might see if I can give you a hand. I sometimes hear of vacancies going begging."

"Thank you," said Gary. "How was Mr Welsh?" he asked changing the subject.

"He's the sort of a man you want to solve a case for because he's so fragile – and hurt," said Francesca. "I can understand how George Brett felt."

· · ● · ·

"Can I get you a drink?" Jo asked Debra that night when they were on their own together in the flat.

Debra looked at him. "Something's up," she said. "You don't normally ask me that."

"No," said Jo. "It's just that I think I've got some good news about myself but it might not be what you want to hear."

"Oh – then if I don't want to hear it don't tell me about it." It seemed a perfectly simple explanation to her.

"I have to," said Jo. "It will impact on you. Francesca and I are going to live together. It means I'll be leaving here – and potentially you'll be on your own."

"You are living together already," said Debra. "That's not new. I think I'm doing very well living on my own."

"Well, the thing is you needn't," Jo said. Francesca had told him of Gary Clarke's situation, "There is someone who might like to move in here."

"Oh. Who?"

Jo swallowed hard. "Gary Clarke," he said.

"What?" Debra spoke louder than he had ever heard her before.

"You heard," said Jo. "What do you feel about that prospect?"

"I hadn't considered it."

"Of course not."

"He can be quite nasty."

"I think he's learnt his lesson now after the roasting Francesca gave him for the way he questioned you."

"All the same – he's not like you or Mr Rivers. Why do you want someone to move in with me?"

"We weren't sure how you'd manage on your own."

"We?"

"Me and Francesca."

"I'm managing quite well at the moment."

"But the rent?" said Jo. "You wouldn't be able to pay it all."

"Oh," said Debra. "I didn't think of that." She thought for a moment. "I think I've been getting on well by myself," she eventually, "so let me manage my own affairs. There's no need for you to foist someone on me to look after me. Besides, I don't think Gary Clarke would do that. I tell you what. I know I won't be able to afford the rent on my own but let me advertise for a fellow tenant and choose whom I live with myself."

"Deal," said Jo offering his hand for her to shake. She took it.

"Now let's have that drink," she said. "You and Francesca do have something to celebrate. I'm happy for you."

Jo poured the drink. Later on that evening when Debra had gone to bed, he telephoned Francesca and told the Gary Clarke move was off. "She says she'd like to take care of things herself," he said. "I think we should let her."

CHAPTER TWO

Jo was listening to the news on the radio the following morning while at the flat he was still sharing with Debra. After telling her of his decision to move in with Francesca, he had decided to spend a last night in her company. The lead item was about a major demonstration against the Government's immigration policy. It highlighted how people who had been living in the UK for years had suddenly been removed from their homes to face deportation procedures. He could recall from his time living in Calicos Island in the Bahamas how the father of a friend of his had come over to the UK as part of the Windrush generation and had ended up being deported from the UK some forty years later because he could not satisfy the demands of Home Office officials for proof that he was in the country legally. He had lost his home, his job and – his dignity. Months later, when an apology was issued, he had decided not to go back to the UK because of unhappy memories of his deportation. He had died penniless.

"It's not right," he said to Debra as she emerged from her bedroom and went into the kitchen to make herself some breakfast. He rang Rivers at his home. "Are we busy today?" he asked.

"No, not particularly," said Rivers. "I'm planning to make a start on investigating the Jennifer Welsh case but I don't need you to help me. If anything else comes in, I'd like to hand it over to you, though."

"It's just that I've been listening to the news today and there's this major demonstration against the Government's immigration policy. I feel I'd like to be there."

"I can't see any problem with that," said Rivers. "I can always call you if I get that desperate – but you should come into our new premises as soon as possible and see the office I've set aside for you."

"Is that a gentle chide that I should have already visited it?" he asked.

"Not so gentle," replied Rivers, "but I do understand your feeling the need to go on this demonstration. What does Francesca think about your decision?"

"I haven't told her," he said. "I've been at the flat. I was telling Debra about my decision to move in with Francesca."

"Wow," said Rivers. "So it's that serious?"

"You don't mess about with a woman like Francesca."

"No," said Rivers reflecting that he had once had the idea that he would like to start a relationship with her. They had decided against it – not least because Rivers was still married to Nikki – but were still good friends. "You should tell her about going to the demonstration," he added.

"I will," said Jo, "just as soon as I've put this phone down." He was as good as his word and caught her before she left home that morning to go to the police station. He explained his decision to go on the demonstration. "You don't have any issues with that?" he asked her.

"That's a loaded question," she said. "It seems to anticipate there is just one answer that I can give."

"All right," said Jo. "What do you think of my decision?"

"I have no quarrel with it. You're not a seasoned demonstrator. I can't imagine any circumstances in which you would seek to cause trouble. Go – and go with my blessing."

"Thanks," said Jo.

• • ● • •

"Mr Rivers is not in yet," Debra told Rick Harper when he arrived at the private detective's offices that morning. "I don't expect he'll be long. Would you like to wait?"

"Yes, I will Thanks." he sat down opposite the reception desk.

"Have you got what I asked for?" said a voice coming up the stairs.

"Yes," he said. "The names of all the people I know who were at the dance."

"Good. Let me have them."

Rick Harper pulled a piece of paper out of his pocket and handed it to Rivers. "All the ones I remember are there," he said.

"Go through them with me."

Rick nodded. "Well, first there was the band. Jay and the Sundowners. Jay is the lead guitarist. He's a friend of mine. Softly spoken, quiet kind of guy. I can't imagine him ever losing his rag and killing somebody. Jimmy Atherton is the lead singer – great voice. He'll go places. I think he was on the verge of signing a professional contract. I think there was an agent there that night but I don't know his name – and presumably the agent wouldn't know anything about Jennifer because he would never have met her before. There's Steve Mayhew, the bass player, Renee Hick, the organist and Vince Williams on drums. I seem to remember Jennifer had been chatting to Jimmy Atherton earlier in the evening but I don't know what about. Jay's father – Mr Bannon – is the manager of the band. He's what you would call a wide boy." He turned to Debra and said: "I don't mean by that he was fat – he was – well, it's a silly expression anyway. He's not a boy, either."

"Don't do that," said Rivers.

"What?"

"Be patronising to Debra. Like anybody else, if she doesn't understand something, she'll ask – if, that is, she's interested in your opinions anyway."

"My opinions?" said Rick. "I'm just telling you like it is."

"She can take care of herself," intervened Debra sounding a little embittered.

There was an awkward silence for a moment before Rick carried on. "I've included a few of the ordinary dance-goers, too," he said. "There was a guy called Duncan Hamilton Very straight laced. Training to be a police officer, as far as I can recall. Quite quiet Like Jay really – except he was no fashionista. I mean, he wore a white shirt and a suit. Then there's this guy." His finger moved down the list. "Thomas Saunders. He wouldn't have been interested in Jenny. He was gay. He's been troubled, though, recently. I think he was consulting a therapist. His father is a pathologist often used by the Hertfordshire police. I don't think he could accept his son was gay but I hardly think that's relevant. As you can see I've got his address and that of Duncan Hamilton. No guarantee that they're still living in the same place, though. The address I've got for Thomas is his parents' – though if he'd any sense he would have move out by now. Duncan's address is a flat that he had after moving out of the police section house while he was training. You've got to remember I haven't been around for at least three years. A lot can happen in that time. Then there's Tim Rathbone. You know about him – he's a friend of mine." he paused for a moment. "Or I should say 'was'. I went round to his place last night. He was embarrassed to see me. We left almost accusing each other of murder."

"I thought I told you not to go and see him," said Rivers. "I wanted to take him by surprise with the information that a new investigation had been set up."

"Well, I just thought that – as he was a mate – I should tell him," said Rick.

"Mr Harper, I don't make these requests for fun," said Rivers. "I make them to give my investigation a better chance of coming up with the true version of what happened to Jennifer Welsh and – what was her name? – Lesley Peters. If you're going to take steps that could frustrate my investigation, then this is not going to work."

This time Rick Harper did look penitent. "I'm sorry, Mr Rivers," he said.

"I see there's one more name on the list."

"Yes. Stan Wightman. I think he's the only person who's ever been sweet on Lesley Peters – but I think he got dumped by her. Too many people forget Lesley died as well that night – you couldn't even remember her name a few minutes ago. Stan's a very quiet, reserved person but I think a lot of brooding goes on under the facade of a quiet man."

"Thanks," said Rivers.

"You know, when I went to see Tim Rathbone, he referred to it as the Welsh/Peters murders. He thought she was as important as Jennifer. If we had accepted Jennifer's invitation first off, I think he would have gone for Lesley while I went for Jennifer."

"I don't intend to forget that Lesley Peters was killed, too," said Rivers.

"Good," said Rick. "Well that's it. I would add that if you want to know any more about Jennifer, there's a guy you should talk to. Graham Hands. He's a disc jockey. Works for an employer that runs a pop radio station for its employees. For most of the time, Jennifer didn't mix in the same circle as me – but she did move in the Graham Hands set. He'll know more about her relationships than me."

"Thank you," said Rivers. "You've done well I've got my work cut out now."

"What should I do now?" asked Rick.

"Just wait to hear from me," he said, "but – if anything comes to mind – give me a ring. Also, if there are any more threats against you. We should probably log them with the police."

"None so far," said Rick. With that, he turned on his heels. He was just about to leave when Rivers called him again. "Yes?" he asked.

"I forgot one thing, the deposit?"

"Sorry?"

"We agreed – one week in advance and then weekly payment."

"Er, I haven't got the money on me at the moment. I'll get it by the end of the week."

"You're a student, you haven't got a job. Are you sure you can afford me?"

"Yes." The word was uttered without conviction.

"By the end of the week or this whole thing's off."

"Right."

"Bank of Mum and Dad?" Rivers asked softening the mood between the two of them.

"Something like that."

Rivers smiled and waved him goodbye. He hoped Rick would get the money by the end of the week. He was looking forward to getting his teeth in the case. He decided he would make initial enquiries before the payment.

• • ● • •

Debra was just about to clock off work for the day when the telephone rang. She thought she had better answer it – the agency still had only one investigation on their books – the Jennifer Welsh murder – and, if she had judged the conversation between Rick Harper and Rivers correctly, there was a question mark hanging over that.

"It's Jo," said the voice on the other end of the line. "Is Rivers there?"

"No, he's out."

There was silence for a moment. "Debra, you've got to help me," he said.

"Yes, Jo, of course."

"I need help. I've been arrested. You know I was on this demonstration?"

"Yes."

"Well, they kept a load of us prisoner just off Trafalgar Square. I tried to get out and have been arrested for assaulting a police officer I need a solicitor. Can you get me one?" He gave her the address of the police station. "I'm refusing to answer any more of their questions until the solicitor gets here," he said.

"There's a firm downstairs. I'll go and get them," said Debra.

"Good girl. When you've done that can you tell Rivers what's happened – and Francesca? They only allow me one telephone call."

"Of course." With that, Jo hung up and Debra imagined him being marched down a corridor into a cold, uninviting interview room much like she had been when she had been suspected of a murder some months previously – when the detective interviewing her, Gary Clarke, had been determined to trap her into a confession. In the end, she gave him what she wanted simply to get out of the room and the harassing form of questioning she was undergoing. She could not let the same thing happen to Jo. She could not conceive of him assaulting a police officer – or assaulting anyone for that matter. She breathed a deep sigh, got up from her seat behind the reception desk and made her way downstairs to the offices of Gallagher and Diamond – the solicitors who were the main tenants in the office block she worked in. There was no-one in their reception area when she got down there.

"Hello," she shouted. No-one answered. "Help," she shouted a little bit louder,

A man came out into the reception area. "How did you get in?" he asked sternly.

"I, er, I work upstairs – for the Rivers detective agency."

"Well, its 5.30," he said looking at his watch. "What do you want at this time of night?" he asked irritably.

"One of our detectives is in trouble," she said. "He needs a solicitor urgently."

"Well, I can't help. I've got loads of paperwork to get through."

"I can," said a voice behind him. It was a woman. "Go back to your desk, Stephen, if you can't help." The last few words were spoken with heavy emphasis. "I'm sorry," she said offering Debra a handshake. "Rosemary Gallagher."

"Oh. Are you the Gallagher of Gallagher and Diamond?"

"One of them," said Rosemary. The man named Stephen had now disappeared back into his office. "He's a Diamond," she said nodding back in the direction of Stephen's office," and I don't mean that to be an assessment of his character. He should have treated you with more courtesy. Anyone can see you really are worried."

"Yes. It's Jo," she said. "He's one of the detectives. He's been arrested." She took a scrap of paper from her pocket and gave Rosemary the address of the Central London police station where Jo was being held. "He was on this demonstration today – about immigration."

"Oh, what was he investigating?"

"No, he wasn't working. Just protesting. One of his friend's father in Calicos Island was wrongly deported. He felt strongly about it."

"I'd better get down there as soon as possible," said Rosemary. She went back into her office and emerged moments later with a briefcase and made her way towards the door.

"Could I come with you?"

Rosemary paused for thought. "There may be a lot of waiting around," she said.

"Yes, but he's all alone," said Debra. "It will do him good to know that there's a friendly face just a few yards away." She knew that if her flatmate Sue – who had sadly been killed – had been around on the night she was questioned by police it would have made a huge difference to her confidence.

"You're probably right," she said. "You can explain what happened to Jo along the way."

"The police tried to hold them prisoner just off Trafalgar Square."

"They call it kettling." Debra looked at her as if she had lost her marbles. "I know," said Rosemary. "It's a silly name – but that's what they call it." As they made their way to Rosemary's car, the solicitor noticed Debra had more details written on her scrap of paper. "Do you have the name of the person in charge of the case there?" she asked. Debra nodded. "Sergeant Bowers," said Rosemary reading the name off the scrap of paper. "I'll ring them and let them know we're on our way. We'll take the train. It'll take over an hour but Jo will just have to hang on."

"He will do," said Debra. "He's a very determined man."

● ● ● ● ●

Rivers had taken the time that afternoon to go and see Francesca at the police station. Before he embarked on the case, he thought he would like to know how seriously the police were taking the investigation into Jennifer Welsh's murder.

"Congratulations," he said by way of greeting when she had ushered him into her office.

"Congratulations?" she asked surprised. "What for?"

"For finally getting it together with Jo – and moving in together."

She smiled. "A relationship's either going somewhere or it's not going anywhere," she explained. "I felt Jo and I had something. I've not felt that for a long time."

"I know," said Rivers ruefully. "Anyway," he added. "That wasn't what I came for."

"No."

"The Jennifer Welsh/Lesley Peters murders. It looks as though I shall be investigating them. Rick Harper has asked me to clear his name."

"I know. I was at your party when you received the phone

call, remember? I thought then it would be too interesting an opportunity for you to turn down."

"If I get paid for it," mused Rivers.

"What?"

"Well, he's an out of work student, he's not exactly flushed with cash." Rivers halted. "But I didn't come here to tell you that. You are right. It is too interesting a case to turn down. If you think that, though, why aren't you investigating it?"

"It's four years old. Manpower. We have difficulty enough coping with what's happening today without spending time on something that was thoroughly investigated four years ago."

"Ah, but was it?"

"Off the record?" Rivers nodded to put her at ease. "George Brett, the detective who investigated it, had a breakdown a few months later and was invalided out of the force. He was assaulted – nothing to do with this case – just before his breakdown but the fact that he hadn't brought anybody to justice over the death of these two girls was weighing heavily on his mind. Still is, according to Gary Clarke."

"Gary Clarke?"

"Yes, he spoke to George over the weekend. George came in here wanting to report that Rick Harper was back in town. Seemed to think we should interview him again."

"And you thought?"

"We have nothing new to ask him. There might be a case for monitoring him for his own safety. I suspect you know he was the victim of a minor attack in a supermarket at the weekend?" Rivers nodded. "Well, that was the first time he had been seen in public for more than three years here. I gather he stayed at Uni rather than come home and see his parents while he was studying for a degree. You don't know what could be round the corner. I'm sure there are quite a few people who harbour ill feelings against him around here – although I don't think he's in any danger from the Welsh family. The mother and surviving daughter want their father to lay off the case. He came in here and I'm convinced he only wants to see justice done – even though I can't imagine him wanting to have a quiet drink with Rick Harper in the next few weeks. He's too old and infirm to be a vigilante, though."

"Good. What about the Peters family?"

Francesca swallowed. "I have to admit I don't know," she said. "They've kept themselves to themselves. Lesley was their only daughter but apart from a routine interview at the start of the case nobody seems to have bothered them. Goes with the character of the girl. She was a mousey, quiet sort. Jennifer was the gregarious one, by all accounts."

"That's the picture I get," said Rivers.

"Tell me something," said Francesca leaning forward in her chair as if she wanted to carry out a confidential conversation. "What happens if you find that Rick Harper is guilty – or at least can't clear his name?"

"I will tell him that," said Rivers, "and then face a battle to get paid for my work." he laughed. "Now you tell me something – how committed are you to carrying out a renewed investigation?"

"I'm going to wait to see what you come up with and – if you unearth any new leads – I'll investigate them."

"Quite a cushy number, then."

"You'll get mentioned in despatches if you find a lead – which I'm sure you will."

"You flatter me."

"No, not necessarily. I unflatter – if that's a word – George Brett."

"Why?"

"I said that he had a breakdown. From what I can make out, he wasn't functioning on all cylinders even before he was assaulted."

"Sounds as if I should start my enquiries with him. Do you have his address?"

Francesca fiddled around with her computer and then printed it out for Rivers. He pocketed it. "I'll be off then," he said.

"Good luck," said Francesca to the departing detective. "And I hope you get paid."

• • ● • •

"Are you sure you want to rake that all up again, darling?" said Janet Harper after her son had told her of his decision to hire a private detective to investigate anew the Jennifer Welsh murder.

"Yes," he said firmly.

"Sometimes it's best to let sleeping dogs lie," she added.

"That would be an option if the dogs were sleeping," said Rick firmly. "They're not. One of them spat at me in the supermarket – a woman I don't even know. Then Tim Rathbone, someone whom I'd always counted as a friend, looks so nervous at my arrival at his house that I could have been forgiven for thinking he thought I was going to kill him. Worse still, by the time we'd finished whatever brief conversation we'd had, we both ended up virtually accusing each other of murder."

"I'm sure it wasn't that bad," she said. "Anyhow, you've got lots of friends round here. Why not contact one or two others?"

"I haven't, mother."

"It's not been easy for us either," she carried on. "Furtive glances whenever I went shopping. 'She's the mother of that guy who killed those two girls', they seemed to be saying. We rode it out, though, your father and me. Gradually it died down."

"Can I ask you, mother, do you think I killed those two girls?"

"No, of course not, darling?"

"Do you think I should be able to walk the streets of Hertford, go into supermarkets and cinemas unimpeded? Live the life of an ordinary Hertford resident?"

"Well, yes, of course," she said. Janet seemed flustered now as if she did not know how to deal with Rick's request.

"Well, I can't," he said. "And I won't be able to until we find the person who killed Jennifer and Lesley."

"It should be the police's job," she protested.

"Oh," he said – adopting an icy tone, "And you think they're doing that job effectively, do you?"

"Well, I don't like criticising the police."

"But?"

"Well, they don't seem to have got anywhere. I'll agree with you there."

"That's because they're fixated with the idea that I did the murder – a fixation that can't be backed up by any of the facts."

"Well, you did go to that girl's house that night? Why did you do that, Richard? Why didn't you just come home?"

"Because I wanted to get my leg over."

It was a conversation stopper. Janet recoiled in embarrassment. Eventually she managed to recover some equilibrium. "I hope you didn't adopt that tone with the police," she said, "or tell them that. No wonder they thought you did it."

"Of course I didn't. I just meant to emphasise to you there's no point in going down that path. It doesn't lead anywhere. Except aggravation."

"I don't want to talk about it anymore, Richard. It's just too upsetting for words."

"Yes. It is upsetting. It's been upsetting for me for the past four years. I wish sometimes that somebody could show me some sympathy for the plight I'm in. But you can't, can you? It's all 'let it blow away, darling', 'it'll all be over soon', 'just don't mention it again and it'll be forgotten'." You don't really believe I didn't do it, do you?" At this juncture Janet started to cry. "You wish I hadn't come back from Uni, don't you? You wish I'd gone and stayed with one of those myriad of friends you think I had. Then you could have carried on with your life – ignoring those knowing looks in the supermarket and pretending you didn't have a son who was the prime suspect in a murder case."

"Cut it out, Richard. Can't you see your mother's upset?" It was the voice of his father who had just returned home from work.

"Why should she be upset?" continued Rick. "She's not the one who's been accused of being a murderer."

"What's brought all this on?" Rick's father asked him.

"I've engaged a private detective to investigate the Welsh/ Peters murders." He adopted the phrase Tim Rathbone had used to describe the crime. "But I can't afford to pay him. He wants a week's money up front."

"That's not unreasonable," said Roger Harper thoughtfully. "Is he bona fide?"

"He's got an office in the centre of town and he's got a card showing he's the member of some kind of professional association for private detectives. More than that, I don't know."

"How much is the money?"

"£500 a week – plus expenses."

Roger Harper was a stockbroker in the City of London. "Doesn't sound unreasonable," he said. "What do you think, darling?" he added, turning to his wife.

She wiped her eyes and tried to recover her composure. "I don't know. I suppose not."

"An investigation?" Roger thought aloud. "There hasn't really been one for four years. You know, listening to the two of you a moment ago made me think. There are people that are affected even more by the fact these murders have remained unsolved, the girls' parents, for instance. A new investigation could help to bring some closure to them."

"I think he is professional – this Rivers guy," said Rick to his father. "He made it clear that if he thought the evidence pointed to me again, he would not hesitate to say so."

"Good." Rick recoiled at his father's reaction. "No, I'm sorry," he said. "I didn't mean to imply that I thought it would. I meant that could be a strong pointer to getting acceptance for the investigation from all parties involved – the girls' parents, for instance. Yes, I think on balance it's a good idea."

"And you'll pay for it, dad?" Rick asked tentatively.

"Initially," he said. "Let's hope this Rivers chap comes up with some quick results, though."

"I have no doubt he will give it his top priority. Thanks, Dad." He left the room but stopped to touch his mother on the arm as he made it upstairs to his room. His father moved across the room to put his arm around her. She snuggled up to him – the tears subsiding.

"I do know it's been difficult for you," said Roger. "I can go to work. Escape. Go away and set up business deals, but you – you're in the community all the time. Ever watchful for that snub, that look of suspicion, even hatred. That's why it's wrong to put up with the current stalemate. Look at this optimistically; a fresh pair of eyes are bound to come up with some new leads."

She smiled and retained hold of his hand for a while before departing to the kitchen and pouring the two of them a drink.

• • • • •

Rosemary Gallagher arrived at the police station where Jo was being held about an hour and a half after leaving Hertford with Debra in tow. "I'd like to see Sergeant Bowers," she said as she approached the reception desk. "He's holding a client of mine."

"Would you sit down over there?" said the desk sergeant indicating a couple of empty seats. "I'll see if I can raise him."

"Do that," said Rosemary. They sat down and within a couple of minutes the desk sergeant was back again – protesting that he could not find the sergeant. "He must be on a dinner break," he said. "He doesn't have to sit here every minute of the day waiting for you to turn up when your client is being uncooperative."

"How did you know my client wasn't answering any questions?"

"Pardon?"

"I said how did you know my client wasn't answering any questions. It's not likely to be common gossip around the station. You must have just had a word with Sergeant Bowers."

"He's on a break."

"Well, in that case, I'll see my client while I'm waiting for him to return."

"I'm not sure Sergeant Bowers would like that."

"Tough," said Rosemary. "I think you'll find I have a right to see my client. I telephoned Sergeant Bowers to say I was coming. I gave him my name and here's my card to show you that I am who I say I am." She got a card out of her purse and showed it to the desk sergeant,

He gave it a perfunctory glance and then got up from his seat. "Follow me," he said grudgingly. "Your colleague will have to stay here."

"Of course," said Rosemary. "She's a friend of my client. Works for the same detective agency." Rosemary thought it would do no harm to give Debra a little status in the eyes of the police. The desk sergeant said nothing, though, and Rosemary followed him down a corridor to the cells. She gave a parting look to Debra who smiled – and motioned the thumbs up sign. This was one impressive solicitor, she thought. She would show these London cops that they could not treat her as a country bumpkin.

She settled down for a long wait – and started by trying to contact Rivers on his mobile phone. It was still on answerphone, though.

Meanwhile, the desk sergeant unlocked the door to the cell where Jo had been placed.

"Hello," said Rosemary. "I'm Rosemary Gallagher. I'm going to be representing you this evening. I work for the solicitors on the ground floor of your office in Hertford." Jo was ushered into an interview room with Rosemary following behind. When the officer closed the door she sat opposite him and took out her notebook, "So what's been happening to you?"

"I was on the immigration demonstration and thousands of us got herded into a place just off Trafalgar Square. I actually wanted to go to the toilet but the police weren't allowing anyone to leave. I argued forcefully that I should be allowed to leave. I said I had an important meeting to go to in the evening but it didn't cut any ice. We all had to stay there."

"Go on."

"I put my case strongly to leave. I think I said the place would be a mess if they continued not allowing people to go to the toilet. At one stage I argued that this was a public street and I was entitled to move along it freely. I made as if to go and then this police constable grabbed hold of me and warned me that I would face charges if I continued to try to leave. This constable then wrestled me to the floor where I was warned I would face charges of assault and handcuffed. I realised nothing would cut any ice with this guy and so just remained silent while I was bundled into a police van and brought here."

Rosemary nodded. "Were others arrested?"

"I think so," said Jo.

"What happened to them?"

"They were brought here and. I don't know what happened to them then. I guess they must be facing charges, too."

"And released on bail, too, I would assume," said Rosemary. "None of the other cells seemed occupied when I was brought here. By the way, your work colleague Debra is here. She said she thought you might find it reassuring to know that there was a friendly face just around the corner."

At that juncture the cell door opened and a plain clothes officer walked in. "I'm Detective Sergeant Bowers," he said. "Who are you?"

"Rosemary Gallagher, solicitor. This is my client." She pointed to Jo as she spoke.

"Well, we're ready to interview him again. I would advise you to make sure he's a bit more cooperative this time or we could be in for a long night."

"Thank you for that," said Rosemary, "but I don't really need your advice."

Bowers shrugged his shoulders. "Follow me," he said.

"I need another couple of minutes with my client before we start," said Rosemary.

"I told you I'm ready."

"I know you did but I'm not. It'll only take a couple of minutes." Bowers shrugged his shoulders again. "And by the way," added Rosemary, "in future it would be good if you could see your way clear to knocking on the cell door before you barge into a confidential meeting between me and my client."

"So we're going to be difficult, are we?"

"No," said Rosemary. Bowers left the room at that leaving Rosemary alone with Jo. "I just wanted to say you can answer all the police's questions this time. You won't incriminate yourself with the story you've told me. If we get into difficulties, I'll just touch your arm and then advise you on what to do as you are entitled to speak to me in private at any time."

The custody sergeant came at Rosemary's knock and they then left the cell and made their way back to reception where the sergeant was waiting to take them to the interview room. Jo spotted Debra while they were in the reception area and moved to go over and talk to her. A police constable who had accompanied them from the cell laid a restraining arm on his shoulder. Jo stopped in his tracks. "Hi Debra," said Jo. "Thanks for coming." Debra had been engrossed in conversation with two young men – both of whom looked as though they had been on the demonstration rather than serving police officers. She looked up. "Hi, Jo," she said before he and Rosemary were taken off to the interview room.

Sergeant Bowers took charge of the proceedings. Jo was warned he was facing a charge of assault arising from the demonstration. A decision as to whether to charge him would be made after the interview. There was a police constable in the room – the man whom Jo had allegedly assaulted.

"My client would like to make it clear before this interview starts that he at no stage during the demonstration assaulted anyone," Rosemary stated.

The police constable then read from a notebook that he had taken from his pocket. "Your client was one of a number of people held just outside Trafalgar Square during a demonstration over immigration on the grounds that there was a threat of violence," he said.

"Thousands," said Jo. "Not just a number."

The two policemen ignored his comment. "He then tried to leave the confined area and on being told that was not possible proceeded to try and push his way out shoving me and punching me in the chest in the process."

"No," said Jo.

"You deny this?" said Bowers intervening.

"Most certainly. I did try to get out as I wanted to go to the toilet but I was restrained. I stopped trying then – realising that rational argument would not alter my situation."

"We then ended up grappling on the floor and – perceiving that I was danger of being assaulted again – I made an arrest, handcuffing him and escorting him to a police van."

"Those are polite words to describe your constantly aggressive behaviour towards me," said Jo.

"You deny you scuffled with the officer?" said Bowers.

"I may have scuffled with him but that was because he was pulling me down on to the pavement."

"Is that all the evidence, constable?"

"Yes, sir."

"In which case I should like to apply for my client to be bailed until such time as charges are brought against him in a magistrate's court," said Rosemary.

"Noted," said Bowers, "now if you would allow us to withdraw, we shall consider the circumstances of this case." The two officers then left, leaving Rosemary and Jo on their own.

• • ● • •

"George Brett?"

The retired policeman looked curiously at the man who had just rung his doorbell. Rivers took it by the look on his face that he did not receive many day-time callers asking for him by name. "Yes," he said cautiously. "And who are you?"

"Philip Rivers, private detective. I'm investigating the murders of Jennifer Welsh and Lesley Peters. I've been hired by Rick Harper to clear his name." Brett squinted at Rivers as if sizing him up. "You'll have a job," he added. "The lad's as guilty as sin."

"And if he is I shall have no hesitation in saying so."

"You won't get your money."

"Let me worry about that." He smiled politely. "Do you think I could come in? There are a few questions I'd like to ask you."

Brett shrugged his shoulders. "I don't know what good that will do," he said.

"You must want this murder cleared up," said Rivers, "and it doesn't seem as if the police are going to give it any priority any more. I may be your only chance to get to the bottom of what happened."

"There is that," said Brett. He gave a shrug again. "You might as well come in." He led Rivers into his living room and invited him to sit down. He even offered to make him a cup of tea. Rivers thought the ice was breaking between them. He sipped his tea. "Now, what do you want to know?"

"You've always been sure that Rick Harper was guilty," Rivers began. "Why?"

"He was there."

"You had no evidence he went into Jennifer Welsh's home."

"I don't buy this thing about not knowing her address. If Jennifer had wanted him to come round that evening, she would have told him."

"You could have proved that theory one way or the other by

51

asking Tim Rathbone whether the girls gave them their address. Did you?"

Brett hesitated for a moment. "No," he said.

"Why not?"

"He would have lied to save his friend's skin."

"There's no evidence of that. So why do you think Rick Harper killed the two girls?"

"It's obvious. She changed her mind about sex and he just lost the plot."

"Bit drastic, though, isn't it – to kill her?"

"I'm not saying he meant to kill her. It could have been an accident. He lost his temper."

"He has no history of violence."

"He was the only person seen in that close that night."

"You're sure? You asked people whether they'd seen anybody else."

"Not in so many words. I asked them what they'd seen and two or three of Jennifer's neighbours said they had seen Rick Harper."

"Did you ever consider anybody else a suspect?"

"There was a young lad there. Bit of a nutter. Thomas Saunders. He'd had a bit of a breakdown but his dad's our pathologist. Asked me to go easy on the kid. Said he was going through a bad patch."

"You only suspected him because you thought he was a nutter?"

"No, he had been near Rick Harper when Jennifer Welsh invited him back to her place. He could have overheard and gone back there thinking there was going to be a party – but then again there would be no motive. Thomas Saunders was gay. He would have had no interest in Jennifer Welsh."

Rivers nodded. "I've been given a list of names of people who were there that night." He took it out of his pocket and handed it to Brett. "Duncan Hamilton, Stan Wightman, Jimmy Atherton and the other members of the band. Did you question any of them?"

"All of them, I think, if I remember rightly. You can rule out the band. They all went back to Jay the lead guitarist's house after the dance to unwind. All except Jimmy Atherton. He was offered a professional contract at the end of the evening by an agent who was there. They went off together to talk about his future."

"What was the name of the agent?"

Brett shook his head. "Can't remember." He looked at the list. "Duncan Hamilton. Nice lad. Training to be a policeman. Couldn't think of anything against him. Stan Wightman? Former boyfriend of Lesley Peters. Bit creepy. Well, not so much creepy as dull and slow-witted. I suppose he could have been angry that Lesley was inviting a boy back for the evening – if he knew about that. There was no evidence to suggest he did. Anyway, I was pretty sure it was Jennifer who was the killer's main victim. Lesley just copped it because she saw what had happened to Jennifer. I don't envy you your task. All roads lead back to Rick Harper, in my book."

"What about Tim Rathbone?"

"What about Tim Rathbone? He decided to go home to bed that night."

"Who told you that?"

"Tim Rathbone."

"Exactly," said Rivers. "Suppose he changed his mind but was a bit late and Jennifer refused to let him in."

"If he'd killed her as a result of a scuffle on the doorstep, the neighbours would have heard."

"Or she let him in and then said no. Do you not think he could have got as mad as you think Rick Harper did and killed her?"

"His mother said she heard him coming in about 11pm that night. That would have been just when the dance ended."

"And she's likely to be reliable because she's a neutral observer?"

"I don't like your attitude, Mr Rivers."

"And I'm not so sure I'm impressed by the thoroughness of your investigation."

Brett winced. "There was one more bit of information I was given during the course of my investigations," he said. "In private, mind you."

"Go on," said Rivers.

"Professor Saunders, Thomas' dad, said that Rick Harper was a bit of a bully at school. He even cuffed a boy who he thought was slacking when he took him out on a cross country run. He and Thomas went to the same school as each other."

"From school bully to cold blooded murderer is a bit of a journey," said Rivers. He thought for a moment and then asked: "Tell me, did you come across a Graham Hands during the course of your investigations?"

"No, who's he?"

"Someone who knew Jennifer and her circle of friends quite intimately. Someone who could give you the kind of information that you got from Professor Saunders about Rick Harper. Someone whom I intend to speak to as soon as possible." Rivers got up to go. "Well, I think that's all for the present. Thank you for your time."

"Thank you," said Brett. "I wish I could say it's been a pleasure meeting you but I do wish your investigation well and hope it's a success. I'd rather have somebody with a bias towards Rick Harper investigating the murder than no-one at all."

"I've told you – I don't intend to cover up any of the facts," said Rivers as he departed.

• • ● • •

"Debra, it's so good of you to come," said Jo again as he sat down next to her in the forecourt of the police station. He kissed her on the cheek – whereupon she blushed.

"It was nothing," said Debra. "I just remember how frightened I was when I was all on my own being questioned by the police last year.It made me say things I should never have said just to get away."

"And incriminating yourself in a murder case," said Jo. "Yes, I remember."

"So I thought if you knew I was here and was going to stop here it might make you feel better."

"It did," said Jo.

"So what's happened?" asked Debra.

"The police have withdrawn to consider whether to charge Jo," said Rosemary. "We're just waiting to hear what they're going to say."

Debra nodded. "I've been putting my time here to good use.

I was chatting to a couple of the protesters who were arrested at the same time as Jo. They said there were twelve of them arrested. You were the thirteenth." Jo grimaced. "They're all clubbing together to have the same solicitor representing them. They wondered whether you would want to join with them."

Jo thought for a moment and glanced at Rosemary. "It's your decision," she said. "I would warn you this is an area of law I have not specialised in. We don't get much call to represent demonstrators in Hertford."

"No, I guess not," said Jo, "but I think you did a pretty good job in there. You showed them you weren't going to put up with any bullshit."

"I seldom do," said Rosemary wryly.

"I'm also a bit worried about throwing my lot in with the other twelve," he said. "Don't get me wrong – I'm glad I joined the demonstration; the more the better. But I got the feeling they were expecting trouble and quite welcomed it as a chance to take a political stand against the police tactics. In my case, it's a bit simpler. It's just that I didn't hit the police officer I'm accused of assaulting."

"And I think even with my limited knowledge of proceedings in these kind of cases, our firm can defend you on that."

At that moment Sergeant Bowers and the police constable who claimed Jo had assaulted him emerged from the depths of the police station.

"Mr...." Sergeant Bowers looked at his notebook."..... Rawlins Clifford, we're ready to see you now."

"Rawlins Clifford?" said Debra surprised.

"It's a long story," said Jo. "I prefer just to be known as Jo. Rawlins and Clifford are my parents' surnames. I didn't know which one to choose for my passport and they weren't around to help me."

"It does make you sound like the product of a minor public school," said Rosemary. "It enhances the public image."

Jo looked genuinely surprised. "I never thought my two surnames would end up helping me," he said. So saying they left Debra in the reception area and followed the two policemen to the interview room.

"One thing," said Bowers, "we forgot take an address for you beforehand. Could you oblige?"

Jo nodded and gave them Francesca's address without thinking about it. After all, from this evening, he would be living there. There was no point in giving them the address of the flat he had been sharing with Debra.

Bowers nodded. "We are of the opinion that we have enough evidence to charge you with assaulting a police officer. You will be released on police bail seeing as you are of previous good character and not thought to be a flight risk," said Bowers. "A final decision on whether to charge you will be communicated to you as soon as possible. Have you anything to say?"

"Nothing," said Jo, "except for the fact that your constable knows very well that I did not assault him."

"I'll take it you'll be pleading not guilty, then."

"You take it correctly and if there's any justice in this world – that will be an end of the matter and this lying scumbag." Rosemary laid a restraining hand on his shoulder. Jo nodded as if understanding why she felt the need to restrain him.

"If you could show a little civility towards my constable," said Bowers.

"I'll be civil towards him if he'll be civil towards me – and tell you I didn't do it."

"This is not the forum to discuss this matter," said Bowers. "I suggest we adjourn now. Our differences may be resolved in court."

"What a good idea," said Jo sarcastically.

● ● ● ● ●

Rivers glanced at his watch. It was early evening. Probably a good time to catch the Welsh family in, he thought. He knocked on the door and a woman who looked as if she was in her twenties answered the door.

"You must be Anne Welsh," said Rivers. She was immensely attractive. That was Rivers first thought. More attractive than her sister, Jennifer, who – according to photographs he had seen of her – seemed to be suffering weight-wise from the excesses of party life. Anne had the kind of features that Rivers would have described as striking rather than beautiful. She was wearing a grey trouser suit – as if she had not changed out of working attire.

"That's not a difficult conclusion to come to," said Anne. "There is only one person of my age living in this house. "And you are?"

"Philip Rivers – private detective." He showed her his card.

At this stage her father, Arthur, emerged behind her. "Let the man in, Anne," he said. "We need to talk to him."

Anne showed Rivers into the living room and bade him sit down. "Can I start by offering my condolences to you over the death of your daughter?" he began.

"Thank you, Mr Rivers, but that was four years ago," said Arthur Welsh.

"I've...."

"We know why you're here," Arthur said, cutting in. "The police have told us that you're conducting an investigation into Jennifer's murder at the behest of Rick Harper, I believe, who wants you to prove him innocent. A tough task, I would think."

"So everybody seems to think."

"Let me say this, Mr Rivers," Arthur continued. "I hold no brief for Rick Harper. If he's guilty, I hope you help them lock him up and throw away the key," By this time, his wife Sylvia had joined them in the living room. She slipped her hand into her husband's as if to offer him support. Anne just stood there passively – not reacting to what her father had been saying.

"If he isn't, though," he went on, "I have no wish to see an innocent man hounded for a crime he has not committed."

"May I ask you what your feelings are about the case?"

"I received the courtesy of several briefings from Detective Chief Inspector Brett while he was investigating the case. I think you'll know, therefore, what my erstwhile conclusions are. Over the last four years, Mr Rivers, I haven't had that much peace. My wife and daughter think I should let it go." He paused. "I can't."

Rivers was aware of Sylvia squeezing her husband's hand

again. Anne also moved across the room to place a hand on his shoulder.

"This is a difficult question," said Rivers, "but I wonder if you could paint a picture of the kind of girl that Jennifer was."

"She wasn't like me," said Anne – the first member of the family to volunteer any information. "I've been at university studying for a degree. My studies have always taken priority over my private life – more so since Jennifer's death. Jennifer would never have turned down an invite to a party because she had some studies to complete."

"Who was her closest friend?"

"As parents you never really get to know the answer to that question," said Sylvia. "She had been going out with this policeman, trainee policeman for a while."

"Duncan Hamilton?"

"I think that was the name." Anne nodded assent.

"Then there was that singer – what was his name? – Jimmy Atherton. Most unsuitable."

"Mother," said Anne reproachfully.

"He was an invalid. You don't want to get yourself saddled with that at such an early stage of your life."

"He walked with the aid of a stick because of an injury he's suffered early on in his life," said Anne, "and he was black." She smiled at herself. "Still is, I expect."

"That was never an issue," said Sylvia.

"Of course not, mother," said Anne in a tone that denoted she thought it was. "He was quite a charismatic guy. I went to a couple of the dances that he was performing at – when I managed to drag myself away from my studies."

"How would you describe their relationship?"

There was silence from the Welsh family. Eventually Anne piped up. "Friendly," she said. Rivers realised it was embarrassing for them to talk about their daughter's personal life. The parents wanted to preserve as pristine an image of her as was possible. Best for him to wait to see this Graham Hands fellow to get more precise information on that score. "That night," he said. "Where were you?"

"We went to visit some friends in Chislehurst for the weekend," said Sylvia. "We left Jennifer and Anne alone in the house."

"And her decision to invite two boys back – would that have had your blessing?"

"We weren't in a position to bless it or not bless it," said Arthur intervening for the first time. "Obviously we wouldn't have approved of it if we had – but we didn't know about it."

"And Lesley Peters was staying for the weekend?"

"Oh, that was all agreed beforehand," said Sylvia, "We were quite pleased, actually. Lesley was such a sensible sort. We thought." She suddenly stopped speaking.

"What Mother wants to say is that they thought Lesley would have a restraining influence on any of Jenny's excesses," said Anne.

"No, dear," said Sylvia, obviously upset that a less than perfect image of her deceased daughter was now being given to the detective.

"Do you think that would have been the case?" Rivers asked Anne.

"Jennifer was the dominant character of the two."

Rivers nodded. "I'm sorry if this sounds too cliched," he went on looking at Anne, "but where were you on the night of the crime?"

"I stayed with friends. I went to a concert at the Royal Albert Hall with two of my girlfriends from university."

"Did Jennifer know you weren't coming back?"

"I don't think I actually told her." Rivers noted that she looked a little shifty in answering this question and resolved to take it up with her at some later date when her parents were not present.

"Will that be all, Mr Rivers?" asked Arthur as a gap emerged in conversation.

"I think so – for the present," said the private detective.

"I'll show you out," said Anne. She ushered Rivers to the door. "I hope you'll get to the bottom of this," she said as she reached the doorstep. "Too many people have suffered for too long as a result of Jennifer's murder."

"You mean your father?" asked Rivers.

"Yes and Rick Harper." Then she mumbled quietly to herself.

"If he didn't do it."

"Which you believe to be the case," Rivers suggested.

"It doesn't matter what I think," she replied.

I think it does, Rivers thought to himself. After all, if you are in a family where you are constantly being bombarded with propaganda suggesting Rick Harper is guilty of murdering your sister, it takes a strong person to resist that tide.

• • ● • •

"Jo?" said Francesca. "What is it?"

She could see from the look on his face that something was troubling him. "Didn't you get Debra's messages?" he asked.

"No, I've been up to my eyes in it. The Chief Constable was giving a pep talk to the troops tonight."

"Oh, good. I hope he told them not to arrest people just because they're black."

"What's wrong?" Francesca asked.

"I have been arrested – and it is just because I'm black. I'm going to be charged with assaulting a white police officer."

"Oh, my goodness. Oh, I'm sorry, Jo. I would have been in touch sooner if I'd realised."

"I know," he said softening his position. "It's not the ideal way to celebrate our first night of living under the same roof, is it?"

"No," said Francesca agreeing. "Do you want me to ferret around tomorrow morning and see what I can find out?"

"I don't think there's much to find out. The police officer lied about the assault. End of story."

"I could see if I could find out anything about the officer concerned," said Francesca.

"It might help my defence if you discovered he was a mad racist," said Jo, "but other than that."

"You could probably do with a drink," said Francesca. "I did go out and get some champagne to celebrate our first official night together in our own home – but it hardly seems appropriate now."

"No," said Jo. "A scotch and ice would be more suitable."

Francesca smiled. She kissed him on the lips. "Coming up," she said. "I'll stick with wine, though. Scotch isn't really my poison. Or rather it would be if I let it." She went into the kitchen to prepare the drinks – whereupon Jo's mobile went off. It was Rivers.

"I've just picked up these messages from Debra," he said, "What's happened?"

"I'm likely to be charged with assaulting a police officer."

"Oh my God."

"I didn't do it."

"No, of course you didn't," said Rivers. "I know you well enough to know that. Have you got a good brief?"

"Rosemary Gallagher."

"Gallagher? Where do I know that name from?"

"From walking into the office every morning. They're on the ground floor."

"Yes, of course. I wouldn't think she specialised in these sorts of cases. I assume the charge stemmed from the demonstration?"

"No, I just went and punched a police officer's lights out on the way home for fun," said Jo sarcastically. "Yes, of course it did. But she's good, really good."

"Okay," said Rivers. "Look, I've had a busy evening – not as hard as yours, I must admit – but I'd like to go home to rest – and we'll have a chat about this in the morning."

Rivers put his mobile phone back in his pocket. He reflected on what Jo had just told him. If Jo was convicted, it would be difficult to sustain keeping a private detective with a conviction for assaulting a police officer on the payroll. At the very least the association that covered private detectives could revoke Jo's membership. At the very worst it could revoke recognition of the agency if he kept him on. He didn't want to tell Jo that – and burden him with further worries – but it was an issue that might have to be faced in future.

Jo, too, realised that the discussions they were going to have about the case the following morning were not necessarily going to be just a cosy chat. He realised there could be implications if a conviction followed. He found it difficult to get to sleep that night – his first official night staying with Francesca. It did not help that, after drinking her glass of wine, she went out like a light.

• • ● • •

Debra arrived home to be followed quickly by a knock at the door. It was Nikki. "Hi," she said. "I've been deserted tonight. I just thought I'd come and see how you were making out on your own."

"Much better than Jo has done on his first night of living at Francesca's," she said. She explained to Nikki what had happened.

"Oh, that's awful," said Nikki. "I wish there was something we could do."

"Well, there isn't."

"Anyhow, I placed an advert for a flatmate for you in the local paper. We've already had four replies."

"Oh." Debra was not sure if she wanted this to happen too quickly. "I'd be all right on my own for a few weeks," she said.

"They probably won't want to move in immediately – and you do need someone to help you with the rent."

"I suppose so" said Debra grudgingly.

"Anyhow, I thought you might like to look at the names and we could arrange a viewing. You'll recognise one of them."

Debra took the piece of paper on which Nikki had written the names. The first was a solicitor who had just started working in Hertford – ironically with Gallagher and Diamond. She had given Rosemary Gallagher as a referee. The second was a teacher, also a woman, who had just started working at a local primary school. The third was a male student who had been studying at the local university for a couple of years and now wanted to move out of student accommodation. It was the fourth name that caught her eye. Gary Clarke – Francesca's number two.

"Oh, my goodness," said Debra. "I don't really want to end up with him."

"You don't have to," said Nikki. "We'll scrub him off the list."

"No," said Debra – a mischievous smile forming on her face. "I would like to see his reaction when he realises it's me that he would have to share with."

"Okay, I'll fix up appointments for Saturday."

CHAPTER THREE

"Hi, hello, how are you?"

Rivers knew immediately he was in the company of a disc jockey – simply by Graham Hands' choice of words in greeting him. "I'm fine," he said and then added – getting into the spirit of things: "Really good you could spare the time to see me."

"No probs," said the DJ with a dismissive wave of his hand. "Would you like to see round the studio?"

Hands worked in a radio station run by one of the country's leading supermarkets. His job was to play music for its employees to make them happier in their work. He read out requests for them – helped them celebrate their birthdays, marriages, engagements and even adopting new pets.

"We have all the music at the press of a button," said the DJ. "The records we'll be playing have all been lined up by the studio staff. We're not on the air yet. My show starts in half an hour's time."

"Great," said Rivers.

"You might think it is small fry to be playing to supermarket employees – but the customers can hear it, too. It's piped all over the country to every outlet."

"Amazing," said Rivers. He paused. "I don't want to press you but you said you were on the air in half an hour. I wonder if it would be best if we started talking about Jennifer Welsh."

Hands nodded. "Yes," he said. "It was very sad."

"Very," said Rivers. "People I have spoken to – Rick Harper, in particular – said you knew her well."

"She was part of our set," said Hands. "Rick wasn't really. Our set was mainly people involved in the music scene."

"Jennifer wasn't," Rivers intervened to say.

"No, but she was one of the hangers on – in the nicest sort of way. We had quite a few girls who followed us round from party to party."

"Was she involved with anyone at the time of her death?"

"You never really knew whether Jennifer was involved with anyone," the DJ said. "She was a kind of free spirit. I think most people in the set would have had a thing about her. In most cases, it would have been harmless snogging."

"But not all." Rivers was sizing up the DJ. He wondered what his motive was for being helpful. After all, it would do his image no good to be seen to have been involved with a girl who was murdered. At first Rivers had thought he oozed insincerity. He was wearing a flowered shirt outside tapered white trousers. His hair was immaculately coiffured – just long enough to touch his collar. A smile never seemed to leave his lips. He did, however, seem to be providing answers for Rivers' questions. Maybe, just maybe, there was a touch of sadness over Jennifer's death and he did genuinely want to see her killer brought to justice.

"Not all, no," said Hands. "There was this trainee policeman."

"Duncan Hamilton?"

"Yes," said Hands. "I grew up with him. I brought him along to some of the parties. I thought he needed to enjoy himself. He'd led a sheltered life. Well, he had a real fling with her but she eventually decided he was too boring. Which he was, really. She dumped him."

"How did he take it?"

"He was morose."

"But still kept coming along to parties and dances where she would be?"

"The party that night. It was more Rick's scene than ours. I wasn't there. Duncan was. He'd dropped out of our crowd and started hanging around with guys like Rick. I was surprised, as a matter of fact, that Jennifer had gone to that dance. Still, she had that girl Lesley staying with her for the weekend. It was more her scene."

"Interesting," said Rivers.

"Oh?"

"Well, I sort of got the impression that Jennifer was the main decision maker in their friendship. Not Lesley."

"That would be true, as a rule." Hands paused for a moment. "I don't think we had anything on that night. I seem to remember

I went to see a film. Can't remember what I saw. It was four years ago. It may have been 'Mamma Mia Two'."

"Any other relationships of note?"

"Yes," said Hands. "Jimmy Atherton The singer with the band that night. There the boot was on the other foot. Jennifer had quite a crush on him but he wanted to portray himself as a single man and available. Thought his records would sell better."

"His records?"

"He signed a contract that night with an agent, Peter Aymes, who promised he could get him a deal with a record company. He was always aiming for the big time – and trying to develop an image that would help him succeed once he got there."

"So he would have dumped her?"

"Nothing so crude," said Hands. "No, he would have ignored her in the hope that she would either go away – or allow him to make her his bit on the side."

"And did he succeed – in the latter?"

"I would think so. There's not a lot that he touched that didn't come off." Rivers looked askance at his choice of words. "I guess I do mean that literally," said Hands – a smile forming on his lips. "She had a fling with a couple of other members of the band. Not Jay – he was a brilliant guitarist but a bit shy when it came to developing relationships. Nor Renee, the organist. He kept himself to himself. He would have walked away." Hands smiled again at this illusion to the one time hit record by the Four Tops.

"Were you surprised when Rick became the prime suspect?"

"Yes."

"Why?"

"Because he didn't do it."

"How do you know that?"

"Because anyone who knows Rick would know that he didn't do it. He's not got a violent bone in his body. Besides, what's the motive? Duncan's got one – he wouldn't like her flirting with another guy. Jimmy's got one – he would have hated it if she had threatened to go public about their relationship. Not Rick, though, He might have liked a one night stand with her but what's the point of killing her over that?"

"Did you offer these words of wisdom to George Brett, the officer in charge of the case?"

"I never saw him," he said, "or let me say – he never came to see me. I think he was fixated with the idea that Rick had killed Jennifer. He was wrong, though." Hands glanced at his watch. "I have to be on air in five minutes," he said, "and the studio like me to concentrate on my show for a few minutes before that."

Rivers nodded. "You've been most helpful," he said.

"If I can be of any further assistance," said Hands. "We DJ's often get a bad press for being shallow – but I would really like to see somebody put away for Jennifer's murder and you seem the best hope of that happening."

Rivers smiled as he made his way out of the studio. Graham Hands had convinced him that he was genuine in wanting to help him with his investigation. Further questions did emerge in his mind. Had Hands himself ever had a relationship with Jennifer, for instance? They would have to wait for another time, though. As he left the studio, he heard Hands starting his show. "Hi, hello, how are you, this is Graham Hands with another bumper three-hour show of your requests and favourite music. Here's one to start us off today – 'Walk Away Renee' by the Four Tops."

Had he made a last-minute change to the running order? wondered Rivers.

• • ● • •

"You do realise the sensitivity of this case?" Bowers asked PC Enderby, the policeman who had accused Jo of assaulting him. "Thousands of people were gathered in Trafalgar Square to protest about the treatment of – mainly – black people by the authorities and you have to go and nick one of them with, as far as I can see, no further evidence to back you up?"

"He assaulted me, sir," protested the PC.

"So you say – but we've looked through all the CCTV of that day and it seems as if your kettling arrangements took place off camera."

"They weren't my kettling arrangements, sir."

"No, but all we've got is some blurred images of what happened. They don't seem to have penetrated the area you were in. We've asked those present to send in any selfies and videos of what went on – but they're more likely to send them in to the defence and catch us with our knickers down rather than help the police with their enquiries."

"Are you considering dropping the case, then, sir?"

"No, I'm not. I've put a file up to the Crown Prosecution Service recommending we charge him." He looked down at his papers and saw the name Rawlins Clifford staring out at him. "Posh boy with assault but I wish – I do bloody wish – we had just one policeman corroborating your version of events."

"We do, sir."

"We do?"

"PC Luke Boatman, sir."

"Why hasn't he come forward before today?"

"He's been off, sir, since the day of the demonstration. He's only back today. He'll corroborate my version of events."

"How do you know?"

"He was standing next to me."

"And?"

"And he saw things the way I saw them."

"You mean, you told him what to say."

"No, sir. He was just asking me what had happened to the guy who attacked me and I said – as far as I knew – we were planning to charge him with assault."

"And you'll admit to this element of collusion when it comes up in court?"

"It wasn't collusion, sir."

"I'm sure it wasn't but you mustn't admit to talking to him before he came forward with his version of events. The defence would have a field day."

"He is going to approach you independently of me with his version of events. I will have nothing to do with that process. And with any luck it will help us put that black guy away."

Bowers narrowed his eyes. "You see, Enderby, it's comments like that that worry me about you," he said. "If it had been a white guy that had attacked you, would you tell me you would take great pleasure in seeing that white guy put away."

"I'm sorry, sir. I only meant it as a means of identification."

Bowers nodded. "Is there anything I should know about your past?" he asked.

"What do you mean?"

"Have you had any complaints laid against you by ethnic minorities about your treatment of them?"

"No, sir. You can look that up on my file."

"I will. And Boatman?"

"I don't think so, sir. I didn't think to ask him."

"It could be the tipping point for the CPS. Corroboration. OK, constable, you can go now."

No sooner had Enderby left the room than Bowers telephoned down to the desk sergeant. "Could you ask PC Boatman to come up to my office?"

"Yes, sir." Within minutes, the PC was knocking at the door.

"Come in," said Detective Sergeant Bowers. "I was told you wanted to see me."

"Yes, sir." Boatman seemed surprised. "I was planning on coming and seeing you."

"Well, you're here now. Why?"

"I wanted to give my account of the incident on the night of the immigration demonstration when PC Enderby was assaulted by a demonstrator."

"A black demonstrator?"

"Yes, sir," Boatman looked uncomfortable.

"Go on."

"Well, PC Enderby explained to him that no-one was allowed out of the area but he got annoyed and protested he needed to go to the toilet and had to attend a meeting. He seemed to be using any excuse to get out of the area and PC Enderby just repeated that this would not be possible – whereupon the man, I don't have his name, shoved PC Enderby in the chest and tried to push past him. PC Enderby told him to stop but he didn't and shoved PC Enderby to the ground whereupon they scuffled and PC Enderby cautioned him he would face arrest and handcuffed him."

"And you've taken two days to come up with this information because….?"

"Because I've been off duty. I didn't realise my evidence would be needed. I thought PC Enderby's evidence would be enough to get the man charged."

"But after speaking to PC Enderby you realised it would not be and decided belatedly to come forward."

"I won't deny speaking to PC Enderby, sir, but I was planning to come forward to the investigating officer and ask if further evidence was needed."

"Which is the right answer," said Bowers. "I'm impressed by your evidence, constable. Firstly, it was presented without any mention of the protestor's race. Secondly, you were honest enough to admit you had spoken to PC Enderby even if that could be used to discredit your testimony."

"Thank you, sir."

"I'll forward your evidence to the Crown Prosecution Service if you give me a written statement as soon as possible and – one thing which is imperative – no mention of any conversation with PC Enderby if you do have to go to court and give evidence."

"No, sir."

• • • • •

"Any news?" Rivers asked Jo as he arrived for work that day.

"No," said Jo. He realised Rivers was referring to the question of whether he had been charged over the allegation by PC Enderby that Jo had assaulted him. What other news could there be in his life? The fact he had moved in with Francesca – possibly one of the most monumental decisions in his life? No, that was insignificant – at least in Rivers' eyes.

"I want to reassure you that I'm sure you didn't do it," said Rivers.

"I feel a but coming."

"Yes," said Rivers. "I'm afraid there is. I can't put it softly to you. If you are convicted, the agency would stand to lose its recognition if we kept you on."

"You'd have to let me go – as the phrase goes."

"Yes."

"And I'd have to go back to Calicos because I doubt if I could find alternative employment here."

"I hope it won't come to that."

"And that would mean an end to my relationship with Francesca. A high flying detective chief inspector wouldn't want to give up her job. All she could do on Calicos would be laze on the beach."

"You're being unduly pessimistic," said Rivers. "I was going to say 'innocent until proven guilty'. I won't suspend you if you are charged."

"That's decent of you." Rivers detected a note of sarcasm in Jo's voice.

"And the agency will pay your legal fees. We'll fund an appeal if that's what it takes."

Jo momentarily picked himself up and jettisoned the aura of gloom that had seemed to surround him. "You'd do that?" he said "I wouldn't have thought we'd had the funds to do that."

"Nikki is earning good money. She can subsidise me for a while if it becomes necessary. Besides we're earning good money from this Rick Harper case."

"Thank you," said Jo.

"Don't thank me," said Rivers. "I hope we don't have to fund an appeal. If there's any justice in the world you'll get off any charge – if you face one."

"That's it, though," said Jo. "There isn't any justice in this world when it comes to black people. We're singled out by the police as troublemakers, cop charges when we're innocent, probably face prejudice from magistrates."

"I know it seems bad," he said, "but justice can sometimes triumph. Let's not get despondent until we've got something to be despondent about. I'm sure Francesca will stand up for you."

"Oh, yes. I'm sure she will support me. Trouble is there's fuck all she can do."

"I'm going to make you take your mind off things," said Rivers. "The Harper case."

"Yes."

"I think we need to interview the parents of Lesley Peters. Too many people seem to forget she was murdered too. I've been to see the Welsh family so I think I should see the Peters family, too. Could you go and interview members of the band – Jay and the Sundowners? Two of them had an affair with Jennifer – the bass guitarist and the drummer. Oh, and pay special attention to the organist Renee. I had a kind of cryptic message from the disc jockey Graham Hands that he may know something about the murders – but he would be reluctant to admit it."

"What?"

"I don't know. It sounds silly but – as I left his studio – he started playing the record 'Walk Away Renee' and – earlier – he said that's exactly what Renee would have done."

Jo's mood seemed to have lightened as a result of talking about the case. It was almost as if the possibility of the assault charge was not hanging over his head, thought Rivers.

● ● ● ● ●

Rick woke up in a cold sweat that morning. He had been screaming just beforehand and sat up in bed to see the anxious face of his mother beaming down upon him.

"What is it, darling?" she asked.

He stared blankly ahead of him and attempted to regain his composure. "Oh, nothing," he said.

"It didn't sound like nothing," his mother insisted. "You were screaming."

"It was a dream. Just a dream. You shouldn't really pay any attention to dreams, should you?"

"Sometimes it might help to talk about them. They can sometimes mean something or focus on something we're worried about."

Rick still looked a little shaken. He had not quite come to that morning and was still ruminating about what he had dreamt. He started feeling a sudden urge to confide in someone. He stopped in his tracks, though. What earthly good would that do he thought to himself. How could he tell his mother that he had been dreaming that he had entered Jennifer's house that night and was just about to deliver a blow to her head when he had awoken from his slumbers screaming. No, he thought to himself, best not to admit it to anybody. It would only sow doubts in her mind as to his innocence. "Don't worry, mother," he said. "It's all right now. It's probably raking up that murder again. That's what's done it."

"I told you that you should have let sleeping dogs lie," she said to him. "It's not doing you any good. All the strain. I do hope this Rivers character comes up with something soon and we can put it all to rest."

"It's not going to be as simple as that," said Rick. He gathered himself. "Now, mother, if you don't mind, it's only six o'clock in the morning. I think I should try and get a bit more sleep."

"Well, if you're sure?" Her voice tailed off.

"I am sure," he said. He was also sure that he would not be able to get back to sleep again. The vividness of the dream was still tormenting him. As he lay there in bed, he started turning things over in his mind. Did the dream mean anything? Was it trying to tell him that – contrary to his recollection – he had been in Jennifer's room that night and that he had brought his hand down to hit her for some reason? The dream did not give him any clue as to why he would have wanted to hit her. Just that he did. Should he tell Rivers about the dream he wondered? After all, the detective was looking for any information – no matter whether it reflected well or badly on him. No, he thought. He should not. The dream didn't provide any evidence one way or the other. It was still the case that no trace of him being in the Welsh household had been found. All the dream had done was to muddy the waters in his mind. Was it possible that he had gone into the house that night but obliterated that fact from his conscious mind?

• • ● • •

Rivers arrived at the road where the Peters family lived. Green Road. He smiled. There was nothing green about it, really. Just a row of semi-detached houses on either side. Very ordinary looking when compared with The Close where the Welsh family lived. He began to wonder why Jennifer had struck up such a friendship with Lesley Peters that her first thought on being left alone for the weekend was to invite Lesley round to stay with her. They were, everybody seemed to be telling him, like chalk and cheese.

It was early evening and there was a chance, he thought, that Lesley's father would have been back from work. He was office manager at a local supermarket – the one where Rick had been spat at by a woman shopper, by coincidence. Rivers approached the door and rang the bell. A man answered his ring.

"Yes?" he asked as if suspicious that someone should be calling round.

"Mr Peters?"

"Yes." He was still dressed in what Rivers thought must have been his office clothes. A white shirt with a check pattern on it and a suit which had seen better days. The trouser turn-ups, he noted, were fraying at the edges.

"My name's Philip Rivers," he said. "I'm conducting an investigation into your daughter's death." He thought he would make his investigation seem personal to them.

"Oh." Mr Peters seemed at a loss for words.

"Could I come in?"

"Who is it?" called out a woman's voice from behind Mr Peters.

"It's a man who says he's conducting an investigation into Lesley's murder," he replied – whereupon the woman behind the voice stepped forward and stood side by side with him on the doorstep. Again, she was conservatively dressed but there was evidence that she took her appearance a little more seriously than he did his. She wore make-up and lipstick and she was wearing a black two-piece suit. It was as if she was still in mourning. Her brow looked furrowed as if she was worried about something.

"You'd best come in," she said. When they were seated in the living room, she took charge of the conversation rather than her husband. "Are you a policeman?" she asked Rivers.

"No," he said. "I'm a private detective. I've been hired to look into the deaths of Lesley and Jennifer Walsh."

"I can't see what good that would do," said Mr Peters. "The

police have long given up trying to find out who killed her."

"Quiet, Arthur," said Mrs Peters, "give the man a fair hearing. Who hired you, Mr Rivers?"

"Rick Harper," he said. He did not elaborate on the name – wanting instead to see what reaction that would trigger off from Lesley's parents.

"The police thought he'd done it," said Mr Peters,

"Yes," said Rivers, "but they have never managed to prove that. Rick Harper has hired me because he wants to clear his name. He thinks a lot of people around here still think he's guilty."

"They do," said Mrs Peters.

"Do you?" asked Rivers.

"Oh, we don't get into that," said Mrs Peters. "We really don't know enough about what happened to say one thing or the other. We've relied on the police for our information."

"And they've kept you in touch with what's going on?"

"We had that Detective Chief Inspector Brett round once. I gather he's gone now," said Mr Peters.

"That's why I was happy to hear that someone was still investigating Lesley's death," said Mrs Peters, "but – if your sole purpose is to clear his name – then I don't know how much good it will do."

"It's not," said Rivers. "I want to find out who committed the murders – regardless of whether it's him or someone else. I find it scandalous, though, that the police only contacted you once." The couple gave no reply. It was as if, Rivers surmised, they did not like to question authority and did not have the confidence to try and question the police handling of the case themselves.

"That's just the way it is," said Mrs Peters.

"The police are very busy people," added her husband.

"Nevertheless," said Rivers. He paused for a moment before changing his line of questioning. "I hate to ask you this," he went on, "but can you think of anyone who bore Lesley any ill will?"

"Lesley?" said Mr Peters as if the question had never occurred to him. "We thought the killer was after Jennifer and that Lesley just got in the way." Rivers could see that perhaps they had comforted themselves with the thought that Lesley had no enemies in the world and had just been unluckily caught in the crossfire between the killer and her friend Jennifer. In one sense, he did not want to disturb this safety valve they had created for themselves – but he did think Lesley's character was one area that had been neglected by the police in their original handling of the case.

"Nevertheless," said Rivers, "if there was someone who held a grudge against her it might be best to tell me. It might only be a case of eliminating whoever it was from my investigation."

"There was that boy," said Mr Peters.

"Yes." Rivers was anxious to encourage him to participate in the investigation.

"Stan Wightman," said Mrs Peters.

"That's him," said Mr Peters almost sounding enthusiastic. "He was a bit odd. Bit of a simpleton, if you ask me."

"No, dear," said Mrs Peters. "He was just shy."

"What happened between them?"

"Lesley dumped him," said Mr Peters.

"She did it very nicely," Mrs Peters hurriedly intervened. "She just told him they didn't really have any common interests in life. He was dedicated to his allotment. She was working very hard at school to try and get into university. She didn't really have time for a boyfriend."

"So there was no-one else?"

"No." Mrs Peters was emphatic.

"How did he take it?"

"He came round once afterwards. Tried to plead with her to take him back. She wouldn't change her mind."

"She was unhappy that she'd upset him," said Mr Peters, "but she had a very stubborn streak in her. Once she'd made her mind up about something that was it."

Rivers nodded. "Do you know why she was so friendly with Jennifer Welsh?" he asked.

"They were at school together."

"They were chalk and cheese, though, weren't they?" continued Rivers."Jennifer constantly flirting with boys. Lesley quite subdued by comparison."

"I wouldn't use the word subdued, Mr Rivers," said Mr Peters.

"She deserves praise for devoting herself to her studies."

"Nevertheless she went to stay with Jennifer that weekend. What did you think about that?"

"She'd just finished her exams. She wanted to go to the dance. We thought she'd worked so hard…." Mrs Peters stopped, and a tear welled in her eye "…. we just didn't think it would do her any harm." At this she burst out sobbing and her husband moved to be by her side and comfort her.

"Just one more thing," said Rivers softly allowing time for Mrs Peters to recover from her grief. "Did you know Jennifer's parents were going to be away that weekend?"

The two were silent for a moment. "No, inspector," said Mr Peters eventually. "We didn't." Rivers declined to correct him about calling him an inspector. He also decided to forgo the follow-up question. It would have been to ask whether they would have changed their minds about the weekend sleep-over if they had known Jennifer's parents had been away. He could see from the looks on their faces that they would have done – and they were still coming to terms with fathoming out why Lesley had lied to them. "I'd better be going now," said Rivers. He moved to the doorway. "Let me assure you – I will keep you abreast of any developments." He had quite warmed to the couple during the interview. They were decent people, he thought. Decent people whose grief should have been respected by Detective Chief Inspector Brett during his initial investigation into the murders.

"Thank you," said Mr Peters showing him to the door. "Thank you for showing an interest." Rivers smiled and touched Mr Peters on his forearm as he left the house – a touch which seemed to embarrass Lesley's father.

• • ● • •

"I think you should be prepared that this may go against us," said Rosemary Gallagher as she and Jo met up to prepare for Jo's summons to the police station. "As I indicated to you last night, they rang me to insist we attend at 11 o'clock." Jo remained silent.

"Don't worry, Jo, it's a case of your word against PC Enderby's with no corroboration on either side," she said. "I find it difficult to believe that constitutes a cast-iron case against you."

"Lots of things in this country are beyond my comprehension," said Jo. "First of them is why I should face charges at all." The police station was quite busy as they arrived. The scene in front of them seemed to indicate that other protestors caught up in the kettling had also been called in by the police to hear whether they would be prosecuted or not. They were listening to a solicitor addressing them before they left the station. "We will be issuing an appeal for anyone who has any video film of the events in that area to come forward," he said to them. "Don't worry. I'm sure we will be able to challenge the police's version of events." As the protestors dispersed, Rosemary made her way over to the solicitor. "Are you involved in this demonstration thing?" he asked.

"Yes, I have a client who may be charged with assaulting a police officer." She pointed to Jo. "Jo Rawlins Clifford."

"Funny how they all have posh names. I've got a Claud Fortescue-Green among my clients."

"Jo is not posh," said Rosemary firmly. "He grew up piloting a boat in the Caribbean. Just decided he wanted to put both his parents' names on his passport."

"I had eighteen clients before today," said the other solicitor. "Fifteen of them have been charged. They'll all be represented by the same person. Do you want to throw your lot in with me? I'd love to represent Jo whatever his name is."

"No," said Rosemary. "Jo doesn't want to. He's worried his case will be seen as part of a political plot against the police if he throws in his lot with you."

"He is the only black person to be charged. If I didn't know better, I might have been tempted to think the police were being sensitive in the way they handled the demonstration. After all, it mainly was to protect black and ethnic minorities from the heavy hand of the state when it comes to immigration. The heavy hand of the state seems, in the main, to have been laid off. My defendants are almost all middle class students. One mixed race but mostly white."

"Sensitivity obviously failed in Jo's case," said Rosemary.

"That should be your trump card – accusing the police of racism in singling out your client for arrest."

"My trump card is that he's innocent and didn't assault the officer he's accused of hitting."

"If I might say so, that's a trifle naive," said the other solicitor.

At that juncture Detective Sergeant Bowers entered the reception area. "Jo Rawlins Clifford," he called as if it was a doctor's waiting area. Jo got to his feet and linked up with Rosemary to accompany her into the custody suite – where the custody sergeant was waiting for them. Jo was immediately cautioned and charged with assault. "Do you have anything you wish to say?" said Bowers after he had completed the formalities.

"Only that we will be contesting the charge," said Rosemary laying a restraining arm on Jo to prevent him from replying directly to the detective sergeant. "We find it odd that you only have PC Enderby's word to rely on to present the case against my client."

"No," said Bower. "I think you'll find our case is stronger than that. We have supporting evidence – of which we will notify you in due course." He picked up a file of papers from the desk. "We're done here now," he said. "You will be provided with the prosecution statements in due course," he said before inviting Rosemary and Jo to leave the room. Jo gave PC Enderby a long hard stare before leaving the room. Enderby, for his part, remained silent.

"Enderby's obviously convinced at least one of his colleagues to back up his version of events," said Rosemary after they had left the room.

When they were outside, Jo reached for his mobile to tell Rivers what had happened. "I was going to interview members of the band about the Welsh and Peters case," he said. "I suppose I should drop that now."

"No," said Rivers quickly. "Remember what I said. Innocent until proven guilty. You carry on with the job until you're convicted of the charge – if you ever are."

• • ● • •

It was later that afternoon that Francesca Manners received a call in her office asking her to report to the Chief Constable's office. She frowned. There was no major case on her books at that precise moment so she could not think what he was calling about. However, as she had been summoned, she was duty bound to attend.

"Rory," she said on entering Chief Constable Gleeson's office. She extended a hand to him which he ignored.

"Sit down, Francesca," he said. She noticed he was avoiding eye contact with you. "I've just had notification from the Met that someone giving your address has been charged with assaulting a police officer."

"Oh," said Francesca. It was the first she had heard of Jo's fate. In all the hullabaloo of going to the police station and then trying to put it out of his mind by continuing to pursue his murder enquiry, Jo had forgotten to call her.

"You don't seem surprised," said the Chief Constable. "There's no rush to deny it, either, I notice."

"No, sir." She wondered how frank she could be with Gleeson – they had had a close working relationship up until then, after all.

"Who is he – this...." He looked at a piece of paper on his desk,"....Jo Rawlins Clifford?"

"He's my partner, sir." Francesca thought she had better revert to the more formal way of addressing the Chief Constable. Any sense of intimacy or friendship between them seemed to have evaporated from the moment she had entered the room.

"And?"

"And what, sir?"

"Tell me more about him – what he's done."

"Jo works for the Philip Rivers detective agency. He was born and brought up on Calicos Island in the Bahamas."

"He's a black man, then?"

"I don't see why that's relevant, sir," she replied a trifle haughtily.

"It's information, detective chief inspector. Information."

"Yes, he's black and he felt angry enough to go on a demonstration against immigration laws because he had a friend whose family were part of the Windrush generation and who faced being deported from the UK."

"And, whilst he was on this demonstration, he assaulted a police officer?"

"He didn't do it, sir."

"Oh, please. Spare me that. Let justice take its course. I don't want some kind of schoolgirl pleading that my boyfriend didn't do it. You're a grown-up police officer. It's not for you to question the decision of the Met when you have no knowledge of the case."

"I know Jo, sir."

"And I expect Dr Crippen's daughter said she knew him and he couldn't possibly have done it." Gleeson paused. "Let's keep emotion out of this. I am presented with a dilemma here, detective chief inspector. I do not like the idea of one of my senior officers being involved in a relationship with a hardened criminal." Francesca opened her mouth to protest but Gleeson waved her aside. "I don't want you living at the same address as him. Do I make myself clear?"

"Crystal."

"So, I can expect you to ask him to move out as swiftly as possible, can I?"

"No, sir. Do I make myself clear, sir?"

"Francesca." Gleeson reverted to her first name again. She saw it as an attempt to soften her up to take the decision he wanted her to make. "Francesca," he repeated. "I cannot tolerate the idea of a senior officer of mine living with someone who has a criminal conviction for assaulting a police officer. I cannot put it clear than that."

"We have a system in this country. Innocent until proven guilty. In that case, I am living with a man who is currently innocent of a charge of assaulting a police officer. Why should I kick him out?"

"Do I take it from your words that you will review the situation should he be found guilty of this charge?"

"Yes."

"And you will leave him or kick him out – as you so succinctly put it – should he be found guilty?"

"I have given you my assurance that I will review the situation."

"Well, we shall have to leave it at that for the present, but be in no doubt as to what I shall expect you to do if he is found guilty."

"I won't be, sir."

Gleeson nodded. "You can go now," he said to her.

Francesca left his office and made her way to the office she shared with Detective Constable Gary Clarke Upon arrival, she kicked a desk and shouted: "Damn! Damn! Damn!" at the top of her voice.

Gary looked up from the papers he had been reading. "May I ask what's the matter, ma'am?" he asked. He had dropped the more informal approach of using her first name to address her when they were on their own together. He detected this was not a moment for such niceties.

"No," she said firmly as she sat down behind her desk.

● ● ● ● ●

As luck would have it, the band was all together practising that evening at the Bannon household. Jo had put all thoughts of the charge he was facing out of his mind as he knocked on the door. A man whom Jo would have put at being in his late fifties, answered. He was slight with slicked back greased hair and an obvious East London accent.

"Hello, darling," he boomed. "What can we do for you?"

"I rang," said Jo. "I wanted to talk to the band."

"Oh, yes. About the Jennifer Welsh murder."

"The Welsh/Peters murders, yes," replied Jo. "And you are?"

"John Bannon. Manager to this modest band Jay and the Sundowners. They're all here tonight."

Jo nodded. "May I come in?"

Bannon nodded and shepherded him into the room where the band was rehearsing. "They're not quite the same as they were four years ago," he said. "Jimmy Atherton, the singer, has gone on to bigger and better things. He's got a recording contract and is on tour at the moment. He comes back to us occasionally but we have Simeon as our singer now." Bannon introduced Jo to a tall gangling youth who had been engaged in singing a soul number for all it was worth. He stopped on being introduced to Jo.

"This is my son," said Bannon, indicating a pale youth strumming a guitar. He had red locks going down to the collar of his shirt but his hair was beginning to thin out on top.

Jo shook him by the hand. "I think it would be better if I could talk to them all individually." he said.

"Of course," said Bannon. "Come on, Jay, you go first."

Bannon ushered them to another room – a dining room, it looked like – and left Jay and Jo together in there to talk.

"Those murders," said Jay. "They were a long time ago."

"Yes," said Jo. "Did you know the girls?"

"I knew Jennifer, or let's just say I was friendly with her. She came to one or two of our gigs and.... "His voice tailed off.

"And?" prompted Jo.

"Well, it's probably no secret. She did have a fling with members of the band."

"Members?"

"Steve Mayhew the bass player. He's still with us. He's in the other room. Vince Williams the drummer He's left us now. They probably had a couple of dates – I don't know – it was all so long ago."

"Can you remember what you did that night after the dance?"

"What we always do. Come back here to chill out, have a couple of beers and something like a pizza."

"How long did they stay here?"

"Ooh ... until about three." Jo looked surprised. "We're night owls, man. You can't just go to bed and sleep after a gig."

"So, they would have had time to go back to the Welsh household afterwards?"

"And kill those two girls? No. My dad drives them home at the end of the night. Steve lives in West Hampstead and Vince was in Camden Town, then. They wouldn't have had the time or inclination to go back and commit murder, man."

"What about Renee and Jimmy Atherton?"

"They went their own separate ways. They didn't come here. They never do – although Renee's become a bit more sociable now Jimmy Atherton's left the band. They went out to celebrate that night. An agent had promised to sign Jimmy up. He deserved it. He was a really great singer. My dad, of course, was livid. Thought he should have had some loyalty to the band. My dad's a hard man to say no to – but Jimmy managed it that night."

Jo nodded. "And you?"

"Me?" said Jay. "No, I never say no to Dad. That's why I'm still stuck in this band four years later."

"Stuck? I would have thought it was quite a cool way of making a living."

"We don't earn much. I still have to have a day job."

"Oh, yes?"

"I'm an accountant," said Jay blushing.

"I didn't really mean whether you said 'no' to your dad. I meant what did you do that night and what was your relationship with Jennifer?"

"I came back here and went to bed when they'd all gone. No, I never dated Jennifer. She was out of my league, man."

"What was your reaction when you heard Jennifer and Lesley had been murdered? Were you surprised?"

"Of course."

"And when you heard Rick was the main suspect?"

"No, man, he's cool. He was a good friend to me." Jay paused to allow a smile to form on his face. "Always prepared to listen when I wanted to grumble about my old man."

"Good," said Jo. "Thanks, Jay. Could I have a word with Renee now?" Jay nodded and brought the group's organist in to see Jo. "Hi," said Jo. "You know why I'm here?"

"Yes, you're investigating those murders."

"I wanted to ask you what you did on the night of the murders."

"It's a long time ago."

"Jay seemed to think you went out with Jimmy Atherton to celebrate."

"Celebrate what?"

"You tell me."

"Oh, yes," said Renee. "Jimmy had won a contract. An agent had come to hear him sing. Peter Aymes."

"Did he go out to celebrate with you?"

"I think he was there for the first part of the evening. Then Jimmy and I went home. To Cricklewood. We carried on partying there. We shared the house with a couple of other musicians."

"And they would support your alibi?"

"I wasn't aware I needed an alibi."

"Everybody does," said Jo, "This is a new investigation."

"I haven't the faintest idea where they are now. I can barely remember their names."

"If you remember them, it would be good if you could forward them to me Tell me, what did you think of Jennifer?"

"Honestly?"

"Honestly."

"She was a bit of a slut. I wouldn't have touched her."

"And Jimmy?"

"Jimmy's my number one friend."

"No, what did he think about Jennifer?"

"You'd have to ask him that," said Renee.

The interview was drawing to a close but Jo had the distinct impression that Renee was hiding something from him. "Is there anything else you'd like to say?" he asked.

"No," he said.

"I may need to speak to you again," said Jo. "Are you going to be around for the next few weeks?"

"I've been in the band for five years now. I'm not going anywhere."

Jo nodded and thanked him for his help. He asked him to send Steve Mayhew in. He felt obliged to ask him some questions on account of his previous relationship with Jennifer – but it soon became apparent that he had no insight into the events of the night of the murder. As Jo left the dining room, John Bannon emerged to see him out.

"Oh," he said just as he was about to leave. "I should ask you what you did on the night of the murders."

"I killed them," he said. Then he smiled. "Only joking."

"This is no joking matter," said Jo sternly.

"No, I suppose not. Well, I was ferrying the boys around and finally got home about four o'clock. Why are you asking me?

What motive have I got for killing them?"

"I haven't discovered one yet," said Jo. He decided he didn't like John Bannon. Anyone who tried to make a joke out of murders irritated him.

• • • • •

Rivers had decided his next task was to go and interview Thomas Saunders. He knew the former school friend of Rick Harper's was unlikely to offer any insight into the murders. He was gay and could not possibly have had any motive for killing Jennifer or Lesley. Nevertheless, he was on Rivers' radar as one of the names Rick had given him when accounting for who had been present that night.

His address was an 18th century cottage in a little village outside Hertford. Someone obviously had money, thought Rivers. It was not the sort of place he could ever have aspired to. There was a long driveway leading up to the front door. Rivers rang the doorbell and was greeted by a smartly dressed woman wearing a bee-keeping outfit.

"Can I help you?" she asked – a pleasant smile forming on her face.

"My name's Philip Rivers," he said. He showed her a card. "I wondered if I might speak to your son, Thomas."

"Why?"

"Well, I'm investigating the murders of Jennifer Welsh and Lesley Peters and I was given his name as someone who had attended the dance on the night of the murders."

"And your reason for singling Thomas out to speak to?"

"It's because I'm trying to trace and speak to everyone who was there that night."

"I don't believe you. Thomas is in a very fragile state of mind. You shouldn't bully and harass him."

"I have no intention of bullying or harassing him – merely asking him a few simple questions."

"Who has asked you to conduct this investigation? I note you're not a policeman."

"That's true. Rick Harper."

"You should have said that at the beginning. We have no intention of helping that young man in any way at all."

"This is the beginning of our conversation. I had no intention of hiding anything from you."

"Rick Harper has ruined my son's life. Don't you realise that?"

"No. How?"

"Well, if you don't know I'm not going to help you. Good day, Mr.... whatever your name was."

At this juncture, the door slammed in his face. As he turned to walk down the driveway, he noticed the twitching of a curtain in the upstairs room of the house. That, he thought, was Thomas Saunders. He walked back to his car and settled himself down for a long wait. At some stage, surely, Thomas Saunders would attempt to go out. When he did, Rivers would be waiting and follow him to his destination.

The first person to leave the house was the woman who had treated him so abruptly when she had answered the door. He assumed she was Thomas' mother. She was followed after about 15 minutes by a young man in his twenties. He was good looking but his face was lined and drawn and he looked furtively about him as he left the house. Rivers allowed him to get a head start down the road from the cottage before following him. He left the car after he had been following him for about ten minutes and carried on by foot. Eventually Thomas led him to a cafe in the village where he went in and ordered a cup of tea and a bun.

"Thomas Saunders?" asked Rivers as he approached the table the young man was sitting at.

"Who wants to know?"

"Philip Rivers. I'm a private detective." Thomas got up as if to leave the table. "No," said Rivers putting a hand on Saunders' arm, "I'm not going to hurt you. I just want to ask you the same kind of questions that I'm putting to all the people who were there at the dance on the night of Jennifer Welsh and Lesley Peters murder."

"So I went to the dance? So what?"

"And afterwards?"

"I went home."

"Did you know either of the girls?"

"What kind of question is that? Of course I did. Everybody knew Jennifer but I wasn't interested in her like everybody else because I'm gay."

"I'm struggling with a couple of things. I wonder if you could help me. Your mother said Rick Harper had ruined your life. How? Also, why are you sitting at home all day when you seem like a perfectly healthy individual who should be enjoying life a bit more?"

"Being gay and enjoying life aren't compatible in my parents' eyes. They say I've had a breakdown and should rest."

"And have you?"

"Yes," he said hesitantly, "but not for the reason they think. They think I was forced into a gay relationship and that's what's caused my depression. I know it was because I was in a relationship with somebody I loved – who just casually announced he wasn't gay and broke it off. "

"And that person was?"

"Rick Harper."

Rivers nodded. "I should have guessed. So you and your mother would be agreed on one thing – Rick Harper ruined your life."

"Yes," said Saunders.

"But it must have been a long time ago?"

"It was – but there are some things you just don't get over. She thinks Rick forced me into a gay relationship but I went into it quite willingly. It was the first I'd ever had. It was the first time I realised I was gay."

"And your parents don't thank Rick for that."

"They're old-fashion Christians. They believe being gay is an abomination."

"Why don't you leave them? Find a more sympathetic environment?"

"I haven't had the courage to do so because of my depression. They'll only be happy if I tell them I'm not gay – but I'm not about to do that. I am."

"And what feelings do you harbour about Rick Harper?"

"I wish he'd come to terms with himself. Ask yourself – has he got a girl-friend? The answer's no."

"He wanted to have Jennifer Welsh that night. Did that upset you?"

Saunders declined to answer. "I have to go home," he said.

"Why?" asked Rivers. "Does your mother not let you leave the house?"

"Oh, I get out and about but I told her I was resting because I didn't feel well. Wouldn't be good if she found out I'd gone out by myself." With that, he got up and left the table – leaving Rivers deep in thought. Was Thomas Saunders so disturbed that he might have killed Jennifer Welsh just to get back at Rick Harper – and why hadn't George Brett unearthed this line of enquiry? Or had he done so only for Saunders' father, the eminent pathologist, to warn him off from pursuing it?

● ● ● ● ●

Francesca could see that Jo had already arrived home when she drew up outside her house. The lights were on in the kitchen and – as she approached the front door – she could hear the sounds of Bob Marley and the Wailers playing on her outdated CD player.

"Hallo, darling," she said as she opened the door. "I'm so sorry to hear you've been charged. You should have rung me."

Jo came out into the hallway. "I know I should but I thought you'd have a lot on your plate. How did you know?"

"The Chief Constable told me. Someone had alerted him to the fact that my address had been given as the home of someone who had been up in court. You."

Jo gave Francesca a quizzical look. "Does that give you a problem?" he asked.

"No," said Francesca, "I would have expected you to. After all, you live here. No – it gave him a problem. He doesn't want a senior member of his staff living with a known criminal."

"And that's what I am?"

"In his eyes, yes." She approached him and gave him a hug. "Not in mine."

"So where does that leave us?"

"Nowhere until the end of the court case I said I'd think about what he'd said if and when you were found guilty – but that I believed you were innocent."

"I am," said Jo, "but that doesn't change the fact that I might be found guilty at the end of the day because of the lies of a toe rag of a policeman." He paused for a moment. "Who now has someone else backing up his version of events. How did he react to you expressing your faith in me?"

"He virtually accused me of school-girlish immaturity for believing the police could possibly be wrong."

"Charming."

"Jo," Francesca said seriously. "I believe in you. You are not guilty no matter what the courts say and I am not going to desert the man I love and know to be innocent if the courts find otherwise."

"Nice speech," said Jo, "but what does it mean in practice?"

"I'm sure we can find a way round his ultimatum." She squeezed his arm again "What about you?" she said. "What are the consequences for you?"

"Oh, Rivers said he'd have to get rid of me if I was found guilty. Something to do with him losing his professional support if he kept me on. He doesn't intend to suspend me until the hearing and I've been working on the Welsh/Peters murder case this afternoon and evening. It did help take my mind off things."

"How's it going?"

"Well," he said. "I think we're beginning to realise there were others apart from Rick Harper who could have had a motive to kill Jennifer Welsh – or could have attacked her in an angry moment."

"Keep me posted when there's an arrest that needs to be made."

"If you're still in your job."

"Oh, don't worry. I will be. I have one or two ideas up my sleeve for coping with the chief constable."

"And they are?"

"Best kept under wraps until they have to be unveiled."

"You're not contemplating being devious are you? You're always so straightforward. An honest policewoman who can be relied upon."

"Straightforwardness is always the best policy if it works. I can do deviousness if it becomes necessary, though."

• • ● • •

Rivers was in the office early the following morning. He wanted to jot a few ideas down on his computer to get it clear in his head as to the way the investigation was going. No sooner had he arrived than he heard Debra's footsteps coming up the stairs. She was surprised to find him in. Normally it was any excuse to keep away from his desk.

"Cup of tea?" she asked knowing that her boss had a preference for tea over coffee.

"That would be great," he said. When she had made it, he retired with it to his office to try and collect his thoughts. It was only a few moments later that he was disturbed by the sound of a loud booming voice in the reception area.

"Is your boss in?"

"Yes," said Debra. "If you'll just hold on a minute, I'll get him for you. Who shall I say it is?"

"Saunders. Professor Matthew Saunders."

Rivers could hear the exchange and decided not to wait for Debra to officially inform him about his visitor.

"Professor Saunders," said Rivers extending a hand of friendship as he came out into the reception area. It was ignored. "What can I do for you?"

"I think you know."

"Would you like to come into my office?"

"No," said Saunders, "what I've got to say can be said out here. Lay off my son."

"As far as I'm concerned, I didn't think I was laying anything on him."

"You've been bullying him."

"No, I've been asking him a few routine questions – the same ones that I've been asking anyone else who was at the Jay and the Sundowners dance on the night Jennifer Welsh and Lesley Peters were killed."

"He was in a state last night after speaking to you. You stirred up unhappy memories for him."

"I can't be responsible for the emotional state of people when I ask fairly routine questions. It says more about them than me, don't you think?"

"He's not guilty of any crime."

"I didn't suggest he was."

"You have one obvious suspect for the murders. Why don't you put him under the same scrutiny that you put my son under?"

"I take it you're referring to Rick Harper?"

"Of course."

"The man who's hired me to clear his name?"

Saunders gave Rivers a glare. "I see," he said, "so this is a whitewash job aimed at clearing his name?"

"No, it's a thorough investigation that will leave no stone unturned. Unlike the one mounted by Detective Chief Inspector Brett."

"George Brett saw sense and realised my son had nothing to do with it. He was a close friend of mine. He soon determined that Rick Harper was the guilty party."

"That's why he charged him, is it?" said Rivers sarcastically.

Saunders, who was quite a physical presence and all of six foot five inches tall, moved a step towards Rivers "All right," he said, "he may not have had enough evidence to charge him but it's there. It's there."

"In which case I'll find it but I have to say I think you're basing your supposition on a wing and a prayer rather than hard facts."

"I'll have you know the Chief Constable is a very good friend of mine," Saunders continued.

"I'm happy to hear it. On second thoughts, though, I couldn't give a toss. You could try threatening George Brett with that but it won't wash with me. The Chief Constable has no jurisdiction over me." He took one of his cards out of his pocket. "See what it says," he said showing it to Saunders. "Private detective. I operate privately – independently of any police force."

"I can still make life very difficult for you. That co-operation that you possibly had in the past from the police. It can be withdrawn."

Rivers decided it was time to stop counter-acting Saunders' hectoring with his own goading. "I'm sorry we've got off on the wrong foot," he said, "and I'm sorry your son is upset. I can promise you I will give him no harder a time than anybody else involved in the investigation but I can't go further than that. At present he is not a suspect."

They were the wrong words to pacify Professor Saunders, though. "At present?" he shrieked. "What do you mean by at present?"

"Precisely what the words mean," said Rivers. "At the moment I have no evidence connecting him with the murders in the same way that I have no evidence connecting Rick Harper with the murder. I cannot foretell the future but that may change – as far as either of them and others are concerned."

Saunders grunted. "I find your attitude deeply unsatisfactory," he said. "I'll be off now but let me warn you, you haven't heard the last of me."

And your son may not have heard the last of me, thought Rivers. He wondered why bullies never realised that their attitude might make people more suspicious of the people they were trying to protect than less.

CHAPTER FOUR

"Thomas?" said Rick surprised at the identity of his caller when he opened the door. "What are you doing here?"

"I want you to call him off," said Thomas walking past Rick into the sitting room before he had been invited in. He sat down on the settee It was obvious that he was feeling uptight.

"Call who off?" asked Rick. "Do come in, by the way."

"That private detective. He came around to question me."

"Good."

"What do you mean?" Thomas contorted his face in agony.

"I gave him the names of everybody who was present at the dance. The idea was he would question them all as to what they did on the night of the murders. I'm glad to see he's doing just that."

"But why did you give him my name?"

"Because you were there."

"But why would I want to kill Jennifer Welsh?"

"Don't ask questions when you don't know what the answer would be. You could be in for a shock."

"My father says you did it."

"He also thinks you're not gay. He can be wrong about things."

Thomas swallowed hard. "He's been helping me out of my depression – caused by you," he said.

"Thomas, all that was nearly eight years ago. What's the point of raking it up again? I told you. I'm not gay. It was just something I dabbled in while I was growing up. I'm sorry I dabbled in it with you and hurt your feelings but – get over it. Also, I don't think your parents have been helping you out of your depression – rather plunging you further in it. As far as I understand it, they refuse to believe you are gay. That can't be helping you. Why don't you leave home – try to meet some people who would be more sympathetic towards you?"

"I can't," said Thomas. "I have no money. No job. No qualifications. All down to you and the breakdown you caused at a time when I should have been focussing on getting qualifications and securing a career. My parents have at least ensured that I have a roof over my head. If you really believe I would be better off in the company of like-minded people why don't you do the same. Offer me a roof over my head. Somewhere I can stay and be myself."

"No, Thomas. I'm the last person you should turn to for help. I let you down. Remember? Besides, I haven't exactly struck out successfully on my own myself. I've returned from university and am living with my parents. I don't have a job yet and a lot of people – like your parents – think I'm a murderer."

Tears welled in Thomas' eyes. "But I still love you, Rick," he said.

"No, you don't," said Rick emphatically. "You feel emotion towards me because you still see me as the source of your unhappiness. But what happened eight years ago? Two gropes in a school toilet and then I called it off. It wasn't the relationship you have conjured up." He swallowed hard. "Thomas, I think you had better go now," he said. "You're not doing yourself any good here." Thomas arose from the settee and made his way towards the door when Rick stopped him in his tracks. "By the way, what did you tell Rivers?"

"What do you mean?"

"About what you did after the dance?"

"Oh, nothing, really. I just told him about our relationship."

"You were there, weren't you, when Jennifer asked Tim and me to go back to her house?"

"What?"

"I remember it distinctly. That must have upset you. Given your state of mind."

"What are you trying to get at?"

"Did you go round to Jennifer's house to try and stop us? Did it all get too much for you?"

"You think I killed her?"

"No," said Rick thoughtfully, "but all I would say to your father and all the others that are seeking to blame me for the murder is that someone like you had more of a motive for wanting to kill her than I did."

"I wasn't seen outside her home."

"True," said Rick, "but remember – nobody can show that I was inside her home."

Thomas looked downcast. "This wasn't a good idea," he said. "Coming to see you."

"No," said Rick. "Look," he added. "I'm sorry for the way you are but I'm not the answer to your problems." He thought for a moment. "And nor are your parents."

"Will Rivers want to see me again?" he asked, changing the subject.

"I don't know," said Rick. "That's up to him. Depends on whether he thinks you've got any more information that could be of use to him." Rick realised his words failed to give Thomas any reassurance but then, he thought to himself, that was not his problem.

• • ● • •

"Another cup of tea?" said Nikki to Debra once her third potential flatmate had made her way from her home.

"I think I'm in danger of overdosing on it," she said, "but – go on then."

"What do you think?"

"I don't want the student," said Debra definitely. "I think he was just seeking to leave his student digs so he could have a wilder social life. Not my scene, really."

"And the teacher?"

"She's teaching at Sue's school. It would bring back too many painful memories." Sue had taken Debra under her wing and offered her a home. They had been living together when Sue had been murdered.

"And the solicitor?"

"She was all right and she could give me a lift to work in the mornings – but this would just be a temporary stopover for her. She'd be looking to buy a place of her own and then we'd be in the same boat. Looking for somebody else."

"So you're not terribly impressed?"

"No," said Debra.

Nikki smiled. "We still have one person to see," she said.

"Gary Clarke."

"Yes."

"The man who thought I was guilty of killing Sue and then tried to frighten me into making a confession."

"You'll think differently about him when you see him in his pyjamas cleaning his teeth in the bathroom in the morning," said Nikki – a smile emerging on her face. "He won't be so frightening then."

"He's not frightening," said Debra. "He's been quite kind to me since then."

Nikki glanced at her watch. "He'll be here in five minutes," she said.

"I'm not sure I'm going to learn anything more about him through seeing him again," said Debra.

"Philip would probably want you to take him on as a lodger," said Nikki. "He'd think you could wheedle some secrets about the police force out of him."

"Philip?" queried Debra.

"My husband."

"Oh, sorry. Of course." Debra had momentarily forgotten her boss' first name. He always seemed to introduce himself to people just as Rivers. "I wouldn't want to do that," said Debra. "It wouldn't make for a happy atmosphere at home if one of us was acting as a snitch."

"Possibly not," said Nikki. There was a ring at the doorbell. "That'll be him," she added. She got up and made her way over to the door. It was Gary Clarke. She had met him once before in Rivers' company and he seemed to be trying to remember why her face was so familiar to him.

He came into the sitting room and spotted Debra on the couch. "You," he said surprised to see her.

"Me," said Debra.

"I didn't realise it was you," he said. "It just said ask for Debra on arrival."

"Well, that's me."

"Surely?"

"You don't think she'd want you as a flatmate after the way you treated her in that murder enquiry?" said Nikki.

"Well, no."

"You were trying to make a name for yourself," said Debra. "I don't think you'd be questioning me about anything if you moved in here as a co-tenant."

"No. Probably not."

"Can I ask you – why do you want to move in here?" said Debra, getting down to business.

"I'm living in the police section house at the moment," he said. "It's rather like a boarding school dormitory." Debra looked quizzically at him. "Sorry," he said, "I went to a minor public school as a boarder," he said. "I didn't enjoy the experience. I just want to get away and strike out somewhere by myself."

"Do you see this as a stopping off point before you get somewhere else?" Debra liked order in her life. She didn't want change after change as far as her co-tenants were concerned.

"No," he said. "I suppose I might eventually want a place of my own without a co-tenant but I can't see that happening for a while – not with the price of property around here."

Debra smiled. "What would you think about having me as a flatmate?"

Gary swallowed. "Well," he said, "following our first encounter – which was a disaster and my fault – I think we've rubbed along okay. I'm not as brash as I was. Also, I'm no longer the Chief Constable's nephew out to make a name for myself." His uncle, the former Chief Constable, had been forced to resign after making a number of passes at women police officers. "I think I could make it work," he said. "Also, you'd have the protection of the law on tap if anything did happen here." He had meant the latter to be a joke but he could see Debra had taken it seriously.

"I'm not sure I'd want to think of myself as being cossetted by the long arm of the law," she said.

"Point taken," said Gary. "What I meant to say is that I think I could make a go of it."

"So could I," said Debra.

"And I know if I erred, I'd have people like Jo and Rivers down on my back like a ton of bricks."

"And Francesca," added Nikki.

"And Francesca," he echoed.

Debra offered him a handshake. "It's a deal, then?"

"It's a deal," he said accepting her handshake.

"I'll just show you round," she added. "I doubt if it'll make you change your mind." It didn't.

• • ● • •

Rick sighed as the doorbell rang again at his parents' home. He hoped it was not Thomas Saunders returning. It was not. "Mr Rivers," he said on finding out the identity of his caller.

"May I come in?" asked the private detective.

"Of course," he said. "How are things going?"

"Well, I seem to learning a lot," he said. "A lot about you."

"Oh. Thomas Saunders?"

Rivers nodded. "Your gay lover," he added.

"I wouldn't put it quite like that. A couple of fumbles in a toilet when we were teenagers which – sadly – meant more to him than they did to me."

"He's quite disturbed," remarked Rivers.

"I wouldn't use the word 'disturbed'," said Rick. "Mixed up, yes."

"We're beginning to build a case which shows that you're not the only person with a motive to kill Jennifer Welsh. And I stress Jennifer Welsh. We haven't so far come up with any motive to suggest that Lesley Peters was the main target – although we still have some more enquiries to carry out."

"So, tell me, who are these other suspects?"

"I have to say Thomas Saunders is one of them. He could have killed Jennifer Welsh in a fit of rage because of the relationship she had with you."

"Or didn't have with me. I didn't go there that night if you remember."

"I think that's immaterial. He thought there was something between the two of you."

Rick nodded. "And he did overhear Jennifer inviting me and Tim round that night," he said.

Rivers' ears pricked up. "Are you certain of that?"

"Yes," he said. "He came around this morning – ostensibly to ask me to call you off. He confirmed that during his visit, though."

"Right," said Rivers. He made a note of it in his notebook. "Then there was something going on with Jimmy Atherton."

"Jimmy Atherton? I know Jennifer had a thing for him."

"I haven't got round to talking to him yet," said Rivers, "but Jo – my assistant – has talked to Renee, the organist."

"Yes, I know Renee. He and Jimmy Atherton were as thick as thieves. After every gig, the rest of the band – and me – used to regroup at Jay's dad's house. Renee and Jimmy used to go off by themselves. They lived together and, I think, quite liked to go to a night club to wind down after a gig."

"Jimmy was celebrating that night. He's just been signed up by an agent. The agent could have wanted to go out celebrating, too. Could Jimmy have heard Jennifer inviting you round?"

"I don't know. Why?"

"Well, he could have thought it was a party and tried to gate-crash it. I can't think he would have gone round otherwise. Jennifer's parents might have been in. Not the sort of scene that he would have been looking for. Anyhow, we'll have to do a little more delving on that score to find out what happened." Rick nodded. "How are you bearing up?" Rivers asked – changing tack.

"Me?"

"Yes, this must have brought the murders back to you in a more focussed way than you've had to deal with over the last few years."

"I suppose it has." Rick remained quiet for a moment then added: "Actually, it has very much so." He leaned forward. "Can I tell you something, Mr Rivers?"

"Please," said Rivers. "I'm all in favour of people doing that."

"I had a dream last night."

Rivers chuckled. Rick's intonation reminded of the famous

Martin Luther King speech. "Oh, yes," he said when he had gathered his composure.

"I dreamt I was in Jennifer Welsh's house that night and I was just about to hit her. Then I woke up. Mr Rivers, it was scary."

"Did it make you think that you might have been responsible for the murders?"

"It threw me," he said. Then he added: "Yes, it did." He breathed a sigh of relief. "God, I'm glad I've told somebody about that," he said.

"I wouldn't tell too many people," said Rivers.

"Because?"

"It may confirm their suspicions that you are the guilty party."

"And you?"

"I've never concluded a case by finding someone guilty as a result of what they have been dreaming."

"So?"

"It's just the pressure you're under with it all coming back to you. Until you remember something consciously that links you with being in Jennifer's house, I wouldn't worry too much about it."

"Thank you, Mr Rivers."

"By the way, drop the Mr. It's much too formal. Most people just call me Rivers."

"So, two new avenues of investigation then. Anymore?"

"I've still got one or two people to interview. Duncan Hamilton, the trainee policeman."

"Yes, I haven't seen him since the night of the murders. I don't know where he lives."

"Graham Hands does."

"Graham?" said Rick suddenly smiling. "You've seen him?"

"Yes."

"Was he at all helpful?"

"He alerted me to the Jimmy/Renee axis. By the way, he's adamant you didn't do it. You're too nice a bloke, apparently. Not everybody thinks you did it. Jay Bannon, for instance and the Peters family don't hold a grudge against you."

"You've seen them?"

"Yes."

"What are they like?"

Rivers thought it was a rather strange question. The character of Lesley's parents didn't really have any bearing on the case. "They're very nice people," he said. "Ordinary – in comparison with the Welsh family. But nice. And when I use the word 'nice' I don't in any circumstances mean it to be patronising."

"Any other people you need to see?"

"Well, there's this guy called Stan Wightman. Lesley's ex."

"I know him," said Rick. "Bit of an oddball. Well, not so much of an oddball as slow witted. I think Lesley did well to ditch him."

"That's the first time I've heard you talk about Lesley."

"She was a nice girl." He smiled. His description of her mirrored the way in which Rivers had described her parents. "No, she was. I'm not damning her with faint praise either. A nicer girl than Jennifer."

"Yet you were prepared to contemplate going to bed with Jennifer and not with Lesley?"

"Male hormones. Besides, Lesley would not have let me into her bed."

"So this Wightman fellow would have no cause for jealousy with Lesley?"

"No," said Rick. "I suppose not." He reflected for a moment.

"Two other people to see," said Rivers. "Tim Rathbone – although you've rather ruined the element of surprise there."

"Sorry," said Rick.

"And Anne Welsh."

"Surely you don't need to see her?"

"Why not?"

"Well, she didn't do it."

"How can you be so sure?"

"I just am. Anyway, she's been through a lot." There was a look on his face which seemed to signify more than just empathy with her pain at losing a sister.

"I have to interview her if I want to be thorough – not just to eliminate her as a suspect. She might have some important information that she doesn't even realise about Jennifer."

"I suppose so." He still seemed reluctant to accept the idea that Jennifer's sister should be interviewed.

"Do you know her well?" Rivers asked him.

"No, not really," he said. "I've always thought." He stopped in his tracks.

"Go on," said Rivers encouragingly.

"Well, that she was more attractive as a personality than Jennifer but I never had the chance to find out. That's one of the reasons I want you to clear my name. Oh, yes, I want those gossips to stop spitting at me in the street. I want Thomas' father to stop having an irrational hatred of me. But I'd also like to find out if Anne Welsh is as attractive a personality as I think she is. Silly, really."

Rivers smiled. "Not silly at all," he said.

• • ● • •

"Thank you for agreeing to see me, Chief Constable," said Professor Saunders as he was ushered into Rory Gleeson's office.

"That's all right," said Gleeson. "I don't believe we've met before so I thought it was about time I should make the acquaintance of our chief pathologist."

Saunders grimaced. He would not have wanted that conversation to be repeatedly outside the confines of Gleeson's four walls. After all, he had been making the point to those he sought to bully that he and the Chief Constable were close friends. "How's Adrian Paul – your predecessor?" he asked.

"Haven't a clue."

"I used to have a good relationship with him. It was a pity he went in the circumstances he did."

"He shouldn't have tried it on with the women police officers he assaulted," said Gleeson quite gruffly. "Now, what was it that you wanted to talk to me about? No point in us reminiscing about old times. We don't have any history together."

"No," said Saunders. He was beginning to think it would be hard work currying favour with this new chief constable. "It's a murder case that you're involved with," he said.

"I wasn't aware we had any on the go at present," said Gleeson.

"That's precisely the point," said Saunders. "There is one and you should be more involved with it. Would it mean anything to you if I said it was the Jennifer Welsh and Lesley Peters murders?"

"Yes, of course. Four years ago."

"But still no-one caught in connection with them."

"That's true," said Gleeson. "You're going to tell me you have a lead on them?"

"Not really," he said, "but I think everybody is convinced they know who the murderer was and he's still out there laughing at us."

"Is he?"

"Rick Harper."

"You'll have to forgive me. Rick Harper is who?"

"The teenager who was spotted outside Jennifer Welsh's house on the night of the murder. She'd apparently asked him round after a dance was over."

"Right."

"But after taking him in for questioning nothing else happened and now you seem to have ceded the enquiry to a private detective. A most unsuitable chap called Philip Rivers."

"Unsuitable?"

"He's been harassing my son."

"Has your son got something to do with the enquiry?"

"No," said Saunders almost shouting. "Oh, he was there at the dance but so were 150 other people. I think if you haven't got anything else on – and you say there are no other murders in the county – that you ought to be redoubling your efforts to find the killer."

"The trouble is – and I remember the details of this case now – is there was no evidence linking Rick Harper to the scene of the crime. No new evidence has come forward at all and it is four years since the event."

"My son has had a breakdown – all as a result of that Rick Harper trying to persuade him he was a homosexual."

"I'm sorry," said Gleeson. "Have I missed something? I thought Rick Harper had been invited round to Jennifer Welsh's house with the prospect of heterosexual sex in mind but now you say he's gay?"

"He's both but that's not the point. He's guilty. My son is not."

"How do you know he's guilty?"

"Your detective chief inspector – George Brett – told me he was. He didn't see any need to speak to my son about the murders because he knew he wasn't involved in them. I just wanted to ask you to reopen your enquiries into the deaths because I fear Philip Rivers may be missing the point."

"Which is that your son is not guilty?"

"Amongst other things, yes."

"We've never closed the enquiry, Professor Saunders, but I'll tell you what I'll do. I'll ask our current Detective Chief Inspector, Francesca Manners, to step up her enquiries and also keep an eye on the investigation this Philip Rivers is carrying out. Would that help?"

"Yes."

"After all, Professor Saunders, I'm sure we're on the same side here and we both want the killer brought to justice as soon as possible."

"Thank you, Chief Constable."

Gleeson got up and offered the professor a handshake – which he accepted and went on his way. Gleeson then marched into his outer office. "Get me Francesca Manners on the telephone as soon as possible and tell her to come upstairs and see me," he told his secretary.

• • ● • •

Rivers rang the doorbell a second time. He could see a man – presumably the occupant of the house, Duncan Hamilton – was playing in the back garden with three young children as he looked through what was the window to the sitting room and saw through to the other side. It was a small maisonette, tastefully decorated. Duncan Hamilton had obviously struck out for himself and bought his own first home. Equally, he appeared to have forgotten about his crush on Jennifer Welsh and settled down with somebody else. As he rang the doorbell for the second time, the man in the garden looked up, gathered the children together and made for the sitting room. "I'm coming," he said in a voice barely audible to Rivers. Having parked two of the children in the living room, he arrived at the front still clutching the eldest of his litter.

"Can I help you?" he asked Rivers as he struggled to hold the three-year-old in a position he found comfortable.

"Yes, I hope you can," said Rivers. He got out his card. Duncan squinted and digested the information on it. "Philip Rivers, private detective," said Rivers. "I'm investigating the murders of Jennifer Welsh and Lesley Peters."

"Gosh," said Duncan – finally giving up the struggle to hold the child in a comfortable position. "That was a long time ago."

"Four years," said Rivers.

"You'd better come in." He ushered Rivers to a seat in the sitting room. Within seconds of the private detective sitting down, a toy car – thrown by the eldest child who must have been no older than three, Rivers surmised – was aimed direct at the private detective. (The other two – Rivers was fairly confident they were twins – probably were aged about two.) The toy car struck the private detective in his private parts.

"Chloe," said Duncan sternly. "Behave." He smiled at Rivers. "Sorry, I've got the kids today. My wife's mother's not too well and she's gone off to see her. I've got the day off work."

"Was that easy?" asked Rivers. Duncan stared at him as if not comprehending the remark. "It's just that I know a bit about policing. It isn't always family friendly in its hours."

"Oh, no," said Duncan. "I'm not a police officer. I work for an engineering firm. In its sales department."

"But you were training to be a police officer, weren't you?"

"Yes, I gave it up. Too many unsocial hours," he said. "And it went down like a lead balloon when you told people what your job was at parties."

"Right," said Rivers smiling. "You ought to have become a private detective. That doesn't seem to have the same effect on people." He paused for a moment. "I won't beat about the bush. I've come because I was given your name as one of the people attending the dance Jennifer and Lesley went to on the night of their murder."

"Yes," said Duncan hesitantly.

"And that you had had a relationship with Jennifer Welsh."

"It was over by then," said Duncan.

"But you were cut up about that, I understand?"

"She was a beautiful girl."

"Were you with anybody that night?"

"No, I went on my own. I knew a few friends of mine would be there."

"And Jennifer?"

"And Jennifer. I did ask her to dance but it was obvious she only accepted out of politeness – nothing more. I danced instead with the woman who has now become my wife. Diane."

"What did you do when the dance finished?"

"I went home."

"With Diane?"

Rivers thought he detected a moment's hesitation before Duncan replied. "Er, no," he said.

"So there's no-one who can corroborate that for you?"

"No," he said. "I lived in digs at the police section house while I was on the police training course. No-one would have heard me come in, I'm pretty sure of that."

"Were you asked for an alibi at the time?"

"Yes. And Diane. She stayed with friends she was at the dance with. The police never followed anything up with me. I think the detective in charge accepted what I said." He put heavy emphasis on his words – as if to suggest that Rivers should do, too.

"But you must have got together with Diane fairly soon afterwards."

"I'm sorry?"

"The children," said Rivers pointing to them playing away with their toy cars on the sitting room floor. "Your oldest must be three."

"Approaching four – and the other two are twins. Took us by surprise."

Rivers went back to questioning Duncan about the night of the dance. "Did you hear Jennifer inviting Rick around after the dance was over?" he asked.

"No."

"Are you sure? It's just that Rick noticed you were nearby when the invitation came."

"I'm sorry – but I didn't," he said firmly.

"What would you have thought if you had heard?"

"I would probably have been angry – but, seeing as I didn't, that's immaterial, isn't it?"

"Angry enough to do what?" Rivers persisted.

"Sulk probably. Not kill her. Sulking's more my style."

Rivers nodded. "Well," he said, "I don't think there's anything more I need to ask you."

"You didn't tell me why you were investigating the murders four years after everybody else has given up on the case."

"Rick Harper asked me to."

"Rick?"

"You sound surprised?"

"I wouldn't have thought he'd have wanted it all raked up again."

"He thinks people still believe he killed the girls. He wants to clear his name."

The conversation between them dried up at this point. "Well, if that's all, said Duncan.

"Yes," said Rivers. He made for the door. Once outside he began thinking about his conversation with Duncan Hamilton. The former trainee police officer had seemed a little reticent to co-operate, he thought. That could have been as a result of his character, thought Rivers. After all, everyone had seemed to be agreed that he was pretty dull. Monosyllabic answers could have been the norm for him. Then again, thought Rivers, they would also be the refuge for somebody who had something to hide.

● ● ● ● ●

Rivers had tried to fix an appointment with Jimmy Atherton through his management but the best they could come up with was to offer him the chance of catching the singer on the hop as he prepared for an evening gig at the Hammersmith Apollo. As he exited from the tube station, he saw a poster advertising the concert. Jimmy Atherton was top of the bill. He had obviously come a long way since his days with Jay and the Sundowners.

Rivers did not really pay much attention to current pop music any more. Suffice it to say, he had not heard of Jimmy Atherton. The poster he passed on the way to the reception area at the Apollo seemed to suggest that perhaps he should have done if he did not want to be dismissed as being square.

"I've come to see Jimmy Atherton," he said to the woman on the reception desk.

"You and five thousand others tonight," she said unimpressed.

Rivers showed her his card. "I'm not a groupie," he said.

"Nor are they," the woman replied emphatically. "I don't think he'll speak to you."

"Could you at least try?" asked Rivers civilly. "It's just that I asked his management team for a chance to interview him and they suggested I roll up here. Could you tell him – or whoever you speak to – it's about Jennifer Welsh?"

The name meant nothing to the woman on reception but she did as Rivers had asked. To her surprise, whoever was on the other end of the telephone asked her to send him upstairs.

"They're happy to see you," she said surprised. "Take the lift and go to the first floor. Someone will be waiting for you and they'll take you to his changing room." It was as she had said and Rivers soon found himself confronted by the singer. He had a charming smile on his face and got up from his seat to come over and greet the private detective. He walked with the aid of a stick.

"Philip Rivers," he said extending his hand. Jimmy shook it warmly. "I've come to talk to you about Jennifer Welsh and Lesley Peters."

Jimmy nodded. "Tragic," he said. "It was tragic." He sounded as if he meant it sincerely.

"I've been asked to investigate their murders by Rick Harper."

"Rick? How is he?"

"I can't give you a glib answer," said Rivers. "He's still hounded by people who think he did the murders. He wants to clear his name."

"Nice guy," said Jimmy. "I got on well with him. He was a sort of roadie to us – helping us out on gigs. He knew a lot of people himself. Got us a few gigs. I'm sorry he's still plagued by this thing."

"Sounds as if you don't think he did it."

"What does it matter what I think," said Jimmy philosophically. "I just remember he and I could talk about things – politics, news, events. Our music scene wasn't great for encouraging that. Conversation dried up after you'd talked about the latest hit records. Not with Rick. You know, he used to be a disc jockey at a hospital radio station. I did my first interview there with him. Nice times." Jimmy laughed. "He played my first record," he said. "Only trouble was most of the patients were too ill to go out and buy it. Still, he put me in touch with Graham Hands. I gather they both used to work on the hospital station. You haven't come here to listen to me reminiscing, though."

"In a way, I have," said Rivers. "Though I want you to reminisce about the night of Jennifer Welsh's murder."

"She was at the dance," said Jimmy.

"You'd had a relationship?" prompted Rivers.

"I think Jennifer thought we still had. She asked me early in the evening whether I'd like to come back to her place after the dance. I said no."

"Why?"

"It was over and I don't believe in hanging on to things once they're over. Besides I knew there was an agent at the dance who'd come to listen to me to see if he could offer me a contract. I was pretty sure I should put some time aside to talk to him after the dance was over."

"Is that what happened?"

"Yes, we went to a night club, had a chat and then I went home with Renee. We shared a flat."

"Did you hear Jennifer invite Rick and his friend round?"

"No."

"If you had?"

"I would have been happy. It would be a sign she was moving on. It's just that – if I was going to start making it – I didn't want to have to cope with a relationship at the same time. I'm sorry if I hurt Jennifer."

"She had another boyfriend, I believe?"

Jimmy blushed. "You couldn't accuse Jennifer of going without boyfriends," he said. "You mean Duncan?"

"Yes."

"She was well off without him. He was a bit clingy – and that's not the sort of guy Jennifer liked."

"On a scale of one to ten, who posed the most threat to Jennifer – you, Rick or Duncan."

"Me and Rick nought. Duncan, three maybe. But I don't like the idea of speculating as to who killed her."

"What about Thomas?"

"Thomas?"

"You don't know him."

"No."

"Gay friend of Rick's."

"No," said Jimmy. "I never met him. Anyhow, why would a gay bloke hold a grudge against Jennifer?"

"Same reason as everybody else. She'd pinched his lover."

"I don't really know of any gay bloke in that scene," said Jimmy. Rivers decided not to enlighten him. He got up to go. "Before you leave," said Jimmy interrupting him, "I've got a few tickets left for tonight's concert. Would you like a couple?"

Rivers had to confess he would have liked to find out more about Jimmy's singing. It seemed a genuine invitation, too, and not something Jimmy felt obliged to do. It was too short notice, though, to ask Nikki who was on a fashion shoot. "Another time," he said as he left the singer's changing room.

• • ● • •

"Francesca," said Gleeson – a smile forming on his face. "Do come in and sit down." He waved her to a seat.

Ah, thought Francesca. Very different to last time. He obviously wants something from me. She chided herself for such uncharitable thoughts. It was, after all, the usual way that the Chief Constable greeted her. The conversation about Jo had been an aberration. "Thank you, sir," she said. After her last meeting with him, she felt she could not slip into Rory and Francesca with him so easily.

"The Jennifer Welsh and Lesley Peters case," he said. "Where are we on that?"

She was tempted to say "nowhere and you damned well know it" but decided that would be undiplomatic. Instead she stuck to the facts. "A new investigation into it has been launched by the private detective Philip Rivers," she said. "In the absence of an abundance of police time being available, I'm waiting to see the results before deciding what action to take."

"He seems to be upsetting a few people."

"Who? Rivers?" Gleeson nodded. "I would be tempted to say 'good'. That's just what the case needs."

"I've had a visit from Professor Saunders, the eminent Home Office pathologist. He says Mr Rivers is bullying his son."

Francesca thought to herself for a moment. Would it make a difference in Rivers had been bullying someone connected to someone who wasn't eminent? she pondered. Sadly, from the tone of Gleeson's voice, she thought it would. Of course, they wouldn't have come to see the Chief Constable in the first place. She sighed. Rory Gleeson seemed to be going the way of too many chief police officers she had known – protecting the privileged.

"I don't find the words 'Rivers' and 'bullying' synonymous with each other," she said. "Maybe his son is a suspect."

"Professor Saunders doesn't seem to like the fact that Rivers is not treating Rick Harper as a suspect."

"Harper is his client."

"Precisely."

"I know Philip Rivers well enough to know that he won't baulk at pointing the accusing finger at Harper if he finds any evidence against him."

"The point is – is he looking?"

"Maybe you ought to be interviewing him, sir, rather than me."

"I thought you said you were keeping tabs on how his investigation was going."

"Yes, but I'm not watching his every move."

"Maybe you should be taking a closer interest. It shouldn't

be too difficult. After all, your boyfriend works for Rivers' organisation."

"I thought you wanted me to ditch him, sir."

"You've convinced me you don't have to do that just yet." A certain iciness entered Gleeson's manner at this juncture.

Oh, yes, thought Francesca. Use him as a snitch and then dump him. Thank you, sir. She was enough of a realist, though, to know she should keep those opinions to herself. "I will endeavour to find out how their enquiries are progressing," she said.

"That's all I ask," he said. "Oh, and bring Rick Harper in for questioning. That should do the trick."

"On what pretext?"

"Think one up."

"I'll send Gary Clarke round to interview him."

"No," said Gleeson. "You do it. That'll convince Professor Saunders we're taking his complaint seriously."

"Why do we have to convince him of that?"

"He moves in circles which could make things nasty for us. I'm not asking you to charge Harper or anything like that."

Just waste police time, Francesca thought to herself. There was no point in quarrelling, though. She could see that. She and Gary would go round to Rick Harper's on the pretext of asking him if he felt he needed protection and take it from there. "If that's all, sir," she said, getting up from her seat.

Gleeson waved her away but then interjected: "What about the other matter?"

"My relationship with Jo?" she asked. Gleeson nodded. "The trial hasn't come up yet, sir," she said – and this time she did turn on her heels – fairly quickly – and exited his office.

• • • • •

Jo was in the office early the next morning. Rosemary Gallagher had wanted to see him to tell him the trial date had been fixed for the following Tuesday. A letter would be sent to his home – the one that he shared with Francesca. She had been in touch with the solicitor representing the other arrested demonstrators and their appeal for witnesses had unearthed someone who had seen the confrontation between him and PC Enderby. The witness was suggesting Jo did not hit the police officer. "I'm not sure how reliable a witness he is," said Rosemary.

"Rather him than a racist wanting to strike at black people," Jo had interjected. "You think the latter is more likely to be believed?"

"Sadly, that may be true but it probably doesn't matter that much. I gather he is reluctant to give evidence," said Rosemary. "I will do my best for you – or, actually, the barrister I've commissioned will do his best for you. Charles Clayton. You'll meet him at the court on the morning of the case. He'll go through a few things with you."

"Good," said Jo. "I'm sorry if I sound a bit tetchy, Rosemary," he added. "It's just that I really don't think I should be having to go through this – and sometimes that gets to me."

"I know," said Rosemary. "At least, though, the suspense will only last another week."

Jo nodded and left Rosemary's office to go upstairs to his. Debra was there ready to make tea for the two of them They were interrupted by the arrival of a woman. She was in her twenties, Jo surmised, and looked a bit, well, mousy, he thought. She was dressed in a sober grey suit and nervously ran her fingers through her hair as she approached the reception desk. "Can I help you?" Debra asked.

"My name's Diane Hamilton," she said. "I wondered if I could see Mr Rivers."

"I'm afraid he's not here at the moment," said Debra.

"I'm his assistant. Can I help?" said Jo butting in. "Are you the wife of Duncan Hamilton?"

"Yes. You know about him?"

"I know my boss went to see him yesterday. We're working on the case together. Won't you come into my office?"

"Thank you," said Diane.

Jo looked at Debra. "Could you stretch to a third cup of tea?" He turned to Diane. "Or would you prefer coffee?"

"No, tea would be fine," she said. "It's just that there's something my husband didn't tell your boss when he visited him yesterday," she began after she had been offered a seat.

"Go on."

"Well, the night of the murders. He said he went home alone to his digs but that's not true. He smuggled me in and we spent the night together."

"I see," said Jo. "and why didn't he tell Mr Rivers that yesterday?"

"We weren't supposed to be seeing each other. I told the police at the time that I'd spent the night at a friend's. I didn't want to admit to my parents that I'd been with Duncan. I signed a statement to that effect – that I'd been with a friend. Duncan didn't want it to come out that I'd been with him. They're not allowed to take women back to their digs at the section house. He would have faced disciplinary action. Anyhow, it wasn't as if we were suspects. Nobody came to question us again. I told my friend to back me up – which she did."

"The police may not have told your parents what you said."

"They took the statement at their house. I had to tell them what I'd said and that seemed the easiest thing to say. My friend lived alone in a flat so no-one else was involved."

"So why have you come forward now?"

"Duncan said Mr Rivers seemed to be treating him as a suspect. I thought it was time we came clean."

"Or offered him an alibi to get him off the hook," suggested Jo.

"No, it wasn't like that. Actually, I think my first child was conceived that night."

"Your first child?" said Jo.

"We have three children. A girl aged three and twins aged two. The girl arrived just nine months and a few days from the date of the dance."

"Right," said Jo. "Just one thing – can you give me the name of the friend who you said you were staying with?"

"Why do you want to know?"

"To corroborate your new evidence and confirm that you weren't staying with her on the night of the dance."

"She's moved away I'm no longer in touch with her."

"Nevertheless."

"All right. It's Alison Palmer. She went to university – Cardiff,

I think – soon after the dance."

"Do you know where her parents live?"

Diane thought for a moment. "No, I don't think so," she said hesitantly.

"Okay," said Jo. "We'll follow it up. I imagine either Mr Rivers or I will want to talk to your husband again."

"Yes," she said. "I told him I was going to do this. He's looking after the children until I get back." With that, she left the office.

"Fascinating," said Debra when she had gone.

"You were listening?" asked Jo.

"Not really. I couldn't help overhearing. You left the door open."

"I must remember not to next time I'm seeing a client. What did you make of her? Is she telling the truth?"

"I think so," said Debra. "Her parents aren't going to be too pleased with her. Telling a lie for all those years."

"On the other hand, they must have already been annoyed about the baby," said Jo. "If she's right about him being conceived that night, it was before she got married."

● ● ● ● ●

"Tim Rathbone?" asked Rivers when a young man answered his knock at the door.

"Yes? Who wants to know?"

"My name's Philip Rivers, I'm a...."

"I know who you are. You're a private detective. You've been hired by Rick Harper to try and prove him innocent of the Jennifer Welsh and Lesley Peters' murders."

"He got to you first," said Rivers grinning.

"You could say so. Virtually accused me of murder."

"And you were upset by that?"

"Yes, of course. Wouldn't you be?"

"Yet a lot of people have been accusing him of murder over the past four years."

Tim sighed. "I suppose you're right. You'd better come in," he said.

"Do you think Rick did it?" asked Rivers once he was seated.

"In my heart of hearts? No, I suppose not."

"Exactly. So that's where I come in. Trying to find out whether you're right."

"Put that way," said Tim.

"What do you remember of that night?"

"I remember the invitation from Jennifer. I remember feeling I didn't want to go. For a start, it would be difficult to explain to my parents where I'd been for half the night."

"There is that," said Rivers.

"And, for another thing, it seemed that Lesley Peters had been earmarked for me. She was a nice girl, but..."

"Not your type?"

"I don't know that I had a type."

"How would you have felt if it was Jennifer that had been earmarked – as you put it – for you?"

"She'd never have fancied me," said Tim. "I was too boring. I wore a sports jacket and a tie. Sartorial elegance and fashion were not my strong points."

"Would you have tried it on with her?"

"Not with Rick around. They were so obviously more suited to each other."

"So you just went home?"

"We were outside my house when I told Rick I fancied going home to bed. We don't live far from the Welsh's house."

"And Rick went off to their house all on his own?"

"I didn't realise that. I thought he went up the road back to his home. He must have had second thoughts, though."

"So – as far as you knew – you would be the only one going back to Jennifer's house Rick was out of the way. You could have made a pass at Jennifer. Did you know where they lived?"

"Yes," said Tim. "My parents were friendly with Jennifer's parents. "

"So did you?"

"Did I what?"

"Go round to Jennifer's house after thinking about it for a while?"

"No."

"We only have your word for that, though. Oh, no, of course, there were your parents – dutifully waiting in for their son to come home."

Tim smiled ruefully. "Actually, they'd gone out for the evening. I was in bed by the time they came home."

"Or at Jennifer's?"

"No, I've told you. I didn't go round. Anyhow, if I had committed a double murder, don't you think I might have made more of a noise when I finally came home. Enough to waken them. I'd have had to clean my blood-stained clothes. Or maybe I could have waited until the morning and my parents could have gone along with a cover up."

"It has happened before."

"What?"

"Parents covering up an offspring's crime."

"Don't be ridiculous."

"Look," said Rivers. "I may believe you but the truth is you can't prove you were in bed at the time those two girls were murdered. I may believe what you've said – but then, equally, I may believe Rick Harper when he says he never went into their house and had nothing to do with their murder. He's no more obvious a suspect than you. It just shows how easy it is to build up a case against someone."

"But, on your theory, a lot of people could become suspects."

"Yes," said Rivers, "so the next thing we look for is motive. Who would want to kill Jennifer and Lesley? On that score, I would rule both you and Rick out. You could have gone round later. Maybe Jennifer was in her night clothes. It was too late and she told you to go home. I don't see that as motive enough for you to have killed her."

"I've told you before."

"We're hypothesising. Similarly, with Rick. He goes round, gets in. Jennifer changes her mind. Okay, he's annoyed. You can imagine in such a case he might try and force himself on her in frustration. That could lead to him killing her because he would be worried she would accuse him of rape. But he didn't. There was no evidence that Jennifer – or Lesley for that matter – was subjected to a sexual attack. And I can't believe that Rick would kill her without mounting a sexual attack."

117

"I didn't know that. That's interesting," said Tim.

"So, the best advice I can give to you is go and make up with Rick. He needs friends right now. People still think he murdered Jennifer." Tim tried to interrupt Rivers but the private detective gestured to him to be silent. "Rick got the impression that your parents would be unhappy if you continued to see him," he continued. Tim nodded "Well, stuff them," said Rivers. "You're a grown man now. Do what you want to do."

"I was feeling guilty about the fall-out Rick and I had," admitted Tim. "Thanks."

Rivers nodded and got up to go. At least he was becoming clearer in his own mind as to who hadn't committed the murder even if he felt he was no closer to being able to name the real suspect.

• • ● • •

Jo reached for the bottle of white wine and poured himself a second glass and then wolfed down a sizeable amount. "Sorry," he said to Francesca. "Tricky period."

"Yes, I know," she said. "I haven't really wanted to ask you to focus your mind on what might happen at the trial but I have decided that – should you be found guilty – you should continue living here. I'll give my address as the house you shared with Debra."

"Surely it makes more sense for me to move back?"

We'll spare Debra having to put up with that if I move. Besides," she said, placing a hand on his arm, "I don't intend to sleep at Debra's place all the time."

Jo managed a smile. "Good," he said. "There is a problem, though. Jo's new co-tenant."

"Why?"

"Hadn't you heard? It's Gary Clarke."

"Gary? Debra and Gary sharing a house?" Francesca could not suppress a giggle. "Well, so long as he doesn't take to questioning her!"

"But you do understand, don't you?" continued Jo. "You might place him in an awkward position if he was questioned about whether you really were living there."

"I don't think it would come to that," said Francesca.

"You didn't think it would come to an ultimatum for you to ditch me from your nice new chief constable."

"Point taken," said Francesca. She reflected for a moment. "By the way, the chief constable is suddenly taking an interest in the Welsh/Peters murders again. He's under pressure from the pathologist Professor Saunders, Tom Saunders' dad. He wants me to question Rick Harper again."

"Will you?"

"I think I'll have to."

"I don't think you'll learn much. Our enquiries seem to be taking us in a different direction. It seems George Brett overlooked a lot of potential evidence. At least two people had better motives for wanting rid of Jennifer Welsh – jilted lover Duncan Hamilton and singer Jimmy Atherton who was just about to launch a new career marketing himself as a solo artist while Jennifer was inconveniently throwing herself at him. We've a long way to go yet but we haven't found out anything particularly incriminating about Rick Harper."

"Interesting," mused Francesca. "I thought a way into the interview might be by offering him protection."

"Does he need it?" asked Jo. "After all, it was only one old lady in the supermarket who attacked him. I know it shook him up but – talking to people – there don't seem to be many who bear him a grudge. Which makes it all the more surprising that George Brett was so fanatical in his belief that Rick was the prime suspect."

• • • • •

As luck would have it, Rivers found Anne Welsh was in on her own when he called round to the family home that evening. "I'm sorry," he said, "but there are just one or two questions I need to ask you about the night of Jennifer's murder."

"I'll try and help you if I can," she said. Rivers looked at her as he sat down on the settee in the living room. The word "striking" would be the best one to describe her appearance, he confirmed to himself following his thoughts on his previous visit to the Welsh household. Not a bubbly blonde like her sister Jennifer. Strong features, he thought, which seemed to tell of an intellectual mind rather than a party going animal. "What is it you want to know?"

"I'm sorry to sound like a clichéd detective," said Rivers, "but where were you on the night of the murder? Your parents, I know, were away for the weekend. Jennifer, though, seemed confident you wouldn't be returning to the family home that night – or she wouldn't have invited Rick and Tim back. Also, she'd given your room to Lesley Peters for the evening."

"Yes," said Anne. "She asked me to stay away for the evening so she could invite friends round. I thought it was a bit cheeky of her – asking me to stay out of my own home – but that was Jennifer."

"Did you like her?"

"I'm sorry, Mr Rivers, but is that relevant?"

"I take it the answer is a 'no', then."

"I didn't dislike her but we were like chalk and cheese. Are you suggesting I might have wanted to kill her? Presumably you think I also killed Lesley. Why was that? For sleeping in my bed?"

"I'm sorry," said Rivers. "I'm just trying to build a picture of all those who knew Jennifer. Can I change the subject? How do you feel about Rick?"

"I don't think he did it," she said immediately. "I liked him but Jennifer got in the way there. They had a brief fling at a dance about a year before her murder. He didn't want to continue it."

"He told you that?" said Rivers. "So why do you think he toyed with the idea of accepting the invite to go back to her place – your place – on the night she died?"

"Why do you think he did?"

Rivers was caught out by the question. "I'm asking, you," he said.

"Sex, Mr Rivers. Pure sex."

"So you don't have a high opinion of him?"

"Not many men would refuse the offer if it came from an attractive blonde that they fancied."

"That they fancied? I thought you said he had indicated he didn't want to be involved with her."

"They're two different things. Involvement and a one-night stand. I don't blame him for wanting to accept her offer." She smiled at Rivers. "It's not the sort of offer I would make. A candlelit dinner and at least a couple of dates are more my style when seeking a romance with somebody."

"You never tried that with Rick?"

"I never got the chance."

"You know he likes and respects you."

"And now there's no Jennifer to come crashing in between us." She gave another ironic smile. "You know, you're building up a very good case for why I might have wanted my sister out of the way."

"I didn't mean to," protested Rivers,

"Quite neat, really, though if I had come back that night and found the two of them together I don't think it would have enhanced my prospects of ensnaring Rick if I had killed her."

"No, but if he wasn't there. If he was telling the truth about that night."

"I wouldn't have wanted Jennifer dead because she would have done nothing to get in the way of a relationship between me and Rick."

"Which is what you wanted?"

"I would not have said no were he to have asked me out. I don't know now," she continued. "I haven't felt able to approach him because of my parents and because of him being the prime suspect in enquiries into Jennifer's murder. I don't know what's happened to him over the last four years. Whether all this has changed him."

"I think he'd like to give you the opportunity to find out, By the way where did you stay that night?"

"With friends. I can give you their names."

Rivers nodded. Anne went to a bureau in the corner and took out a sheet of paper. She wrote down a name and address on it. "There you are," she said.

"Thanks.""

Anne smiled. "I'd like to take that opportunity to find out what Rick feels," she said – recalling their previous conversation, "but it may still be too early. I could hardly invite him round here while there's still a chance he may be a suspect in the murder enquiry. My father's a changed man since the murder. He was the life and soul of the party before – a cheerful man for an undertaker."

"Perhaps he needed a release valve because of the day job."

"Yes," said Anne, "but since then he's been morose. Not socialising much. Just hoping that somebody would be arrested for what they'd done to his favourite daughter."

"Favourite?"

"The rest of my family don't share my rather academic outlook on life. That, I think, is why my father rather approved of Jennifer's life-style. Of course, he probably didn't know the more sordid details of it."

"You mean the sex again."

"Not just that," she said. "That set that she was in. Drugs were freely available. Certainly cannabis. Probably cocaine, too."

Rivers began to take a closer interest in what she was saying. "You think Jennifer was into that?"

"I'm sure of it."

"Who did she get the drugs from?"

"Some of the people Jimmy Atherton mixed with. Some of the people Graham Hands mixed with. I don't think either of them was into drugs. They may have dabbled but they were not serious users."

"And Jennifer was?"

"I don't have proof but – when I attended their parties – it was made clear I could indulge, too."

"By whom?"

"I'm not sure I should be telling you."

"I'm not the police," said Rivers quickly. "You wouldn't be getting anybody into trouble over that. It just may be crucial evidence."

"Well, the person who offered me drugs was Renee Hick – the organist in Jimmy's band."

"Yes, I know him." Rivers paused. "But there were no traces of drugs in Jennifer's body in the post mortem as far as I know. That, though, doesn't rule out some of the suspects from dabbling."

CHAPTER FIVE

"You again?" said George Brett unenthusiastically as he opened the door to find Rivers waiting outside.

"Me again," confirmed Rivers. "Can I come in?"

"I suppose you'd better as your investigation does seem to have the backing of the police."

"Thank you," said Rivers. "Just a few lines of enquiry that have come up that I'd like to run past you."

"Okay," said Brett indicating to Rivers he could sit down. The private detective noted there was no offer of a drink – tea or coffee – and wondered just how illuminating the conversation was going to be.

"Firstly," Rivers began. "It seems to me there are a couple of other people who could have had a motive for killing Jennifer Welsh. Jimmy Atherton, for example."

"Nice guy," said Brett.

"Yes," said Rivers without being deflected from his aim, "but she could have been an embarrassment to him. He wanted to market himself as a solo artist with this new contract he'd got – but she was besotted with him."

"I think that's an exaggeration," Brett butted in. "Jennifer wasn't besotted with anybody. Anyhow, how would it help him if he murdered her? Surely, there was a chance it would get out?"

Not if you were doing the detecting, thought Rivers. He refrained from comment, though, instead asking: "Did you ascertain where he was on the night of the murder?"

"He went to a night club with the group's organist Renee Hicks and they went home together. They live together."

"Did you check that out with the night club?"

"One of my detective sergeants went to the night club and confirmed they were there with the night club owner."

"Which night club was it?"

"You mean there are so many in Hertford you're afraid you won't be able to find it?"

Rivers smiled. "Touché," he said.

"I can't remember the name of it but it had live blues bands. Near Hertford East station."

"I'll find it."

"You're still refusing to believe Rick Harper committed the murders? Still, I suppose he is your employer. He who pays the piper."

Rivers refused to rise to the bait. "Then there's Duncan Hamilton," said Rivers. "Jennifer's ex His wife – she wasn't his wife then, just girlfriend – has come forward to give him an alibi for that night. Says she was with him when previously she told people she had stayed with a friend."

"I believe she did say that she had stayed with a friend but she wasn't central to the enquiry so we never followed it up. I didn't know she had been in a relationship with Hamilton at the time. Neither of them told me."

"And you just accepted Hamilton's word he had gone straight home to bed after the dance?"

"He wasn't seen anywhere else. In The Close where Jennifer lived or anything like that. I saw no reason to disbelieve him."

Rivers digested the information "Of course, there is one more suspect." he began. "Thomas Saunders, but his dad had told you to back off from interviewing him. Pity you didn't follow it up. He had a gay relationship – if you can call it that – with Rick Harper."

"His father denied he was gay. What do you mean "if you can call it that?"

"It was a couple of teenagers experimenting, Rick Harper found out he wasn't gay – or at least didn't want to pursue a gay relationship." Rivers took a deep intake of breath. "Which made Thomas extremely resentful of him. Resentful enough to have killed someone he perceived to be having a relationship with Rick? He's mixed up. His parents refuse to believe he's gay and he doesn't appear to be strong enough to move away from their apron strings."

"I doubt that's enough motive to commit murder," said Brett.

"What did Thomas' father say to you that made you drop that line of enquiry? Was it purely the influence he had with senior police officers?"

"He convinced me his son wasn't hung up upon Rick Harper."

"Whereas if you'd asked Thomas himself?"

"I didn't," said Brett emphatically. "All right?"

"Not really," said Rivers. "Let me go back to Jimmy Atherton, though. One of the people I've interviewed seemed to think he was involved in the drugs scene and could get drugs for Jennifer."

"Jimmy?" Brett sounded incredulous.

"Yes," said Rivers emphatically.

"No," Brett replied. "Look," he said moving forward in his chair as if to denote he was about to release some important information to Rivers. "Jimmy Atherton is clean living. I'd put money on it. Okay, I might have been a bit lax in not pursuing Thomas Saunders. I accept that but I'd have got no thanks from the chief constable at the time if I had done – but Jimmy Atherton? No."

"Renee Hicks?"

Brett was silent for a moment. "I have to admit it's more likely," he said. "I never managed to work that guy out."

Rivers laughed inwardly. It seemed to him there were quite a few people that Brett hadn't managed – or perhaps bothered – to work out. Still, it was interesting to note that even this staunch supporter of the line that it was Rick Harper and nobody else who was responsible for Jennifer and Lesley being murdered, had question marks over the character of Renee Hicks.

"Thank you," said Rivers. "I think that will be all for now." He wondered as he left how George Brett was feeling about the scrutiny of his original investigation. It seemed to him that – coming towards the end of their conversation – he was at least thinking that there might be an alternative scenario to Rick Harper being the guilty party.

• • • • •

"Rick Harper?" asked Francesca as she and Gary brought out their warrant cards. "I'm Detective Chief Inspector Francesca Manners and this is my colleague, Detective Constable Gary Clarke. We are investigating the murders of Jennifer Welsh and Lesley Peters. May we come in?"

Rick looked at them puzzled. "I suppose my hiring of Philip Rivers has made you lot wake up again," he said. "I suppose you'd better come in."

"We understand that you were attacked in the supermarket a couple of weeks ago," Francesca began.

"An old lady spat at me. It didn't hurt me. I was just rather upset about it."

"Of course, sir. That's why initially we wanted to ask you if you felt you needed protection from this kind of thing."

"Protection?" said Rick. "You've changed your tune. Last time your lot spoke to me they wanted to lock me up and throw away the key."

"They?" queried Francesca.

"Well, Detective Chief Inspector Brett," said Rick.

"Who is no longer on the case."

"Good," said Rick.

"Have there been any other incidents?"

"No," said Rick. "I mean, my friend Tim Rathbone got close to accusing me of being a murderer but that was only a row that got heated and I think we've sorted our differences out now."

"So you don't feel you need protection? I was wondering if you could describe the lady who spat at you. We could go and have a cautionary word with her."

Rick smiled. "I don't think that will be necessary," he said. "I think she's got whatever it was off her chest I doubt if she'll do it again. To be honest, she didn't look the violent type. Will that be all, inspector?"

"No," said Francesca. "I just wanted to chat to you about the case. Have you had any thoughts about it since you were last interviewed by the police?"

"It hardly ever disappears from my mind," said Rick. "You'd find it would if you'd been accused of murder after spending hours in a police interview room. I wish I'd never tried to find Jennifer's house that night. If I hadn't I'd never have been considered a suspect."

"I don't think you can guarantee that," said Gary butting in. "You'd have still been invited round to her house on the night she died."

"That evidence would have been even more flimsy that the evidence which led to me being interviewed."

"Possibly," conceded Gary.

"Have you had any thoughts?" Francesca persisted.

"About who did it?" Rick asked.

"Anything would be helpful," said Francesca. "It's a baffling case."

"My private detective seems to be making some progress. Perhaps you should ask him that question."

"I will," said Francesca. "Well, perhaps we ought to leave it at that, then?"

Francesca and Gary opened the door. As they were about to bid farewell to Rick Harper, a photographer emerged at the gate. He took a quick picture of the three of them and then made off before they could gather themselves together for a response.

"Thanks a bunch," said Rick.

"What do you mean?"

"Well, it's an obvious set up, isn't it? I didn't invite that guy round."

"I didn't either," said Francesca. She noted, though, that Gary remained silent.

"He's probably from the local paper and they'll run a story about how you're reopening the investigation. There'll be a pictured of me on the front page, saying 'police question Rick Harper as part of the new investigation'. Another old lady will spit at me." His voice tailed off. "Just get out of my sight," he added a moment later and slammed the door in their faces.

"Gary?" said Francesca when the two of them were on their own. Gary remained silent. "Come on," said Francesca. "Are you responsible for that photographer appearing?"

Gary looked sheepish. "I rather think I might be," he said.

"How?"

"Well, the chief constable's office rang for you this morning to ask if you'd set up the interview with Rick Harper yet. I said we were going to do it this morning. He must have rung the press. I'm sorry."

"It's not your fault," said Francesca. "I doubt if I'd have been able to brazenly lie or withhold information from the chief constable if I'd been asked the same question. I'm beginning to see a new side of him. He's quite Machiavellian, isn't he?"

"That's how he got to be chief constable, I suppose," said Gary.

And that's how he created the vacancy by getting rid of his predecessor. Gleeson had warned Francesca that Adrian Paul – Gary's uncle – was a "randy old goat" or words to that effect. As a result, Francesca had tape-recorded their dinner together and – sure enough – Paul had made a pass at her.

• • ● • •

Jo had been given a description of Charles Clayton by Rosemary Gallagher – young, bespectacled, fresh faced, fair haired and undoubtedly wearing a pin striped suit. It was easy to pick him out at their arranged meeting spot at the magistrates' court. He looked every inch the product of the private education system, thought Jo. His name should be double-barrelled not mine. He recalled an earlier conversation he had with Rosemary when she had said, "he'll be defending you."

Jo had looked puzzled as Clayton offered him his hand. "Can't you defend me?" he had asked Rosemary. "After all, you know all about the case."

"That's not the way I work. I act for you, prepare the case and then hire a barrister who specialises in advocacy to present your case to the court. I've worked with Charles for some time. You'll be safe in his hands."

Jo shook his head. "I'm not sure I like the system," he said.

"You're not the only one," confided Rosemary.

"Mr Rawlins Clifford?" said Clayton – extending a hand to him as if his double-barrelled surname made him "one of us".

"I've read through the case notes. It seems a straight case of one person's word against another's."

"Except for the second lying toad they've got to give evidence. PC Luke Boatman. By the way, call me Jo."

"What?" said Clayton reacting to Jo's description of "a second lying toad". Jo eyed him up and down. He was young, exuded keenness but obviously had not devoted himself to catching up with the latest developments in the case.

He looked through his papers. "Ah, yes, I've found him," said Clayton. He scan read the document. "We'll get him on collusion. Don't worry, Mr Rawlins Clifford," he said. It was obvious Clayton had not listened to a word he had said. Jo had to pinch himself for a moment before realising Clayton was addressing him. The way Clayton addressed him it sounded as if they were members of some elite society that ordinary people could not aspire to join. "I'll be giving the case my all," he added. "You are of previous good character, aren't you?"

Jo sighed. "I am," said Jo, "but I served a prison sentence in Calicos for the manslaughter of a guy who was threatening the life of a friend of mine. I was cleared on appeal some time later.""

"Ah," said Clayton. "We need not go into it." He paused for a moment. "Oh, and drop the attitude when we put you in the witness box. The judge won't like it."

"Attitude?"

"Yes, you shouldn't really call the second police officer a lying toad and let's have no mention of the fact you think you're of previous good character but went to prison for manslaughter. Won't go down well with the magistrates, I'm afraid. Any questions?"

Only how the hell are we going to win this case if we can't criticise the police or refer to me as a nice guy, thought Jo. "No," he said smiling, "but I'd like to give evidence."

"We'll see but let's get into court now. We're up now." Jo was escorted into the dock for the accused and Clayton took up his seat on the front bench. He smiled at the prosecuting counsel who then rose to outline his case.

"The accused was taking part in a demonstration against

government immigration policy," he said. "The police perceived there was a threat to order and decided to isolate one group of protestors in a road just off Trafalgar Square." He picked up a map from the papers in front of him and highlighted the street where the protestors had been kettled with a biro mark. His clerk took the map to the magistrates. "They decided it was too much of a threat to public order to allow this group to mix freely with the rest of the demonstrators and took the decision not to allow individual protestors to leave the street. This angered the defendant who insisted he had a meeting to go to and wanted to go to the toilet as well. He tried to push the police officer who had refused him permission to depart out of the way and shoved him in the chest causing him to lose his footing. The two of them ended up on the ground still grappling with each other whereupon the officer, PC Ray Enderby, arrested the defendant who was subsequently charged with assaulting a police officer." The prosecutor then took a rest from his narrative and sipped a glass of water. "I should now like to call my first witness," he said. "PC Ray Enderby." Enderby was sworn in and waited for the prosecutor to start asking him questions. He confirmed his name and rank and the duties he had been performing on the day of the demonstration. "When did the defendant first come to your notice?"

"When he was trying to leave the road," said Enderby. "He refused to accept that he could not leave the area and tried to shove me out of the way – aggressively."

"Did he hit you or cause you injury?"

"It was more of a scuffle," said the PC, "but I could see that he wasn't going to stop until he had got past me. That was when I took the decision to arrest him. I handcuffed him and escorted him to a police van with the help of another officer and subsequently questioned him with Detective Sergeant Michael Bowers at the police station. I was bruised but my injuries did not require hospital treatment."

"Thank you, officer," said the prosecutor. He turned to Lambert. "Your witness."

"A moment," said the chief magistrate who resembled a benign academic with greying hair and a beard. "Why was this group singled out for being kettled?"

"They were perceived to be a danger to public order, sir," said Enderby.

"Did they look dangerous to you?"

"I'm sorry, sir?"

"Did you perceive them to be a threat?"

"I was only following orders."

"Ah, the defence of the reluctant Nazi under Hitler." The magistrate paused for a moment. Jo smiled for the first time. "Carry on, Mr Clayton."

Clayton nodded and rose to his feet. "You were policing this demonstration on your own, were you PC Enderby?"

"I'm sorry, sir?"

"Well, I struggle to work out why one of your fellow officers didn't come to your aid when you were grappling with my client on the floor?"

"PC Luke Boatman, who I believe is to give evidence later, did help me escort the defendant to the police van."

"But no-one perceived my client to be a threat before then – except you?"

"It all happened quickly. There were a lot of people there. It was probably difficult for my colleagues to see what was going on."

"You know my client was the only black person to be arrested that day?"

"I believe so, sir."

"So, in the main the demonstration was peaceful and orderly? – bearing in mind the protestors were mainly from ethnic minority groups who felt strongly about the issue. "Jo raised an eyebrow at this. It sounded as if Clayton expected people from ethnic minorities to be violent.

"There were more than a dozen arrests."

"All of them in the area that you were policing. Might that not suggest it was the police tactics that were wrong rather than the demonstrators?" PC Enderby opened his mouth as if to speak but Clayton was in quickly with a follow up. "No further questions."

"Call your next witness," said the chief magistrate to the prosecutor

"I call PC Luke Boatman," said the prosecutor. The other PC took the stand and was sworn in. "Were you on duty with PC Ray Enderby at Trafalgar Square of the day of the demonstration against government immigration policy?"

"Yes, sir."

"And did you notice the defendant?"

"Yes, sir."

"When did you first notice him?"

"I saw him struggling with PC Enderby and trying to get past him. He shoved into him and the next thing I noticed was that they were grappling on the ground as the defendant tried to leave the street."

"Did you offer to help your colleague?"

"I made my way over to where he was grappling on the ground with him but by the time I got there PC Enderby had handcuffed and arrested him. I helped PC Enderby escort him to a police van and then the police station."

"In your view, was what you witnessed an assault on PC Enderby?"

"Most definitely."

"No further questions."

Clayton got up from his desk and turned to the officer in the witness box. "Why were you the only other police officer to notice that PC Enderby was in trouble?"

"We were outnumbered by the demonstrators. I think everyone had a lot to cope with."

"I gather that you had not come forward by the time my client was being interviewed about the alleged assault."

"I came forward when I returned on shift to the station – two days later."

"Did you speak to PC Enderby?"

"Well, I've seen him in the police station but I didn't speak to him about the events surrounding the demonstration."

"Are you sure?"

"Yes, sir."

"Only it seems a tad too convenient for PC Enderby that he is in need of witnesses to back his story up and – at that very time – you come forward with your story corroborating what he has said. You did not collude with PC Enderby at any time?"

"No, sir."

"I don't believe you." Boatman opened his mouth as if to say something but Clayton was quick to intervene. "No further questions," he said.

The prosecutor rose to his feet but the chief magistrate waived at him to sit down. "I ask you the same questions I asked PC Enderby – did at any time this group you were policing seem dangerous?"

"I don't know, sir. I was concentrating on doing my job."

"You don't know. In other words, no." Boatman seemed to be thinking of what to say again. "There's no need for you to respond," said the chief magistrate.

"That concludes the case for the prosecution," said the prosecution counsel.

"Mr Clayton?" asked the chief magistrate.

"Would you give a minute with my client, sir?" The chief magistrate nodded. Clayton walked over to Jo. "We've won the argument. They don't like the way the demonstration was policed. There's no need to give evidence."

"But I'd like to."

"Honestly, you could lose it for us."

Jo realised his knowledge of the UK judicial system was not great. "Well, if you're sure."

"I am." Clayton turned to the chief magistrate. "The defence will be calling no witnesses," he said. Jo looked nervous in the dock. "We submit that our client was going about his business – peacefully protesting. He had two concerns: one, he had a meeting to go to and two, he urgently needed to visit the toilet. He made a stride towards leaving the street where he was, whereupon PC Enderby grabbed hold of him, presumably believing that was the best way to stop him. What followed was, in fact, a scuffle but was caused by the heavy handedness of PC Enderby – not my client."

Clayton sat down and the magistrates retired to consider their verdict. It was 15 minutes before they returned.

"It's too late now," said Jo as they returned to the courtroom. The chief magistrate ordered him to stand.

"Joseph Rawlins-Clifford, we are satisfied that you are guilty of the offence of assaulting PC Ray Enderby on the day of the demonstration against the Government's immigration policy. You must be made aware that assaulting a police officer is a serious crime. However, we have heard enough today to question whether the police tactics over the demonstration of refusing to allow people to leave the scene were correct. Because of that, we believe that you were not – as the charge states – assaulting a police officer in the execution of his duty. The duty was misconceived. We are reducing the charge to common assault. You may well have had an urgent reason to leave the area and for this reason we intend to impose a fine rather than a prison sentence. You are fined £500 and bound over to keep the peace."

Jo looked forlorn. Charles Clayton sped over to them having gathered his papers. "Never mind," he said. "No prison sentence, Joseph Rawlins Clifford."

"Except my life has been ruined," he said. "I won't keep my job – and my partner's employer will insist she gives up on me."

"Must go now," said Clayton. "I have a busy rest of the day."

Jo looked after the departing Clayton. He just thinks it's all a game and I'm a figure of fun to him, he thought to himself. Joseph Rawlins Clifford. I was christened Jo. My friends all call me Jo. Still, I guess he's not my friend.

• • ● • •

Rivers looked at the Welsh household before he started his house-to-house enquiries to find out if anyone else knew anything about what had happened on the night of the murders. It could do with a lick of paint, he thought to himself, but then that had possibly not been a priority for its occupants. In a way, he was surprised the family had not moved away and bought somewhere new to live. Perhaps it was a case of not wanting to leave memories of a happy childhood with Jennifer and Anne behind. He could understand that. He had had the same feeling when giving up the flat he and his previous partner – Joanna – had lived and died. Best, though, to start afresh with Nikki somewhere else, he had eventually decided. In some ways just looking at the Welsh household brought back memories of his life with Joanna. Those last days when she had been suffering from her cancer. Snap out of it, he thought to himself. You're here to do a job. Do it. He was surprised how thoughts of Joanna could still unlock emotions in him. Six years on. He walked on to the house next door and rang the bell.

"Yes?" said an elderly lady as she answered his ring.

"My name is Philip Rivers. I'm a private detective investigating the murders that took place four years ago."

"Yes," said the woman. "I've heard all about you from the Welsh family. I don't want anything to do with you."

"Oh. Why?"

"Because you've been hired by that…."Words seemed to fail her.

"Rick Harper," Rivers said informatively.

"That Rick Harper. And he's no good. He killed those girls."

"You know that for a fact, do you?"

"Yes."

"How?"

"What do you mean 'how'?"

"The police have been investigating the case for four years and they haven't been able to pin anything on him," said Rivers.

"Well, he was here on the night of the murders. I saw him."

"Did you see him go into the Welsh's house?"

She stopped for a moment. "Well, er, no," she said, "but what other reason could he have had for being here?"

"He says he couldn't remember the house number and went home."

"And you believe him?"

"It's not a question of me believing him, ma'am," said Rivers politely. "It's a question of evidence – one way or the other – and we don't have any. Did you see him leave the square that night?"

"Er. " She thought for a moment. "Yes."

"So if you're right and he killed them he must have killed them while you were awake – possibly even watching from the window. You heard nothing?"

"Like what?"

"Screams? I imagine they wouldn't have just sat back and let him kill them."

"No, I suppose not," she said after giving the matter thought for a moment.

"So you might be wrong then?"

"I didn't see anybody else in the close that night," she said fiercely.

"In fact, you didn't see anything except a teenager looking around him trying to work out where the Welsh's lived and then going away. If I were you, I'd think twice before spitting on anyone again in future."

"What makes you think that was me?"

"It's written all over your face. Besides, even the Welsh family haven't got as much hatred for Rick Harper as you have. Anyhow, I really don't want to fall out with you. I am trying to find out what happened that night and – if the evidence points to Rick Harper being guilty – I shall be the first to say so." He paused for a moment. "Think, Mrs....?"

"Hardy. Barbara Hardy."

"Just think if you heard anything else that night."

"I went to bed after Rick Harper left the close. I did hear the slamming of a car door in the early hours of the morning and the revving up of a car engine."

"Did it sound like somebody in a hurry to get away from the close?" asked Rivers.

"I don't know," she said. "I suppose it could have been."

"You didn't take a look and see what kind of a car it was?"

"No," she said.

Rivers nodded. "Tell me," he said. "Are there many people living here now who would have been there then?"

"I don't know," she said. "There's been a lot of coming and going. The Archibalds, though, on the other side from the Welsh's.

They've been here for years. They're retired so they'll probably be in."

"Thanks," said Rivers. With that, he left Mrs Hardy ruminating as to whether she had been too hasty to come to the conclusion that Rick Harper was the killer. As she shut her front door, Rivers was busy ringing the doorbell of the Archibald's house. Rivers explained his mission to a man he guessed was in his seventies and tall and slender with a slight stoop. "Were you in on the night of the murders?" he ended by asking.

"Yes, yes, we were," said Mr Archibald, giving the impression he had had to think before giving his answer.

"Did you see or hear anything?"

"Really, Mr Rivers, we gave a statement to the police at the time."

"I know," said Rivers sympathetically, "but I am reopening the investigation and I'd rather hear the evidence from your lips personally than rely on the police's interpretation of what you said."

Mr Archibald nodded as if he sympathised with Rivers' aim. "I thought at the time the police were rather dismissive of what I had to say," he said.

"Go on."

"Well, I saw the young lad in the close. The Harper boy. He was singing as he arrived in the close. Soon stopped – but really he ought to have had respect for us at that time of night."

"Seemingly he did, though," said Rivers. "He didn't go around knocking on doors trying to find out where Jennifer Welsh lived."

"I suppose that's true." Mr Archibald paused again. "I told them – the police – about a car I heard in the early hours of the morning. Not so much a car. I looked out of the window. It was a stretch limousine. You know, one of those long thin things."

"Yes," said Rivers. "Did you see the occupants?"

"Not clearly. By the time I'd got up and looked out of the window, one of the occupants had been up to the house next door and was coming away again."

"Did he go inside?"

"I don't know. I shouldn't have thought so. It wasn't long after it had arrived in the close."

"Did you hear the engine revving up and the car driving away?"

"I didn't hear it revving up. Those stretch limousines, they don't really make that much noise."

"That's interesting," said Rivers. "Did you hear another car revving up during the course of the evening?"

"Yes, I think I did."

"Thanks. And when was that?"

"Earlier. Not long after the Harper boy had left."

"And you told all this to the police."

"Yes," he said. "They said they couldn't trace the car that had revved up its engine. I had no details and nobody else had mentioned it. As to the stretch limousine, they said they couldn't find anybody connected with the case who had a stretch limousine, so they'd had to drop that line of enquiry, too."

"Thanks," said Rivers. "You've been most helpful.," He continued his house-to-house enquiries around the close but most of the rest of the residents either had not been living in the close at the time or preferred to stall all questions by saying they had not heard anything. Still, he thought, at least he now knew there had probably been two cars in the vicinity of The Close on the night of the murders that had not belonged to any of its occupants – and an occupant of at least one had tried to gain entry to the Welsh household.

• • • • •

Jo had first rung Francesca on being convicted that day – but had only got through to her answerphone. "Guilty," he said – leaving a curt message. "Going back to the office and then home." He could do with being on his own, he thought. He was pleased to see Debra on his arrival at the office, though.

"What happened?" she asked.

"Guilty," he said. "A £500 fine."

"What does that mean?" asked Debra.

Jo smiled. "It fucks up my career and my life." He swallowed. "Sorry for swearing," he said.

"That's all right" said Debra. "I probably would do, too."

"No," said Jo. "You'd have reached for a saucepan and banged the chief magistrate on the head with it. Far more effective." It had been the way Debra had dealt with an intruder when she had found him in the Rivers' flat when she was staying with them.

"Best not to," said Debra. "Philip will be back in a minute. He's just rung to say he's finished his house to house enquiries into the Welsh' and Peters' murders."

"I should probably go home," said Jo. "I've told Francesca that's what I'm planning to do – although it might not be home for very much longer. She's been told the police force won't wear her living with a convicted criminal."

"Stupid arses," said Debra. She blushed and then added: "Sorry."

"No," said Jo. "As ever, you are entirely accurate in your analysis of their characters." He made his way to the door only to find Rivers on his way up the stairs.

"Good news," said the private detective. "We now know there were at least two visiting cars in the street on the night of the murders."

"I was found guilty," said Jo.

Rivers stopped. "Oh, I'm so sorry." He reached out to touch his friend and work colleague. "Thoughtless of me. I got carried away with what I found out this afternoon."

"Life goes on," said Jo. He looked at Rivers. The private detective's enthusiasm seemed to sum up the kind of feelings he could muster up at time about the job. "So I resign," he said.

"Resign? Why?"

"You told me – you couldn't keep an employee on your books who had a criminal record," said Jo.

"Yes, I know and I've been feeling bad about it ever since."

"I thought I'd resign to make it easier for you," said Jo.

"Have you thought of appealing against the conviction?"

"It's a bit too soon for that," said Jo. "What could I use in an appeal?"

"I don't know. You tell me."

"Well," thought Jo. "The barrister representing me wouldn't let me take the stand. The magistrates never had the chance to hear me tell my side of the story."

"I'm not sure they'll wear that," said Rivers. "It's a tactical decision by the defence – rather than an error by the judiciary. Anyhow, why wouldn't he let you give evidence?"

"He thought I was too volatile. He thought I'd accuse them of being racist and obviously they weren't."

"Nevertheless," said Rivers. "If you are contemplating an appeal, I think I could stall on taking any action against you. I will have to if the sentence stands at the end of the day but – for the moment – withdraw your resignation, please."

"Ok," said Jo. "But now I think I should go to Francesca,"

"Of course," said Rivers.

Jo made his way down the staircase to the street. He summoned a cab to take him to Francesca's – or what had been his and Francesca's home that afternoon. On arrival, he went straight to her drinks cabinet and poured himself a stiff whisky. He sat back in the armchair and did not have to wait long before Francesca arrived home from work. "I'm so sorry, darling," she said kissing him as she made her way into the living room. "I got away as soon as I could."

"The barrister didn't give me a chance to go into the witness box," he said. "Said I was a liability for thinking this was racist."

Francesca nodded. "Well, we've got to decide what we're going to do," she said.

"I'll move out."

"No, you stay here. I'll tell them I moved into Philip Rivers' house for the time being."

"Won't they think it's a bit odd that you've left your house?"

"Why should we bother about what they think?" asked Francesca. "Anyhow, I don't intend to stay in Philip's house every night." She smiled and moved over to him and gave him a kiss.

• • ● • •

"We're going out to a night club tonight," said Rivers to Nikki as he arrived home that evening.

"Oh, really? Where?"

"In Hertford."

"I didn't know they had such places here," she said.

"That's because you just haven't been looking," he replied. "There are two. Discoland and the Jaded Pearl."

"Right. Which one are we going to?"

"The Jaded Pearl. It has live blues music, apparently. I think Discoland is aiming at a slightly younger audience than us."

"Why are we going? I take it it's not just to enjoy ourselves."

"Correct," said Rivers. "A couple of the suspects were there on the night of the murders – or at least say they were. We're going to check their alibis out."

"Are you sure there will still be people there who remember that night? I would have thought they might have quite a high turnover of staff."

"You might be right," said Rivers, "but it's got to be worth bothering to find out. Are you on for it?"

Nikki nodded. "I'll just get my coat," she said.

"I've ordered a cab to pick us up in 15 minutes time. We can both enjoy a drink that way."

The cab took them to the Jaded Pearl in the centre of the town. They passed Discoland on the way to it. A young lad was being sick on the pavement and they could hear the thud of disco music even though they were in a cab going past it. It seemed to feature strobe lighting as well. It confirmed their suspicions about the clientele it was trying to attract. By contrast, the Jaded Pearl was quite dark. A three-piece band were singing a soul number as they made their way to the bar. Rivers brought out his card. "I wonder if you have any employees who were here four years ago," he asked the barman. "I'm making enquiries into a murder."

The barman looked at him as if sizing him up. "Jake," he said calling to an older man with straggling grey hair who was serving down the other end of the bar. "These guys would like a word with you."

"Yes," said the man. "Jake Prescott. Owner of the Jaded Pearl. Can I help?"

"That depends on how long you've been here," said Rivers.

"I'm the owner," he said. "I've been here since it opened eight years ago."

"Good," said Rivers. "I wonder if you remember the Welsh and Peters murders?"

"I do. Four years ago. We gave evidence to the police at the time."

"Right," said Rivers, "because two of the – well, I'd hardly call them suspects – but people of interest were here at the time."

"Three," said Jake. "Look, you guys, how about having a drink while we talk about this? On the house."

"That's very kind,"said Nikki. "I'll have a dubonnet and lemonade."

"Mine's a pint of bitter," said Rivers.

Jake furnished them with drinks and motioned them over to a table. He opened a bottle of beer himself and then sat down next to them."I felt sad that they never caught anyone in connection with those murders. One of the girls, Jennifer Welsh, used to come here quite regularly."

"You said there were three people the police were interested in that were here that night."

"I didn't say the police were interested in them. They seemed to be going through the motions."

"Two people I have spoken to gave this place as their alibi – the singer, Jimmy Atherton, and the organist in his group, Renee Hicks."

"Yes."

"They were here, then?"

"Yes."

"They said they went home after they left here?"

"I don't know where they went – but they didn't leave together."

"Ah. Then we come, I suppose, to the third man. Who was he?"

"I don't remember his name. He was a flash git, though. He'd just signed Jimmy up and was going to represent him." Jake thought for a moment. "Actually, I think his name was Peter Aymes. I remember seeing him in the paper."

"Thanks," said Rivers. "So who left with whom?"

"Renee went off by himself. I think he went over the road to the taxi rank. Jimmy went off with his agent. He had a stretch limo."

Rivers' eyes lit up. "Do you think they were going on elsewhere?" he asked.

"I couldn't tell you."

"Did you tell the police this?" asked Rivers.

"No." Rivers raised an eyebrow. "They didn't ask," said Jake. "It was a young detective constable. He said he wanted to confirm two people's alibis – Renee Hicks and Jimmy Atherton. He said they had both told the police they were here that night and he just wanted to check their alibis. Of course, they were both here. Their alibis checked out. He asked what time they left and I told him that as well."

"What time was it?" asked Rivers.

"About one o'clock. He never asked whether they left together so I never told him about the other guy. You learn in a place like this not to volunteer information to the police. Just answer their questions accurately."

In Hertford? thought Nikki. You withhold information?

"This is a tricky question. "Rivers began.

"Ask it," said Jake.

"Drugs," said Rivers. "Do you ever have trouble with drugs?"

"We don't tolerate the use of drugs on the premises. Of course, if people bring them in with them, we don't always know."

"Did you have any reason to believe that any of the three of them were dabbling in drugs?"

"If you want my honest assessment?"

"Please."

"I would have thought it a near certainty the Aymes character was a user. I would imagine that Renee was, too. I think he quite possibly could get hold of them and pass them on to other band members. Jimmy? I don't know. I don't think so. He was quite a clean living lad. I doubt whether he would have wanted to have a drugs image."

"Which makes me ask the question: why did he fraternise with Peter Aymes?"

"The lure of a professional contract. I've seen musicians take drugs to get in with people who could supply them. Not Jimmy, though. As I said, I was pretty sure he was a clean living lad."

143

"Sixty-four thousand dollar question. Could any of them be associated with the deaths of Jennifer and Lesley?"

"I don't like and I don't trust Aymes. I don't trust Renee. Jimmy, no, I'd stake my mortgage on that."

"Thanks."

"Is that all?"

"Yes, but we'll have another drink," said Rivers. "We'll pay for it this time. I'll have a beer. Would you like one, too?" Jake went off to get the drinks. "Don't let them say I never mix work with pleasure," said Rivers after Jake had returned. "This is not a bad place."

Nikki smiled. "Thanks for the night out," she said. "We should do it more often."

Jake returned with the drinks and placed them down on the table. "I wish you luck," he said. "The killers of that girl don't deserve to get away with it."

"Killers?" queried Rivers.

"Or killer. It could be more than one if it was a drug fuelled killing."

"There's no chance that Renee Hicks went away with Peter Aymes and Jimmy Atherton went home, is there?" asked Rivers.

"No," said Jake. "I'd love to tell you yes in the hope it would help you to wrap your murder case up but that didn't happen."

"Just a thought," said Rivers.

• • ● • •

"Sorry, Francesca, the chief constable wants to see you again," said Gary Clarke as his boss arrived for work that morning.

"There's no prize for guessing what that's about," she said. "Honestly, I wish he could take more of an interest in our active investigations than stressing out about the thought that one of his senior detectives may be living with a criminal."

"Honeymoon period over?" suggested Gary.

"For both of us, it seems," said Francesca. "I was hoping he was going to be a breath of fresh air after...." She looked at Gary. ".... sorry, Gary, your uncle."

"You mean the groper?" said Gary trying to indicate to his boss that he did not feel in any way offended by the disparaging reference to the previous chief constable, his uncle, who had been forced to resign after allegations of sexual assault against him by – among others – Francesca.

"Yes," she said blushing. "I also thought he rated me."

"He probably does," said Gary. "That's why he's insisting you should have a whiter than white image to the public. There are still one or two people around who resent the fact that you did for the last chief constable. They could be only too happy to put the boot in if they found you were living with a criminal." He paused for a moment and then added: "And I'm not saying you are. It's just that the law says you are."

"Thanks, Gary," she said as she left the office for her meeting with the chief constable. She reflected on Gary for a moment. He had come a long way from the gauche detective constable who had tried to make a mark for himself by being objectionable to most of the members of the public that he met. By the time she had succumbed to these thoughts, she found herself outside the chief constable's office. "Francesca Manners," she said to his secretary upon arrival.

Rory Gleeson looked up from his office and saw her standing in the doorway. He came out to meet her. "Do come in," he said. She smiled and took a seat in his office. "Can I first say how sorry I am that your partner was found guilty of the assault on the police constable?" he said. "I have to add, though, that it does bring us back to the debate that we were having before his trial."

"Which means I have to leave him to keep my job."

"I didn't say that – exactly," said Gleeson. "Just that I couldn't stomach one of my senior officers living with a known criminal."

"In which case, I'll move out. I'll be going to stay with Philip Rivers and his wife whilst I sort things out. I'll notify the office of the address."

"Why not let.... " Gleeson looked at his papers to find out the name of Francesca's partner " .... Jo move out."

"I think I could cope with it better. I think Jo needs a period of stability in his life following the conviction. Anyhow I beg to point out that the mechanism by which we lead separate lives has nothing to do with the police force."

"Just so long as you realise the force won't tolerate the two of you living together."

"I think I've got that message loud and clear, sir."

"Good."

"Is that all then, sir?"

"Yes."

"May I then thank you, sir, for arranging to get me caught on camera when I went to interview Rick Harper in line with your instructions?"

"What?"

"I think you heard, sir. It would be helpful if I could carry out my enquiries without the intrusion of the press."

"You should be above trying to cut a sarcastic tone with me, Francesca," said Gleeson. "It won't do the image of the force any harm if we are seen to be re-opening a four-year-old murder enquiry into a particularly brutal killing – and trying to get it solved. I am given to understand the story and the picture are likely to feature on the front page tomorrow. It would probably not have done without the picture." He looked at her squarely in the eyes. "That is all," he said.

"Sir."

• • ● • •

"There's a Winston Samuel waiting for you in reception," the receptionist said on calling Rosemary Gallagher just as she was about to leave her office.

"Winston Samuel?" She racked her brains. "I don't think I know him."

"He agrees that's right – but says he's got important information for you."

"I'll come out." Rosemary walked out into the reception area to be greeted by a tall Afro-Caribbean man with a firm handshake. "What can I do for you?"

"It's a question of what I can do for you," he said. "I have some information which could help your client, Jo Rawlins Clifford."

"You'd better come in to my office." Once inside, Rosemary instructed her secretary to make tea for the two of them. "Now, Mr Samuel," she began.

"I am – or rather was – a police officer – working alongside PCs Enderby and Boatman and helping to police the demonstration during which your client was arrested."

"Was?" said Rosemary.

"I've resigned," he said. He adopted a matter of fact tone and then cleared his throat. "Let me take you back to the morning of the demonstration. We all assembled at the police station before going on duty on the streets. I overheard a conversation in which PC Enderby used extremely racist language. It was obvious he didn't approve of the aims of the demonstration."

"What did he say?"

"Basically, in much cruder terms, he said he was going to make sure he nabbed one of those ...." Samuel hesitated.

"Go on," said Rosemary softly.

"One of those nignogs for making him work overtime on his wife's birthday. I'm sorry about the language."

Rosemary brushed his apology aside. "Who was he talking to?"

"No-one in particular. Just to anybody who'd listen"

"Did anyone complain?"

"No. They were too busy preparing to go out on to the street."

"PC Boatman?"

"Was next to him when he was speaking but I have to admit he didn't respond. I was in the same theatre of operation as Enderby throughout the demonstration. I saw the arrest of your client. He never laid a finger on PC Enderby. All the aggression came from Enderby. He prodded your client and shoved him back into the midst of the demonstration. When your client got up and tried to talk to him again, he grabbed his arm and scuffled with him until he could get handcuffs on him."

"Why didn't you come forward beforehand?"

"I thought it would all come out at the trial and that there wouldn't be enough evidence to convict your client. I thought he'd get off."

"But you should have reported PC Enderby for racist behaviour."

"I know but – I'm ashamed to admit it – I was worried about the effect on my career of laying a complaint against a brother officer. When your client was found guilty, I did a lot of soul searching. I realised I had to come forward. I decided to resign from the force. I didn't want to go through their internal channels for airing grievances. I thought I'd come straight to you instead."

"And I thank you for that," said Rosemary. "What about PC Boatman? He lied on oath, then."

"Yes. He was not in a position to see what happened. I was the officer nearest to your client and PC Enderby."

"He was taking a great risk then displaying such racist behaviour in front of a black police officer."

"I have to say it's not the first occasion on which I have witnessed him making racist comments. He may have thought I would never do anything about it."

"Or perhaps he's just unthinking of the consequences." Rosemary looked at Samuel squarely in the eyes. "Are you prepared to give evidence to this effect should there by an appeal?" she asked.

"Of course," he said. "Resigning would be rather a futile gesture if I didn't."

"Right," she said. "May I take a written statement from you outlining what you are prepared to say which I can then use in my grounds for an appeal?"

"Yes."

• • ● • •

"Thank you for coming to see me, Detective Constable Clarke," said Rory Gleeson as he offered his detective a seat. "I have a task I'd like you to carry out for me."

"Yes, sir."

"You're aware of Detective Chief Inspector Manners' situation?"

Gary feigned ignorance. "Sir?"

"Her partner has been found guilty of assaulting a police officer?" Gary nodded. "Good," he said. "Well, a rather difficult situation has presented itself. The force is anxious she should not be found to be living with a criminal. She assures me she is not and that she has moved out of her home to live with this...." He looked at a note on his desk. ".... this private detective Philip Rivers."

Gary smiled. He knew there were some forces where the senior brass would have been almost as unhappy at the thought that one of their senior detectives was living with a private detective. "Yes, sir," he said.

"You knew that?"

"I overheard her organising it on the telephone."

"I'm not sure I believe her." Gary eyed him suspiciously. "I want you to find out whether she's telling the truth or whether – in reality – she's still living with this guy."

Is it really that big a deal, Gary thought to himself. "In other words, you want me to snoop on her, sir," he said.

"I wouldn't put it quite like that. You're a detective. You should be able to find ways of determining whether she's telling the truth without – as you put it – snooping on her."

"Sir?" Gary began tentatively.

"Yes." Gleeson's tone was neither encouraging nor discouraging.

"Is it really the best use of police resources to have one officer snooping on another? Surely, I would be better off investigating real crimes?"

"Believe it or not, I have Francesca's best interests at heart." He sighed. "I can't tell her that. Besides, she wouldn't believe me. There are still one or two senior officers and people involved at a high level with the police force who resent her part in the downfall of my predecessor, your uncle. I don't want her to give them any ammunition to discredit her."

Gary smiled. "I told her that might be why you're acting the way you are, sir," he said.

"Thank you, detective constable, but you should really keep those thoughts to yourself," said Gleeson. "Will you check for me whether she really has left this guy?" He smiled. "Actually, it's not a request. It's an order," he added.

"Yes, sir," said Gary. At that he was dismissed from the Chief Constable's presence. He glanced at his watch. It was getting late – about eight o'clock. He thought he would go home and pick Debra up and go round to Francesca's house – pretending that he had just called round on the off chance that she and Jo would like to go round for a drink.

"You're inviting me out with you?" said Debra suspiciously when he put his plan to her.

"I've got to go round and see Francesca," he said. "I thought it would be nice if you came too."

Mmm, thought Debra. This is a far cry from the man who a year ago was questioning me until two o'clock in the morning. "Thank you," she said.

"I'll drive," said Gary as they made their way out to the car. It was superfluous to say that, thought Debra, seeing as she did not possess a car. The drive to Francesca's house only took ten minutes. Jo answered his knock on the door.

"Gary?" he said. "What brings you round here?"

"We thought you might like to be taken out of yourself," he said. By this time Debra was standing by his side on the doorstep. "We thought you might like to go for a drink."

"Right," said Jo. "That's nice."

"Is Francesca with you?"

Jo remained silent. He looked embarrassed. A voice sounded out behind him. "Francesca is with him," it said. At that Francesca emerged in the hallway. "Is that what you really wanted to know?" she said.

Gary acted as if flustered. Debra looked quizzically at him. "What's going on here?" she asked.

"I think you'll find your friend is checking up on me. He doesn't really want to go out for a drink. At least that's not his primary concern."

"It is now," said Gary. "Let's talk."

"We can talk here," said Francesca. "Unless you feel that would be compromising you."

"No," said Gary.

"Would somebody mind telling me what's going on here?" asked Debra.

"Precisely," said Jo.

Francesca invited them both in and – when she had poured drinks for all of them – suggested to Gary he should tell them the real reason for his visit.

"All right," he said. "The chief constable has told me to check whether you really have left Jo."

"Left Jo?" said Debra as if concerned by the idea.

"Yes, Debra," said Francesca. "The chief constable does not think one of his senior detectives should be living with a man with a criminal record so I told him I had moved in to live with Philip and Nikki. As you can see, I haven't." She paused. "Yet." The last word was spat out in Gary's direction. "The ball is in your court, I believe," she said.

"And I have no intention of telling the chief constable you've reneged on your promise to him – but I would warn you that there are elements in the police force who would like to see you come a cropper. Friends of my uncle." He then turned to Debra. "The former chief constable whose downfall she was responsible for. I come to warn you they may check on you, too, and they won't be as pliable as I am."

"Gary," said Francesca. "I'm sorry if I gave you a hard time. You're one of the good guys."

"And so is the chief constable. He just doesn't, can't show it."

"I will move out," said Francesca, "but I have to tell you any interruption to our relationship won't be long term." With that, she placed a hand on Jo's knee.

"What does that mean?" asked Gary.

"I'm as interested as you in the answer to that," said Jo.

"If I can't live with my partner if I remain a member of the police force, maybe I'll have to think of something else to do," she said.

• • ● • •

Renee scrutinised Rivers' card. "Your agency again," he said unenthusiastically.

"I suppose I shouldn't expect warm welcomes," said Rivers. "I'd like to have a further word with you. May I come in?"

"I suppose you might as well," he said. "What do you want?"

"I want you to tell me the truth about what happened on the night of the murders."

"Why should I? I've already told you what you need to know."

"Which was a lie." Rivers paused for a moment. "You said you and Jimmy went to the night club in Hertford – and then went home. Well, you might have done but Jimmy didn't."

Renee eyed him accusingly. "What do you mean?"

"I think you understand English."

"Don't take that tone with me," said Renee threateningly.

"Sorry. I didn't mean to disparage you."

"On the grounds of my colour?"

"No. I merely meant to say I know – having spoken to the night club owner – that there were three of you in that night club that night. You may well have gone home. Jimmy didn't. He stayed with Peter Aymes, his new manager. They went on to somewhere else. Do you know where that was?" Renee remained silent. "Well, do you?" asked Rivers.

"I don't. No."

"Would you like to hazard a guess?" Renee eyed him intently. "Jennifer Welsh's. Peter Aymes had a stretch limo. A stretch limo was seen outside Jennifer's home later on that night. It doesn't take a genius to put two and two together."

"But it depends on what they make."

"Did you never question Jimmy about what happened?"

"He said they didn't get in. He went because he overheard Jennifer inviting Rick round. He thought there might be a party."

"But there wasn't. And what did he do when he found that out?"

"He was at home when I woke up the following morning." Renee paused again. "I'm telling you the truth, man."

"And Peter Aymes?"

"He doesn't live here." He grinned. "Besides there's no room for a stretch limo in these streets."

"What kind of state were they in?"

"What do you mean?"

"You know. Look, Renee, I'm not the police. I don't care if you take drugs, peddle drugs or whatever. I'm just trying to solve a murder."

"Well, don't try and pin it on Jimmy. A nicer man you couldn't meet. He wouldn't dabble in drugs. He was clean, man, that day. And every day."

"And Peter Aymes?" Renee remained silent. "Your silence speaks volumes," said Rivers.

"Then you should be able to hear what the volumes are saying."

CHAPTER SIX

"I tried to get hold of you last night but you weren't answering," said Rosemary in mitigation as she finally tracked Jo down on his mobile the following morning. "Good news – a witness has come forward and told us that PC Enderby was lying and is a racist."

"So tell me something I don't know," said Jo.

"Jo, don't be so dismissive," said Rosemary reproachfully. "It's grounds for appeal – and I'm pretty sure we'll be successful. At the very least I would have thought it helped towards saying the guilty verdict was unsafe."

"Who is this witness?"

"A black police officer. He's resigned from the force which, he says, makes him freer to relate what he saw."

"And why didn't he come forward before?"

"He didn't want to get involved in disciplinary procedures against Enderby. He also thought you'd be found not guilty so it wouldn't matter. Where are you, Jo?"

"I'm at home. At least I'm at Francesca's house. She's not here by the way. Police etiquette insists she shouldn't be having anything to do with a known criminal."

"You still sound…."

"….Pissed off. Is that the word you're looking for? Yes, I am. I've done nothing wrong – yet my relationship has been torn apart and my job's in jeopardy."

"That could all be over soon. Go back to Rivers and tell him what's happened. It'll convince him he was right to keep you on."

"Yes, but how many more times is this going to happen?"

"I'm sorry, Jo, I don't follow."

"No, you wouldn't, Rosemary. You're a nice middle class girl from Hertfordshire. Nobody's ever going to single you out for arrest if you go on a demonstration – which I bet you haven't. I still want to do in my life what my heart tells me is correct –

go on a demonstration protesting about the way people with the same pigmentation of the skin as I have are treated by the immigration service. At least if I was back in Calicos this wouldn't be happening to me."

"Treat your problems one step at a time," said Rosemary. "First we'll get the conviction quashed. That will allow you to rest easy in your job and for Francesca to return home and live with you. And, by the way, I have been on a demonstration. I demonstrated against the Iraqi war way back when."

Jo smiled. "I'm sorry, Rosemary, I didn't mean to disparage you. I was just trying to point out that you can't quite experience the worries that I do."

"Point taken and no harm done."

"And talking about people who can't quite experience the worries that I do, could I have a different barrister this time?"

"I'll see what I can do," promised Rosemary. "You ought to tell Francesca what's happened, though, as soon as possible. It'll put her mind at rest."

"Yes," said Jo, "she was talking about quitting her job last night which would be a shame." He reflected. "More than a shame, in fact. She would be a great loss to the force."

"Do that – and get yourself off to Philip Rivers' office and see if you can be of use to him."

"Will do."

● ● ● ● ●

"You didn't have to speak to Anne," said Rick as he ushered Rivers into his parents' living room. "She's been through enough without having to believe she's considered to be a suspect in these murders."

"I have to speak to everyone," said Rivers, "and it's not necessarily that I question them as suspects. I agree there's hardly even a remote chance that she had anything to do with the murders – but she did give me some useful information for the investigation."

"Oh? What?"

"She said she thought Renee was peddling drugs. It subsequently opened up a new line of inquiry. I discovered he'd lied to the police about going home with Jimmy on the night of the murder. They were drinking in the Jaded Pearl night club on the night of the murder. Renee left on his own – he probably did go home. Jimmy and his new manager, Peter Aymes, went off in the manager's stretch limo to Jennifer's place. It was seen by one of the neighbours."

"So I wasn't the only one seen in the close that night?"

"I think George Brett knew about the limo – what he didn't know was who was in it or the fact that Peter Aymes had been doing drugs that night. He should have found out but didn't."

"What drugs was Aymes doing?"

"I don't know but I think it's more likely to have been cocaine than cannabis."

Rick swallowed. "So I'm beginning to look a less likely suspect?" he said.

"You're not off the hook yet but I would say there's more compelling evidence against Peter Aymes or Jimmy Atherton than you."

"Jimmy? No way," said Rick.

"That's what everybody says. Why?"

"He's a really nice guy. Professional. You know, he worked in the civil service before he got this fulltime singing contract."

"And that means he couldn't possibly have done it. You know a word to the wise, sometimes people are not as they seem on the surface. I think I'd better go and try and find this Aymes guy and start questioning him about what he was doing that night."

Rick leaned forward in his chair. "I can see why you had to question Anne," he said. "I just ...." His voice tailed off.

"You've got a thing for her," said Rivers. "I can see it. I think she cares for you, too."

"I should go and see her."

"No," said Rivers emphatically. "Her father may not be one of the out and out Rick Harper haters, but – in his eyes – you haven't been cleared of involvement in his daughter's murder. Let's put it that way. It would be too much for him to have you in his house."

"Then I'll have to go round when he's not there."

"Up to you," said Rivers shrugging his shoulders, "but I would counsel against it."

Rick nodded. "I'll bear in mind what you say," he added. But you'll bloody ignore me, Rivers thought to himself. "Anything else to report?" Rick asked.

"Duncan Hamilton," said Rivers. "His wife is giving him an alibi. Says she was with him and not with friends as she had previously stated."

"In the section house?"

"Pardon?"

"Duncan was staying in the police section house while he was training to be a police officer. It would be almost as difficult to smuggle her in there as it would be to infiltrate Fort Knox. Besides, I don't think they were going out with each other at that stage."

"Could have been the start of a beautiful friendship," said Rivers. He looked at Rick as if asking for a response but got none. "Well, I'd better check her previous alibi out," he added. "She said she was staying with an Alison Palmer but I don't have an address for her and her address is not in police files."

"I don't suppose Brett bothered to interview her. Just accepted what Duncan said – that he went back to the police section house after the dance."

"Do you know whether he did or not?"

"No," said Rick. "I didn't really have access to any of these people after the murder. I tell you who will know how to get hold of Alison Palmer. Graham Hands. She was one of his set."

"Right. I'll try him again."

Rick reflected on the information he had been given. "It makes sense," he said tentatively.

"I'm glad about that," Rivers intervened.

"No, Jimmy would have known Jennifer's address. After all, they had been an item. He probably overheard her inviting me back and thought there was some kind of a party going on there but he didn't kill her. That I'm sure of and – if his drug crazed friend did – why is he still with him, allowing him to be his manager? He must have known that he did. If he did."

"Ambition can do a lot to a man."

"Not that much to Jimmy."

"So who do you think is most likely to be responsible for the murder?"

Rick laughed. "I'm glad I don't have to come up with the answer to that one," he said. "That's why I hired you."

Rivers nodded. He looked at his client. It was good therapy for him to be involved in discussing alternative scenarios for the deaths of Jennifer and Lesley. He could see that. As Rick ushered Rivers to the door, he could see there was more of a spring to his client's step than there had been when he had first hired him.

• • ● • •

"I thought I'd go and see George Brett again this morning," Francesca said to Gary as her detective constable arrived in the office.

"Poor chap will be feeling persecuted," said Gary.

"Why?"

"Well, every time you or Rivers go to see him you expose more flaws in the way he conducted his investigation."

"He's got a thicker skin than that," said Francesca.

"I don't know. Maybe he genuinely wanted to put somebody away for the murders but couldn't see beyond Rick Harper as a suspect," said Gary.

"I don't think analysing how George Brett's brain works – if it does – is going to get us anywhere," said Francesca. She went into her office which was partitioned off from Gary's and spied on her desk the local paper. She picked it up. The front page lead – accompanied by a picture of her and Gary leaving Rick Harper's house – was about how detectives had reopened the murder inquiry. "Bit of journalistic licence there," she said. "We didn't reopen it. It was never closed."

"I think I'd let them get away with that one," said Gary.

Francesca smiled. She put the paper down. "You know, I've got an idea here," she said. "There seems to be quite an appetite for stories about the murders. Why don't I go round and offer the reporter an interview about our investigation? I could say we're looking at new leads. Leave it a bit vague, obviously, because we don't want to finger anyone with any blame."

"We haven't got any new leads," protested Gary.

"But I could have a word with Rivers. He has. What harm could it do?"

"Upset Professor Saunders. He obviously thinks that it's signed, sealed and delivered that Rick Harper is the killer."

"I don't see why I have to worry about him," said Francesca defensively.

"The chief constable does."

"Yes, but surely all Saunders wants to do is to protect his son from any involvement in the murder. If my interview doesn't cast any suspicion on him, he won't care a jot. I'll make an appointment with the journalist who wrote this story," she said jabbing her finger down on the front page lead of the paper. "Would you like to come with me?"

"I think I'm supposed to be tailing you – not accompanying you everywhere."

"Surely that's all at an end now with the discovery of this new witness in Jo's case?" said Francesca.

"What new witness?"

"The black police officer who recalls Jo's arresting officer making racist remarks before the beginning of the demonstration and was near enough to him during the demo to be sure that Jo never lifted a finger to attack him. Quite the other way round, in fact."

"Jo is still guilty of assault in the Chief Constable's eyes until he has all charges against him rescinded."

"Well," said Francesca, "I don't care what hat you're wearing. You're very welcome to accompany me to the interview with the journalist." With that, she strode from the office and made her way by car to George Brett's house.

"At least it's not that private detective again," said Brett on finding out who his caller was.

"Nice to see you again, too," said Francesca. "I wish you could say something positive from time to time."

159

"Retirement's not much fun," he mumbled. Francesca looked at him. He was wearing jeans and a crumpled shirt – which looked as if it had not been washed for some time. She shook her head. "Why don't you go out and spoil yourself, George?" she asked. "Buy some new clothes?"

"You wanted something?" he said gruffly.

"Yes," she said. She had been briefed by Rivers about the latest developments in his investigation. "What about this stretch limo which was in the close where Jennifer lived on the night of the murders?"

"Oh, you've found out about that."

"You knew about it?"

"Yes, couldn't find out who owned it. Anyhow, it was only in the close for about five minutes. No-one went inside Jennifer's house from it."

"Suppose I told you its driver had been snorting cocaine earlier in the evening and its passenger was a former lover of Jennifer Welsh's?" Brett did not respond. "Well, the driver was Peter Aymes, the – for want of a better word – impresario and the passenger was Jimmy Atherton. You could have found that out if you'd just taken a smidgeon of interest in mounting a balanced investigation into the murders."

"Did you just come round to give me a good kicking again?"

"No, I genuinely came round to see if you thought there was a legitimate reason why you airbrushed the existence of the stretch limo out of your investigation."

"I told you. It was only there for five minutes and its occupants never went inside Jennifer Welsh's home."

"In other words, no."

"Let me tell you about Rick Harper, then," he said icily. "Let me tell you why I thought the little toe rag should be locked away. He's not a nice man."

"And that's our criteria for concluding murder investigations?"

"Hear me out. Did you know that he used to go out with Mary Wightman?"

"No," said Francesca. "I don't even know who Mary Wightman is."

"So, you don't know everything?" sneered Brett. "In a sense it doesn't really matter who she is. It was the way he treated her that matters. She is, in fact, the sister of Stan Wightman. You've come across him."

"I believe Philip Rivers has him on his list of people to be interviewed. He is the former boyfriend of Lesley Peters. He also knows Thomas Saunders."

"So you do know something," said Brett. "Right. Rick Harper was friends with Thomas Saunders and they were talking about Mary Wightman one day. Rick said – and I quote; "I often wonder what difference it would make if I said 'I hate you' instead of 'I love you' when I'm with a woman. Would she notice?" Shows us a side of Rick Harper's character that's not quite the sympathetic character that Rivers would have us believe in. If he can mix up hate and love, what could he do when he was making love to Jennifer Welsh?"

"You think he's disturbed?"

"I should say so. He didn't treat Thomas Saunders all that well either. According to Professor Saunders, he pretended to have a gay relationship with him and then just dumped him. That's why I spent so much time and energy trying to prove the bastard guilty."

"Did Mary Wightman ever find out that he'd said that about her?" asked Francesca.

"I don't know," said Brett – once again giving the impression that he wasn't interested in the answer to that question. "I don't think it makes much difference whether she did or not. It says more about his character than anything about her. I do know that Thomas told her brother, Stan. I don't think he was that pleased about it. I think he would have tried to shield his sister from it. He was that type."

"What type?"

"Quiet. Reserved. Didn't seem to want to hurt a flea. So what do you think of your crusade to clear Rick Harper's name now?"

"There is no crusade to clear Rick Harper's name," said Francesca. "I'll just pass this information on to Philip Rivers for use in his investigation."

Brett shook his head. "You'll come round to my way of thinking in the end," he said.

• • ● • •

"Rick!" Anne's voice conveyed a mixture of shock and delight on finding out the identity of her visitor. "What are you doing here?"

"I came to see you. Are you on your own?"

"Yes. My father's gone for a walk. That usually means a visit to a pub. Mother's visiting friends."

"So they're not likely to come back any time soon."

"No." Anne seemed nervous – as if not quite sure what to say.

"Can I come in?" he asked. "It's probably not a good idea for me to be seen standing on your doorstep." He turned to face the house on the left. "Especially by her. She was the one who spat at me."

"Of course." She moved to her side. "Do come in." She ushered him into the sitting room.

"How have you been?" he asked once he was seated on an armchair in the sitting room.

"Not too bad," she said. "It's my father who's taken it the worst." They both looked at each other – neither quite sure of what to say.

Rick broke the ice. "It's been four years," he said.

"Yes."

"I never got round to saying it before but...." he paused to summon up courage. "I've always had a soft spot for you." Anne blushed but still said nothing. She was not going to make it easy for him, Rick surmised. "Part of the reason for that was Jennifer," he said. "She had an uncanny knack of flinging herself at me just when I was plucking up courage to ask you out."

"Don't flatter yourself," she said. "You weren't the only one she flung herself at." She stopped in her tracks. "I'm sorry," she said. "I don't mean to speak ill of the dead."

"You're not speaking ill of her. That was just the way she was. If anything, you're speaking ill of me. I shouldn't have succumbed to it." He wanted to say he had never really fancied Jennifer but

162

thought that might be the wrong thing to do in the circumstances. "Looking at you, I can see why I harboured that soft spot for you," he went on.

Anne broke her silence. "Mixed feelings," she said nervously. "On the one hand I want to tell you I feel the same way about you. On the other, I wonder what would happen if my parents realised that."

"They still believe I was involved in her murder, then?"

"Father has mellowed. He can concede there are other explanations – especially after being visited by your private detective, Mr Rivers. On the other hand, you still haven't been cleared – in his eyes."

"Why do I have to be cleared? I haven't been charged with anything. You believe I wasn't involved, don't you?"

"Yes," said Anne. "I can't conceive of you doing anything like that."

"Well, then," he said. He got up from the armchair and walked over to where Anne was sitting. He bent down to give her a kiss on the cheek which became much more passionate an embrace as she flung her arms around him and insisted on being kissed on the mouth.

"Oh, Anne," he said. "I never thought this would happen." He kissed her passionately on the lips again. "Is there anywhere we could go that would be more comfortable?" he asked.

"Yes, but…." She disentangled herself from his embrace. "It wouldn't be right. I'd feel I would be betraying my father."

"But not Jennifer."

"Jennifer would give it her blessing. Her motto was always 'go for it'. It's no good, though, I can't get round the fact that I would feel guilty. Your private detective seems to be making some progress. Hopefully you'll soon be cleared and then we can start seeing each other. At least we both now know what we want."

"There is that," agreed Rick. "Do you think I should go now?"

"No, stay for a bit. I'm sure my parents won't be back for a while. I'll make us a drink. Coffee or tea?"

"Tea – although something stronger to celebrate the progress we have made wouldn't go amiss."

"There's a bottle of white wine in the fridge," said Anne.

"That'll do."

"It'll have to." She went into the kitchen and poured out two glasses then returned to the sitting room, carrying the bottle as well.

"To us," said Rick raising his glass.

Anne smiled. "To us," she echoed. The two of them were so engrossed in themselves that they failed to notice Anne's father arriving at the front door. It was only when Anne heard the turn of the key in the lock that she realised what was happening. "Oh, my God," she said. "It's my father."

"Hallo, darling," said a voice from the hallway. "I thought I'd come home for a spot of lunch." By this time he had entered the sitting room and noticed Rick quaffing a glass of wine and sitting on the armchair. He looked at Anne with a shocked expression on his face. "What's he doing here?" he said, jabbing a finger in Rick's direction.

"He came round to see me, father."

"And you let him in and now he's drinking my wine. The man who killed your sister drinking wine with you in my living room."

"I did not kill your daughter, Mr Welsh."

"Shut up," shouted Arthur Welsh. "You don't speak to me in my house. Do you hear?"

"I'd better go," said Rick getting up from his chair. He finished his glass of wine – much to Arthur's annoyance – before turning to Anne. "Thank you for inviting me in," he said, "and for believing me." He walked past Mr Welsh to the corridor. "I hope there will come a time, sir, when we can meet in more pleasant circumstances," he said and then repeated: "I did not kill your daughter."

Arthur Welsh said nothing. Instead he went to the coffee table where there was a copy of the local paper. "Detectives have reopened the murder enquiry into the death of Jennifer Welsh," he said reading from its front page, "and who's the first person they interviewed – you." He jabbed his finger down on the photograph on the front page. "Out," he said. "Out now." Rick opened the front door only for Arthur to wrench it from him and open it wider. He virtually shoved Rick out of the front door but ended up gasping for breath as a result of his exertions. "Out," he shouted as he stumbled backwards and fell down clutching his heart.

Rick stopped and turned – a worried look on his face. "No," said Anne. "Go. I'll look after him. What is it, Dad?"

"Heart," he managed to say. "Heart attack, I think. Get an ambulance."

She rushed inside and to the telephone. "Ambulance, please," she said when the emergency service number answered. She gave the address and then went to comfort her father as he lay on the doorstep. "Do you want to come inside?" she asked.

"Just leave me," he said. "I'll wait here until the ambulance comes."

A head popped over the garden fence. It was Barbara Hardy. "What's happened?"

"My father's had a heart attack."

"That man," she began, "that just went. It was Rick Harper, wasn't it?"

"Yes," conceded Anne.

"Well, I'm not surprised, then. Not satisfied with killing your sister."

"You don't know that."

● ● ● ● ●

Francesca and Gary walked into the offices of the local paper – Gary holding a copy of it under his arm. They walked up to the reception desk. "We'd like to see ....," Francesca lifted the newspaper from Gary's grasp and looked at the front page. "Jeff Cantelow."

"Who shall I say is calling?"

Both got out their warrant cards and showed them to the receptionist who nodded as if she appreciated the urgency of the situation. "Jeff," she said on obtaining a reply to her call. "The police want to see you."

"Better send them up."

It was an open plan office, Francesca noted as she obeyed the receptionist's instructions as to how to get to the newsroom. There could not have been more than four reporters around and several empty desks. There was a separate office with a glass exterior which Francesca surmised was probably where the editor worked. Hunched up in the corner were two other members of staff sharing a desk. One of the reporters got up and walked over to Francesca and Gary. They shook hands. "Jeff Cantelow," he said. "I'm afraid we don't stretch to a private office or interview room." He pulled a couple of seats over from an empty desk. "Do sit down, though."

"Thank you," said Francesca. "We read your article."

"Good." He refrained from asking them whether they had liked it. He felt he was going to find out sooner or later – probably sooner.

"I'd like to thank you for your interest in the case."

"Oh." Francesca's reaction had surprised him. He had assumed they had arrived mob-handed to complain about it. "Good," he said again.

"We thought it might be worth sharing our thinking with you about the case for a follow up article."

"Thank you."

"Do you want to take notes?" asked Francesca. "Then we'll start."

Cantelow reached across his desk for a notebook. "Fine."

"You're the interviewer," prompted Francesca. Cantelow seemed so surprised at the friendly approach of the officers that he seemed unsure as to how to take advantage of it. "So fire away."

"Yes," he said, "so what prompted you to reopen the case?"

"We haven't so much reopened it as just revived it. It's always been an ongoing investigation."

"But was there something specific that prompted you to make new enquiries."

"Yes, Rick Harper." She bent down and picked up the paper. "The man in the picture," she said. Cantelow nodded. "He has hired a private detective to clear his name. We felt we shouldn't be complacent and leave it to him to unearth any fresh facts in the investigation."

"This Rick Harper – is he still the prime suspect in the investigation?"

"I don't think I'd ever have referred to him as the chief suspect."

"Your predecessor, George Brett, did. I've been around on this paper for years. He was never reluctant to come forward and steer us in the direction of Rick Harper as the prime suspect."

"There are no prime suspects," said Francesca. "That's why it's misleading to accompany your article with a photograph of us talking to Rick Harper. I can see why you did it. I know you were tipped off about our visit to him. Not by us, though." Jeff remained silent. "You don't have to protect your source," she continued. "It's someone who answers to the name 'chief constable'." She paused for effect.

"I'm not saying anything."

"No," said Francesca. "We now know that a stretch limousine was seen in the road outside Jennifer's house in the early hours of the morning on the night she was killed. One of the occupants may have tried to gain entry to her house."

"Successfully?"

"We don't know yet?"

"Who were the occupants?"

"I can't tell you that."

"But you know who they were?"

"I can't tell you that."

"Also, we are building a picture of the character of Jennifer Welsh – one of the girls that were murdered. She had had relationships with at least two other men who were at the dance in Hertford on the night she was killed. Any of them could have heard her inviting Rick Harper round to her home when the dance finished. Revenge on a lover who had spurned them might have been a motive."

"Do you know who these two men were?"

"We can't go into that."

"Can I assume that one of them was one of the occupants of the stretch limo?"

"Clever question."

"To which I'm not getting an answer?"

"Correct."

"Then I think I know what the answer is."

"Be careful making assumptions," warned Francesca. Gary

admired the way she was treating the interview. She had given Cantelow just enough meat for a follow-up story which could warrant front page treatment again. Jealous lover sought in teenage girl's killing, he thought to himself. Francesca, for her part, hoped the interview would persuade Rick Harper to believe that he wasn't the only show in town when it came to apportioning blame for the killing of Jennifer and Lesley. It also might make one or two fringe players in the enquiry quake in their boots. "I think that's all we can say at this precise moment," said Francesca, "but I'd like to keep communications between the three of us open."

"You've been more than helpful," said Cantelow.

"It goes without saying that we'd welcome an appeal for witnesses to come forward who might have seen the stretch limo and its occupants in The Close where Jennifer lived. Also, if anybody has any further information about the character of Jennifer Welsh, that would be of interest to us."

"Fine," said Cantelow. "Just one more request. Could we take a picture of the two of you visiting our offices?"

Francesca looked at Gary. "I'm not sure that will be necessary," she said.

"Put it this way," said Cantelow. "If we don't have a fresh picture, we'll have to use that one of you with Rick Harper again and that will give entirely the wrong impression. It will suggest he still is very much in your thinking when it comes to investigating the murders whereas my understanding is that you want to get the message across that the net has been widened."

Francesca glanced at Gary. She smiled. "Put like that," she said, "how can I resist?"

Cantelow left them to go and raise a photographer from their separate office. "He'll go far," said Gary once Cantelow was out of earshot.

"I'm not so sure," said Francesca. "He said he had been on the paper for years. Maybe he likes being a big fish in a small pool. Having said that, I agree. He's sharp. He's on the level, too. We can do business with him in future, I think."

• • • • •

By comparison, it had been a quiet day in Philip Rivers' office. Jo had not put in an appearance. Rivers himself had not exactly rushed back after his briefing session with Rick Harper that morning. Debra had been left on her own to hold the fort. There was a call from Francesca for Rivers. Debra said she would pass on the message that she had called. Then there was one from a Professor Saint asking to speak to Rivers. Debra never handed out his mobile number in such circumstances – but she did think it could be important. She resolved to ring Rivers herself and pass the message on.

"Professor Saint," he said. "I recognise the name but I can't quite place it. I'll come back and give him a ring. "Rivers preferred to make important calls from the cosiness of his own office rather than ring people on his mobile from the street where the substance of the conversation seemed to revolve around "you're fading" or "I can't hear you any more". He arrived in the office just before lunchtime. "Did this professor say where he was from?" he asked Debra.

"No," she said. "I think he thought he was that important that you'd know who he was."

Rivers rang the number Debra had given him and was soon put through to the professor. "Professor," said Rivers, "what can I do for you?"

"I don't think we've actually met," he said, "but I was the pathologist operating in Finchley when you were working there. Jill the Ripper?"

"How could I forget?" The case had been one of Rivers' goriest – revenge killings against men who had mistreated women.

"Well, I strayed into your new territory a few years ago. I carried out the post mortems on Jennifer Welsh and Lesley Peters. Of course, it should have been Professor Saunders but he recused himself on the grounds that his son was involved in the police investigation."

Rivers expressed surprise at this. Saunders' whole rationale seemed to have been to try and – successfully – persuade the investigating officer Brett that his son had nothing to do with the murders yet here was evidence that he did take the involvement seriously.

"Well, I don't want to speculate on that," said Saint. "The point was that – for whatever reason – I was asked to carry out the autopsies on the girls. It's just that I heard that you were conducting a fresh investigation into the murders and I thought you ought to have all the facts before you. I got the feeling that the police at the time didn't really pay much attention to my ravings."

"I'm sure they weren't ravings," said Rivers.

"No," said Saint thoughtfully. "Anyhow, I'll pass them on to you for what their worth. Jennifer Welsh didn't put up a struggle. She was killed outright – a single blow to the head and then strangulation. Clean. Clinical. With Lesley Peters, though, it was a different story. She suffered a violent beating before she died. Almost as if it was a crime of passion."

"Go on."

"The conventional explanation for this would be that Jennifer had been the number one target and was killed as she slept. Lesley then disturbed the killer before he could get away and then put up a terrific fight as he tried to kill her, too. That's certainly what Detective Chief Inspector Brett believed."

"Go on."

"But there is another explanation. That the murder of Lesley Peters was a crime of passion. Do you understand what I'm saying?"

"I think so."

"The killer wanted to kill Lesley, was so het up about her that he wanted to inflict as much pain on her as possible. He killed her, waking Jennifer up in the process, realised he'd got to finish her off to escape detection and knocked her out and strangled her. No emotion. Just something he had to do to escape detection. So...."

"So?" repeated Rivers.

"Don't rule out the possibility that you could be seeking somebody with a motive for killing Lesley rather than Jennifer. DCI Brett certainly did."

"Thank you, Professor." Rivers replaced the receiver. Don't forget, he told himself, there were two murders on that night.

● ● ● ● ●

"What happened?" exclaimed Sylvia as she rushed into the accident and emergency waiting area and found Anne sitting by herself – trying to remain calm.

"He's had a heart attack," she said. "They're just taking him up on to the ward. They don't think it's serious but he'll have to take it easy."

"What brought it on?"

Anne grimaced. "You'll find out sooner or later," she said. "Rick Harper came round to see me."

"Rick Harper? Why?"

"He wanted to see me. I think he's always wanted to see me. I let him in."

"Why?"

"He's innocent, mother. I know he's innocent."

"Have you seen the front page of the local paper? He's being questioned again by the police."

"He was being offered protection from people like Barbara Hardy who spat at him in the supermarket."

"Is that what he told you?"

Anne thought for a moment before replying but then determined that she should answer all her mother's questions honestly. "Yes," she said.

Her mother looked at her. "We'll carry this conversation on later," she said. "Right now we must find out about your father."

The two of them were invited up to the ward to which he had been admitted. A doctor met them before they could attend his bedside. "He's had a lucky escape," said the doctor. "If we hadn't got to him so quickly it could have been worse. We've stabilised him and the drugs we've given him means he'll probably sleep for the next twelve hours or so. Best come back in the morning and then we'll know for sure if he's out of the woods."

"Is there any danger?" Sylvia began.

"That he will deteriorate during the night," said the doctor – pre-empting her question. "That's the $64,000 question, but I don't think so."

"I think I'd rather be here with him."

"I'll stay here, too," said Anne.

"No," said her mother firmly. "I don't want your father seeing you when he comes round. It'll bring back what's happened to him. Memories of Rick Harper. You go home. Or visit a friend."

"But I want to find out how he's getting on," said Anne. "You will tell me, won't you?"

"There are more important priorities than keeping you informed of what's going on," said her mother.

"Mother, Rick Harper came round to me. I didn't invite him."

"Then you should have shut the door in his face and told him to go away. Instead, what did you do?"

"I invited him in and offered him a drink. It seemed a civilised thing to do."

"Why bother being civilised with a man like him?"

"Because he was being civilised to me?"

"And your definition of the word civilised is?"

Anne remained silent. It would only light the blue touch paper if she had told her mother what really happened after she had invited Rick in. Just as well they hadn't decamped to the bedroom, she thought. "Giving him a drink and talking to him," she eventually replied. "He's no guiltier than his friend, Tim Rathbone, or any of the other people who were there at the dance that night. A couple of them are into drugs."

"Well, we wouldn't want them coming round either," said her mother. "Can't you see what you've done to your father? If he dies as a result of what happened it'll be on your conscience for the rest of your life – or it should be."

"I'll go," said Anne. "I think I get the point. I'm not the person you want around tonight while father's desperately trying to recover. You've lost one daughter, mother. Don't force the other one away as well. It could just as easily have been father who opened the door to Rick Harper today instead of me."

"Yes, but he would have shut it firmly in his face."

• • ● • •

Francesca and Gary decided to pay a visit to Rivers' office before returning to the police station. As luck would have it, they caught

Rivers before he went out to continue with his investigations. Francesca told him about her visit to the newspaper office while Gary helped Debra to make the tea.

"So they'll be doing a piece next week?"

"Which could put the wind up one or two other people involved with Jennifer Welsh," said Francesca.

"Remember," cautioned Rivers. "There was another murder victim. I've just had a word with Professor Saint – you remember him?"

"Yes, the pathologist we used in Barnet."

"Well, he's of the opinion that Lesley could have been the intended victim here. The bruises to her body make it look as if she was the victim of a crime of passion."

"Interesting," said Francesca. "If that's the case, this murder could be quite easy to solve."

"Why?"

"Well, she's not as complicated a character as Jennifer Welsh. She only had one boyfriend and called the relationship off. Stan Wightman. Have you spoken to him yet?"

"I will do. I got caught up in investigating the stretch limo. My next port of call is Peter Aymes, the cocaine snorting stretch limo driver who also visited Jennifer Welsh's home on the night of the attack."

"So you don't think you should drop everything and beetle off to see Stan Wightman in the light of Professor Saint's evidence."

"Everyone in good time," said Rivers. "That was the mistake George Brett made. To be fixated with just one person. I want to explore every avenue."

"Talking of George Brett, I've just been to see him."

"Poor you."

"I'm sorry?"

"Well, he's not exactly a bundle of laughs, is he?"

"He shed some interesting light on Rick Harper."

"Interesting and George Brett are not words that I would automatically use in the same sentence," said Rivers dryly.

"Apparently, he used to go out with Wightman's sister. One night when he was talking to Thomas Saunders he asked him if

173

he thought Mary would notice if he substituted 'I hate you' for 'I love you' when he was with her."

"Interesting but I'm not sure what it reveals."

"As they would say in a court room, 'goes to the defendant's state of mind'."

"Look," said Rivers, "nobody is pretending Rick Harper was the finished article four years ago. He'd had a gay relationship with Thomas Saunders but decided he wasn't gay any more, he had a relationship with Mary Wightman – but couldn't decide whether he loved or hated her, he was quite happy for a night's snogging with Jennifer Welsh whenever it was on offer even though he really fancied her sister, Anne. He was all over the place but if we decide that anyone who is all over the place is a prime suspect, there's quite a queue. Jimmy Atherton, Peter Aymes, Thomas Saunders – you name them."

"Duncan Hamilton?"

"Yes," said Rivers, "And the strange case of the unasked for alibi. I'd better find out whether Diane Hamilton really did sleep with Duncan or kipped down at her friend's house that night. Apparently, Graham Hands is most likely to point me in the direction of the friend – one Alison Palmer – so I should be able to wrap that one up soon. Or Jo. Where is he, by the way?"

"Is he no longer persona non grata, as far as you're concerned?"

"He never was – but with this realistic chance of a successful appeal I don't feel constrained about using him."

"Good," said Francesca. "He said he wanted to chill out today. I don't know what he means by that. He's still pretty sore that he's had to face all this aggro as a result of one racist police officer."

"I can understand that – but the best way of overcoming that feeling is to knuckle down to some work. By the way, where's the tea we were promised?"

"I don't know. Gary and Debra were making it."

The two of them decamped to the office's kitchen area where Gary and Debra were deep in conversation. "Do you like football?" Gary asked her.

"Obviously a more meaningful conversation that the one we've been having," said Rivers quietly as an aside to Francesca.

"I think I could get to like it," said Debra. Rivers noticed she was shifting from one foot to the other. She was either embarrassed by the situation she found herself in, he decided, or anxious to please her flatmate.

"I've got tickets to Stevenage on Saturday," said Gary.

"That is the worst chat up line I've ever heard," whispered Rivers. "Might as well take her to watch paint dry."

"Great," said Debra.

"You mean you'll come?"

"Yes", said Debra.

Gary was at a loss for words. "Nobody's ever said 'yes' in answer to that question before," said Rivers. "I was going to say I'll pick you up at two o'clock," said Gary, "but I don't have to as we're living together – I mean we're living in the same flat. There's a burger bar outside the ground. We could go there afterwards."

"It's getting serious," Rivers whispered to Francesca.

"Don't mock," said Francesca, "you were young and gauche once."

"What do you mean 'were'?" said Rivers. He decided to break up Gary and Debra's cosy chat. "Where's the tea you promised us?" he asked.

"Sorry, we got carried away." Gary turned around and noted that the kettle had boiled and started pouring out cups for everyone.

• • ● • •

It was the one telephone call that Jo responded to. He had decided to go out and see a movie which was then followed by a couple of pints in the pub. He wanted to unwind. Be on his own. Stop talking about all the ills that were besetting him – as he saw it. Then he noticed that Rosemary Gallagher had been trying to contact him.

"Good news," she said. "They think you've got grounds for an appeal. It'll be heard at the Crown Court in a couple of weeks. It won't be the same magistrate. It'll be a judge."

"And it won't be the same barrister representing me?" he asked.

"No," she said. "I've got a new fellow who we've used a couple of times before. I promise he'll put you on the stand if that's what you want but I think our case is so strong this time there may be no need to."

"I've heard that before."

"But I'm not saying it because I think you'd be an embarrassment in the witness box. I genuinely think you'd give a good account of yourself. I also genuinely think we've got a cast-iron case."

Jo nodded. "At the very least it's one person's word against another," he said. "Mind you, there is PC Boatman as well."

"Whom we can prove couldn't see a thing. I'm rather looking forward to seeing how well he'll stand up to cross examination."

"Will it all be over?" asked Jo.

"Don't count your chickens but you heard what I said."

"I wonder," said Jo. After all, I am still guilty of assault. By the way, she Francesca has left me. She's living with Rivers and his wife."

"I think you should go back to work tomorrow," said Rosemary. "It would do you good."

"Yes," said Jo. "Rivers has been trying to phone me today. I think he needs help on those murders we've been investigating."

"Go for it," said Rosemary.

• • ● • •

"Thank you for coming to see me, Gary," said Rory Gleeson. "Have you anything to report – about Detective Chief Inspector Manners?"

The words of thanks were superfluous, thought Gary. If the chief constable said he wanted to see you, you went to his office as quickly as you could. "Not really," said Gary.

"What do you mean by that?"

"Well, there's nothing to report. She appears to have left her home and be living with the private detective Rivers." Gary blushed for a moment. "Although there's nothing untoward there," he said. "Rivers is still living with his wife."

"I have evidence to the contrary," said Gleeson frostily.

In that case, why have you got me stalking my own boss, Gary thought to himself. "Oh," he said.

"Messages picked up that Rawlins Clifford and Manners are still seeing each other."

"Well, to be honest with you, sir"

"I hope you will be, Clarke," said Gleeson.

"The first time I went round to Francesca's house both she and Jo were there. I chatted to her and she said she would move out immediately. I assumed she had."

"That's not what I asked you for. Assumptions." Gleeson thought for a moment. "You may not believe me – and I know she won't – but I do have her best interests at heart. However, if you are going to be at best slapdash in your monitoring of her, I think there are others who will be more diligent in the task.

"Let me get this straight, sir, is another branch of the force – presumably Special Branch or MI6 or some such organisation monitoring Francesca?"

"I can't really go into details," said Gleeson, "but I believe they're monitoring Rawlins Clifford not her. However, they do come up with information about her which is of interest. As far as you're concerned, though, I don't think your services are required anymore." He got up from his desk and started pacing up and down the room. "Perhaps you could advise her, though, that if she persists in seeing this man, it will come to my attention."

"Yes, sir." It wasn't his place to ask but he was anxious to know what Gleeson would do with the information. Mainly, though, he was relieved he no longer had to shadow his boss. He excused himself from the chief constable's presence and returned to his office where Francesca was busy reading some documents. "You'll be pleased to know I'm no longer being asked to spy on you," he said.

"Oh, good."

"But the only reason that's happened is because somebody else is monitoring your activities. Somebody infinitely more important than me."

"Don't tell me. Special branch."

"I got the impression from Gleeson that they were tapping Jo's phone. You should warn him."

"In a couple of weeks it won't matter."

"What do you mean?" His mind went back to earlier when she had hinted that she might consider leaving the force. He fervently hoped this was not the case.

"Jo's been granted leave to appeal and we have a witness – a serving police officer at the demonstration – who says he did not assault PC Enderby."

Gary inwardly gave a sigh of relief. "That's excellent news," he said, "but be careful until then."

"Are you giving me orders, DC Clarke?"

"I wouldn't presume to," he said, "but I would value your advice on another subject."

"Yes?"

"Debra Paget."

"Your flatmate?"

"Yes," he said – and then seemed to be wrestling with himself as to whether to say anything further. "I'm getting on very well with her," he said.

"Good."

"You remember me questioning her last year? I was told she was a vulnerable person."

"She is," said Francesca. "She has a simplistic view of life and she believes what people say – quite literally. I assume by 'getting on very well' you mean you fancy her."

"Yes."

"And you want me to advise you as to whether you should do anything to take your relationship further?"

"Yes."

"Well, I'm not going to. What I would say is if you're unsure about what you want to do, don't do anything. On the other hand, if you are sure then you should go for it."

Gary nodded. "Yes, ma'am – I'm sorry, Francesca." It was the first time he had used the form of address that Francesca hated for a while. She did not rebuke him. It stemmed, she thought, from the confusion he had in his own mind about how to deal with his feelings for Debra.

• • • • •

Rivers looked up. They were quite plush offices – but then what should he have come to expect with a Mayfair address. Jimmy Atherton was not Peter Aymes' only client. The man seemed to be doing well for himself, Rivers thought. He approached the reception desk. "I'd like to see Mr Aymes," he said.

"I'm sorry, sir, Mr Aymes is busy. He's with a client."

Rivers showed the receptionist his card. "It is quite a delicate matter," he said, "connected to a criminal investigation I'm conducting."

"You're not the police, though."

"No, but I would appreciate you telling him I'm here."

She sighed and picked up the receiver beside her. "Marjorie," she said when somebody answered at the other end. "I have a Philip Rivers wanting to speak to Peter. He's a private detective. He says it's to do with some sort of criminal investigation." Silence followed and Rivers assumed Marjorie – whoever she was – was approaching Aymes with the news that he wanted to see her. "Yes," said the receptionist after an interlude that lasted two or three minutes. "Yes, I quite understand." She put the receiver. "Mr Rivers, Mr Aymes does not want to speak to you," she said. "He says he knows who you are and he does not think he has any information that will be of use to you."

"He's wrong," said Rivers.

"I beg your pardon?" said the receptionist.

"Sorry," said Rivers waving his hand as if to apologise to her. "Those thoughts weren't really for public consumption."

"So would you like to leave?"

"The honest answer." asked Rivers. "No. I'll wait for him to have a free moment."

"I don't think you heard what I said. He doesn't want to see you."

"I have to say I don't like negotiating with you – because I don't think you should be put in that position – but if he doesn't see me, I shall have to pass on the information I have about him to the police and I think they'll want to question him about it. On the other hand, if he can reassure me about it, that could be an end to the matter." The receptionist looked at him as if he was some dirt on her shoe that she would like to remove. She did nothing, though. "You could tell Marjorie that," he said.

She grimaced and pick up the telephone. "Marjorie, he won't leave," she said. "He insists on seeing Peter." She was silent for a moment. "Well, all right," she said when Marjorie finally returned with a message. "She says I must call security and have you removed from the building," she said.

"Well, all right then but then I might have to reveal the information I have on him – and, believe me, that wouldn't make him look good."

"Are you threatening me?"

"No, him."

The receptionist sighed and picked up the telephone again. "Marjorie, I think Peter should see him. He said he's going to reveal the information he has on him – and it won't make him look good."

"Thank you," said Rivers.

The two of them waited for Marjorie to come back to the telephone. There was a longer break this time which indicated to Rivers that his comments were being passed on to Aymes. Eventually Marjorie returned. "Yes," said the receptionist. "Understood." She looked at Rivers. "You've got five minutes – and Marjorie will come down and collect you."

"Thank you," said Rivers, "And I am sorry to have put you in that position."

The receptionist did not react but returned to reading some files which were on her desk. At the same moment, a woman soberly dressed in a black two-piece suit and sporting pearl earrings emerged from the inside of the building. Marjorie was not the epitome of what Rivers would have expected from the secretary to a man who was at the heart of the pop music industry. "Mr Rivers?" she asked.

"Yes."

"Will you follow me?"

"Thank you." She escorted him to an open plan office where about three secretaries were busy working. The others, Rivers observed, looked far more like rock chicks than Marjorie. She ushered him to an office at one end of the room which had transparent windows.

"Mr Rivers?" said the man he assumed to be Peter Aymes. "What is it that is so urgent?"

"Back entrance," said Rivers.

"What?"

"I said you must have a back entrance," he said. "I was told you had a client and could not see me but they appear to have gone. Thank you for not using it to escape me."

"Stop blathering on and get to the point," said Aymes irritatedly.

Rivers eyed him up and down. Again, he came to the same conclusion as he had done with Marjorie – he was not a typical example of someone involved in the rock industry. He was in his late thirties, Rivers guessed. Slightly balding with grey tinges to his moustache and beard. He was wearing a dark blue suit and light blue shirt. He was thin – almost to the point of being gaunt. Perhaps that was as a result of his flirtation with cocaine, Rivers surmised.

"All right," said the private detective eventually. "You were snorting cocaine on the night of the murder of Jennifer Welsh and Lesley Peters and you drove your stretch limo round to their house in the early hours of the morning. You were seen in The Close where they live by some of their neighbours."

"You can substantiate this?"

"Yes."

"How?"

"Private detectives are like journalists. They never reveal their sources. The point is – given the state you were in did you gain access to Jennifer's house and – if you did – did you kill her?"

"The police have never had cause to question me about the murders."

"That's because they didn't know you were there out of your head on cocaine."

"I wasn't out of my head."

"So you do admit to taking cocaine that night?"

Aymes ignored the question. "All right," he said, "so my

181

limousine was seen in the area that night. What does that prove?"

"You were there?" said Rivers "It at least gives you as much opportunity as the police's prime suspect Rick Harper to carry out the murders."

"I never left the car."

Rivers swallowed. "Go on."

"Well, I didn't."

"Why drive all the way there and just sit in the car?" asked Rivers.

"Jimmy got out. He thought Jennifer was having a party – but it looked all quiet. He got out of the car and knocked on the door. There was no response."

"I see. And do you remember what time this was? Roughly?"

"About two o'clock in the morning – possibly a little bit earlier."

"Had Jimmy had any cocaine?"

"Not to my knowledge. Look, Mr Rivers, we were only there for five minutes and we did nothing. You said to the receptionist that – if you were convinced by my explanation that nothing untoward had gone on – that that would be an end of the matter."

"I did."

"So is it an end to the matter?"

"I'm not convinced by your explanation. I may have to speak to you again."

"And in the meantime?"

"We'll leave it at that for the time being. I've said that when I've completed my investigation I shall pass on the information I have to the police. We're not at that stage of affairs yet."

"Thank you, Mr Rivers."

"Don't thank me for anything. Information about what happened that night seems to be coming out in dribs and drabs. First, I inherit a brief which makes no mention of your limo being in the area. Then I find out it was. Then I find out you had been taking drugs. What will I find out next?"

"Nothing, Mr Rivers Nothing."

"I think we'll have to see about that." With that, he turned on his heels and left the office. Marjorie came over to him to escort him from the room. She could not help but notice that her boss seemed to be shaking with fear.

CHAPTER SEVEN

"So what have you discovered?" Graham Hands asked Rivers as he entered the studio.

"You could have been right about Renee walking away. He left Peter Aymes and Jimmy Atherton at the night club that evening – and they went over to Jenny's."

"Shrewd guess," said Hands. "I had no inside knowledge. I have a feeling that his walking away covered something more serious than that." He paused then added: "So why have you come to see me?"

"I need more help," admitted Rivers. "Duncan Hamilton. His wife Diane has given him an alibi for the night of the murder."

"I didn't know he needed one."

"Nor did I," confessed Rivers. "She says she was with him that night."

"In the police section house?"

"Yes."

"Be a bit difficult getting out in the morning without being seen," said Hands. He sifted through a pile of requests on his desk. "Just choosing the songs for my show. Don't mind me."

"I'm trying to track down the woman she originally said she was with. An Alison Palmer."

"Yes," said the disc jockey. "She left the country to work in Australia soon after the murders. Back now. She looked me up. Apparently, it's cool to be seen to be going out with a disc jockey so she thought she'd give it a try."

"And was it?"

"Cool? You'd have to ask her that. We only saw each other the once but I've got an address for her if it helps." Hands fiddled around with his smart phone for a while before coming up with it. "My crowd always seem to want to stay in touch with me. I think they believe I can hand them some freebies from my musical collection."

"Bayswater? You could have seen her again if you'd wanted to."

"Yes," said Hands in a non-committal way.

"What's your take on this alibi?"

"Does Duncan need one?"

"It would help put him in the clear if he had one – but I've found nothing against him except he used to have a relationship with Jennifer Welsh. She dumped him. Not surprising, really. He hardly inspires the earth to move. He was quite cut up about it, apparently."

"So if he heard Jennifer inviting Rick round?"

"He could have been upset by it. On the other hand, if he went round himself, he'd be thinking he would have had to deal with the two of them – and possibly others in Lesley Peters and Tim Rathbone."

"Right." By now Hands had an earnest expression on his face. "I'm not sure that his relationship with Diane had started by then," he said. "It was very soon after the demise of his fling with Jennifer. On the whole, I'd probably opt for saying its odds against him being with Diane that night – but you find out for yourself."

"I will." Rivers hesitated for a moment. "Did you know Renee had supplied Peter Aymes with cocaine on the night of the murder?"

"I'm not surprised."

"He's not a nice man."

"Who? Renee or Peter Aymes?"

"Peter Aymes. He was on the verge of throwing me out of his offices when I just mentioned I might be about to blab about his habit if he did so."

"And?"

"He came clean – but said he was only outside Jennifer's for five minutes and never got out of the car."

"Too stoned?"

"Well, I hope not. He was driving." Rivers changed tack. "What about Anne Welsh's friends? She said she was staying with someone on the night of the murders."

"Can't help you there. Not my crowd. To use the words of a song again – she's too far above me. Intellectually. So would her friends be – academically. It's Tommy Steele, by the way. The song. From 'Half A Sixpence'."

"I won't have any difficulty corroborating her alibi," said Rivers. "If you were to pick a song to describe Diane Hamilton's actions, what would it be?"

Hands smiled. "Now that's a difficult one," he said. "'Silence is Golden'. She may have overegged the pudding by coming forward with an alibi." He smiled again. "If I were to pick one for you, it would be the theme for an old cop drama which they were re-running on Sky – 'No Hiding Place'."

"Thanks for the compliment," said Rivers.

● ● ● ● ●

"We have a problem," said Peter Aymes the next time he met up with Jimmy Atherton. "He knows we were there. He knows I'd been snorting cocaine. I told him I never got out of the limo but I don't think he's going to let the matter rest there."

Jimmy was sitting relaxed on a sofa in his suite at the plush London hotel where he was staying while his tour took in venues around the capital. Not for him a cab ride back to the flat he still sometimes slept over in and shared with Renee in West Hampstead after the show. He lived a different lifestyle now. He had acquired a quite upmarket mansion in the country but tended not even to stay there on the nights of his concerts. It was just too far to go – the rigours of touring didn't leave him with enough energy to pursue that option. "Rivers spoke to me, too," he said. "I told him I knocked on Jennifer's door and there was no response so we went away again. I don't think anybody else saw us doing anything else beyond that."

"So the great singer – the man who's everybody's friend – is not above lying when it comes to the crunch."

"I don't think it would throw any more light on the case if I told him any more about what happened that night." He picked a boiled sweet up off the coffee table where he was sitting. "But you're right, I was struggling with my conscience over not telling him the whole truth. If the police become involved, of course, the

185

stakes get higher. If we lie to them, we could ultimately end up being charged with committing perjury – and that could lead to a prison stretch. Not good for my image." Jimmy thought for a moment.

"So, what are you going to do?", asked Peter Aymes.

"On reflection, I think I should ring Rivers and tell him the whole story."

"Ouch."

"I don't know what you're worried about. It doesn't land you in it in any way."

"Rivers might not see it that way. He knows I was sitting in the car having snorted coke He may think I just can't remember what happened next."

"He may be right."

"What do you mean?"

"When I returned to the limo, you'd gone. I mean, not disappeared but wasted. You were kind of hallucinating – as if you were having a bad dream. You were mumbling. I couldn't understand what you were saying. I yanked you out of the driver's seat and drove you home myself."

"I don't remember any of that," said Aymes. "I remember waking up in my own bed the next morning. I wasn't sure how I'd got there but assumed I must have driven myself. You'd gone and the stretch limo was on the gravel path leading up to my house. I assumed you must have got a cab home."

"I did get a cab back to Renee's – hence him offering himself as a witness to the fact that I was at his home that night. He didn't, of course, know what time I'd got in."

"Why didn't you take the limo? You'd got the keys."

"I think one or two eyebrows would have been raised if I'd left the limo parked outside my house all night. They don't do stretch limos in West Hampstead. It might have got stolen or smashed up. It was safe at your house in Richmond."

"Of course. If I was out of it when you got back to the car, though, you could have been lying about the amount of time you'd spent away from the car."

"And you could have been lying about the amount of time we

spent in that close. But, before you get too worried about all that, remember that an unbiased observer – a resident in the close – thought that we were only there for a short while. No-one heard any sounds of violence while we were there. I don't think Rivers will put two and two together and come up with us as culprits even if we tell him the truth. And, remember, lying to him is tantamount to lying to the police. He's going to pass on all the information he gets to the police If we don't then correct it, then we're effectively lying to the police as well as him."

"So you're going to tell him?"

"The truth, the whole truth and nothing but the truth."

• • ● • •

"Good to see you again," said Rivers as Jo came through the door of their offices.

"Sorry about yesterday," said Jo. "I needed to clear my head."

"That's okay – let's get down to work now. There are some things that need doing."

"Fine," said Jo.

"The pathologist who did the autopsies on the two girls says he saw evidence that the killing of Lesley could have been a crime of passion – which sheds a whole new light on proceedings. If she was the intended victim, then her boyfriend – Stan Wightman – becomes the prime suspect. You need to go and see him."

"Right."

"I've got an address for him. He still lives with his parents."

"Right."

"Also, we have some new dirt on our employer – Rick Harper. Apparently, he was going out with Wightman's sister, Mary. He told Thomas Saunders one night that he wondered what would happen if he told Mary he hated her while they were...."

"Having sex?" suggested Jo.

"I don't know if it went that far Let's say canoodling."

"Oh, I say, how jolly spiffing," said Jo in a mock upper class English accent.

"I'm sorry, Jo?"

187

"Don't mind me. Just glad to be back at work."

Rivers looked perplexed but decided to continue. "Romantically engaged rather than he loved her."

"And we know this because?"

"Professor Saunders told Detective Chief Inspector Brett."

"Ah, two of the most reliable people we've come across during this investigation."

"I take your point, Jo, but take it as true for the moment and ask Wightman if he'd heard this and what his reaction was."

"What will you be doing?"

"I'm following the cocaine trail," said Rivers. "We now know that cocaine snorting Peter Aymes had driven over to Jennifer Welsh's house that night in the company of butter wouldn't melt singer Jimmy Atherton. They say they only stopped for a few minutes while Jimmy Atherton got out of their stretch limo and rang Jennifer's doorbell. On not getting a reply, he went back to the limo and they drive off again. No-one can prove any different."

"Right."

"I've also got an address for the friend of Diane Hamilton that she originally said she was staying with. She now says she wasn't and that she spent the night with her future husband, Duncan. We have to find out which version of events that night is true." Rivers waited for a moment to help Jo take in what he had just said. "I somehow feel your mind isn't a 100 per cent on the job," he added. "If that's the case and you want me to carry on single handed for the time being, just say so."

"No, I'll be all right," said Jo. "I have got one or two things on my mind but I'll be able to major in on the investigation." His mobile phone went off. "Excuse me," he said. "I have to take this. It's my solicitor." He confirmed his identity to the person on the other end of the phone and then – after a pause – exclaimed: "What?" He moved out of earshot of Rivers to continue taking the call. After a few moments, he returned to Rivers again. "That was my solicitor," he said.

"So I gathered. She could have come upstairs."

Jo ignored the remark. "Someone's threatened my new witness and he's had to go into hiding."

"Is he still going to give evidence?"

"Yes, but…."

"But what? It could help your case if you can tell the court that."

Jo sighed. "I suppose so, but, well, I just wonder what I'm dealing with here." He shook his head. "My accuser seems to have one of two low-life friends."

"Your accuser is a racist. He therefore has racist friends. They don't like black coppers and they don't like a black man riding to the rescue of a black copper, trying to get him off his conviction. Don't be surprised. Just deal with it." He smiled. "Deal with it by going out to interview Stan Wightman without a care in the world. Well, possibly not quite that but make sure you focus on Stan Wightman and not on some perceived threat to your witness."

"It's not perceived, it's real."

"I know," said Rivers laying a fatherly hand on Jo's shoulder, "but it may be that your witness is a very determined man. He doesn't seem – from what you tell me – to have been put off by the threat."

"No."

It was Rivers' turn for his mobile to ring. "Hang on," he said. My turn to take some time out. Who is this?" he asked of the caller.

"It's Jimmy Atherton. I need to talk to you again."

"Okay. Where are you?"

"I'm rehearsing for a show in Croydon tonight. Could you come over and see me?"

Rivers thought for a moment. It was obvious the singer could not spare the time to come dashing across London and see him. "All right," he said. "I'll be there as soon as I can."

• • • • •

Gary arrived late for work that morning and Francesca could detect immediately that his mind was not on the job. "Have you been asked to spy on me again?" she asked him by way of breaking the ice.

"No, nothing like that," he said. He then went into silent mode

189

which prompted Francesca to look at him as if inviting more comment. "Oh, it's Debra," he said. "I've suggested we go to the cinema tonight. There's a film I particularly want to see."

Francesca waited long enough to give him time to continue. "And she replied by saying?" she eventually said when it became clear he was not intending to elaborate on his previous statement.

"Well, she's agreed," he said tentatively.

"Good," said Francesca.

"Yes, but I'm not sure as to how to handle the date. It's been a while since I took somebody out," he said.

"It'll come back to you. Look at me and Jo. He said he was better at ending relationships than starting them. I hadn't had a serious relationship for years. Now look at us."

Gary smiled. "You forget," he said. "I don't have to anymore. Which is just as well, or I might feel duty bound to tell the chief constable what I know."

"Seriously, though," said Francesca, "you'll be all right. Just be yourself." She thought for a moment. "Not the yourself of last year who was intent on grilling Debra until the early hours of the morning determined to get a confession out of her. Be the new man that seemed to emerge soon after your uncle resigned from his job as chief constable."

Gary smiled. "You're probably right," he said. "It's good to know that you and Jo are still together – even if you are having to reside in separate houses for the time being."

Francesca put her fingers to her lips. "Remember," she said. "The walls have ears."

Gary nodded. Francesca picked up some papers from her desk. "If you want to take your mind off worrying how you'll approach Debra tonight, there was a robbery at a chemist's in Fore Street over the weekend," she said. "Drugs taken. Better look into it. At least it will get you out from underneath my feet."

Gary strode over to her desk and took the papers from her. He then strode purposefully from the office.

• • • • •

Rivers made his way to the venue in Croydon where Jimmy Atherton was performing that evening. He went up to the reception desk and was soon being escorted by a steward to a changing room where Jimmy was resting between rehearsals. As Rivers entered the room, he noted that Jimmy looked relaxed – not what he would have expected from someone planning to make a confession of some sort. "You wanted to see me?" the private detective began.

"Yes," said Jimmy. "I want to come clean with you."

"You mean you haven't been so far?"

"I want to tell you the whole truth about what happened on the night of the murders."

"Go on."

"You know I said we parked the stretch limo in The Close where Jennifer lived and I went to the door and got no reply?"

"Yes."

"Well, that's not strictly true." Jimmy swallowed as if he was finding the right words to say. Rivers decided not to make it any easier for him. "It's true," he said, "there was no response to my knock on the door. What I didn't tell you was that the door was open. I pushed it and then went inside." He heaved a huge sigh. "I saw them both."

"Jennifer and Lesley?"

"Yes, they were both dead. There was a lot of blood around Lesley's body in the living room, Jennifer was lying in her bedroom. There was no blood."

Rivers nodded. "What did you do?" he asked.

"I went back to the car." He waved his hand as if to stop Rivers intervening. "I know, I know," he said. "I should have called the police there and then but think about it for a moment. I was on the verge of a new career. My new manager was high on drugs in the car. At the very least it would have been embarrassing for him. The police might have come to the conclusion he had something to do with the murders. Any sane person would. We would probably have been taken to the police station for questioning. I didn't want to start my new career with Peter Aymes like that."

"You're right that any sane person might have come to the

conclusion that the two of you had something to do with the murders."

"Meaning you have?" asked Jimmy.

Rivers did not reply to his comment. "Just go on with your story," he said.

"Well, there's not much more to tell. As I said, I went back to the car. Peter seemed out of it. He was kind of rolling around making no sense. I think he must have taken more drugs. Certainly, in that state he would never have been able to drive the car from Jennifer's place. I shoved him from the driver's seat to the passenger seat. I took the keys from him and drove off."

"Where to?"

"His place. I left the car there and ordered a cab to take me home to Renee's. That's how I was back there when Renee woke up in the morning. I thought it would look suspicious if there was a stretch limo parked outside my flat in West Hampstead. We don't often see them – unless it's a drug dealer calling."

"It would have been," intervened Rivers.

"Peter's not a dealer," said Jimmy.

"No, I know," Rivers responded. "Renee is."

Jimmy ignored the comment. "That's it," he said, adding a phrase he had uttered beforehand: "That's the truth, the whole truth and nothing but the truth."

"What if I don't believe you?"

Jimmy looked at him surprised. "Why should you jump to that conclusion?" he asked.

"I'm not saying whether I've jumped to that conclusion – but your story has changed somewhat. I've been involved in cases where someone has altered their statement and put themselves in a position closer to the crime. By dribs and drabs, it's then emerged that they were the actual criminal."

"That's not the case here," said Jimmy emphatically. "No way."

"Okay, then answer a couple of queries for me. You insist you only stayed at Jennifer's house for five minutes yet – during that time – Peter Aymes went from somebody you were quite happy to let drive you about to a kind of shuddering, gibbering wreck out of it on drugs."

"A slight exaggeration of what I said but – essentially – yes."

"Rubbish," said Rivers.

"He probably took some more drugs while I was in the house."

"It still would have taken him longer to get into that state." Rivers looked at Jimmy for a response. There was none. "Also, are you sure Peter Aymes never got out of the car?"

"As sure as I can be. He never came into the house. What are you suggesting? That the girls were alive when I went into the house. That he killed them while I looked on and watched him."

"It's quite possible that – if he was in the state you say he was in – the girls rebuffed his advances and in a temper he lashed out, striking Jennifer and killing her. Then, as Lesley attempted to come to her rescue, he fought with her – killing her, too."

"And I just stood there and watched it happen?"

"He then asked you to clean up the mess which you helped him to do – quite effectively. After all, your contract depended on it."

"No, Mr Rivers, it didn't happen like that."

"You were anxious to retain your newly-won contract?"

"Yes, but not at all costs."

"When I was interviewing Peter Aymes I noticed he was shaking as I left."

"He's worried that it will come out about him and the cocaine habit."

"A rock impresario worried about that? No, I think he's worried that he will become a main suspect in the murder enquiry. It makes more sense that a crazed drug addict would commit the murders – rather than my client, Rick Harper."

"I can see that but what I'm telling you now is the truth." Rivers nodded. "What happens now?" asked Jimmy.

"Nothing," said Rivers. "I have said that – at the end of my investigation – I shall hand over all my information to the police – which I will do. It'll be up to them to decide what to do with it."

"So Peter's cocaine habit will become public knowledge?"

"Not necessarily," said Rivers. "It may be that the police won't pursue it if he's not directly responsible for the murders. It may be they question him as to who his supplier is. In which case, I would think Renee is in a more vulnerable position than he is."

"And me?"

"Your big mistake was in not informing the police about discovering the bodies. You could face charges over that, I suppose I can't read the police's minds. One thing, did you attempt to clear anything up in the house after you'd found the bodies?"

"No, I just high-tailed it out of there."

"So they won't find your prints anywhere in the house?"

"I don't think they found any prints anyhow," said Jimmy.

"No," said Rivers, "but they could organise another search once I've given them fresh information." He looked at Jimmy intently as he said this but detected no reaction. Certainly, there was no air of panic about him. Maybe Jimmy had been speaking the truth this time, he thought to himself. "I'll let myself out," he said as he got up from his seat – still weighing up the pros and cons of what Jimmy had said.

• • ● • •

Jo remembered what Rivers had told him. Thomas' parents were very protective of him. A straight call on his home would have had a protective mother fielding the enquiry and yielded nothing. He had to wait for Thomas to leave the house and follow him and then pick a spot where he could best approach him. It never got that far, though. Within minutes of Jo setting off behind Thomas, the latter turned round and said to him accusingly; "You're following me."

"What makes you think that?" replied Jo.

"One, you're following in my footsteps and two, we don't have many black people living round here so it stands to reason that any black person has come here for a reason – and is not just here to do the shopping."

"You're right," said Jo. He produced his card. "I want to have a word with you about the Jennifer Welsh and Lesley Peters' murders."

"Again?" said Thomas. "Your boss has already questioned me."

"New evidence is coming up all the time. I wanted to discuss it with you," said Jo. He decided that treating Thomas as a mature person who could contribute to the inquiry rather than a suspect was the best way of dealing with him.

"I thought my father had dealt with you and that I was not to be questioned again," said Thomas quickening his stride.

"That's not the way it works," said Jo. "My boss, Mr Rivers, and I work independently of the police." And of your father, he thought but declined to mention it. "You have nothing to fear from talking to me," Jo continued. "If you just relax and let me talk to you, you'll see."

Thomas looked suspiciously at Jo. They had just come to a bench beside a bus-stop. "All right," he said reluctantly. "Let's sit down."

"Thank you," said Jo. "We've been talking to ex Detective Chief Inspector Brett."

"But he's one of the good guys," interjected Thomas.

You mean useless at his job and not probing enough, thought Jo. He decided against putting his thoughts into words. "That's as maybe," said Jo. "He told us that he'd had words with your father about Rick Harper – that Rick had had a conversation with you about Stan Wightman's sister, Mary. Do you remember it?"

"Yes," said Thomas. "He said he wondered whether she could tell the difference if he said he hated her when he should have been telling her he loved her – or something like that."

"That's right, said Jo. "What did you make of that?"

"Make of that?" He seemed to be weighing up whether he could be trapped in any way if he answered the question. "I didn't make anything of it. It wasn't directed at me."

"It's stuck in your mind, though?"

"Well, yes. I thought it spoke volumes about Rick," he said. "He doesn't know whether he loves people or hates them. It's all the same to him. He doesn't...." Here Thomas stopped to search for a word ".... empathise with people. He just uses them. Me, Mary and Jennifer as well. You know he snogged her once then didn't want anything to do with her?"

"I gather you had a relationship with him when you were younger, too."

"Yes, he said it was experimental. He wanted to find out whether he enjoyed gay sex." Thomas looked a little wistful as the memory of the relationship came back to him. "It turned out he didn't but I think we could have made something of it if we had persevered with it."

"What did you do about the information you had?" Jo asked – ignoring Thomas' comments about his relationship with Rick,

"Do?" questioned Thomas.

"Yes – like did you tell anybody about it?"

"I told Stan."

"You knew Stan?"

"We were at school together." Thomas smiled for a moment as if recalling happier memories. "You know, he was never judgemental about things. He said I was better off out of it if Rick was going around saying things like that."

Jo was beginning to despair. Again Thomas Saunders was reacting as if the comment only affected him. "What did he think about Mary?"

"She was his sister," said Thomas – not understanding the question.

"Yes, I know – but did you discuss how she might have felt about it?"

Thomas looked surprised at the tone of the question. "I don't think so," he said. "Not really."

"So why did you tell Stan what Rick had said?"

"I wanted to talk to someone about it."

"And it was just a coincidence that that person was the brother of the person the remarks had been aimed at?"

"He was my closest friend at the time."

"Do you think he told his sister?"

"I shouldn't have thought so."

"Oh. Why?"

"Well, it would have hurt her feelings."

"Or it could have been a warning to her not to get too involved with Rick? Surely that would have been a good thing?"

"I suppose so," said Thomas, shrugging his shoulders.

"Do you think Stan might have done anything else with the

information he had?"

"What? Like punched Rick's lights out?"

Jo stalled for a moment. "Possibly," he said eventually.

"Stan's not like that," said Thomas. "He reacts slowly to things. He doesn't forget them, though."

"Stan had a girlfriend once, didn't he? Lesley Peters?"

"I think you already know that," said Thomas. "Why are you asking me about that?"

"Just chatting," said Jo.

"No," said Thomas. "Everything you ask, you ask for a reason."

"Okay. I'm just trying to build a picture of everybody involved in this enquiry."

"Involved? You think Stan's involved?"

"Well, he was there on the night of the murder. He has a reason to dislike Rick – and maybe take it out on someone who had replaced his sister in Rick's life – and Lesley."

"No," said Thomas. "You're just trying to put words in my mouth." No, thought Jo, I'm desperately trying to coax words out of your mouth. "Stan wouldn't have held that sort of grudge against Lesley."

"But she broke it off?" Jo decided to be more direct in his questioning.

"He wouldn't have done," conceded Thomas. "He would just have got a bit broody about the situation, not violent."

"Thanks," said Jo. "That's very helpful. And Mary?"

"Mary?"

"What would she have done about the situation – that Rick had said those words?"

"That's always assuming she knew," said Thomas.

"Let's assume that for a moment," said Jo.

"They're very stoical as a family She'd have just got on with life, I guess."

Jo nodded. "Thanks," he said again "I think that's all I need to know at this time."

"At this time? You may want to question me again, then?"

"If further evidence emerges, yes."

"But my father." Thomas' voice tailed off.

"Has no influence on the conduct of our investigation." He realised his words had upset Thomas. "I'm sorry but that's the truth. If it makes you feel better, what I've said to you is only the same as I've said to everyone else involved in this investigation. Even Rick Harper who is employing us. You're not a special case."

Rather than reassure Thomas, it seemed from his reaction that he was alarmed by Jo's comments. The private detective immediately went on his way after uttering those words. Thomas quickly took his mobile out of his pocket. "Father," he said on getting through to the person he was ringing, "those detectives – Rivers and his sidekick – they were questioning me again about the murders. I thought you were going to stop them."

"I've had a word with the police, Thomas, and – if you look at the front page of the local newspaper – I think you'll find Rick Harper is still at the centre of their investigations. Don't worry about Rivers and his lot. They're not the ones who'll be charging the killer at the end of the day."

Thomas turned off his mobile without another word to his father. He got up and continued his walk down the road and reached a local pub where he immediately ordered a double whisky and downed it in one.

● ● ● ● ●

The flats in this particular block would have been way beyond his price range, Rivers reflected as he approached the private estate in St John's Wood where he had been told Alison Palmer lived. She was, he had been told, the fashion editor of a magazine – a choice of occupation which Rivers felt was entirely in keeping with someone who purported to be a member of the Graham Hands' set.

"You're lucky to catch me in," she said as she answered Rivers' ringing of the bell. "I have a fashion shot in Fulham in two hours' time."

"I'll be as quick as I can," sad Rivers. "Graham Hands gave me your address." It was said to reassure her – and seemed to have the predicted effect.

"Ah, Graham," she said fondly. "Delightful man."

Rivers smiled as if it was a description he recognised. "He thought you could help me with a case I'm investigating," he said.

She bade him sit down and offered him a cup of tea or "something stronger". He accepted the tea and studied her carefully as she made her way into the kitchen to make it. You would have expected a fashion editor to be elegantly dressed, he thought to himself, and she did justice to the stereotype: black leather trousers, stiletto shoes and a gold satin shirt with the top two buttons undone to reveal just a hint of breast. He could not help thinking that here was someone from a different social strata to Diane Hamilton, a woman with three children and a husband whose job as an engineer did not exactly set the pulses racing.

"I'm intrigued, Mr Rivers – or may I call you Philip?"

You could call me Rivers like everybody else, he thought to himself, but – outwardly – he acquiesced to her suggestion they should use first name terms. "There was a murder – well, two murders – four years ago," he began.

"You mean Jennifer Welsh and…." she hesitated for a moment …." Lesley Peters."

"You remember it?"

"Yes, Jennifer was one of our set." There was a sense in which great importance was attached to that status, her tone indicated. "I think I had to give an alibi to the police for a friend of mine, Diane Chesney."

"Hamilton as now is," said Rivers.

"Oh," said Alison. "She married that little guy?"

"You sound a bit surprised?"

"He was rather boring," she said. "Training to be a policeman, I believe."

"He's become an engineer," Rivers confided in her. "She's got three kids."

"Oh, how nice," said Alison in a tone of voice that would have you believe she didn't mean a word of it.

"Yes," said Rivers. "You did give her an alibi for that night – although I'm not sure it was strictly necessary. She was never a suspect. Did she ask you to give her an alibi?"

"Ask me?"

"Yes," Rivers said without elaborating.

"Are you suggesting I gave her a false alibi?"

"Put it like this," said Rivers. "She now says she didn't spend the night with you – but was with Duncan Hamilton all night."

"How intriguing," said Alison. "Do tell me more. Is he a suspect?"

"He was at the dance they all went to before the girls were killed," said Rivers. "In a sense anybody who was there is a suspect until proved otherwise."

"I see. Well, I find this difficult," said Alison. "I mean, she was with me all night I was at the dance, too."

"So why do you think she would have come up with this false alibi?"

"She must have thought Duncan did it – the murder, I mean."

That was candid of you, thought Rivers. "Do you remember much about those times?" he asked.

"Some of the parties were pretty good," she said. "Best not to remember what happened in the morning."

"Would Diane have taken the same view?"

"She was, how shall I put it, slightly more conservative than I was. She would have had less that she did not want to remember. I'm surprised she married Duncan Hamilton, though. She could have done much better for herself – although I can see her in the role of mother of three. Lapping it up."

Rivers smiled. "Was she with Duncan at that particular dance?"

"I think she danced with him. I'm not sure. I had my own particular fish to fry."

Yes, thought Rivers, and I bet you fried it to perfection. "Did you keep in touch with her afterwards?"

"Not for long. I got a chance to work for a fashion magazine in Australia – through one of the fish I managed to fry – and left the UK. When I came back, she was no longer living in the same place. I heard from friends that she'd got married – I didn't know to whom – so I kind of deleted her from my contacts book."

"Were you aware of her being with Duncan after the dance and before you went to Australia?"

"I suppose. To be honest, I found her a bit boring too so we didn't hang around with each other much after the dance."

"Sixty-four-thousand-dollar question. Can you imagine her living with a guy for four years knowing that he'd committed a murder?"

"Darling, I can't imagine anyone doing that – but I guess it happens."

"Fair point."

"What I can't understand is why she'd come to his rescue after all this time. If she thought everything was okay for four years, why suddenly turn round and tell a different story."

"That, I think, I can explain to you. The police were convinced someone else had done it. That person – Rick Harper. "He paused to see if any recognition of the name registered on her face but it did not, "hired me to clear his name. I began digging up some facts that weren't known about what happened on that night."

"But it's so stupid. I mean, someone was bound to check her original alibi."

"She thought not. She knew you had gone abroad and didn't know you'd come back. She probably thought the police wouldn't track you down half way across the world." In fact, thought Rivers, Detective Chief Inspector Brett probably wouldn't manage to track you down to a different part of London.

"So do I have to do anything now?"

"No, I'll present all my evidence to the police. They may well want you to corroborate your original alibi for her. I don't know." He got up as if to go. "Enjoy your fashion shoot," he said. Years ago, he thought to himself, she was the sort of woman he would make a pass at. Years ago? He meant two really – before his marriage to Nikki. Alison Palmer still provoked a frisson of excitement in his veins but the days of making passes were long gone.

• • ● • •

Debra was finding the day quite boring. Both Rivers and Jo were involved in chasing people out of the office and she was beginning to realise that Hertford was not the kind of place where people walked in off the street and hired detectives to sort out their lives.

She had brought a book to read with her that day in the thought that it might have its quieter moments. Somebody had given her an anthology of Ruth Rendell mysteries to read as a Christmas present and that was what she was reading that afternoon. She put it down beside her as someone arrived in the office.

"Can I speak to Mr Rivers?" The youth with longish straggly blond hair asked.

"I'm afraid he's not in today," said Debra. "Can I help you at all?"

"The name's Thomas Saunders." He paused after speaking to see if the name registered with her. It did not. "Thomas Saunders," he repeated in firm tones. Again it did not register with Debra. "You must know who I am," he insisted. "Your boss is hounding me over this murder," he continued, "and it's got to stop." With that, he brought his hand down heavily on the reception desk – startling Debra.

"There's no need for that," said Debra curtly. "I'll tell Mr Rivers."

"I said it's got to stop," continued Thomas Saunders. With that, he picked up a plant pot on the coffee table in the foyer and flung it past Debra with all the forced he could muster.

"Careful," she said as she ducked out of the way. "That could have hurt me."

"As if I care," he said. He looked around the room for something else to throw. He noticed there were a couple of magazines on the coffee table and tore them into pieces – scattering them around the reception area as he did so.

"I want your boss to understand he's got to stop this hounding of me," he said. "Do you understand?"

"I understand I should give him a message saying he should stop following you," said Debra, "but I refuse to tell him to stop hounding you because I know Mr Rivers and he wouldn't hound you. Now would you please go?"

Thomas Saunders was still looking around him. He noticed Debra's computer on the other side of the reception and lifted the flap which gained him access to her side of the desk and made his way over to where it had been placed. However, as he tried to pick it up, Debra picked up her volume of Ruth Rendell mysteries and brought it down with a smack on the back of his head. Dazed, he stumbled around for a few seconds before a second thwack from Debra sent him spinning to the floor. Before he could pull himself together, she was on her mobile phone to Gary's office. "Help, Gary," she said when he answered. "I'm being attacked in the office."

"We'll be there as quick as we can," came the reply. "Get help from one of the other offices in the building in the meantime." By now, Thomas Saunders had risen quite groggily to his feet. "Help," shouted Debra as loudly as she could in the hope that someone would hear her in the solicitors' office below. Meanwhile, Thomas Saunders put all thoughts of throwing the computer around out of his head and moved towards Debra in a menacing way as if he was going to punch her. She picked the Ruth Rendell volume up again – a move which was enough to stop him in his tracks. At this juncture, Rosemary Gallagher and one of her male solicitor colleagues came bursting through the door.

"Are you all right, Debra?" shouted Rosemary.

"No," she shouted pointing at the still groggy Thomas Saunders. He took one look at the odds and stumbled past Rosemary and her solicitor colleague and made his way out of the door and down the stairs – escaping into the street. Debra sat back, clutching the Ruth Rendell volume. "I don't know where that came from," she said. "He just came in here and accused Mr Rivers of hounding him and started to smash the place up."

"Can I get you anything?" asked Rosemary. "Have you called the police?"

"Yes, Gary's coming." As she sat back, she looked at the Ruth Rendell volume and the inscription inside the front cover which read "From Nikki with love, merry Christmas You'll understand Philip's job a bit more if you read these.". "Thank you, Nikki," she said, "that was a marvellous present."

Rosemary was just pouring Debra a cup of tea when a couple of uniformed constables arrived on the scene and started taking details of what happened. Gary arrived moments later. "Are you all right, Debra?" he asked.

"Yes," she said.

"Good. What happened?" Debra explained in great detail, ending with the bit where she hit him over the head with the Ruth Rendell mysteries. "It was quite a crack," she said. "I think he might have to go to hospital to be checked out for concussion."

"You're priceless," said Gary – reminding himself of a couple of previous occasions when she had fought off intruders successfully. He moved towards her and put his arms round her waist and kissed her firmly on the mouth.

The two constables seemed astonished by what had happened. "That never happens to me when I call the police," added Rosemary.

As Gary sat down next to Debra – holding her hand – he thought to himself: Ah, well, that saves me from having to decide when to make a pass at her at the cinema tonight. The relationship has started.

• • ● • •

Francesca read the local paper with interest on the Thursday. She and Gary were pictured on the front page with a lead story saying that the net had been widened in the hunt for Jennifer and Lesley's killers. It said detectives were considering a number of possibilities – including the idea it could have been the work of a jealous ex-lover. She smiled. Not exactly what Professor Saunders had ordered but it could put the wind up a number of people who had been at the dance that Saturday night. The telephone rang. It was Rory Gleeson's secretary. Could he see her right now? "Of course," said Francesca.

"What's this all about?" said Gleeson as she entered his office. He pointed to a copy of the paper on his desk. "I've already had to field one complaint already."

"Professor Saunders?"

"Yes. He says the description of jealous ex-lover could apply to Thomas who Rivers' sidekick – the man who was your partner – was harassing yesterday."

"One point, sir," said Francesca. "I am not responsible for what my ex-partner does." There was a heavy emphasis on the word "ex". "May I remind you, you told me to dump him and I have moved out of what was my home?" she continued. "Two, the phrase jealous ex-lover could apply to Duncan Hamilton and Jimmy Atherton equally as well. It could even apply to Stan Wightman if you consider Lesley Peters was the target of the killer."

"I don't know who these people are." protested Gleeson.

"They've all been linked romantically to one or other of the victims."

"All right." Gleeson nodded "This business, though, of not being responsible for your ex. I can see it on one level but if – as you have said – you are going to rely on the evidence brought up by this detective Rivers then in a kind of way you are. Anyhow, what's he doing still working for that man Rivers? We could put pressure on to get that agency closed down."

"Whoa!" said Francesca. "I'm staying with Rivers at present. Rivers takes the view that until Jo's appeal is heard, he's quite entitled to employ him. "

"I'm not sure he's right about that."

"I don't wish to debate it with you, sir. What Rivers decides and what Jo does are nothing to do with me. You'd be ridding the area of a very good and upstanding detective agency if you tried to get it closed down. Some might say it was an act of vindictiveness towards me."

"You don't understand, do you, Francesca? There are people in high places who think you're too zealous. Detective Chief Inspector Nick Barton at Brighton, Chief Constable Adrian Paul at Hertford. Who's next on your hit list, they say?"

"You are talking about a man who was prepared to let an innocent man go to jail for life for murder and a man who sexually assaulted his underlings. Not behaviour that I would have thought you condoned for one minute."

"Of course I don't, Francesca. Just be aware, though, Professor Saunders is likely to go to the Police Commissioner if he finds any reason to support the argument that you have been harassing his son."

"That's one good reason why we're letting Rivers get on with his investigation. He doesn't have to worry about ruffling people's feathers and – if he comes up with concrete evidence which we have to act upon so much the better."

"So, what do I tell Professor Saunders if he gets back to me."

"That I was merely checking out evidence supplied to me by Philip Rivers. He's going to have to learn that he can't run the police force in the same way as he did when Detective Chief Inspector Brett was here."

"One of these days, Francesca," he said, "you're going to be promoted to a position like mine and you'll realise it's not as easy as you thought it was."

"I do realise that, sir."

"Good, that'll be all, then." Francesca left the office in reasonably good spirits. She felt Gleeson had understood some of her arguments. Gleeson picked up his telephone receiver. "Professor Saunders, please," he said. "Professor," he added when Saunders answered, "I've had a word with the investigating officer and she says all she was doing was checking out some information the private detective Rivers had supplied her with. The jealous ex phrase could apply to a number of people other than your son."

"I'll tell him that, then shall I?" said Saunders. "He really was most disturbed this morning, I was very worried about him."

Francesca went back to her office. Gary had arrived by now. "What are you doing this morning?" she asked him.

"There was a break-in at the Rivers detective agency. A guy called Thomas Saunders tried to trash the place."

"Oh, no," said Francesca.

"Pardon?"

"It's just that his influential father has just complained that we are harassing him over the Welsh and Peters' murders. It's going to look great if we go and arrest him today for trashing the Rivers place."

"I could go and have a quiet word with him," said Gary. "It was Debra who witnessed the brunt of the damage. She's not exactly mad keen to press charges."

"Did he cause much damage?"

"No."

"How did she stop him?"

"Banged him over the head with one of Nikki's Christmas presents – a volume of Ruth Rendell mysteries."

Francesca laughed. "She's ingenious, that one. You'd better watch her. How are you getting on with her?"

Gary made the sign of fingers being crossed to Francesca.

She smiled. "Now, about Thomas Saunders" she said.

"Yes?"

"I'm not the sort of person who thinks we should drop a case just because the person involved in it has friends in high places."

"No."

"What would we do if the son of a railway clerk, say for example, had trashed a place?"

"We'd go and caution them, at the very least."

"Then go and do the same with Thomas Saunders."

● ● ● ● ●

Francesca and the Saunders family were not the only ones avidly reading the papers that morning. Rick Harper, who was expecting a visit from Rivers, was also doing so. He liked what he saw and told Rivers so in no uncertain terms when he arrived for their interview.

"At long last, it really does seem I'm being treated equally to everybody else," he said.

"You're not out of the wood yet," cautioned Rivers.

"I know, I know," he muttered, "but at least I know one or two things – that, when I am out of the wood, Anne Welsh is ready and waiting for me. Honestly, Mr Rivers, you don't know what that means to me."

"She's the one, then?"

Rick smiled. "Yes," he said, "I've always fancied her. She's a couple of years older than me and I didn't have the courage in those days to ask her out."

"You'd have saved yourself a lot of trouble if you had," observed Rivers. "You wouldn't have been invited round to Jennifer's house for a shag if you had been going out with her." Rivers noted a look of protest coming over Rick. "Oh, come on, Rick, don't beat about the bush. That's what it was – from both your points of view."

"Well, maybe. I don't like casting aspersions on Jennifer now she's dead."

"You're not casting aspersions. She was a robust teenager. Full of life. Ultimately, that was probably her downfall."

"Who do you think killed her, Mr Rivers?"

"I'm not remotely near there yet," he said. "There's lots of evidence to sift through. Including new evidence against you."

"Me?"

"How's Mary Wightman?"

"Mary Wightman? Why do you bring her up?"

"You had a relationship with her."

"I wouldn't put it like that. "

"You went out a few times. You even told her you loved her."

"Who's told you that?"

"You said to a friend that you doubted whether she'd notice if you said 'I hate you' instead of 'I love you' when you were together. Not nice."

"Thomas Saunders," said Rick. "I should never have said anything to him. Doubtless he made a mountain out of a molehill – as usual."

"Why did you say it?"

"Mary was boring. Her parents insisted she be in by ten o'clock every evening. We went to the cinema one night and she wasn't allowed to stay out until the film finished. She never thought to question her parents. I was angry. I wanted to see the film. I marched her home from the cinema in silence. I never asked her out again. I happened to be with Thomas Saunders the following evening." Rivers raised an eyebrow. "Don't read anything into that. Our experimental sex was long over by then. I happened to say what you said I said. I was angry. At the time I didn't like her for what she had done."

"Bit of a coward's way to treat her," said Rivers. "Why didn't you tell her you wanted to go out with someone who could stay out a bit longer with you? She might have learnt something if you had tried to do that. Do you know what effect your treatment of her had on her?"

"No. Stan was a bit cool to me for a while afterwards. I guess she was a bit upset. Tough."

"Where is she now?"

"Like Stan, still living with her parents. She has been away to university, though. I guess she manages to stay out until the end of movies now. I've no idea whether she has a boyfriend or anything like that. I wouldn't want to see her again. No point. There's not an awful lot to reminisce about."

"Do you think Stan told her about what you'd said?"

"Probably." He smiled. "It would have been something for him to talk about with her. He hasn't got great powers of conversation."

"You see. There you again. People say you're disdainful of other people. They can see you getting annoyed with Jennifer and losing your temper if she refused you."

"It never came to that. Anyway, if I had have got into the house that night, she wouldn't have refused me. Not in her character."

Arrogance again, thought Rivers, but he decided this time not to tell his employer that. "Well, I've got work to do," he said getting up from his chair. "Jealous lovers to see. Cocaine snorting impresarios to expose."

"Pardon?"

"Peter Aymes was out of his head on cocaine outside Jennifer's house at around 2am that morning. Jimmy was with him."

"Not Jimmy," said Rick. "No way."

"You mean."

"As a murder suspect. The guy's too nice."

"Ambitious, though."

· · ● · ·

"I tried to get round to see Stan Wightman this afternoon but there was no reply from his house," said Jo. "He still lives with his parents. I could go round and try again this evening."

"I'm sure it could wait," said Francesca. "Rest up for the appeal tomorrow. Rivers will understand."

The two of them were at an Italian restaurant in Hertford. Francesca had resolved to drive back to Rivers' house after the meal. "It could be the last night we have to spend on our own," she had said.

Jo had smiled. "Don't you think we're behaving rather like schoolboys and schoolgirls?" he had said.

"Not quite."

"What makes you say that?"

"I don't think my boss would approve of the two of us even having dinner together. So we are sort of bucking the system before any thought of our behaviour comes into the picture."

"Good. I'd hate to think we were a slave to it." He had toyed with his fork at that juncture – keeping his thoughts to himself. "Rosemary's given me a description of this new barrister I've got," he said – still toying with his fork. "She's told him in no uncertain terms that I want to give evidence. Apparently, he will let me. A guy called Peter Lambert. Ever come across him? He does a lot of cases in Hertfordshire, apparently."

"Can't say that I have," she said. "Jo," she then said with more urgency in her voice. "I've taken the day off tomorrow. I can be with you. I've left Gary in charge." She smiled. "Not as frightening a thought as I once believed it to be."

At that stage Rivers entered the restaurant with Nikki. "I hope you don't mind," said Francesca. "I invited her."

"We wanted to be with you on your last night before the appeal," Rivers said to Jo. "We didn't want you getting all maudlin."

"What? With Francesca as company?"

Rivers grinned. "Probably not." He and Nikki quickly ordered pastas. Jo and Francesca were already starting the main course of the meal.

"Business for a moment," said Jo. Rivers nodded. "I tried to get to speak to Stan Wightman this afternoon. He wasn't in. I know it's urgent that we contact him."

"Don't worry," said Rivers, "I'll have a try tomorrow. Anyhow, let's raise a glass – of water in my case – to success tomorrow."

"Success tomorrow," they all chorused. Nikki squeezed Jo's hand. He got up from the table and made his excuses. "Got to go to the toilet," he said.

"Me too," said Rivers.

"No," said Jo. "I want to be on my own for a moment."

Rivers acquiesced with Jo's wishes but when he had not reappeared after what seemed like an age he decided to follow him to the toilet. Jo was standing by the wash basin. "You guys," he said – his voice faltering just a little. "You're terrific. You've bent the rules for me." Rivers made as if to protest. "No, you have," he said. "And Francesca. I'm sure her boss knows why she's taking the day off tomorrow. Big risk. Nikki, too. She's never questioned whether I was in the wrong." He sniffed into his handkerchief. "But it's not enough," he said.

"What do you mean?"

"No, I don't mean you could do more. You couldn't. It's not enough for me. I keep wondering when is it going to happen again? There's racism out there. If they don't get me this time, they will next. And they'll keep on coming until they do."

"No," said Rivers.

"Yes," said Jo firmly. "Back in Calicos, this wouldn't happen."

"It wouldn't be that rosy," said Rivers.

"But I could walk down the street and say 'hi' to the fellows I met – instead of wondering whether I should take a short cut down a back alley." He motioned Rivers to silence. "I know what I'm saying, Rivers," he said. "It's only if you've lived in another part of the world where racism isn't an issue that you feel so badly about it here. Calicos is tempting."

"There's one thing that Calicos doesn't have," said Rivers.

"Yes?"

"Francesca." Another tear formed in Jo's eyes. "Think about it, Jo," he said. "She's one of the best coppers we've got in the UK. What would there be for her in Calicos? Besides, if there was, we wouldn't want to let her go." He quickly added: "Of course, we wouldn't want to let you go either."

Jo looked Rivers straight in the eye. "You rate Francesca, don't you?"

"Yes."

"You fancy her?"

"Yes," said Rivers. There was no point in saying otherwise, he

211

felt. "But we've been through that and decided we were not made for each other."

"But if I left?"

"I would still rate Francesca. I would still fancy her and I would think – if she ever found another man – he would be one hell of a lucky guy. But I hope she would never be in that position because I think – no, I'm sure – the man for her is you. And I'm equally sure that the woman for you is Francesca. Think about that if you're contemplating going back to Calicos."

"I will," said Jo.

"Come on," said Rivers. "We'd best get back to the others. They'll wonder what's happened." He clasped Jo to him and patted his shoulder as he led him out of the toilet. Jo immediately went to his seat next to Francesca and put his hand on her knee.

"Sorry – little wobble," he said.

• • ● • •

Gary Clarke wolfed down a piece of toast before leaving home that morning. "I'm going to give that lad Saunders a caution for trying to wreck your office yesterday," he shouted back at Debra as he made his way out of their home.

"I'm a bit embarrassed about it now," she replied. "I gave him a fair whack with the books."

"Don't worry," said Gary. "It won't come to court. I won't be charging him with anything."

Debra was in her nightshirt. He paused at the door to turn round and give her a passionate kiss on the lips. "Enjoy your day," he said to her.

"I'll enjoy the evening even better," she said smiling. She clasped his hand and then let him go to get into his car and drive to the Saunders household. It was only about a fifteen-minute drive, but it was in the heart of the countryside. Quite isolated, in fact. It spoke volumes of the wealth of the people who lived in it. Gary drove up the driveway – hoping to himself that Thomas was in and that his parents were out. He knew how sensitive they were about visits from the police. Francesca was right, though, he reasoned. You shouldn't let the lad off because of the powerful connections his parents could muster.

"I've come to see your son, Thomas," he said on being greeted by Mrs Saunders answering the door.

"And you are?" Gary showed her his warrant card. "Oh, not again," she said. "My husband has had words with your superiors about harassing our son. He's told you all he knows about the murders."

"This is not about the murders," said Gary. "I'm sorry – but your son damaged property in the office of Philip Rivers, a private detective, yesterday afternoon. I have to talk to him about it." Gary could see beyond Mrs Saunders into the house and noticed a door at the end of the hallway, which looked as if it led into the kitchen, was ajar. He thought he could see Thomas Saunders there. He had been buttering some toast but – when Gary started speaking – he put the knife down and tried to listen. As it began to dawn on him that he faced being questioned by the police again, he began to look a little restless. As Gary indicated he would have to talk to him about Rivers' office, he let the knife slip to the floor and suddenly ran out of the back door. "Excuse me," said Gary – almost pushing Mrs Saunders out of the way as he headed towards the kitchen.

"Don't you need a warrant or something before you can barge your way into my home?" said Mrs Saunders. By now, Gary had reached the back door of the kitchen, which Thomas has slammed shut as he made his way out into the garden. Gary opened the door and saw Thomas sprinting out of the garden towards the canal bank at the bottom of the garden. Gary sighed. There was no way of catching Thomas, he decided. He turned on his heels and went back into the house. The best thing to do might be to drive towards a bridge across the water which he remembered going over as he had driven to the house that morning. Thomas would have to run past there, he concluded.

"Wait a minute," said Mrs Saunders. "What do you think you're doing?" Gary was in no mood to bandy words with her and got into his car and revved the engine up. Mrs Saunders immediately reached into her jacket pocket and brought out a mobile phone.

"Darling," she said when the person she had called answered, "the police have come round again and Thomas has run off. Can you come home? I don't know what to do." She was reassured by her husband that he was on his way immediately.

Gary, meanwhile, tried to speed off in his car but became stuck behind a tractor – which slowed him down. As he approached the bridge, he became aware of two young boys trying to flag him down. He stopped and rolled down his window.

"Mister, mister," said one excitedly. "There's a man in the canal."

Gary got out of the car as quickly as he could and ran to the canal bank. The boy was right. A man – Gary assumed to be Thomas Saunders – was floating along the far side of the canal, his head buried below the water line. Without waiting to think, Gary jumped into the canal and swam over to where Thomas' body was. He dragged him to the canal bank and out of the water. At the very least he was unconscious, at worst Gary feared he could be dead. He tried to give him mouth to mouth resuscitation and – when this appeared not to work – he telephoned for an ambulance. He then tried pumping his heart but recognised to himself he did not really know what he was doing and certainly appeared to be having no effect on Thomas. He stood back from Thomas' body and called the two boys over. "Did you see what happened?"

"He was running along the canal and he fell, banging his head," said one. "He just slid into the canal."

"No, no," said the other boy. "He jumped into the canal. He didn't fall. Then he banged his head. Almost deliberately."

The sound of an ambulance siren could now be heard. Within two minutes, two paramedics were trying to revive Thomas. One looked grim. "We'll have to get him into the ambulance as soon as possible and into the hospital," he said. So saying, they lifted his body onto a stretcher and took him away to the ambulance.

Gary followed them. "What does it look like?" he asked.

"Not good," said the lead ambulanceman.

"Shit," said Gary. He felt he should inform Francesca of what had happened right away. Then he remembered she was accompanying Jo to court that morning. She had enough to deal with, he thought to himself. He rang the police station instead and secured two constables to come down and cordon off the scene – while they awaited an expert to carry out a forensic examination. Another constable was sent to the hospital to find out how Thomas was. Someone, he thought to himself, should go to Mrs Saunders and tell her what had happened. Oh, well, he thought. Might as well be in for a penny as a pound. He drove back to their house and knocked on the door. It was Professor Saunders who answered. "Yes?" he said irritably.

"I'm afraid your son has had an accident," said Gary. "He's fallen into the canal. He's been taken to hospital. I thought you ought to know."

"How badly hurt is he?" asked Mrs Saunders.

"I'm not a medical man," said Gary. "I don't know. I just thought you might want to go to the hospital to be with him." Best not to offer any more information, he thought.

"Yes," said Professor Saunders. He pushed past Gary to get to his car – which was also in the driveway.

"Come on, darling," he said to his wife. She joined him at the car. Before he got into the driver's seat, Professor Saunders turned to speak to Gary. "Don't think you're out of the woods," he said. "Rest assured I shall hold you responsible for whatever happens to Thomas."

• • • • •

"Jo's appeal is today," said Rivers as he and Nikki breakfasted together that morning. "I did think of taking the day off and going to the court to support him – but I'm falling behind on the murder investigation. Jo didn't manage to get to see Stan Wightman yesterday – he's the guy who was Lesley Peters' boyfriend."

"You should see him," said Nikki. "Nobody seems to have thought much about Lesley up until now."

"This guy could also have harboured a grudge against Rick," Rivers added. "He was rather cruel towards Wightman's sister. He'd been going out with her – but made a statement to the effect he wondered if she would notice if he said 'I hate you' instead of 'I love you' when they were cuddling up to each other."

"You do pick the most delightful clients." said Nikki.

"At least he didn't say it to her."

"Who did he say it too?"

"That oddball Thomas Saunders. The guy who trashed my office yesterday. – though that's got nothing to do with it."

"Why did he trash your office?"

"He thinks I'm hounding him."

"Are you?"

"I wasn't," he said ruefully but then hastily added. "And I won't – but it does make me wonder. His father says he's nervous about the police. He's had some kind of a breakdown and he gets unsettled when we question him. I just wonder."

"Wonder what?"

"Whether he's nervous we might discover something – rather than just nervous about being questioned. It would make sense."

"Discover what? That he had something to do with the murders."

"It's possible. He resented Rick because he broke off a gay relationship with him – well, it wasn't really as much as that. It was a teenage experimental grope that meant more to one participant than the other." Rivers thought for a moment. "I can't see that that would make him kill Jennifer to teach Rick a lesson but stranger things have happened. Maybe he knows something about the murder – but he's frightened to tell us because he's frightened of the killer. At any rate, poor chap. I guess we'll have to question him again to find out.That won't please his father." Rivers got up from the table. "Ah well, I'd better get on," he said. "I gather Stan Wightman doesn't have a job at the moment and spends most of his time on his allotment. Maybe I'll have better luck than Jo today."

"Eh?"

"Sorry – I didn't mean better luck than Jo at the appeal. You know, I spoke to him for quite some time last night. He's thinking of quitting now regardless of the outcome. Britain, he says, is a more racist society than the last time he was here."

"What does Francesca think about that?"

"He hasn't told her. I told him he should stay because of her. He'll never find a better woman than her for a partner."

"You think they should stay together?"

"Of course. Don't you?"

"There was a time."

"When I had designs on her myself? Yes, but I soon came to realise that meant giving up on you – and I wasn't prepared to do that." He moved back into the centre of the breakfast room and put his arms around her waist. He held the pose for a moment and then kissed her. She responded by clasping him to her. "Shame," said Rivers, "but I really ought to go."

"Thank you," said Nikki. "For those words just now."

"It's the actions that speak louder than words." he said as he kissed her again.

• • ● • •

"I'm sorry," said the surgeon after he had taken Professor Saunders and his wife into a side room. "We did all we could. There was nothing for it, though. He was dead on arrival at the hospital. Please accept my condolences."

Professor Saunders nodded at the surgeon. He gripped his wife's hand tightly. "What killed him?"

"There'll be a post-mortem," said the surgeon, "but basically he drowned. He hit his head on concrete as he slipped and fell into the canal. He was unconscious and although the policeman rescued him from the canal as quickly as he could there was nothing he could have done, either."

"I'll get him," vowed the professor, "and the woman who sent him to see Thomas. There was no need to chase him. In fact, there was no need to call on him at all."

"I'm sorry, sir" the surgeon began.

"No, no," said the professor waving him away. "There's no need for you to get involved in this. I accept you did what you could."

"Thank you, sir." The surgeon exited the room. Saunders immediately reached for his pocket and brought out his mobile phone.

"What are you doing?" asked his wife.

"I'm phoning the chief constable. Make sure those two get what they deserve."

"I want to see Thomas first."

"Oh, all right, then. But we must make sure we strike while the iron's hot."

Mrs Saunders hailed a nurse who was walking past her. "I'd like to see my son if that's okay," she said. "Thomas Saunders."

"Of course," said the nurse. The professor reluctantly followed his wife into the operating theatre where Thomas was still laid out on a bed. A police constable who had been despatched to the hospital to monitor progress left. Once outside, he rang the police station and asked to speak to Gary Clarke. "You asked to be kept informed of developments on the Thomas Saunders case," he said. "Unfortunately, the lad has just been declared dead. I shall be coming back to the police station to make a report."

"Thank you, constable," said Gary. Oh God, he thought. What the hell do I do now? I must let Francesca know. He rang her but her mobile but it was on answerphone. She was obviously still at the court hearing with Jo. He put the phone down. It immediately rang again. "Chief constable's secretary here," said the voice at the other. "Can you come and see him immediately?"

"Of course," said Gary. He was in Gleeson's office within minutes.

"I've just had an extremely disturbing call from Professor Saunders. He tells me his son is dead. He blames you and Detective Chief Inspector Manners."

"Yes, sir." Gary was not surprised to hear what the chief constable had to say.

"I need a bit more than 'yes, sir' from you, Clarke. What the hell happened?"

"I went to see him this morning. He was responsible for trying to trash the offices of Philip Rivers, the private detective, yesterday evening."

"So this is nothing to do with the murders?"

"Not directly, no, sir."

"I'm sure you'll explain what you mean by that in good time." Gleeson sounded exasperated. Gary realised he had not got off on the best of footings with him. "Carry on," said Gleeson.

"He trashed the office because he was angry about Rivers questioning him."

"There's no doubt it was him?"

"No, sir. There are witnesses."

"Did he assault anyone?"

"He frightened the receptionist and destroyed furniture."

"So you went to see him? Off your own bat?" Gary reflected for a moment. "The truth, Clarke, the truth," said Gleeson drumming with his fingernails on the table.

"No, sir." said Gary. Then he realised his comment could be misconstrued. "I don't mean 'no, I won't tell the truth'. I meant it was Detective Chief Inspector Manners who said we ought to go and caution him. That was all I was going to do, sir."

"Except you killed him in the process."

"When I arrived, his mother answered the door. He was in the kitchen. As soon as he realised who it was, he legged it."

"Legged it?"

"Ran out of the back door. I gave chase. I realised I had no chance of catching up with him so I went back to my car. It seemed obvious he was going to run along the canal bank. The next thing I knew I was confronted by two small boys who told me there was a body in the canal. It was Thomas. I jumped in and fished him out but there was nothing I could do. My attempts at resuscitating him were in vain."

"Right. I take it you had no search warrant for the Saunders property?"

"I didn't consider the offence serious enough to get one. Besides, I wasn't searching for anything."

"But you shouldn't have entered their property without being invited in. They may have a case there." Gleeson cleared his throat. "Detective Constable Clarke," he began. "I have no alternative but to suspend you from duty pending an investigation into your conduct."

"Yes, sir," said Gary forlornly. "And Francesca?"

"You shouldn't be so familiar with your senior officer," said Gleeson.

"Sorry, sir."

"It is nothing to do with you what happens to her. I shall take time to deliberate on the matter. Is she here?"

"No, sir, she's taken leave."

"Have you contacted her?"

"I've tried to, sir. Her phone is on answerphone. She's at the appeal into her partner's assault charge."

"Her one-time partner?"

"Yes, sir. I stand corrected."

Gleeson nodded. "Hand me your warrant card," he said, "then you can go. Leave the station and do not communicate with anyone in it. Is that clear?"

"Yes, sir." Gary handed over his card. "Before I go, sir, I should like to say one thing."

"Make it brief."

"When she suggested I go and caution Thomas Saunders today, Detective Chief Inspector Manners said that – if it was anybody else – we wouldn't have a moment's thought about going to caution them. If we didn't go, it would be solely because he had friends in high places. I think that is an important principle, sir." Gary came to a halt – surprised by what he perceived to be his eloquence.

"You've made your point." Gleeson looked down at some papers on his desk and Gary took his cue to leave. No sooner had he gone than Gleeson reached for the phone on his desk. "Professor Saunders?" he said when the person on the other end answered.

"Yes," came the reply.

"Chief Constable Gleeson here. I thought I should inform you I have suspended the officer who visited your house this morning."

"Thank you. And that woman?"

"I take it you are referring to Detective Chief Inspector Manners?"

"You know who I am referring to."

"That is a more complicated matter. She is not here today so

I shall to wait and speak to her and reflect on the matter further."

"She should be suspended, too,"

"You may think that. As I said, I have to reflect on the matter."

"Not good enough," said Professor Saunders. "I notice from the local rag this week that she's quite a prominent figure locally. If you don't suspend her, I may have to go and see them and give them my views on the matter."

"That's your prerogative, sir. It doesn't change the position."

"We'll see," he said. "Now, if you'll excuse me, I must go and comfort my wife."

• • ● • •

Rosemary had described Peter Lambert, Jo's new barrister, accurately to him. Three-piece blue suit, buttoned up waistcoat. Long blonde hair combed back.

"Jo Rawlins Clifford?" he said extending a hand to Jo. "Peter Lambert."

"Just call me Jo."

"Okay." He was carrying a set of papers and rested one foot on a bench while he got the papers out of his brief case. "Let me see, you want to give evidence."

"Yes, I didn't in the original trial. I think it could help to clear me."

"Okay," said Lambert. "I think, though, that the most important evidence for us will come from Winston Samuel but I can't see any harm in you going into the witness box. Just don't show your dislike of the police too obviously."

"I don't dislike the police," said Jo. "Just one or two officers."

Lambert nodded. "That's okay." It was only then that he noticed Francesca standing just behind Jo. "Who is this?" he asked.

"Francesca – or to be more precise Detective Chief Inspector Francesca Manners. My partner. One of the reasons I don't dislike the police."

Lambert smiled. "Well, I'd better get togged up. I'll see you in court as they say." Jo and Francesca made their way into the court room. Jo's was the first case that morning so the usher asked him to step into the dock. Francesca took a seat in the public gallery. Within minutes, the court was in session. Jo – like everybody else – stood when the judge entered the court. The judge was a man in his late fifties or early sixties, Jo surmised. He had a greying beard and owl-like spectacles but whatever style of clothing he was wearing was obscured by his robes – making it difficult for Jo to assess him.

The prosecuting council, a Mr Roscoe, rose to his feet. "Your Honour, it is the crown's case that the accused, Jo Rawlins Clifford assaulted a police officer, PC Ray Enderby, on the day of the national protest demonstration against the government's immigration policies – June 24," he said. "A group of demonstrators were being held in a street off Trafalgar Square in an attempt to minimise the threat of disorder. When the accused was told he could not leave the area, he became abusive and pushed PC Enderby which led to a scuffle between the two men and the arrest of the accused. We will be bringing forward witnesses to verify this version of events. I call PC Ray Enderby to the stand."

PC Enderby took the oath and waited for Mr Roscoe to address him. "You will have heard that a new witness has come forward to say that the accused did not attack you but that – on the contrary – you attacked him. Do you still stand by your testimony that Rawlins Clifford attacked you?"

"Yes, sir, he was angry that I would not let him leave the cordon."

"Not even to go to the toilet?"

"If I'd allowed him to go to the toilet, how many others would have wanted to go? I felt I had no choice."

"It is being alleged that you were vowing earlier in the day that you'd like to arrest one of these ethnic minority demonstrators for forcing you to work overtime on your wife's birthday. Is that true?"

"No, sir."

"Are you racist, PC Enderby?"

"No, sir, no way, sir."

"Thank you. Mr Lambert?"

Lambert rose to his feet. He peered at Enderby before asking his first question. "You're saying our new witness, who was also policing the demonstration on that day, is lying then, PC Enderby.

222

In other words, it's your word against his – and therefore cannot be proven one way or the other."

"I'm telling the truth. Anyhow, my version of events is backed up by PC Boatman."

"A man who couldn't see what was going on from where he was standing?"

"I don't know where he was standing, sir, but he says he saw me bring attacked." "What reason do you say the witness has for coming forward after the trial and giving a false account of what he saw?" "I have no idea, but I saw what I saw"

"Thank you, PC Enderby, that will be all."

Roscoe called his next witness, PC Boatman, who merely affirmed he could see what was going on – but when Lambert asked him to point out where he was standing, he seemed to have difficulty identifying the spot.

"And can you tell me where PC Samuel was standing?"

"No, sir, I'm not sure."

"Do you accept that he was nearer to the appellant than you were?"

"I don't know, sir".

Boatman was followed by Detective Sergeant Bowers into the witness box. "You were the person to question Mr Rawlins Clifford on the night of his arrest, were you not?" asked Roscoe.

"Yes, sir."

"Were you satisfied you had enough evidence to charge him?"

"Not then, no sir," said the detective sergeant. "I was aware this was a sensitive case. We could be accused of racism if we brought charges against a black man demonstrating about oppressive behaviour against black people and he was subsequently found innocent. It was only when PC Boatman came forward with his evidence that I believed we had enough evidence to go ahead with a prosecution and the Crown Prosecution service concurred."

"Thank you, detective sergeant."

Lambert rose to his feet for the defence, "Tell me, detective sergeant, if you had had the evidence from Winston Samuel available at the time of your decision to charge my client, would the result have still been the same?"

"I'm sorry?"

"Would you have still have charged him?"

"But I didn't have the evidence available."

"But if you had? A straight yes or no will suffice."

"The question doesn't arise. I didn't have the information available."

"Thank you, detective sergeant. I think the fact you were unable to answer 'yes' to that question speaks volumes. No more questions."

Roscoe shuffled to his feet. "That concludes the prosecution evidence."

"Thank you," said the judge. "Mr Lambert?"

"Your honour," said Lambert rising to address him. "Since the passing of sentence on my client some important new evidence has emerged from another witness to the events. You have a written statement from our new witness, Winston Samuel, and I should like to call on him to give evidence."

"Be my guest," said the judge.

"I call Winston Samuel." The name reverberated round the court room and eventually Winston emerged from the waiting area and sat in the witness box. He glanced around him nervously before taking the oath. Winston was a practising Christian so he had no difficulty taking the religious oath.

Lambert briefly shuffled his papers and then got up to go through the formalities of identifying his witness. "Now," he said after completing them, "on the day of the demonstration where were you?"

"I was on duty as a Metropolitan police officer. I was assigned to the street where a number of protesters were being held to prevent them taking part in any disorder."

"Was there any disorder?"

"No."

"In your mind, was it necessary to hold the protesters in this street?" Lambert pointed to the street after selecting a road map from his brief case.

"I didn't question the order at the time."

Lambert nodded again. "Did you see my client at any time?"

"Yes, I was about ten feet away from me. He started arguing with PC Enderby ..."

"The alleged assault victim?"

"Yes," said Winston. "I then saw PC Enderby shove your client in the chest to push him back into the crowd of people held in the street. Your client stumbled and then got up and started talking to PC Enderby again whereupon PC Enderby forced him to the ground. They scuffled and your client was handcuffed and – I deduced – arrested."

"Did he show any sign of being violent towards PC Enderby?"

"No, sir."

"A second police officer, PC Boatman, confirms PC Enderby's interpretation of events. Are we to believe they are both lying and you are telling the truth?"

"PC Boatman could not have seen what happened. He was several yards further away. His view of events would have been obscured."

"Thank you, Mr Samuel. You said you were a serving police officer on that day?"

"Yes, sir."

"Are you now?"

"No, sir. I resigned in order to come forward and give evidence. I didn't want to get bogged down in all the disciplinary proceedings I would have faced had I stayed in the force."

"Is that why you didn't come forward in the first place?"

"That and the fact that I sincerely believed justice would be done and your client would be acquitted. When he was found guilty, I knew I had to come forward."

"Thank you again.

"I see," said Lambert. "Tell me, did anything happen with PC Enderby before you went out to police the demonstration?"

"He was boasting about how he'd like to arrest one of the ethnic minority demonstrators for forcing him to do overtime on his wife's birthday."

"Thank you," said Lambert. "That will be all. Your witness, Mr Roscoe."

The crown's barrister got to his feet slowly

"Thank you." Roscoe paused. "Did you sympathise with the aims of the demonstration?"

"Pardon?"

"It's a simple question. Did you sympathise with the aims of the demonstration?"

"As police officers, we are taught to remain neutral."

"Yes, I know all that – but most of the demonstrators were of a similar ethnic origin to you, Mr Rawlins Clifford was of the same ethnic origin to you. Let's face it, you might have thought it's a bit much to get arrested for standing up for the same values as you believe in. So you're doing your best to get him off."

"And I've sacrificed my career as a result of this belief?"

"You wouldn't have been popular if you'd stayed in the force, would you? Accusing a fellow officer – an officer with an impeccable record – of conspiracy to pervert the course of justice. That is what it amounts to, isn't it?"

"I have just told the truth as.…"

"Thank you. No further questions."

"Thank you Mr Samuel – your honour, may this witness be released?"

"Yes, thank you for attending Mr Samuel, you may go or stay as you wish."

Lambert remained on his feet. "I call Jo Rawlins Clifford to the stand." Jo took the witness box and affirmed. Lambert began to question him. "Describe the situation on that afternoon in your own words," he said.

"We were being held by the police in a street off Trafalgar Square," said Jo. "I was desperate to go to the toilet. I was also aware I was letting my employer down if I stayed away from work all that day so I told PC Enderby I had a meeting I had to go to."

"And his response was?"

"To shove me in the chest and back in the crowd. I steadied myself and then started arguing with him again."

"Aggressively?"

"No, but forcefully. He pushed me again and I fell to the ground and before I knew it I was handcuffed and arrested and taken down to the police station."

"Did you at any stage use force against him?"

"Nothing other than the power of argument. Which didn't work."

"Thank you, that will be all. Please stay there as there may be more questions"

Roscoe stood up slowly and addressed Jo. "You must have been angry that day. First of all, your fellow countrymen are being harassed and even deported from the country, then this upstart policeman gets stroppy with you – refusing you permission even to go to the toilet when you could see no reason for stopping you. I can understand you wanting to just lay one on him and get out of there."

"Except I didn't."

"You were seen by another police officer."

"We have just been told he wouldn't have been able to see what was going on by a fellow countryman of yours."

"I see. According to you, all blacks are liars." Lambert shook his head ferociously in a bid to try and persuade Jo to calm down.

"In this case, perhaps," said Roscoe. "Mr Roscoe, please remember where you are" the judge intervened sharply.

"Sorry your honour. That concludes my cross examination."

"And the defence evidence," said Lambert.

"Very well then," said the judge. "In that case, if you would like to summarise, Mr Roscoe?"

Roscoe rose to his feet. "We believe you should dismiss the evidence of Mr Samuel," he said. "He merely wants to come to the aid of someone he sympathises with for protesting against this country's immigration laws. If you dismiss his evidence, then you have no alternative but to uphold the verdict of the original court."

"Mr Lambert?" said the judge.

"We maintain that – at the very least – Winston Samuel's evidence casts doubt on the prosecution's case at the original trial. In fact, we would go further and say it destroys it. PC Boatman had no answer when it was put to him that Mr Samuel was nearer the incident and Mr Samuel has no axe to grind in this particular case. He does not know the appellant; he has given up his career in the police force as a result of the injustice he witnessed. These are strong reasons to believe this witness and his evidence completely corroborates the appellant's account which has remained entirely consistent. In view of this, I submit that your honour has no alternative but to overturn the original conviction."

"Thank you, gentlemen," said the judge. "I shall retire to consider the matter."

"Court rise," said an usher. They all did so.

Peter Lambert made his way over to Jo when the judge left the room. "You should feel fairly confident," he said. "I think the Crown made the wrong pitch. It may have played well with a bunch of racist EastEnders to suggest Winston was merely lying to protect someone with the same colour skin as him – but I doubt whether it impressed the judge. We shall see, though."

They did not have to wait long. The judge returned after twenty minutes. When the courtroom had settled down and was seated, he delivered his verdict.

"I find the evidence of Mr Samuel compelling and believe he deserves a hearing – although I wish he had seen fit to give evidence at the original trial. I concur with Mr Lambert that it was telling that Detective Sergeant Bowers could not say with any confidence that he would have been happy to go ahead with the prosecution had he been aware of Mr Samuel's evidence at the time of the original decision to charge. I therefore allow this appeal and order that the previous finding of guilt against Mr Rawlins Clifford be overturned so that he leaves this court without a stain on his character." Jo gave a sigh of sheer delight and looked for Francesca in the public gallery. He caught sight of her and she blew him a kiss. "Just one thing more," said the judge. "Could I ask Detective Sergeant Bowers to come forward and stand before me?" The detective did as he had been asked. "Detective Sergeant, can I ask you to pursue with as much vigour as you have shown in this case, the case against PCs Enderby and Boatman of conspiracy to pervert the course of justice?"

"Yes, sir."

• • ● • •

Rivers was luckier than Jo when he knocked on the door of the Wightman home – Mrs Wightman answered his call. "I've come to see your son, Stan," he said. "My name's Philip Rivers. I'm investigating the Welsh and Peters murders. There's just one or two questions I'd like to ask him."

"He's not here," she said.

"Where might I find him?"

She gave a little giggle. "If you knew him, you wouldn't have to ask," she said. "He's on our allotment. It's just round the corner. Turn left at the bottom of the road. He spends all his spare time there."

"He's not working, then?"

"No," she said. "He hasn't for a while now. At first it was because he was sad about breaking up with Lesley. Lovely girl. Used to take him out of himself. He went to university after the break-up but he dropped out. Said he couldn't concentrate on his studies. He was at York. He's always found it difficult to get to know new people. We've got high hopes of him, though. He's enrolled on a gardening course at Capel Manor in Enfield. Starts September."

"Do you know – did he split up with her or was it her with him?"

"Oh, I don't really go into those sorts of things. He just knew we were around and that we would support him."

Rivers nodded. He looked about him. The house looked extremely like the Peters' household. Both, he would deduce, were lower middle class. Getting on with their lives without any flamboyance. A closely-knit family, perhaps, but one in which there was not much querying of what anybody was doing. Stan could spend his days on his allotment but his parents would not know if he was growing anything or merely just turning over the weeds. "How's Mary?" he asked, changing the subject.

"Mary?" Mrs Wightman sounded shocked. "What's she got to do with any of this?"

"My client, I believe, used to go out with her. Rick Harper."

Mrs Wightman immediately adopted a more antagonistic tone. "Don't you go mentioning his name in this household," she said angrily. "He proper upset my Mary." She'd dropped her guard – revealing a more working class or possibly rural upbringing, he thought. "Wicked – the things he said."

"You knew?"

"Stan told us. Told Mary as well. I think he felt she ought to know. To my mind, he shouldn't have bothered. What she didn't know wouldn't hurt her."

"How did she react?"

"Upset at first," said Mrs Wightman, "but she's got a really nice boyfriend now. Doug. She works in a bank, too."

"Good," said Rivers. He felt he had just about completed the topics of conversation he had wanted to raise with her now. "Well, I'd best be getting off to the allotment now," he said. "See Stan."

She waited at the door until he had departed down the street. It didn't take him long to find the allotment – or Stan. He was turning over some weeds, picking up dead twigs, putting them in a barrow and then emptying them into a dustbin.

"Stan Wightman?"

"Yes."

Rivers showed him his business card. "I'm investigating the murders of Jennifer Welsh and Lesley Peters."

"I wondered when you'd come."

Rivers looked surprised at this answer. "Why?" he asked. "How did you know about me?"

"Thomas Saunders," he said. "Most people dropped him after…." he paused as if he had information he did not want to impart to the private detective but then continued " ….after his breakdown. I remained friends. You see, I know what it's like."

"You had a breakdown, too?" said Rivers trying to sound sympathetic.

"Depression really, just didn't want to do anything. It helped me, though, listening to Thomas' worries. Still, you don't want to know about my problems. What do you want to know?"

"Where you were on the night of the murders, Stan?"

"Very Agatha Christie," he said. "I went to the dance."

"I know that," said Rivers. "It's after that that I'm interested in. Did you dance with anybody?"

"I asked Lesley for a dance but she wasn't interested. We'd only just split up."

"Did she dance with anybody?"

230

"Rick."

"Rick?"

"Yes, he was dancing with everybody. Ended up with Jennifer at the tail end of the evening. Lesley was on her own."

"Did you think it was worth another try with her?"

"I told you I asked her – but she wasn't interested. She chatted to Rick's friend, Tim Rathbone, for part of the evening."

Rivers nodded. "Hence the invitation," he said.

"Invitation?"

"To Rick and Tim from Jennifer to go back with her and Lesley," he said. "Did you know about that?"

"I overheard it."

"Were you jealous?"

"No."

"So where did you go at the end of evening?"

"If you must know, I went down to the allotment here with Thomas. We chatted for a while." He blushed. "We'd bought a bottle of vodka from the off-licence. I went home after we'd finished it."

"Finished it? You got through a whole bottle of vodka?"

"We discarded the bottle before we'd finished it to stop us from drinking it all."

"What time did you get home?"

"I can't remember."

"Would your parents know? Or Mary?"

"Keep Mary out of this." He suddenly seemed to become angry. "She had nothing to do with the girls' murder."

"You say that as if you did?"

"No," he said firmly, "I'm just protective of her. She's done very well since she stopped seeing Rick. I wouldn't be surprised if she gets married soon – so I don't want anything to spoil that."

"You haven't always been like that, have you?"

"What do you mean?"

"Protective over her. You told her what Rick had said about her,"

"I thought she ought to know – know what kind of a guy he was."

"Did you and Thomas talk about Rick and Mary? Lesley? What?"

231

"We talked about everything. And then we went home,"

"Which is where Mary – and your parents – come in. Would any of them know what time you got in?"

"I don't know," he said. "I didn't see any of them."

Try the mother, thought Rivers. They often stay awake until they are sure their offspring are safe and secure.

• • ● • •

"You're home early," said Debra as she returned from work to find Gary lazing on the sofa. "That's nice for a change," she added.

"You won't think it's nice when I tell you why I'm home early," he said.

"Why?"

"I've been suspended."

"Suspended? Why?"

"Thomas Saunders is dead. He died running away from me. I went to caution him this morning over his attempt to trash your office yesterday. He was in the kitchen and he just fled when he heard it was the police at the door. I ran through the house to try and catch him but he got away. He ran along the canal bank, tripped and fell in banging his head. He was unconscious and he drowned."

"Oh my goodness," said Debra, "but why suspend you?"

"His father is an influential man," said Gary. "He made a complaint. I was suspended."

"But you didn't do anything. I hit him over the head as hard as I could twice with a heavy book and nothing's happened to me."

Gary managed a smile. "I don't think he's told anyone about that," he said. "Anyway, they couldn't suspend you. You don't work for the police."

"I'm going to tell them they shouldn't have done it," said Debra firmly.

"It won't help," said Gary.

"They should know how I feel. If they listen to Thomas' father, they should listen to me. What does Francesca think about all this?"

"I don't know," said Gary. "She's been at Jo's appeal all day. I've left messages but she hasn't got back to me."

"She asked you to go and caution Thomas, didn't she?"

"Yes."

"Well then."

"Well then what?"

"It's as much her fault that Thomas died as yours. If she hadn't sent you, then he wouldn't have been running away from you."

"I don't think it helps pursuing that line of enquiry," said Gary. "She was quite right to send me."

Debra placed her hand in his as he remained seated on the sofa. "How long will it take before you know what's happened?"

"There'll be a disciplinary hearing next week. I guess they'll have to talk to the Saunders family, too. Maybe I'll find out next week but these things usually take longer than you think."

"It's not right," said Debra. "I should do something. Thomas' family look after him and his problems. I should look after you."

Gary placed her hand in his. "Trouble is, they can do something about him," he said. "You can't about me."

"Watch me," she said.

Gary looked at her. For a moment, a picture of her hitting Rory Gleeson over the head with her volume of Ruth Rendell mysteries until he changed his mind came into his head. "Be careful," he said.

• • ● • •

Francesca and Jo left the court hand in hand that lunchtime. "Back to my place?" said Francesca smiling when they were on the train back to Hertford.

"You mean to my place?" said Jo.

"All right. I think we're agreed on where it is even if there's been a little bit of a debate over whose it is," said Francesca. She took her mobile phone out of her pocket. "I'd better just check if there are any messages for me," she said. "Oh, my goodness, five, and two are from the Chief Constable's office." She began listening to them and Jo could tell from the look on her face that something serious had happened. "Thomas Saunders is dead," she said. "It happened after Gary went round to see him this morning – at my behest."

233

"What happened?"

"Tripped and fell into the canal – banging his head – running away from Gary."

"Stupid sod."

"Who? Gary?"

"No, Thomas, of course," said Jo – irritated that she should think he was casting aspersions on Gary.

"His father has lodged a complaint. Gary's message says he's been suspended as a result."

"Professor Saunders would complain if you so much as got up in the morning and passed by on the other side of the road from Thomas."

"He wants to see me. The chief constable, of course. I'd better go and sort this all out." She turned to Jo. "Back to normal, then? We can live together but nobody will allow us the time to be together."

"We'll find it some time," said Jo reassuringly. "I should get back to Rivers and tell him that I come with no strings attached. See you later."

Francesca jumped into a cab at the station and went straight to the chief constable's office upon her arrival at the police station. "You wanted to see me, sir," she said as she presented herself to him.

"Are you surprised?"

"Of course not."

"All hell's broken lose – and I've had to suspend Detective Constable Clarke."

"I know."

"What? You mean you've been in touch with him? You know that's against the rules."

"Which is why I haven't been," she said firmly. "It's easy to pick up information like that. You're not the only source of knowledge." She neglected to tell him it was actually from the answerphone message left on her mobile by Gary. "Why did you suspend him?" she continued. "He was acting on my instructions."

"I know and Professor Saunders did demand that I suspend both of you. I decided, though, that it was a legitimate instruction for you to give Gary in view of the fact that Thomas Saunders had been guilty of a crime the previous evening – the trashing of Philip Rivers' office."

"Oh." She thought that his answer was the first indication that he had decided not to suspend her over the incident.

"You sound surprised?" he said. "I am capable of independent thought."

"Yes, sir. But you suspended Gary? Why?"

"He entered the Saunders' household without permission and without a warrant."

"Oh," said Francesca.

"He saw Thomas in the kitchen but the bloke ran before he could get to him. He charged past Mrs Saunders but realised when he got into the back garden he could not catch him and so gave up the chase. He saw that Thomas was making a beeline for the canal towpath and so went back to his car with the express purpose of catching him further along the towpath. However, the next thing he knew was two small boys telling him Thomas had fallen into the canal. We've got Professor Saint doing an autopsy on the body – though I don't suppose that will tell us anything we don't already know. It's just a tragic accident."

"Yes, sir," said Francesca. "So what do you think will happen to Gary, er, Detective Constable Clarke?"

"There'll be a disciplinary hearing – probably next week. We'll find out the result soon afterwards."

"Can I say something, sir? Gary wouldn't have been there if I hadn't told him to go. If I hadn't told him to go, Thomas Saunders would still be alive."

Gleeson looked perplexed. "Are you making out the case for disciplining you?" he asked.

"No, sir. I'm just repeating what you said. This is a tragic accident. It's no-one's fault. The second thing is Gary was not chasing him along the canal. Thomas could have stopped running at any time. No-one would have caught up with him."

"But Gary did run through the Saunders' house initially."

"Yes, sir, but are we saying that the next time a police officer sees a suspect running away from them, they just shrug their shoulders and say 'ah, well that one's got away from me' and decide not to give chase? That's the message we would be sending out if we disciplined Gary for what he has done."

"Sounds as if you should give evidence to the disciplinary panel."

"I'd be glad to."

"I'm sure you would. Now, out of politeness, I should inform Professor Saunders of my decision not to discipline you. If you would excuse me."

Francesca smiled and got up from her chair. As soon as she had left the room, Gleeson was on the phone to Professor Saunders. "I have to tell you that I have decided not to discipline Detective Chief Inspector Manners over the events of this morning. I have decided it was a legitimate instruction to tell Clarke to interview your son over the criminal damage he caused to an office in Hertford yesterday afternoon. My condolences obviously go out to you over the loss of your son but I am afraid they do not extend to disciplining one of my senior officers."

"Not good enough," said Saunders.

"I'm afraid it will have to suffice. You do realise your son was engaged in a criminal activity the previous afternoon?"

"No, I didn't."

"Well, he was and I can't condone that."

"It's not proven."

"There is a witness he threatened."

"I said this is not good enough. I shall be taking this matter further."

"That is your prerogative." With that, Gleeson replaced the receiver.

• • ● • •

Rivers busied himself by tying loose ends up after he left Stan Wightman in the allotment, His mother answered his knock at the door and greeted him with an 'oh, you again'. Rivers smiled inwardly. He wondered how rich he would be if he gained a fiver every time someone had greeted him with those words.

"I've just seen Stan at the allotment," he said, "and I was

wondering if you could help me with something. What time did he get home on the night of the dance?"

"Oh. Difficult for me to recall. I should say about 11.30pm."

"That can't be true," said Rivers. "He didn't leave the dance until about 11pm and he said he went to the allotment with Thomas Saunders for a chat." There's only one reason you would give me such a wildly inaccurate answer, Rivers thought to himself, and that's if you thought the real answer would incriminate him.

"What time did he say he got back?" Mrs Wightman asked Rivers.

"He doesn't know."

"Well, I wasn't clock watching," she said.

"Come on, mothers know when their children are out at night. They never relax until they get home. Constantly looking at the clock. Worrying about what might have happened. You can't tell me you didn't look at the clock."

Mrs Wightman sighed. "Well, I suppose the last time I looked it was ten to two. He came in soon after that."

"Thank you." Rivers was none the wiser, though. If he and Thomas Saunders had made serious inroads into that bottle of vodka, it could have been that late by the time he got home. "Another question: what was he like the following morning?"

"That one's easier to answer," she said, smiling. "Grumpy. Like a bear with a sore head. He didn't get up until 11 o'clock. I remember that. He said he didn't want any breakfast because it was too near lunchtime."

"Perhaps he really was a bear with a sore head," suggested Rivers. "Did he seem hung over?"

"He said he had a headache," agreed Mrs Wightman.

"What about his clothes?"

"Oh, the first thing he did on the Sunday morning was put them in the washing machine. Said he'd been sitting on some damp leaves in the allotment. It had been raining the day before."

"You didn't see them?"

"What?"

"His clothes."

"Why are you interested in them all of a sudden?" Suddenly

realisation dawned on her. "I get it. You think he killed those girls and there might have been traces of blood or something on them. He didn't, Mr Rivers. My Stan would never do that. Besides, if there were traces from the murder scene on them, surely he would have stuck them in the machine immediately he got home – and not waited until the following morning?"

"He would have drawn attention to himself. You would have come downstairs and asked him what he was doing. My mother always stayed awake when I went out for an evening, so he would have known that about you."

"I can't win with you, can I? Whatever he did, you think it's suspicious. The other police officer never asked questions like this."

"And did he find the murderer?" There was no reply from Mrs Wightman. "The answer, in case you'd forgotten, is 'no'."

"And you have?"

"Not yet but, rest assured, your Stan is not the only person I'm asking these kind of questions about." He paused. "And I will find the murderer. I'm confident about that." With that, he dismissed himself from her presence. Once out in the street, he reflected that Lesley's parents only lived a couple of streets away. It would be polite to drop in on them and inform then how his investigations were going.

As he walked up their driveway, he noted – not for the first time – how similar the Peters and the Wightmans homes were. Lesley's mother answered the door. "Oh, Mr Rivers," she said – as if delighted to see him. "Do come in." He would not have been a rich man if he gained a fiver every time he received a similar greeting to that, Rivers reflected.

"I was just passing and I thought there were one or things I would like to clear up," he said. "After Lesley's death, did you see anything of Stan?"

"You mean, did he offer his condolences?"

"And did he attend the funeral? "

"The answer is no on both counts, Mr Rivers. I thought we might have seen him but then their relationship was over. I suppose he thought it was nothing to do with him."

Or everything to do with him, thought Rivers. Instead of

intimating openly what he was feeling, he decided to change tack with her. "We now have a number of suspects for the murder," he said, "but I was just wondering – was there anybody else in Lesley's life after Stan?"

"No, Mr Rivers. Nothing like that."

"I was wondering if there was anybody who would have reacted badly if they had overheard Jennifer inviting Rick Harper and Tim Rathbone back to her home with Lesley on the evening of the murders."

"Only Stan," said Mrs Peters.

"You think he would still have been hurt?"

"He could be a moody person at the best of times. I would imagine he wouldn't have felt too pleased about it."

Rivers nodded. "Well, that's probably as far as I can take it for the time being," he said. "I will keep you in touch with how things are going."

"Thank you, Mr Rivers."

With that he turned on his heels and left her home, reflecting that – if he were to pay a return visit – he should double check he was at the right address and had not gone to the Wightman's by mistake. He chuckled to himself. Now he was on his own, though, he took his mobile out of his pocket to see if there had been any calls. The most important voicemail was from Jo, he thought to himself, telling him the appeal had succeeded and the assault charge was overturned. He returned the call. "Well done," he said when the other man answered. "So you really are available for duty now. I've been to see Stan Wightman while you were in court. He's another man without a perfect alibi. He says he went on a drinking spree with Thomas Saunders until the early hours of the morning."

"Getting that confirmed is going to be more difficult than you think," said Jo. "You haven't heard, have you? Thomas Saunders is dead."

"Dead? How come?"

"He tripped on the canal bank and hit his head before falling in. He was trying to escape being questioned by Gary Clarke over trying to bust up your office."

"Good grief."

"Gary's been suspended."

"And Francesca?"

"She's just left me to go and see the chief constable. It's not good," said Jo shaking his head.

"I was thinking that Thomas' paranoia about the police might be because he was hiding something about the murder," said Rivers. "I guess we'll never know now."

"He might have confided in his father."

"And you think Professor Saunders is likely to open up to us? No way. Besides, I don't think he and Thomas had the kind of father and son relationship where they opened up to each other."

"Most probably not."

"Listen, if you've got some time to kill before Francesca gets back, you could go and visit Anne Welsh and get the names of the girls who were her alibis for the night of the murder. I haven't done that because I was pretty sure it wasn't important but we shouldn't leave any stone unturned."

"Okay," said Jo.

"And no more thoughts about quitting and going back to Calicos?"

Jo declined to answer the question. "I'll get on with my work," he said.

• • ● • •

Francesca was just about to leave work for the day when she spotted Debra sitting on a bench in the reception area of the police station.

"Debra," she said. "What are you doing here?"

"I've come to see the chief constable."

Suddenly, the desk sergeant leant forward and addressed Francesca. "Do you know this woman?" he asked.

"Yes," said Francesca,

"Can you tell her that not every Tom, Dick or Harry can walk in here and demand to see the chief constable? She's wasting her time sitting out there."

"I'm not every Tom, Dick and Harry. I'm Gary Clarke's girlfriend and he's just suspended my Gary," said Debra indignantly.

"Which makes it even more unlikely you'll get a hearing," said the desk sergeant.

"Why?" asked Debra.

"Security."

"You're afraid I might hit him or something? Do I look threatening?"

Francesca smiled. "You have left your saucepan behind?" she asked frivolously. The desk sergeant looked non-plussed

"Yes," replied Debra, "and my volume of Ruth Rendell novels."

"Oh, I haven't caught up with that one," said Francesca.

"It's what I hit Thomas Saunders over the head with yesterday."

"He was trashing her boss' office," said Francesca helpfully to the desk sergeant. At that moment Rory Gleeson strode out into the reception area from his office. "That's him," said Francesca. "I'll deal with this."

She was too late. Debra needed no second invitation to go after the departing Gleeson. "Excuse me," she said. "Are you the chief constable?"

Gleeson was not used to being harangued by members of the public. He kept his eyes clearly focussed on the way to the exit door. "I'm busy," he said staring ahead and not turning to face Debra as she approached.

"I'm Gary Clarke's girlfriend," she said. "I want a word with you."

The tone of her voice sounded menacing to the desk sergeant. He came out from behind the bench and went over to where she was standing before she had time to approach Gleeson. "Madam," he said, "I am going to ask you to leave."

"That's the same direction as he's going," Debra said, pointing to the chief constable. "Maybe we could talk as we walk."

"I only see members of the public by appointment" began Gleeson.

"So what would happen if Professor Saunders walked in here now?" asked Debra. "Would he be ushered out by the desk sergeant and told he had to make an appointment – an appointment which I'm sure would never be made once I consented to go and ring up for one in the morning."

"Professor Saunders has just lost his son."

"And my Gary's in danger of losing his job … "

"Wait a minute," said Francesca, "there's a better way of dealing with this. Debra is actually right. You would find time to see Professor Saunders. And why? Because he's an influential man – important to the police force. You won't see Debra, though. Again – why? Because she has no influence. Nobody is going to do as she tells them. Rory, surely you can spare her five or ten minutes for an interview so she doesn't have to chase you round corridors?"

Gleeson stopped his tracks. "All right," he said. "Ten minutes. There's an interview room here – by the side of the exit doors. Let's go inside." The desk sergeant gave him a look which could be summed up as 'are you sure you want to do this?' "I'll be all right," said Gleeson. "Detective Chief Inspector Manners will be with me." With that, the three of them trouped into the room he had indicated. Gleeson and Debra sat opposite each other. "Now," said Gleeson, "what was it that you wanted?"

"I'll bet Professor Saunders got a cup of tea when he came to see you," said Debra.

Francesca laughed. "Don't push it," she said.

"No," said Debra. "I was just saying."

"I repeat," said Gleeson, irritation sounding in his voice, "what was it you wanted to say?"

"You've suspended my Gary," she said, "but what has he done? He went round to interview Thomas Saunders this morning. Why? Because Francesca told him to." Gleeson registered surprise at Debra using first name terms to describe the officer sitting with him. "Did he hurt Thomas Saunders? No. He never touched him. He didn't hurt him as much as I did when I belted him with a book the previous evening. Yet I'm not facing any sanctions. What did he do wrong? He took the quickest route in what he thought was going to be a chase. So, what message do other police officers take from this. If you see a suspect running away from you, don't run after him. Just let him go."

"Thank you ..." He realised he did not know her name.

"Debra Paget," she said.

"I'm sure your thoughts on this will be put to the disciplinary panel when it comes to discuss the case next week."

"By me if no-one else," said Francesca, "although we won't be pursuing you over the book attack on Thomas Saunders. Make sure you tell Gary I will be putting those points on his behalf."

"You could do it yourself. He'd love to see you," said Debra.

"I would but I'm not allowed to communicate with him during the course of these disciplinary proceedings."

Debra shook her head again. "I bet Professor Saunders isn't limited in the number of people he's allowed to speak to," she said.

"Er, no," said Gleeson. He was thinking of Saunders' threat to take the issue up in the press. That would be another source of annoyance to Debra, he thought. "Well, if that's all?" said Gleeson. Debra nodded. She got up to leave. "Would you wait a minute, Detective Chief Inspector Manners?" Gleeson asked.

Francesca nodded. "Well, that didn't go badly," she said when Debra had finally departed. "Thank you, sir," she said. "She would only have harboured a grudge if she'd been refused access to see you. You know, we ought to think about things like that. How our actions seem to those who have no voice in society."

"I'm glad I saw her, too," said Gleeson. "Quite a plucky character. Detective Constable Clarke is a lucky man."

"I'm not sure he feels that right now."

• • • • •

Jo arrived at the Welsh household in the early evening. To his surprise, his knock on the door was answered by Anne's father. "You've been released from hospital," said Jo – stating the obvious. "How are you?"

"I've been told if I take it easy, I'll be all right," he said ushering Jo into the sitting room.

"But there's a fat chance of that," said Anne who was in there sitting watching television. "He seems to think he's got to solve Jennifer's murder single-handedly."

"Leave that to us," said Jo.

"I just feel there should be something I could do," he said. "I've done my share of moping around but that hasn't helped. Maybe if I went to talk to one or two of the people involved. "

"I've told him that would be dangerous," interrupted Anne.

"They're not likely to kill again. They think they've got away with it."

"Until you turn up on their doorstep."

"Your daughter's right. Best leave it to us. Anyhow I just came round to ask you for the names of the people you stayed with that evening, Anne."

"So I'm still a suspect?"

"Just being thorough."

"I'm glad you are," Arthur Welsh butted in. "Give him the names."

"I was going to." She wrote them down on a piece of paper and handed it to Jo. "Three girls sharing a flat. Of course, they're not there now. That's their new addresses I've written down."

"Thanks." He pocketed the paper. "I'd better go."

"You're not going to share the fruits of your investigation before you do?" asked Arthur.

"Best not. We don't want to alert anyone to the idea we suspect them. That's why we still keep the net wide."

"Tell me," said Anne. "Is Rick still a suspect?"

"I detect an ulterior motive for asking that question," said Jo.

"Yes," said Anne. Jo looked at Anne as if to confirm that she really wanted this discussion to continue in the presence of her father. "My father knows about us," she said. She sighed. "It's what caused his heart attack."

"I can't rule him out yet," said Jo, "but that's only because we still don't know who did it."

"Sounds as if you're trying to tell her – and me – that it's okay to go out with him," said Arthur.

Jo smiled. "There are people with stronger motives who could also have been here that night," he said. "That's as far as I'm prepared to go."

Anne smiled. "Thanks," she said. She saw Jo to the door. "Well, Dad?" she said.

"Yes."

"I'm convinced he didn't do it. Why would he want to see me and go out with me if he had? He would surely have wanted to stay as far away from me as possible."

"I'd like a stronger reason than that before I gave you my blessing to see him. But I think I had it in a roundabout way from Jo. You can see him. Let's not have things hidden behind closed doors."

"Thanks, Dad." She moved over towards him and squeezed his hand.

"But I meant what I said. I am going to be asking people a few questions from now on – beginning with some of Jennifer's ex's. Jimmy Atherton and Duncan Hamilton for a start. "

"Be careful, Dad," cautioned Anne.

"If not being careful identifies the killer and brings him to justice, it will have been worth it."

CHAPTER EIGHT

"Professor Saint," said Francesca on spotting the pathologist in the reception area of the police station. "I thought I'd left you behind once I left Finchley. Who have you come to see?"

"You," he said. "I was told to ask for Detective Constable Clarke but I'm told he's in disgrace at the moment and you're handling his cases."

"He's not in disgrace with some of us," said Francesca.

"I didn't mean to intrude into the personal politics of the situation," said the professor. "I've come about the Thomas Saunders affair. Hmmm. Sounds like a movie starring Steve McQueen."

"I think you'll find that was 'The Thomas Crown affair'."

"Remarkable. I wouldn't have expected your generation to know that."

"Thomas Saunders," said Francesca trying to steer him back to the task in hand.

"Yes," said Saint. "I was brought in because Saunders recused himself again. Well, I suppose it's obvious. It was his son. Poor man is probably grieving at the moment." He quickly got the message, though, that Francesca was not interested in small talk. "He drowned."

"That's hardly earth-shattering news since he had to be pulled unconscious from the canal."

"What you want to know is did he fall or was he pushed."

"Well, not exactly. There was no suggestion that he was pushed. Two small boys found him. There was no-one else around at the time."

"Which brings me on to our next dilemma. Did he fall accidentally or did he throw himself into the water on purpose? This, I warn you, is only guesswork."

"Go on."

"There's no doubt that he caught his head on concrete,

concussing him before he fell into the water. I am of the opinion that he slipped on the grassy bank, banging his head accidentally before plunging into the water. I can't rule out the other option but the general consensus is that he was running along the canal bank before the incident. It would have been extremely unlikely that – in that state – he could have selected a bit of concrete to hurl his head against thus becoming the architect of his own downfall. No, I think you'll have to opt for a verdict of accidental death."

As he finished speaking, the Chief Constable walked by on his way to the office. Saint glanced at his watch. "All right for some, coming in to work at 11 o'clock."

"I've been at a meeting since nine o'clock," growled Gleeson.

"Never mind, I'm sure you'll get your reward in heaven. Now, I've got an important meeting to attend. Wonderful golf course you've got here out at Wadesmill. Beautiful view. One of the reasons I decided to drive over with the results of the post mortem rather than invite you to the mortuary and conduct this little conversation while trying to show interest in the dead body. Anyhow, toodle pip." With that, he was gone.

"Nothing much we didn't know, I gather?" said Gleeson once he had gone. He looked after him. "One of the old school," he said. "We don't make them like that anymore."

"No." She held back from saying "thank goodness". There were times when his witty repartee could be quite refreshing and relieve tension. At the moment, though, having to do without Gary was putting a considerable strain on her ability to keep up with the level of crime in the neighbourhood.

"I suppose someone had better tell the Saunders family," said Gleeson.

"I could do that "began Francesca.

"But since I've done away with your deputy, you're a bit hard pressed. Don't worry, I'll do it – and I'll see if I can get someone seconded to help you."

"Thank you," said Francesca. "That would be most appreciated."

• • • • •

247

"Jeff Cantelow, please," said Professor Saunders as he approached the reception desk of the local newspaper.

"Who shall I say wants to see him?" asked the receptionist.

"Professor Saunders." Cantelow needed no persuading to see him when informed who his guest was. Professor Saunders soon found himself in the newsroom standing next to Cantelow's computer.

"Take a seat," said the reporter. "I would guess you're Thomas Saunders' father?" Saunders nodded "Let me say how sorry I was to hear about your son."

"Thank you." Professor Saunders was not used to talking to journalists. Cantelow detected he would have to put him at his ease if he was to get him to unbutton himself to the newspaper. "Could I ask you your first name?" he asked.

"Is that absolutely necessary?"

"It helps to humanise you in the eyes of the reader," said Cantelow. "They can identify with you if they know who you are."

Saunders nodded as if he appreciated the fact. "Michael," he said. "Michael Saunders."

"Good. Now why have you come here?"

Saunders noticed a copy of last week's newspaper lying on the desk. "You seem interested in this murder case," he said, "and in Detective Chief Inspector Manners?"

"Yes," said Cantelow. "It's a sad story. Our readers identify with it. They'd probably like to help solve it if they could."

"My son's been killed because of it."

Cantelow looked at him. "What?"

"Hounded by the cops investigating this case." He noticed a copy of the previous week's paper was also lying on Cantelow's desk." He picked it up. "This is more like it," he said. He jabbed his finger at the picture of Rick Harper. "This is the guy that did it," he said. "For months he was the prime suspect while this woman Manners' predecessor was investigating the case. Now they've lost the plot. Cast the net wide is their mantra. Well, they cast the net so wide they started questioning my son as to whether he was involved in it. No evidence, mind you. He's – he was – a vulnerable soul. He couldn't take it. He killed himself."

"But I gather his death didn't have anything to do with the murder. The police wanted to question him about an entirely separate matter. The trashing of a private detective's office in Hertford."

"Just think about how much damage had been done and ask yourself was it necessary to send a police officer round to our home so early in the morning. Was it necessary for that officer to chase through our house after him – without having gained permission to enter it? It was a minor matter. It could have been sorted out later when we could have explained to Thomas why the police wanted to see him. They admit now they only wanted to caution him. They've suspended the policeman who came to our house – but he wouldn't have adopted those tactics if he hadn't been told to in advance by his superior. I blame her. But butter wouldn't melt.... They've done nothing about her role in all this. The police literally hounded my son to death."

Cantelow's eyes lit up at the last remark. It would make a good headline, he thought to himself. "You say your son was vulnerable?" he said.

"Yes, he'd had a breakdown after a relationship went wrong." Saunders bit his lip. He knew he would now have to explain what that relationship was and he didn't want anyone to know Thomas had been in a gay relationship. Maybe, though, he thought to himself, the time had come to abandon his sensitivities about that. After all, Thomas was now dead. He would have to co-operate with the newspaper to get justice for Thomas even if the truth was unpalatable in some ways to him. He found himself telling the whole story to Cantelow. "So you see," he said when he had finished, "there was a connection with Thomas' death and the murder investigation," he said. "He wouldn't have trashed that newspaper office if he hadn't been driven to desperation by both the police and this private detective agency focussing on him. He wouldn't have been visited last Thursday morning if he hadn't trashed that office."

"So what do you want now?"

"I want an investigation into the investigation, if you like," he said. "And I want that...." He seemed to be searching hard for the right word to describe Francesca – "that woman to be suspended while any investigation take place. Let's see how she responds to a little bit of hounding."

"Got it," said Cantelow. "Now, if you could furnish me with a picture of Thomas, I think we have the makings of a piece."

"Humanises it again?" he said.

"Yes."

"I haven't got one," said Professor Saunders, "but I'll go home and get one and bring it round."

"No need to go to all that trouble," said Cantelow. "We'll send someone round to collect it. Shall we say this evening? About eight o'clock?"

"Fine," said Saunders.

"Thanks for coming in, Michael," said Cantelow

• • ● • •

"I can't believe Thomas is dead," said Rick when Rivers told him the news. "I've wished he would go away – even cursed the fact that he was still alive in the past – but I can't really take this in."

"It's true," said Rivers. "I'm not investigating it – I'm leaving it to the police – but it does seem like it was a ghastly accident. The thing that I can't explain is why he was so afraid of the police," he said.

"Just didn't want to be hassled, perhaps?" said Rick.

"In that case, why trash my office? He couldn't have done more to draw attention to himself."

"I'm no psychoanalyst," said Rick. "Maybe we have to treat it as just one of life's unexplained mysteries."

"I've never been one for that," said Rivers.

"He did have a near breakdown," Rick said. "Maybe he thought threatening you was the best way to get you to stop asking him questions. I notice he didn't take action against the police. He must have thought that would only have got him into more trouble."

Rivers shrugged his shoulders. "What do we actually know?" he asked. "Thanks to Stan Wightman, we now know he and Thomas went to the allotment after the dance with some vodka and started talking about – things." Rivers paused for dramatic effect.

"That could have been one of the most boring conversations on record," said Rick.

"Why?"

"Well, Stan wasn't exactly the liveliest of company and Thomas was not quite the full shilling."

"But what were they talking about?" persisted Rivers. "What had they both just learned?"

"Well, they probably knew Tim and I had been invited back to Jennifer's to party with her and Lesley. That's what they talked about."

"Under duress, Mrs Wightman acknowledged that Stan didn't arrive home until two o'clock in the morning. It takes about twenty minutes to get from the dance hall to the allotments – and the allotments are just five minutes away from Stan's house. The dance ended at eleven. That means they must have been chatting there for two and a half hours – if they didn't go anywhere else."

"Stan's a bit slow but I don't think even he could eke out a conversation for that long," said Rick.

"You're not taking this seriously," said Rivers. "This is important. It could help you clear your name. So they chat – they think you and Tim are happily ensconced with Jennifer and Lesley at Jennifer's house. Stan doesn't like the idea of Lesley going with Tim. Thomas doesn't like the idea of you going with anyone. So they talk – and think to themselves 'we'll put a stop to this' and either both of them set off to Jennifer's house or one of them does – probably Stan because of the time he got home. They would have thought you and Tim would be there. They get there and find you two aren't."

"Jennifer wouldn't invite them in. She thinks Thomas has a screw loose and knows Lesley had split with Stan." Rick seemed to be warming to Rivers' theme.

"Stan makes a pass at Lesley. It's rejected. He's angry because he knows she was a party to inviting Tim round. He flies into a rage."

"And kills her?"

"It's a possibility. Jennifer tries to intervene but Thomas stops her – pushing her too forcefully or punching her, knocking her out. Stan has killed Lesley. They see no alternative but to kill

Jennifer to avoid her telling anyone about what happened. They are both drunk, remember."

"Right."

"It's a perfectly valid theory – quite plausible," said Rivers. "There's just one problem. There isn't the slightest bit of evidence to support it. And, if it was true, our two drunks at some stage became sober enough to realise they had to spring-clean the place to remove any evidence that had been there. That must have brought them near to the time when Jimmy Atherton and Peter Aymes roll up in their stretch limo."

"Also, why didn't anyone see or hear them?"

"Good point. But, whoever killed them, nobody heard it so maybe it's difficult to pick up noises from inside the house. It's not as if they're semi-detached. The stretch limo was only heard because of the noise of the car. Stan and Thomas would have arrived on foot. And you were seen loitering outside because it was earlier in the evening and people had not gone to bed."

"So what do we do now?"

"We investigate further," said Rivers. "There are still one or two facts we could unearth to help us build up a picture of what happened."

"Like what?"

"Find out what time Thomas Saunders got home that night?"

"Like Professor Saunders is going to tell us."

"I doubt whether he'll give us the time of day. If it's crossed our mind that Thomas may have been hiding something, it will have crossed his, too. He will have rejected the idea, of course, but I reckon I should at least give questioning him – or his wife – a try. If Thomas got home earlier than Stan, it would seem to clear him of any involvement. If they got home at roughly the same time, it could have been a joint enterprise or – alternatively – they could just have had a long session at the allotments. If Thomas got back at a later time, it could mean he was the guilty party."

"Well, I wish you joy in trying to prove any of that," said Rick.

"It's what you're paying me for."

"Right."

"But I think we'll have to go slowly on this one. Give Professor

Saunders and his wife a bit of time to grieve before we start tackling him about his son."

"I can see I'm going to have to approach the bank of mum and dad for another subsidy."

"We're getting there, Rick," said Rivers laying his on arm on his client's shoulder. "It may be taking a long time but we are getting there."

• • ● • •

Jimmy Atherton was at his large mansion house in the Buckinghamshire countryside. The days of sharing a flat with Renee in West Hampstead were fewer and farther between. He was seldom at the mansion house either nowadays. His touring schedule took care of that. His latest tour was at an end, though, and so he had retreated to it. When he was in residence, he had enough money to hire a couple of security guards to make sure no over-enthusiastic fans gained entry to his home. It was one of these guards who confronted Arthur Welsh when he turned up to try and gain access to the singer.

"I'd like to see Jimmy Atherton," he simply said as he approached the sentry hut by the wrought iron gates to the mansion.

"Wouldn't everyone?"

Arthur smiled. "I don't doubt that many of his legions of fans would like to," he said, "but I think if you look at me closely, you'll see I'm not a groupie."

The guard gave him a dismissive look. "So what is your business with him?"

"I'm the father of a girlfriend he used to know when he was growing up."

The guard looked suspicious. "And why are you here? Are you going to claim he got her up the duff? Because if you are, we have quite a few like you and I'd suggest you get on your bike."

Arthur decided not to mention he was driving a car and not on a bike. "That's not my intention," he said. "My daughter was a close friend of Jimmy's. She's dead now. I just wanted to talk to him about it."

It seemed a strange request to the security guard but it must have struck a chord somewhere with him. "I'm sorry for your loss," he said. They were still at an impasse, though, with the security guard reluctant to call Jimmy about Arthur's visit.

"Look," said Arthur. "I guarantee if you mention my name to Jimmy he'll want to see me. If he doesn't, I promise I'll leave. Do I look like a troublemaker?"

The security guard managed a smile. "No," he said. I guess not." He reached for his intercom and pressed a buzzer which brought a voice from the house to answer him. "I have a...." He looked up questioningly at Arthur.

"Arthur Welsh."

"I have an Arthur Welsh to see Jimmy. He says Jimmy will want to see him."

The person on the other end went away for a moment obviously to check whether this was the case. She came back within a couple of minutes and said: "Send him up to the house."

"You're welcome," said the security guard to Arthur who drove his car into the grounds once the barrier had been lifted. He was greeted by a member of staff as he parked his car by the main entrance to the mansion. "I'll show you to Mr Atherton," said the man sent to greet him. He took him through to the mansion's lounge.

"Arthur," said Jimmy offering his guest a warm welcome. "It's been a long time."

"Four years to be precise," said Arthur.

Jimmy knew he was making a reference to the murder of his daughter. "Yes," he said. "I'm sorry."

"I'm sure you are, Jimmy. I'm sure you are." He looked around hm. "Well, things have changed for you."

"Yes," said Jimmy. "I can't enjoy this place as much as I'd like. Touring, you know I've just got a week off between gigs."

"And there's no Mrs Atherton?"

"No. I don't have time to develop relationships." He paused for a moment – mentally kicking himself for suggesting he might have problems when they paled into insignificance behind

Arthur's. "But you don't want to hear me whingeing," he said. "I presume you came to talk about Jennifer."

"Yes, it's been four years," he said, "and I'm no closer to finding out what happened. Jimmy, what do you think happened?"

"I don't know."

"Who do you think killed her?"

"Again I haven't any idea." He paused. "But I will tell you one thing – I think you should park any idea that Rick Harper was responsible for your daughter's death."

"You're the second person to say that to me."

"Oh? Who else?"

"My daughter Anne."

"Anne? How is she?"

"I think she's in love with Rick Harper."

"Oh." Jimmy paused for thought. "Take it from me, Arthur, there's nothing wrong with that."

"Did you see Jennifer on the night of her death?" The question slipped off Arthur's tongue so easily it took Jimmy by surprise. By his hesitation in answering the question, he realised he was leaving the idea in Arthur's mind that he had seen Jennifer that night. "Did you?" repeated Arthur.

Jimmy decided to tell the truth. "Yes, I did," he said.

"And?"

"She was already dead by the time I saw her. It was early in the morning. I was with my manager. We'd just signed a contract that evening. I didn't want anything to spoil that so I just drove away. I'm sorry, Arthur. I have now admitted it to the new investigation launched by Mr Rivers."

Arthur choked back a tear. "I don't suppose you can tell me anything more," he said.

"No," he said – relieved that Arthur hadn't asked him whether he had been with anybody that night and that therefore he had not had to address the question of Peter Aymes' cocaine habit. He wasn't sure how he would have responded. "Let me say one thing, Arthur," he added. "I still felt very warm affection for Jennifer. I would never have done anything to harm her."

"I know," said Arthur sobbing again. "I know." Goodness, he

thought, this is going to be more difficult than I thought.

There was a knock at the door. Jimmy bade his assistant to enter. "Peter Aymes has arrived to see you, sir," he said.

Jimmy nodded. "Show him in," he said. "My manager," he said to Arthur.

"I understand," he said. "I'll be on my way." He got up and walked to the door just as Peter Aymes was ushered into the room.

Aymes gave Arthur a long stare as they passed each other at the door. "Who was that?" he asked.

"Arthur Welsh," replied Jimmy.

"Arthur Welsh? What are you doing entertaining him?"

"He just dropped by. I think he wants to talk to some of Jennifer's friends. He's cut himself off from them for quite a while."

"You didn't tell him anything?"

"I told him I had been there on the night of the murder but that she was already dead by the time I got there."

"Jesus Christ."

"I didn't mention your name."

"Good," said Aymes, "but you really shouldn't be talking to people like him. Something might slip out."

"Like your cocaine habit? Look, I've kept a lid on it for four years. I don't think that' likely to change. Besides, why are you so worried? Lots of people in similar shoes to you have a cocaine habit. It won't discredit you."

"It's the police I'm worried about."

"Well, don't. Look, I don't think Arthur's likely to come back again and I don't think there's been any harm in being civil and honest to him."

Aymes looked as if he did not share his client's confidence.

●　●　●　●　●

Francesca had confided in no-one about the fact she intended to visit Professor Saunders as part of her investigation into his son's death. She knew Rory Gleeson would counsel against it but felt it necessary in order to conclude her enquiries into the young man's death. She was therefore not expecting a rapturous welcome when she knocked on his door. As luck would have it, both he and his wife were in – Saunders having taken some time off work to grieve over his son's death.

"Detective Chief Inspector," he said on recognising his visitor. "What on earth are you doing here?"

"First, I wanted to offer you sympathy over the death of your son," she began.

"You can save your weasel words for some other occasion," he said. "You know I hold you responsible for my son's death. I have laid a complaint against you. In my book, you shouldn't be conducting this enquiry."

"But I am," said Francesca, "and if I am to do it thoroughly I need to know about all the circumstances leading up to your son's death."

"Simple," said Saunders. "He was hounded by the police. Your colleague came here yesterday morning – trespassed on my property – and, to all intents and purposes, caused Thomas to run away – whereupon he slipped on the canal bank and killed himself. End of story."

"Was he frightened the police might find out something he knew?"

"He was just a vulnerable youth. I don't suppose you've had much experience of dealing with them."

Francesca chose to ignore his words. "I don't want to blacken his name," she said. "We just want to find out whether his death had any connection with the murders of Jennifer Welsh and Lesley Peters."

"And it didn't," said Saunders. "You know my opinion on that. Rick Harper's your man and any time spent on trying to pursue another theory is just a waste of valuable police time and money." He looked her in the eye. "You're not getting beyond this door, Detective Chief Inspector, so I would advise you not to try."

Or else you'll call the police, Francesca thought to herself. She quickly dismissed such a mischievous thought from her mind. "If you do think of anything that might help us to solve this ghastly crime, please tell us," she limited herself to saying.

"I can email you every morning, telling you to arrest Rick Harper if you like. Anyway, I thought you were leaving this murder investigation in the hands of that private eye – Philip Rivers."

"Your son's death may be linked to it," she said. "That's why we're pursuing it."

"I have nothing more to say."

Francesca finally acknowledged defeat. She was just about to walk away when Mrs Saunders appeared in the hallway. Francesca nodded to denote her presence. "I just wanted to say I talked to my son a lot over the years," she said. "I don't believe that he was just a frightened, vulnerable youth who couldn't cope with anyone questioning him."

"You believe he may have been frightened by something?"

"Thank you, detective chief inspector, that will be all," said Professor Saunders firmly shutting the door in Francesca's face before the point could be pursued. The comments of Saunders' wife left a question mark in her mind, though. Was she suggesting he was frightened of something? She resolved to pass on details of her conversations to Rivers.

• • ● • •

Jo smiled as he walked up the path to Duncan Hamilton's door. It felt good to be out on the road again – without any fear of what lay ahead now the conviction had been quashed. He had thought that he would find Diane in. After all, she was the mother of three small children. She had given up work to look after them and her husband was in gainful employment as a technician. It was a surprise when he opened the door.

"I'm sorry," said Jo. "I really wanted to talk to your wife. I'm from the private detective agency investigating the murders of Jennifer Welsh and Lesley Peters."

"She's out. Probably gone shopping after dropping the children off at nursery. What did you want to see her about?"

Jo winced. He couldn't work out whether it was worth raising the issue with Duncan. "Well, it's about the alibi she's given you on the night of the murder." He stopped for a moment to scrutinise his reaction.

"Alibi?"

"Yes," said Jo. "You did know she has said she stayed with you in the section house on the night of the murder?"

"Yes."

"Well," said Jo. "Isn't that a bit odd?"

"No," said Duncan. "Why would you think that?"

"Well, she had previously said she was staying with a girlfriend that night. And the woman that she said she stayed with has corroborated her alibi."

"Meaning?"

"Meaning did she stay with you or not on the night of the murders?"

"Yes, she did."

"Why is this other woman still maintaining a lie about where your wife was?" asked Jo.

"I don't know. You'll have to ask her that."

"She insists your wife was with her. Why would she do that?"

"Misplaced loyalty." Duncan continued to work on mending a clock face while he was talking to Jo. It gave Jo the impression that he wasn't really interested in proceedings. "Diane had asked her to provide her with an alibi so that's what she's doing."

"Do the concepts of right and wrong not come into that equation?"

"I'm sorry?"

Jo was surprised that he had to explain his thinking to Duncan. "Well, that it's right to tell the police where you were on the night of a murder – and it's wrong to falsify an alibi. And which one's false?"

"I wasn't aware that I needed an alibi for the night of the murders. Am I a suspect?"

"I wasn't aware you needed an alibi until your wife provided one," said Jo. "She obviously believes you do."

"She's not doing it because she thinks I need an alibi. She's doing it because she is my alibi."

"Which still begs the question – why didn't she say that initially?"

"We're not allowed to have women in our rooms at the police section house. It could have been a disciplinary matter for me. Also, our relationship hadn't started then. It was actually our first night together. We didn't really want people to know we were an item."

"Neither of which points are as important as being truthful when helping the police with a murder enquiry."

"You're entitled to your own opinion," said Duncan. It looked as if he had finally been successful in mending the watch face. He smiled – thus showing more emotion than he had done during the entire interview.

"You had finished your relationship with Jennifer Welsh by the time of the dance?" asked Jo.

"It was more a question of her finishing with me," said Duncan.

"Thank you for your honesty," said Jo. "Were you resentful about that?"

"Yes, I suppose I was – but not resentful enough to kill her. Surely you believe that?"

Jo made no response at first but then responded by saying: "I don't have opinions. I deal in facts." He turned on his heels to go. "I will need to speak to your wife at some stage," he said. "Will you tell her I'll be calling round?"

It was Duncan's turn to offer no response. He just watched as Jo let himself out.

• • ● • •

Arthur Welsh seemed tired when he returned home that evening after speaking to Jimmy Atherton. Anne made him a cup of tea. "You'll wear yourself out if you're not careful," she said, concerned.

"I've been to see Jimmy Atherton," he said. "He told me he saw Jennifer's body that night."

"Oh, Dad," said Anne, "you shouldn't go upsetting yourself."

"No, I'm not," he said. "Jimmy's a decent bloke. He just didn't want to get caught up in whatever happened. Who's to say we wouldn't have reacted in the same way given the same set of circumstances?"

"I wouldn't leave somebody's body like that without telling the police."

"Maybe not," said Arthur, finishing the tea Anne had poured for him, "but it's doing me good to get out and talk to Jennifer's friends. Previously I'd just moped around consumed by grief. At least by talking to Jennifer's friends, I realise there were some good people around her. There's only one person that wasn't a good friend to her and that's the person that killed her." He smiled and patted Anne on the arm. "I'm convinced it wasn't Rick and I'm convinced now that it wasn't Jimmy."

"Be careful, Dad, though," cautioned Anne. "If you keep talking to people, you may at some stage alight on the real killer. They think they've got away with it for years. They won't want you raking up the embers of what they've done."

"Maybe not," he said.

"Who are you going to see now?" asked Anne.

"Now? Oh, no-one. I'll rest for a bit. I would have gone to see Thomas Saunders – but, of course, I read in the papers that he's dead now. I should go round and see Duncan Hamilton, I suppose." He reflected for a moment. "You know, I should go round and see Lesley's mother and father. Offer them my condolences. "

"You never did that, did you father?"

"No," he said. "I didn't think anyone could be suffering as much as I was. I was guilty of…." He stopped in his tracks. "You know, I think I told myself that Jennifer's death was more tragic than Lesley's."

"That's not surprising," said Anne. "She was your daughter."

"But it wasn't the case. Just think about it. Everybody seems to believe that Jennifer was the killer's main target. In which case Lesley was caught up in something that was not of her making. What is more tragic than that?"

As they spoke, Anne became aware of a presence coming up the garden path and ringing the doorbell. "It's Rick, Dad," she said.

"Let him in," said Arthur.

Anne needed no second bidding and ushered Rick into the living room. "Sit down, son," said Arthur.

"I came round to see how you were – and offer my sincere apologies."

"Not necessary," said Arthur.

"But I rather think that I caused your heart attack," he said.

"Your presence sparked it off," acknowledged Arthur, "but it was really me thinking you could have murdered my daughter that was the cause. Anne has persuaded me that I was wrong there."

"I'm glad you believe that," said Rick.

"Yes," said Arthur, "I do." He paused for a moment. "So I've got to find out now who really is to blame for the murder."

"You?" said Rick. "Why? Mr Rivers is trying to work that one out and he's far more qualified than you are to reach the bottom of this. Why, even I wouldn't go around trying to find the real killer. I'd leave that to the professionals."

"It wasn't your daughter that was killed," said Arthur. "Don't worry – I won't be going around trying to confront the real killer. Just a little conversation here – a little word there – could tease something out. I'm a poor old man. Not a threat to whoever it is. They may let something slip to me which they wouldn't tell the professionals."

"You should be careful."

"I have been told that before," said Arthur looking in Anne's direction.

"I mean it."

• • ● • •

Rivers made his way to the Wightman house early that evening. He reckoned if he made it there before dusk there was a good chance that Stan Wightman would still be tending his allotment – and it was not really him that he wanted to see. He wanted to talk to Mary and get an inkling for how she felt about breaking up with Rick and how Stan had reacted to splitting up with Lesley. Mrs Wightman answered his knock at the door.

"Good evening," said Rivers. "Don't worry – it's not about any more questions for you." She showed signs of relief at this. "I wondered if your daughter was in?"

"She is," said Mrs Wightman. "Come in."

"Thanks." There seemed to be no annoyance on her part over the fact he wanted to question her daughter. That's what he liked about families like the Wightmans and the Peters. There were no airs and graces. No sense of why are you taking up my incredibly important time with your meaningless questions. He smiled. No, this was not the sort of reception he would get if he went back to question the Saunders again. Yet he viewed Stan Wightman as just as likely a suspect as Thomas Saunders. It was a question of class, he thought. The Wightmans were a respectful lower middle class family – the Saunders had pretentions to be much more than that. He was brought back to the present by the sound of Mrs Wightman shouting at her daughter to come downstairs.

"Mary, there's a man wants to speak to you," she called. A minute later Mary, now in her mid-twenties, appeared at the top of the stairway. She was, thought Rivers, a very attractive woman. Long brown hair down to her shoulders, she had dressed down for the evening and was wearing jeans and a T-shirt. She was quite tall, too. Eye-catching, he thought, would be the best way to describe her appearance. He could not for the life of him think why his client had been so disparaging of her. Again his thoughts were interrupted by Mrs Wightman. "Do you want me to leave you alone with her?" she asked.

"Yes, that would be good," said Rivers

"Only that's the way they do it on telly."

Rivers smiled. He held out his hand to Mary who shook it. "Shall we go into your sitting room?" Mary nodded. When they were seated, Rivers explained why he was there. "I'm investigating the murders of Jennifer Welsh and Lesley Peters," he said.

"I'm glad someone is," she said. "Lesley was a close friend of mine."

"Even after she dumped your brother?"

"Those sort of things happen when you're in your teens. Stan wasn't the right sort of person for her. She was incredibly intelligent – six A*'s at GCSE."

And Stan wasn't, Rivers thought to himself. "Was Stan as philosophical about the break-up as you were?"

263

"No," she said. "It was his first relationship. You know what they say – 'first love never, ever dies'."

"Would that be true even now?"

"Probably. Stan doesn't really talk about that sort of thing. He hasn't had a girl friend since."

"Has he changed since breaking up with Lesley?"

"No," said Mary after weighing up the question. "He always was a bit of a grumpy old sod."

Rivers laughed. He liked her refreshing openness. "Has he ever confided in you about the break up?"

"Confided in me?"

"You know – said how he felt, how he felt about Lesley, too."

"You mean confessed to me that he killed her?" Rivers spluttered. It was the question he wanted answering but he hadn't thought it the right time to ask it. "No, nothing like that, Mr Rivers," she said. "I can't see him doing that." From the look on her face, she seemed to have given the idea some serious thought – if not now but during the past four years. "He's more likely to act like a hedgehog."

"A hedgehog?"

"Curl up into a little ball and go away and hibernate."

"What did you do after the dance that night?" asked Rivers.

"I didn't go to the dance."

"Oh, I just assumed. Everyone else in the neighbourhood seemed to."

"Well, that would be everybody but me. I knew Rick would be organising it. We had just split up. I didn't want to see him."

"You split up in a cruel way, I gather?"

"He confided to Thomas Saunders that he hated me instead of loved me. Now, that did rile Stan. He couldn't bear to think of someone treating his little sister like that." She paused for a moment. "Come to think of it, Stan was more likely to kill Rick instead of Lesley."

"Could he have gone round to Jennifer's house intent on doing it?"

"Come on, Mr Rivers, I wasn't being serious. Stan wouldn't kill anyone."

264

Rivers noted what she said but thought to himself it could have just been the reaction of an over-protective sister. "So what did you do that night?"

"So now we've ruled out the possibility that I could have lurked outside Jennifer's house all night waiting for Lesley to turn up because I knew Jennifer would be inviting her round?"

"I never thought that," said Rivers.

"No," said Mary. "It was a very dull evening. I just stayed in and watched telly."

"What was on?"

"Casualty "

"How do you remember that from so long ago?"

"It was the night one of my closest friends was murdered. If I had gone to the dance, she might very well have come home with me. She wasn't really interested in having the kind of time Jennifer wanted."

Rivers nodded. "But you didn't because you were still cut up about splitting with Rick?"

"I wasn't cut up about splitting with Rick. These things happen, as I said. I was cut up – no – mad about the way I split up with Rick. So both Stan and I would have had more reason to kill Rick than either of the girls."

"But it would have hurt Rick if his girlfriend had been killed."

"Jennifer?"

"Yes."

"I wouldn't call her his girlfriend. Just someone happy to be shagged by him." Rivers was surprised at her choice of words and showed it in his facial expression. "Well, that was what she was. That was a service I didn't perform."

"Bit difficult to fit it in, so to speak, if you're on a curfew of ten o'clock when you're going to the cinema."

"He told you that?"

"Yes."

"He's right. Since then, I've taken a firmer line with my parents about the idea of curfews."

"Have you had any boyfriends since Rick?"

"What's that going to prove?"

265

"Probably nothing," admitted Rivers.

"Well, yes, do you want to know how many?"

"Not necessary. Any of them turn out to be at all serious?"

"Not really but then I'm only 23."

Rivers came out of his interview with Mary thinking that – if he had been about thirty years younger – he would not have made the same mistake as Rick and dumped her.

● ● ● ● ●

Francesca was sure it would be Rory Gleeson's office on the end of the line when the telephone rang that morning. She was not disappointed. "The chief constable would like to see you now," said his secretary.

"I'm sure he would," she said.

"I'm sorry?"

"I'll come immediately." That seemed to satisfy the secretary. Francesca got up from her desk. She glanced at the local paper again before departing her office. "Police 'bullies' caused my son's death', says professor," its main headline stated. It was, of course, all about the death of Thomas Saunders and went into graphic detail about how he had met a tragic fate running away from the police along the canal bank. She quibbled with a few of the words like "running away from the police". No-one was, in fact, chasing him. Still, she harboured no doubts that the journalist, Jeff Cantelow, had accurately reported what Professor Saunders had said to him. It was, of course, accompanied by a picture of her and Gary Clarke. She wished she had been given the opportunity to put her side of the story instead of relying on a suitably obfuscating quote from a police spokesman to give the story some spurious balance. The police spokesman merely recorded that "enquiries into the death of Thomas Saunders are continuing". The next paragraph said that Detective Constable Gary Clarke had been suspended.

"Quite a splash," said Gleeson as she approached his office. "The front page three weeks running." His mood did not seem particularly anxious. In fact, he appeared to be treating it quite light-heartedly.

266

"I could have done without this one," she said. "Why didn't they give me the opportunity to put my point of view?"

"They asked for you when they phoned up," he said, "and were put through to the press office. I agreed that quote with them."

"Oh." Secretly she was thinking: it must have taken you hours to think that one up.

"I thought an interview with you would risk lighting Professor Saunders' blue touch paper even more."

"Oh," she said again.

"I am right, Francesca," he insisted. "Look, we ride this one out. Professor Saunders has got his anger off his chest. In case you're worried about it, I don't intend that this newspaper article will make me change my mind over my original decision not to suspend you. As I said, we ride this one out."

"Thank you, sir," said Francesca – but without much conviction.

"In the meantime, I'm recommending we unofficially suspend all enquiries into the death of Thomas Saunders – and just let Professor Saint go with the finding that he slipped, banged his head and drowned when it comes to the inquest."

"I'd like to make some enquiries into what was on Thomas Saunders' mind. I think his state of mind may be linked to the Jennifer Welsh and Lesley Peters' killings – not just a phobia about being interviewed by the police."

"No," said Gleeson firmly.

"I have, to that end, attempted to interview Professor Saunders again – unsuccessfully."

"You did what?"

"I tried to interview him again. I think his wife may have got something to tell us."

"No," said Gleeson even more firmly. "Stay away from it. With any luck, Professor Saunders has now released all the powder he has I don't want a follow up story saying 'and now she's bullying me'," he added.

"So we ignore what his wife may want to tell us?"

"Are you sure she has?"

"She intimated as such when I went round to see them."

Gleeson stroked his chin. "You have this friend, this private detective – what's his name?"

"Philip Rivers."

"Yes. He's investigating the murders, isn't he?" Francesca nodded. "Well, get him to find out what she has to say. It goes against the grain to sanction a private detective doing work that should be done by the police but needs must in this case."

"Very well, sir." She got up as if to go but he motioned her to remain seated. "I said this article didn't make me want to change the way I had treated you over this case," he said, "but I have to say it hasn't fallen well for Detective Constable Clarke. It's his disciplinary hearing tomorrow. It may well affect the panel's judgement."

"It shouldn't do."

"I know," said Gleeson. "I know – but this is the real world we're living in." He paused for a moment. "Have you thought of attending the hearing?"

"No, sir. You know as well as I do that I'm not allowed to have any contact with him while he's under suspension."

"This wouldn't need contact with him. I happen to know the panel is convening here tomorrow morning. I think it would be good if – at the very least – you gave it a statement as a character witness."

"I'd be happy to do that," said Francesca.

"My secretary will give you the details of where it's being held."

"Thank you, sir. Now, is that all?" Gleeson nodded. "Just one thing, sir," she said before she left. "Do you want Gary to get off, sir?"

"There's a line from a TV play which covers my response to that question. You may say that, but I couldn't possibly comment."

She smiled. Once back in her office, she rang Rivers. "You're going to love me," she began.

"Is that a prediction?" he asked then mentally chastised himself. Flirting with Francesca was not an option. They had been down that route and decided against it because of Nikki. "I'm sorry," he said. "Why?"

"Have you seen today's local paper?"

"Yes. Not very flattering."

"Well, because of that I've been told unofficially to suspend all enquiries into Thomas Saunders' death."

"Right."

"The thing is I went round to interview Professor Saunders again yesterday."

"Very brave of you."

"I didn't get anywhere but his wife intimated that she might have something to say to us."

"Us being the police force?"

"Or you."

"That's an interesting thought," said Rivers. "I was thinking I should go round and interview Saunders again – but maybe the wife is the key as to what was going on inside Thomas' head."

"Thing is Saunders has taken time off to grieve over Thomas' death. You won't find a way to get to her until he goes back to work."

"That's all right," said Rivers. "He won't delay going back to work for that long."

"So you'll do it?"

"Oh, yes. I'd be delighted."

$$\bullet \quad \bullet \quad \bullet \quad \bullet \quad \bullet$$

Jo sat back in his office chair. "He's a bit of a cold fish, that Duncan Hamilton," he said to Rivers who had just opened the door to find out how his colleague was. "Having said that, he does have a plausible explanation as to why he didn't mention sleeping with Diane when the police first called on him."

"What's that?"

"It isn't allowed to have company of the opposite sex in a police section room. He wasn't a suspect. It was just a casual enquiry from Detective Chief Inspector Brett who was checking up on where everybody was. He didn't see anything wrong in omitting to mention it. Now, though, a more serious investigation has been mounted he thinks he could use all the help he can get."

"There's only one flaw with that argument."

"What's that?"

"Alison Palmer. She still insists Diane Hamilton slept in her spare room."

"Misguided loyalty to a friend?"

"I honestly don't know," said Rivers. "She's one of the Graham Hands set. You know, the DJ who gave us the low down on some of these people at the beginning of this enquiry. His set all have one thing in common. They're supremely confident – arrogant – and you can't tell whether they're telling the truth or not. Let's keep plugging away with this alibi business and see what turns up. Have you spoken to Diane Hamilton following your interview with Duncan and Alison Palmer confirming her original alibi?"

"No."

"I think you ought to have another go at her."

"I was trying to get to her when I got to him – if you see what I mean."

"Then you'd better have another go at trying to interview her." He placed his hands on the back of his head in exasperation. "God, this case is getting difficult to unravel. Brett was lucky. He only knew the half of it and didn't clutter his mind with unimportant things like facts."

"You wouldn't like to be like him, though," said Jo. "Unimaginative and sticking to his own theory of what's what and not seeing any evidence to the contrary. So, if I'm going to talk to Diane Hamilton, what are you going to do?"

"Francesca's work."

Jo looked at him. "What do you mean?"

"She's been told by the chief constable to lay off the Saunders' and leave any questioning of them to me."

"First I knew of that."

"She was only told that this morning – and he told her to give me a ring and ask me to take over the enquiry."

"Is this the privatisation of the police force at work?" joked Jo. "Contracting out interviews?"

"They're not going to pay me anything," said Rivers.

"I think they should," said Jo, "and I'm only half joking."

"We're being paid by Rick Harper. That's the long and the short of it. Anyhow, I was quite happy to take over from Francesca. Apparently, she thinks Mrs Saunders wants to tell us something."

"Well, good luck there. You have to get round the old man first."

"I'll wait for him to go back to work."

"Any more loose ends need tying up?"

"Not at present," said Rivers. "I'm still not a 100 per cent convinced the coke-head is in the clear but I can't see how he did it if Jimmy Atherton is telling the truth and he only spent a few minutes discovering the girls' dead bodies before he fled the scene. The way he described his manager – out of it – I can't see him getting out of his car and focussing enough to murder two women. Also, if Jimmy is telling the truth that he discovered the bodies before he drove Aymes away from the place, that rules out the possibility of Aymes getting back in his stretch limo and driving back to Jennifer's house and killing them – which is one way the coke head could be implicated."

"But you're still not sure?"

"No." He paused for a moment. "Just look at it this way. Two girls are murdered, a guy high on coke goes round to their house that same evening because he wants to bed them – or, rather, one of them. We have no proof of anybody else being there – except, of course, Rick Harper who couldn't find the right house."

"Do you believe that?"

"I'm sorry?"

"Well, he'd known Jennifer for some time. Probably sent her Christmas cards. Surely he knew where she lived?"

"What are you doing? Mounting a case against our own client?"

"It's our job to mount a case against everyone and then accept or reject it."

Rivers smiled. "Point taken," he said.

"Anyhow, I've only just thought of that," said Jo. "I just thought I should share it with you."

"Point taken," said Rivers again. "I will ask Rick if he ever sent Jennifer a Christmas card."

"She was a party girl, too. Surely she had a party at her own house?"

"Also, he can't have been in his right mind when he was being so cruel to Mary Wightman." He described his interview with her. "She's very attractive," he underlined.

"Maybe she wasn't then. She was under her parents' thumb. A testosterone-fuelled guy like Rick was when he was a teenager wouldn't have liked that."

"No," said Rivers. "Anyhow, let me get back to what I was originally saying. Graham Hands said he would be delighted if I could pin the murder on Peter Aymes. A nasty bit of work, he thought. I trust Graham Hands' judgement, He also wanted Renee linked to the crime but he wasn't there."

"He would be – linked, I mean – if he'd supplied coke to someone who became a killer."

"Probably," said Rivers. "Let's get on with it, then."

• • ● • •

"I'll go with you," said Debra as she held Gary's hand across the breakfast table.

"I don't know, love," he replied. "You won't be allowed into the disciplinary hearing and it's a bit difficult having you sit outside in the reception area. It could go on for quite some time."

"A bit difficult? Me supporting you. Why?"

Gary struggled to answer Debra's straightforward question. "They think it's a bit odd. I don't think their wives or partners would support them in that way," he said.

"Are you embarrassed by the thought of me sitting there?"

"If you want the honest truth, I suppose it's 'yes, I am'. Don't ask me to explain it to you. I can't and I suspect if I did I would hurt your feelings. I know last time when you went to see the chief constable you were making a point. My accusers always got access to him so why shouldn't my defenders. Good on you, you achieved something there – but you won't by sitting there today."

"Have you got a defender in your corner today?"

"Yes, a little bird told me Francesca was planning to give evidence on my behalf."

"A little bird?"

272

"Quite a big bird, actually. A black bird. Francesca isn't allowed to have any contact with me so it was done through a rather obvious intermediary – now she's officially allowed to be in a liaison with me again."

Debra shook her head. "I'll never understand the police force," she said. "So many rules. People not just allowed to say what they think."

"I think most people know what Francesca thinks most of the time," said Gary.

"All right," said Debra. "I'll go for a coffee while the hearing's on. I'll have my mobile on. You can ring me if there are any important developments – or, in fact, you just want a chat."

"Thanks," said Gary. He squeezed her hand. "Don't take a saucepan or a set of Ruth Rendell novels with you, though."

"I may take the Ruth Rendell novels. It'll be a chance to read them. I will accompany you to the police station."

The two of them then started to make their way to the police station with Gary driving. Once parked, they both entered the station.

"Morning, Gary," said the desk sergeant. Gary cocked an eyelid. The sergeant didn't normally converse with people as they arrived for work. "It's Room 8A for your hearing. They're here already."

"Thanks," said Gary.

"We're all rooting for you," he added.

Gary smiled. He turned to Debra. "You see, I'm not on my own," he said. "I'd better go." Debra nodded.

"Can I get you a cup of tea or coffee?" the desk sergeant said to Debra. "Cherish that one, lad," he said to Gary. "I doubt if my wife would get off her arse to support me if I was facing a disciplinary hearing."

Debra looked at Gary – as if asking if she should accept the desk sergeant's offer. He nodded.

"That's kind of you," she said. "I'll have a tea."

"And if they ask me to get them one I'll piss in it." Debra looked astonished. "I'm only joking," said the desk sergeant. "Well, half joking." Debra sat down and waited for her tea to arrive. Gary disappeared through a set of swing doors into the interior of the station. He was familiar with the geography of the place and soon found Room 8A. There were three officers in the room – two of them failed to give him any form of recognition, looking as though they were reading papers for the hearing. The third, a senior officer from another force, Superintendent James Bartlett from Oxfordshire, acknowledged him. The other two were middle ranking police officers – one woman and one man.

"Detective Constable Clarke," said Bartlett. "Come in and sit down."

Before he could do so, Francesca appeared in the doorway. It was obvious to her which one of the three of them would be chairing the tribunal. "I wondered if I could ask you if I could give evidence on behalf of my colleague?" Bartlett looked at his subordinates. There was a brief whisper between the three of them. "We had decided that we had completed our enquiries and would need no further evidence," said Bartlett, "However, we would accept written evidence from you."

"Fine," she said. "I'll email you my evidence within the hour." She turned to go and smiled at Gary as she made her way past him. Protocol forbad that she should speak to him.

"You've waived your right to representation from the Police Federation, I understand?" said Bartlett.

"Yes, sir. The facts of the case are not in doubt. I think I can adequately represent my interests."

"Good. Then shall we start?" The other two officers immediately came to the table – sitting on either side of Bartlett.

"The charge is gross misconduct – that you forced your way past a Mrs Saunders and into her house without a warrant or permission from anyone in the family who owned the property. We have spoken to Mrs Saunders and she has verified the facts for us. How do you plead?"

"Not guilty."

"You did not force your way past her?"

"I was in pursuit of a suspect."

"A suspect who had done what?"

"He had attempted to trash the office of a private detective in

274

the centre of town the previous afternoon."

"Is this proven?" intervened the woman officer looking over the rim of her spectacles at Gary.

"There is no dispute that he did it. I think even his family would admit that."

"Is this proven?" she repeated.

"Not in law, no. The young man concerned died before I could obtain access to him."

"Rather a waste of a life?" the woman continued.

"I would agree," said Gary.

The third officer – a bulky detective sergeant – tried to lighten proceedings. "Some would say trashing a private detective's office isn't necessarily a bad thing," he said.

"Not me," said Gary.

"No," said the woman. "We have been told the employee in the office at the time Mr Saunders entered it was a girlfriend of yours. A case of trying to teach him a lesson for messing with your girlfriend."

"No," said Gary. "I think I should point out if you don't already know that it was not my idea to go down and interview Mr Saunders that morning. I was asked to by my superior officer, Detective Chief Inspector Manners. She seemed to think it would be bowing to – I suppose – peer group pressure if we failed to follow up on the crime. It would send out a message that if you're well off and have influence within the force you can use it to protect your family from the consequences of their actions in a way less well-off people cannot do. It is, incidentally, a conclusion with which I would concur."

"Good," said the woman. "I'm glad to clear that up. So you would go into anybody's house uninvited in order to gain access to a suspect?"

"I saw the suspect run out the back door and I gave chase."

"What prompted you to do that?" asked Bartlett.

"Instinct. I think most policemen or women would do the same."

"What were you going to charge him with?" continued Bartlett.

"I was going to interview him about the previous afternoon.

275

In all probability, he would probably have ended up with a caution."

"So, he died over a caution?" intervened the woman again.

"Fundamentally, yes," agreed Gary.

"What a waste. What a waste," said the woman. "You can't be happy with the outcome, detective constable?"

"Of course not."

At this moment there was a knock at the door. "Come in," said Bartlett.

Francesca entered the room. "My statement," she said brandishing three copies of a side of a copy of A4 paper. She smiled at Gary. "I didn't know whether to do one for the accused," she said.

"That's all right," Bartlett continued. "Well," he said, "we seem to have come to an appropriate time for us to adjourn and consider the case."

Left alone in the room with Gary, Francesca no longer felt the need to constrain herself from speaking to Gary. At any rate the proceedings now seemed at an end. "How's it gone?" she asked him.

"As well as can be expected, I think it's one-all with the chair having the casting vote. The woman was harsh on me but I got the impression that the other man was wondering what the hell he was doing here."

"I've just made the point that you were acting under instructions and that no-one is seeking to oppose my decision to send you there to interview Thomas Saunders."

"Thank you." He was about to say "ma'am" – a form of address she abhorred – and reverted to "Francesca" just in time.

"Well, I won't wait for the verdict," said Francesca. "I'll be in the office. Come down and tell me when you know the result. "

As she left, she was replaced immediately by the three panel members. They had sombre looks on their faces, Gary noted. He feared the worst.

"Stand up, Detective Constable Clarke," said Bartlett. He did as he had been bid "We find you 'not guilty' of gross misconduct." Gary breathed a sigh of relief. "However," Bartlett continued. "We do feel the events of that morning should not go unpunished. You were guilty of an uninvited trespass on to the Saunders' property and – in view of the fact this was a relatively minor offence that you were investigating which was likely to end only in a caution – we believe that a reprimand should be laid on your file for the way you behaved."

"Yes, sir."

"Now, go away and be a better police officer," said Bartlett.

"Yes, sir." He hurried out of the room – almost as if he wanted to escape before they could reconsider their verdict." He made his way down to Francesca's office. "A reprimand," he said. "No finding of gross misconduct."

"Well," said Francesca, "that's not too bad. You couldn't count the number of detectives who turned out to be fantastic officers but started out with a reprimand on their file."

"Excuse me," said Gary. "I must phone Debra."

"You must," agreed Francesca. Needless to say, Debra was not over the moon about the verdict. Only a complete acquittal would have satisfied her. "What do they expect of you?" she asked. "Do they expect you to say 'after you, sir' the next time a guilty man runs away from you?"

"I think they probably do," said Gary.

CHAPTER NINE

Rivers thought the best way to make sure of finding Mrs Saunders in on her own was just to park down the road from her house and wait until he saw Professor Saunders leaving. He drove up at about eight o'clock in the morning reasoning that – if the professor was going back to work – that would be about the time he would leave home. He also thought that Professor Saunders was not the kind of man who would want to sit around grieving all day even if his wife would have liked the company. He was right. He only had to wait for about half an hour before he saw Professor Saunders drive out of his home and make his way in the opposite direction to where Rivers had set up camp. The private detective continued to listen to BBC Radio Four Today programme on his car radio for about a quarter of an hour so as to make it a little less obvious that he had been sitting outside waiting for her husband to leave. He chose to leave his car and approach the house just as the programme ended. Mrs Saunders answered his knock.

"You're Mr Rivers, aren't you?" she said. He nodded. "My husband's not in," she added withdrawing inside and closing the door a fraction.

"Actually, it wasn't him I really wanted to see," said Rivers. "I'd like a word with you if I may."

"I'm not sure my husband would approve," she said tentatively.

Sod your husband, thought Rivers. Obviously, he did nothing to indicate to her these sentiments, though. "Mrs Saunders," he said, "I'm investigating a double murder. A lot of people have a question mark hanging over them as to whether they committed those murders. Stan Wightman, Rick Harper, Jimmy Atherton, Duncan Hamilton – to name but a few. I can help put the innocent people out of their misery if I collect all the information I can about the murder and hand it over to the police. It might even help your son Thomas rest in peace if the truth comes out. When Detective

Chief Inspector Manners came to see you and your husband last week, she got the feeling there was something that you wanted to say to her. Now, because of your husband's complaint against her, her superiors have come to the conclusion it would not be wise for her to risk coming into contact with your husband again at present. So, if there is anything you want to say and get off your chest, it would be best for you to confide in me."

Mrs Saunders thought for a few moments and then started opening the door a fraction wider. "You'd better come in," she said – ushering him into her lounge/sitting room. She took a deep breath and motioned him to sit down. "I'm not sure how important this all is," she said – sounding tentative again, "but the night of the murder my Thomas didn't come in until about four o'clock."

"Four o'clock?" Rivers tried not to sound too surprised but wanted to check the information he was being given.

"Yes," she said. "I can be precise about the time because I glanced at my bedside clock when he came through the door."

"Where had he been?"

Mrs Saunders held her hand up as if to denote she wanted to take things at her own pace rather than be forced to answer questions. "I tackled him about it the following morning," she said, "but he was reluctant to talk about it. It was only later on in the day when news of the murders of Jennifer Welsh and Lesley Peters began to emerge that he began to show signs of worry – anxiety even. I was blunt with him. Do you know anything about this? I asked."

"And?"

"He took his time to answer. Then he said he had been with Stan Wightman in the allotments for the best part of an hour after the dance. They were drinking – vodka, I think. He said Stan began to get a bit maudlin – about his relationship with Lesley and that that rose to anger when he started talking about Rick Harper and how Rick had dumped his sister. Thomas admitted Rick had driven him to distraction, too, with this". She hesitated for a moment. "This gay relationship he had had with him. He said he was worried about what might happen. Stan seemed to know that Lesley was round at Jennifer's house and that Rick

279

was there, too. He said Stan almost convinced him that the two of them should go round there and have it out with Rick. In the end they decided against it and Stan said he was going home to bed."

"What time was this?" interjected Rivers.

"I'm not sure. I didn't question him like that. It would have put him on the defensive."

"So what did he do – if he didn't go round to Jennifer's?"

"He didn't go round to Jennifer's – I'm sure of that," she said. "A mother's intuition – added to the fact he told me he hadn't. He said he just sat around brooding after Stan had left him. It was only when he heard about the murders on the radio that he began to get anxious again. I think he thought Stan must have done them. I think he also thought that maybe if he'd got his act together, he could have stopped them."

"You say you think he thought Stan had done them? Mrs Saunders. He had no proof, though?"

"No."

"He never spoke to the police?"

"No. That was why he was so scared of them. He thought they'd be able to wheedle stuff out of him which would have pointed the finger at Stan. Stan was one of his mates. A more loyal friend than Rick Harper had turned out to be."

"Even so – to cover up information about a murder?"

"It wasn't covering up. I mean, he didn't know anything. Look, he knew that at the time Lesley Peters was being killed, there was a guy going around harbouring malicious thoughts about her. I don't think anybody other than Stan did."

Rivers nodded. "Did he ever say anything more about what he did in the hours between when Stan left him and he came home?"

"No," said Mrs Saunders. "I think he may have fallen asleep at the allotments, though. Either that or he just wandered round the streets."

A puzzled expression came over Rivers' face. "Did you tell your husband about what Thomas had told you? Did Thomas speak to his father?"

She shook her head. "No, I think he was a bit in awe of his dad," she said. "He wouldn't have wanted to indicate that he had been drinking until four in the morning."

"Did you?"

"Did I what?"

"Tell your husband."

"I tried to but he was very friendly with Detective Chief Inspector Brett and – as you know – Brett was convinced Rick Harper was guilty."

"So your husband went on a kind of crusade to point the finger of guilt at Rick while his own son was harbouring information that cast suspicion on Stan."

"My husband hated Rick Harper for having had a gay relationship with Thomas. He thought he had led him astray. He's a bit old fashioned in his views."

Not old fashioned, thought Rivers. Merely a bigot. He declined to give voice to these sentiments. "What do you think happened?" said Rivers softly.

"I can't believe the conversation between Thomas and Stan didn't have something to do with the girls' murders."

"How did Thomas react to Stan after the murders? Did they stay friends?"

"Thomas didn't really have much to do with Stan after that night. He became a bit of a recluse."

"Yet he chatted to Rick Harper."

"Fat lot of good that did him," said Mrs Saunders scornfully.

"Did you try and shelter him from the situation?"

"I didn't want him to be acting like a recluse. I felt he was throwing his life away. I didn't want that."

Rivers changed his line of questioning. "Did he do anything when he got in at four in the morning?" he asked.

"Like what?"

"Put his clothes in the washing machine. That sort of thing."

"You mean – try to cover up guilt."

"Yes."

"He was not guilty," she said firmly. "Besides, no – he just went straight to bed."

"Thank you, Mrs Saunders, you've been most helpful," said Rivers getting up as if to leave.

"You won't tell my husband that I've spoken to you?" she said apprehensively.

"Not if you don't want me to."

"So what will you do now?"

Rivers thought for a moment. "I suppose I should have another word with Stan – tell him there are people who think he may have committed the murders." With that, he said his goodbyes and left.

• • ● • •

Jo, too, was involved in door-stepping that morning. He had gone back to the Hamilton home to see if he could track down Diane Hamilton to quiz her on the alibi she had offered for her husband. There was no reply to his initial knock but – after waiting for what seemed ages – he saw her coming around the corner with a pram in tow. He got out of the car and smiled courteously at her. "Jo Rawlins Clifford from the Rivers detective agency," he said. "I spoke to your husband recently and wondered if I could have a word about your alibi for him."

"Is there anything more to say?" she said. "I was with him that night. End of."

"Except that's not what Alison Palmer is saying."

Diane smiled. "Alison is a friend of mine," she said. "I asked her to give me an alibi because it would be more acceptable to my parents if I'd been staying with her. I didn't stay with her, though."

"She is aware that you've given your husband an alibi for the night but she's still adamant you were with her."

Diane smiled again. "It's simple to explain," she said. "Come inside and I'll do it. Would you help me with the buggy?" Jo helped her carry the buggy over the doorstep and into the living room. Once inside, Diane continued: "I had to discreetly exit the police section house early in the morning and went round to Alison's. She saw me in the morning. So I didn't really lie when I told the police I stayed with her. I just didn't tell the whole truth."

"What time did you leave the police section house?"

"It must have been about four or five."

"And Duncan didn't offer to take you home – I mean, to Alison's."

"No. Why should he?"

"I should have thought as a trainee police officer he would have known of the dangers posed to women going home alone at that time in the morning. I certainly wouldn't let my girlfriend trek off on her own at that time of night."

"I got a taxi."

"Oh? Which cab company?"

"I can't remember," she said. "Look, what is this? The third degree?"

"Someone committed two murders that night. We just want to find out who would have been in a position to do that."

"Well, not Duncan. He was with me – or rather I was with him."

"It would be helpful if you could give me the name of the taxi firm so I could check it out."

"I really can't remember," said Diane. "It's pinned up on the notice board in the section house – though whether it will still be there four years later I don't know. Can I offer you anything?"

"Tea would be nice," said Jo.

"Coming up," said Diane. She went into the kitchen and Jo followed her. "Honestly," she said. "Bringing up three young children at the same time is no laughing matter,"

"I'm sure," said Jo. He looked hard at Diane. Her accent told him that she came from a well-to-do middle class family. If she was lying about her alibi for Duncan, it seemed a huge sacrifice to make for a rather dull young lad who, to Jo's way of thinking, had suffered some sort of a charisma by-pass in his formative years. She could, of course face a jail sentence for obstructing the police investigation into the murders if she turned out to be lying. Or could she? he thought to himself. It wasn't so serious an offence to try and mislead a couple of private detectives as to mislead the police. Maybe he should threaten her with going to the police with the information she had supplied. "You do realise the seriousness of your situation?" he said to her.

"What do you mean?" she said as he handed him a cup of tea.

"Well, we'll be handing all our information over to the police at the end of the day. In effect, then, you are telling the police you spent the night with Duncan at a time when the two girls were being murdered. If that turns out to be a lie, I need hardly tell you how serious it would be for you. Duncan, with his police training, should be able to do that. If he turns out to be guilty." Jo's voice tailed off. He looked at her questioningly. He decided to try and put her on the spot. "You think he did it, don't you?" he asked bluntly.

"What?"

"This alibi," he said. "You've given it because you think he needs it. You think he's guilty."

"No. Of course not."

"How can you live with a man for – what is it – four years knowing or thinking he may have killed his previous girlfriend? How can you have three children by him?"

"I don't think he did it. I'm just telling you the truth about where I was."

"Maybe," said Jo. Any hopes Diane may have had that their conversation would be nothing more than a friendly fireside chat had evaporated now. Jo swallowed the last dregs of his cup of tea. "Well," he said. "I must be going now but think about what you're doing. This information goes to the police in about a couple of weeks' time. When they get it, they'll want to question you about it. Get your story straight then." He paused at the doorway and turned back to face her. "I don't think you're a bad person," he said. "I don't think it comes instinctively to you to lie to the police. Tell them the truth when they come calling." With that, he was gone.

Diane sat back in her armchair. How dare he question her commitment to Duncan? Duncan was solid, reliable, dependable – most of the qualities that had been lacking in her previous relationships did not apply to him. She took her mobile phone out of her pocket and scoured down her list of telephone numbers until she came down to Alison Palmer.

"Alison, is that you?" she asked when someone answered the number she had for her friend.

"Who is this?"

"Diane Hamilton."

"At last," said Alison. "I was wondering if you'd call. This alibi you've come up with – do you want me to withdraw mine because I have to say that I don't want to get involved with lying to the police on your behalf?"

"No," said Diane. "I don't want to put you in that position either."

"That's exactly where you have put me."

"I was going to suggest something. Suppose you were to say that you only saw me in the morning? That would mean it would possible to spend most of the night with Duncan before I came on to you."

"Except that's at odds with what I've said previously. I said we were at the dance together and went home with each other."

"Please, Alison."

"I'll think about it – but I don't like the idea that I may be protecting a murderer through what I say."

"You won't be," said Diane. "Honestly. You'll just be making sure the police don't make the mistake of considering Duncan to be a suspect."

"If I want to avoid the police making a mistake, shouldn't I tell them the truth?"

• • ● • •

"Good to see you back," said Francesca as Gary walked into the office for the first time since his suspension.

"Good to be back," he said.

"I'm sorry about the reprimand."

"Don't worry," said Gary with a dismissive wave of the hand. "There are far more important matters to worry about than that."

"Such as?"

"Was I responsible for the death of Thomas Saunders? If I hadn't gone down to his house that morning and chased through the house when he tried to get out of the garden, he would still be alive today. I know I was making sounds about how I'll know in future not to chase a suspect – just let him or her go – but that's not the most important thing to have come out of all this. It's Thomas Saunders' death."

"Thomas Saunders is responsible for Thomas Saunders' death. That's the be all and end all of it."

"Sure," said Gary. "I'll keep telling myself that,"

The two were interrupted by a call from the desk sergeant telling them a Philip Rivers was in reception wanting to see Francesca. "I'll come and collect him," said Francesca.

"Good call on Mrs Saunders," said Rivers as he was escorted to Francesca's office. "She did have something she wanted to get off her chest." He gave Gary a similar greeting to the one he had received from Francesca on spotting him in the adjacent office to Francesca. "Glad to see we're all at full strength now," he said. "I've got Jo back. You've got Gary back."

"We're supposed to be taking a back seat on the murder investigation and on Thomas' death so as to appease Professor Saunders," said Francesca by way of letting Gary as well as Rivers know where things stood. "But tell me about Mrs Saunders."

"Thomas didn't get in until four o'clock on the night of the murder."

"So he could have had time to go round to Jennifer's and kill the girls after Stan left him?"

"Mrs Saunders says not."

"She would do."

"Some evidence, I think, to back her up. He didn't try and get rid of or clean soiled clothing. He just went straight to bed. If you'd just killed someone, would you go straight to bed on getting home?"

"If there were other people in the house who could draw inferences if I didn't, I think I would – yes," said Francesca.

"Maybe," said Rivers. "They had a vodka drinking session in the allotments. We knew that already – but apparently they wound each other up over their respective relationships – Stan got maudlin over Lesley and angry at the way Rick had treated his sister, Mary. Thomas got maudlin over the way Rick had treated him over their gay relationship. Either one of them might have gone over to Jennifer's house knowing Rick was there with the idea of sorting him out."

"Or both?"

"No, I don't think so. Witness the different times they arrived home."

"I wouldn't put too much credence on that. Thomas could just have spent more time moodily worrying about what he'd done."

"Mrs Saunders said he showed no signs of remorse the following morning – but seemed genuinely shocked when news of the murders broke on the local radio. She said she thought he was thinking that he could have stopped them."

Francesca nodded. "So where do we go from here?" she asked.

"You sit back on the orders of your chief constable and I'll do all the donkey work."

"Which means?"

"Another word with Stan Wightman, I guess."

• • • • •

Jo feigned surprise when Debra introduced him to his next visitor at the office. It was Alison Palmer.

"I wonder what you've come to tell me," he said. "Let me guess – your alibi for Diane Hamilton no longer stands up. She could have spent the night at Duncan's." Alison tried to interrupt and speak. "No," said Jo, "I know exactly what happened. Diane rang you and asked you to drop the alibi to protect Duncan."

"When you'll allow me to get a word in edgeways – or do you just want to conduct this monologue and send me on my way?"

"The floor is yours," said Jo with an expansive gesture.

"Yes, you're right. Diane did ring – but I'm not going to lie to you. She did spend the night with me – or at least she was there in the morning when I woke up. What I can't be sure of is the previous night. Yes, we were both at the dance together but what she convinced me of was that we may not have left together. She could have spent some time with Duncan before coming on to my place."

"How did she get in?"

"Pardon?"

287

"You heard."

"Oh, I think I gave her a key earlier in the evening when she said she'd like to doss down at my place."

"Think?"

"All right, I'm pretty sure."

"You can't make that sure, though?"

"It's a long time ago."

"That, in my book, means you didn't give her a key."

"Think what you like – that's going to be my statement to the police. She did come to my house but she says it was in the early hours of the morning and I have no evidence to rebut that claim."

"You didn't hear her come in?"

"No. I wasn't like some mum waiting up for an adolescent teenager. I'd had a bit to drink at the dance and went straight to sleep."

"All right. If that's your evidence I'll amend what you said earlier."

"Thank you," said Alison, getting up to go.

"But I don't believe a word you've said. In fact, far from helping Diane to provide her husband with an alibi, you've done the exact opposite. I'm now as suspicious as hell of the alibi that she's given him."

"That's your prerogative," said Alison with a shrug of the shoulders. So saying, she left Jo's office and departed.

"A classy woman," said Debra to Jo when she had gone.

"Depends what you mean by classy."

"Confident, A go-getter, I should imagine."

"She does modelling shoots – but she's just as capable of pulling the wool over your eyes as to what she really means as the woman next door."

• • ● • •

Rivers, meanwhile, determined to go and visit Stan Wightman on his allotment to discuss with him the information Mrs Saunders had supplied. It seemed to be the most likely place to find him. On arrival, he realised he was not the only person who had had that thought. Professor Saunders had decided to visit him, too. They were talking animatedly and did not notice Rivers arriving at the entrance to the allotments. Rivers decided to remain hidden and glean what he could from their conversation. He hid himself behind a shack a couple of hundred yards away from where the two were talking. He could not hear well but thought he heard Professor Saunders mention his son's name a couple of times. Perhaps he had had a word with his wife and she had told him of the conversation she had had with Rivers. He could imagine Professor Saunders would have been irritated by her decision to speak to him but – if she had reported what had taken place between them accurately- it would surely have reflected worse on Stan Wightman than his son. Still, he really could only pick up one or two threads from the conversation they were having. Then he saw Professor Saunders dip into his pocket and come out with some money which he then handed to Stan. Rivers saw Saunders counting it out – it looked as though he had handed him about £400 in £20 notes. He thought it might be a good time to break his cover. At the very least, he thought, it would embarrass the two men about the transaction that had taken place.

"Morning," said Rivers emerging from behind the shack.

"What do you want?" said Saunders aggressively.

"I wanted a word with Stan actually. Not you," said Rivers.

"I gather you've been pestering my wife."

"I wouldn't call it pestering. She agreed to talk to me. Told me some interesting things, actually."

"Well, you can forget them," said Saunders. "She wants to retract what she said."

"No," said Rivers. "I'm afraid she can't."

"What do you mean?"

"Well, what she said is stored in the memory bank so – unless you've come to tell me she was lying to me when we spoke earlier today – that's where it'll remain."

"I wouldn't go so far as to say that," said Saunders indignantly.

"Anyhow," said Rivers. "I've come to see Stan so if your little transaction is over perhaps you would be good enough to allow me to speak to him in private?"

Saunders moved as if to go but turned round to face Stan again before he departed. "Remember what we said," he told Stan who nodded.

"Why did you pay him £400?" Rivers asked Saunders before he got away. "It looked like about £400 from where I was standing."

"That's none of your business."

"I think you'll find it is. Remember I am passing on all the information I glean to the police. I think they would be very interested to hear that you were paying Stan £400. It's not the friendly Brett police who are in charge now who would swallow every word you said. It's a much more professional outfit."

"Which I have complained about."

"Yes, you would have done," said Rivers. "Heaven forbid that professionals are assigned to this case. Who knows what they might uncover."

"Stan was a good friend of my son's," said Saunders. "He's fallen on hard times. I gave him the money because I thought it would help him in taking up a college course this autumn. I can't help Thomas achieve anything anymore. I could help Stan, though."

"Laudable sentiments." said Rivers, "but – if that's the case – why hand over cash to him in the middle of a field? Why not pay it into his bank account?"

"You read something into everything, don't you?" said Saunders sounding irritated.

"I try to," said Rivers. "Anyhow, I believe you were just leaving?"

"Yes," said Saunders. He left Rivers and Stan Wightman on their own at that.

"Now," said Rivers. "Give me your version as to why you have been paid £400."

"It's as Professor Saunders says – to help me through college."

"Try again. I don't buy that." Stan said nothing. "The real reason I came down here was to discuss with you what Mrs Saunders has told me." Again Stan failed to respond. "So the £400 was hush money for you not to talk to me – or the police." Stan sighed this time. "I warn you," said Rivers, "refusing to talk to me is not a crime but inferences will be drawn if you continue with this stance when the police come around to talk to you – which they surely will do. You may find it easier to talk to me. We can discuss what you're saying. Take a more gentle approach to finding out the truth. I'm going to go now. Think about it. I'll come back at about four o'clock this afternoon. If you want to talk, you'll be here then."

"Okay."

"Be sensible, Stan. Get things off your chest."

• • ● • •

"I don't think you'll find Stan Wightman will be troubling us anymore," said Professor Saunders when he arrived home that afternoon.

"Why? What have you done?" asked his wife.

"I've silenced him."

"What?"

Professor Saunders grinned. "No, not that," he said. "I've paid him to keep quiet. Given him enough money to get through college."

"Why silence him? From what Thomas said to me, it sounded as if Stan Wightman was responsible for the murders. At least that's what Thomas thought."

"I don't want the police and this Rivers character messing around in Thomas' life. It's best no one talks about what happened between Thomas and Stan that night. Some people might make the inference that Thomas was responsible."

"Did he tell you something?"

"You know the lad never talked to me. No, I just thought that – with Thomas' own admission that he was wandering around until four o'clock in the morning that night – someone could make mischief about that and so I paid Stan to keep quiet."

"And Rivers knows you did that?"

"Well, apparently he was skulking around the shacks in the allotment."

"So it is all out in the open – what with what I said to Rivers

291

and you being discovered paying Stan off. You've just made matters worse not better." For the first time in a long while, Professor Saunders was stunned into silence. "You keep telling me you've got everything under control and you've got friends in high places who will sort everything out when the truth is that it's not the people who are in high places that are carrying out this investigation. We would be better off letting this investigation run its course rather than try and interfere with it. That's the truth of the matter. But you, you always want to interfere. First, it was that obsession with trying to get Detective Chief Inspector Brett to put away Rick Harper for the murder. Now you seem to want to stop Stan Wightman being treated as the main suspect when bringing him down would be the best thing that could happen to clear Thomas' name."

"I'm sorry you see it that way. I've always had Thomas' best interests at heart in whatever I've done."

"I've no doubt that you think you have," said Mrs Saunders, "but your actions have made you too many enemies along the way. Rivers, Detective Chief Inspector Manners, why – even the chief constable is no longer dancing to your tune and that lad that came here – who was he? – Detective Constable Gary Clarke was only reprimanded after what happened. Is it worth all the fuss?"

Professor Saunders looked at his watch. "I think I'd better get back to work," he said, changing the subject.

"All right," said Mrs Saunders.

"Well, it's better than engaging in a slanging match with you all afternoon."

"We wouldn't be in that position if you would just occasionally talk things through with me – rather than just bombastically go about your own business."

"You may be right," said the professor. He looked crestfallen.

What seemed to be a sudden change of heart stunned his wife. The change of heart was the last thing she had expected from him. She looked at him. "Do you really mean that, Michael?" she asked.

"I don't know. Maybe. I promise I will consult you in future. Losing a son is bad enough. I don't want to lose a wife as well."

"You won't," she said reassuringly. She moved towards him

and placed her hands on his shoulders. He smiled and kissed her.

"I haven't allowed my emotions to get a look in during all this," he said. "I've always been – right, we must do that or we must do this. I like to pretend I'm in control of the situation but I'm not." He held her in his arms. "I'm so sorry, Margaret." A tear welled in his eye." Thomas is dead, isn't he? And all I can do is make complaints about this, make complaints against that. You know," he wiped the tear from his eye. "You're the strong one. Sitting on your own here grieving. Talking to Thomas when he was troubled. I just wanted to set him up in my image. I never gave a thought about what he wanted to do."

"Do you have to go to work?" she asked.

"No," he said. "I suppose not."

"It's Thomas' funeral the day after next. Would you help me put together a montage of pictures that would capture his life?"

"Yes. I will."

"You know, Thomas has got nothing to be ashamed of. He didn't kill himself. He didn't have any part in the killing of Jennifer Welsh and Lesley Peters. He just got too close to what the real truth was."

"I suppose so."

"Hang on to that thought. He died as a result of a tragic accident which was no more his fault than the fault of the copper who chased him into the garden. He's probably feeling as bad about it as anyone. Thomas wasn't being chased at the time of his death. He just slipped and fell."

"Yes."

"No more complaints, then. Life has dealt us a rotten blow but we're not going to feel any better about it if we insist on making somebody else's life rotten as well."

• • • • •

Arthur Welsh checked out the address he was standing outside to see if the Hamilton's were at home. It was early evening – and there was a man standing in the garden with three young children playing around him. Arthur recognised him as Duncan Hamilton –

the man who had dated his daughter all those years ago. All those years. It was not really that long ago. Four or five years probably. He called to Duncan across the garden fence.

"Duncan," he said. The man looked up. A glimmer of recognition showed on his face. "It's Arthur Welsh – Jennifer's dad," Arthur said.

Duncan was taken by surprise for a moment. "Good grief," he said. "What are you doing here?" It was said out of puzzlement rather than anger.

"I'm connecting with a few of Jennifer's friends. I shut myself away after the murder – for far too long. I'm reminding myself there were some good people in her life as well as one rotten apple. I remember you coming round to our house when you were going out with Jennifer." He looked at the three young children playing in the garden. "I guess things have changed for you?" he said.

"You could say that," said Duncan. "Meet Matthew and Arnold – twins. Nearly two years old. And our oldest, Chloe – three. Would you like to come inside? Have a cup of tea?"

"That would be most acceptable." The entourage traipsed into the living room of Duncan's home where he set about making tea. The twins engaged in a game which featured a fair amount of rolling about on the sofa. "Are you still with the police force?" Arthur asked.

"No," said Duncan. "I'm a sales rep for an engineering firm right now. I think Jennifer's death showed me the police force wasn't right for me. All those intrusive questions when they're the last thing you want to deal with."

"I didn't think they focussed much on you."

"No," he said. "They didn't. Rick was their main suspect."

"I've seen Rick," said Arthur. "Better judges of character than me say he didn't do it. He's going out with my daughter Anne."

"That must be difficult."

"It would be if I let it be, but I agree with her. He didn't do it."

Duncan nodded. "I never really bought into that theory," he said. "So who else have you seen?"

"Jimmy Atherton. The singer."

"We all know who Jimmy Atherton is these days. A mega star.

He was a nice guy."

"No was about it. He still is."

"So those are two examples of the good guys hanging around Jennifer. Who's the rotten apple?"

Arthur said nothing but just looked at Duncan. "Me?" he said. "You can't think it was me."

"I don't think it was anybody in particular. But it was someone."

"Anyhow, I've got an alibi for that night. Diane."

"Diane? That was very soon after your break-up with Jennifer."

"You think I was on the rebound?"

"Not necessarily." Arthur had detected a friendliness towards him from Duncan when he had first arrived but there was a certain coldness inserting itself into his tone now. It was at this moment that Arthur heard the front door open but Duncan seemed not to have heard the tell-tale sign that Diane had returned. "I will admit to you I was cut up by Jennifer ditching me," he said. "I loved her. In fact, I'd go so far as to say she was the love of my life."

"And Diane?"

"She's given me stability. She's given me three great kids but I don't love her in the same way as I loved your daughter."

"I see."

"And because I loved Jennifer I could never have harmed her. Never. So if you're looking for your bad apple you're in the wrong place."

It was at this moment that Diane chose to walk into the room. "So you don't love me?" she said.

"What?" said Duncan surprised. "Did you set me up for this?" he asked Arthur.

"Of course not," said Arthur. "I'm afraid you set yourself up."

Duncan turned to Diane. "How long have you been out there?" he asked.

"Long enough," she said. "Long enough to hear that Jennifer was the love of your life and that you didn't love me."

"I was just saying things that I thought Arthur would like to hear," he said.

"No, you weren't," said Diane. "I know you. I know you were telling the truth when you said all that. Well, as far as I'm

295

concerned, you can kiss goodbye to your alibi."

"What?"

"Your alibi. I'll withdraw it."

"Hang on," said Duncan. "You can't just withdraw it. You'll be charged with wasting police time – or some such thing. You could even go to prison."

"I don't care. People should know the truth about you."

"And what is that?"

"That you killed that girl." Arthur looked horrified on the armchair. "Why else do you think I invented that alibi for you?"

"If you know I was talking the truth when I said I loved Jennifer Welsh, you'll also know I was telling the truth when I said I wouldn't – no, couldn't – have harmed her. Anyhow, why would you have wanted to stay with me if you thought I was a murderer?"

"I loved you," said Diane. "Yes, strange as it may seem, I loved you and we'd had three glorious kids together. I told myself I could live with what you'd done."

"I think I should be going," said Arthur.

"Wait a minute," said Duncan. "What are you going to do about what you've heard here?"

"Tell the police – or Mr Rivers,"

"No," said Duncan. "They'll think I did it."

"Didn't you?"

"No – and they won't have anything they can pin on me. They'll know that Diane gave them a false alibi – but there's nothing to link me with the murder scene. There can't be. I was alone in the section house."

"There's your confession," said Diane.

"Confession? I never made one."

"By the time I've finished with them, I think the police will think you did."

"No. Be reasonable, Diane."

"Reasonable? Is it reasonable to live a lie with me for four years – pretending to love me when all the time you were regretting what had happened to Jennifer."

Duncan turned to Arthur. "This is a case of 'hell hath no fury like a woman scorned', Arthur," he said. "I never killed your daughter."

"I think I should go," Arthur repeated.

"No, don't go. At least until you've given me an assurance that you won't pass on anything that you've heard here."

"Why should I do that? This is the closest I've come to finding out what happened to Jennifer," he said. He made his way to the door. Duncan moved to stop him going but in the end decided to leave him alone. "I'm sorry, Arthur," he said. "I never killed your daughter."

"We'll let the police and Mr Rivers decide that." With that, Arthur was gone. Once outside, he leant against a wall to gather his breath. He was fearful for a moment that he was having another heart attack but – in the end – managed to compose himself and go on his way.

Back inside, Duncan rounded on Diane. "You bitch," he shouted. "How dare you say I confessed to murder."

"You don't monitor your dreams like I do," she said. One of the twins started crying on hearing his parents argue – and Chloe went over to Duncan to reassure him by placing her hand in his. Diane snatched her away from her father. "The best thing you can do is just go," she said to Duncan.

"No," he said. "Please."

"I don't want to hear it Just go."

Duncan sighed and accepted the inevitable. "I'll just go and pack some things," he said. Diane nodded.

Once he had gone she telephoned Alison Palmer. "Alison," she said. "I've just had to withdraw my alibi for Duncan."

"So what do you want me to do?"

"Go back to the Rivers detective agency and tell them on reflection I was there with you for the whole night."

"No. I'd make myself a laughing stock if I changed my alibi again – apart from the fact that normally it is a good idea to tell the police the truth during a criminal investigation."

"But I'm withdrawing my alibi for Duncan."

"That's your decision. I'm not sailing any closer to the wind than I did during my last interview with the detective agency.

They didn't believe me then. They certainly won't if I change my story again."

"Thanks," said Diane sarcastically. "You really are a pal."

"I don't lie for my friends," said Alison. "Besides, have you thought about what you've done? If you've withdrawn Duncan's alibi, you've also withdrawn your own alibi."

"What do you mean?"

"Just pointing it out."

· · ● · ·

"It took me by surprise," Arthur told his daughter, Anne, when he returned from his visit to Duncan's house. "There she was – standing in front of me – accusing her husband of having confessed to Jennifer's murder."

"Do you think she was telling the truth?"

"They were in the middle of a barney. She had just found out he didn't love her and that he was still in love with Jennifer. He'd been trying to convince me he could never have harmed Jennifer."

"And did he? Convince you, I mean."

"Well, I thought he had until the whole thing erupted. At one stage I just wished I'd never started it – but there's definitely something there for the police or Mr Rivers to investigate."

"You should ring him."

"Good idea." Arthur went over to the telephone and dialled Rivers' number. "On answerphone," he said.

"Well, they've probably finished work for the day. I'll ring Rick. He'll have Rivers' mobile number. He's his employer." She dialled the number immediately upon being given it by Rick. "Mr Rivers?" she asked when someone picked up on the other end.

"Yes."

"It's Anne Welsh here," she said. "You know my father has been visiting Jennifer's old friends to try and build a picture of her life."

"Yes."

"Well, he went to visit Duncan Hamilton today and – while he was there – there was a blazing row between Duncan Hamilton and his wife. She withdrew her alibi for him and said he had confessed to murdering Jennifer Welsh."

"Goodness."

"I just thought you ought to know. Apparently, he's been kicked out of the family home. We don't know where he's gone. I think it was all a bit much for my father. He thought he was having another heart attack afterwards. "

"I'm not surprised," said Rivers. "Maybe you should get him to scale back on his visits," he added. "I'll get investigating on this in the morning."

"Do you think it will wait?"

Maybe not, thought Rivers as he put the mobile back in his pocket after concluding his conversation with Anne, but where would Duncan go after being turfed out of his own home? He scratched his head and contemplated giving Jo a ring to see if he had any ideas. Then a thought struck him. "Graham Hands," he said out loud. Duncan had been one of his set and he seemed to operate an open door policy on offering them help. He rang the disc jockey and was put through to his answerphone service. He left a message and was rewarded with a return call a few minutes later. "Sorry," said the disc jockey. "I've got a gig tonight but I've set up a couple of records to run so I can give you five minutes."

"I'll get straight to the point," said Rivers. "Duncan Hamilton has been thrown out of his family home. His wife has claimed he has confessed to murdering Jennifer and Lesley."

"Right."

"I thought – in desperation – he might have come to you."

"Well, I'm not at home. I haven't seen him for months, either."

"If he does come to you, would you let me know? I need to question him."

"Fine," said Graham, "but I reckon he'll 'keep on running'. I promise I will ring you if he turns up at my place but I'm committed to this gig for another couple of hours so he may have moved on by the time I get home."

"You can but try." Rivers paused for thought. "Would you mind if I went round to your place to see if he's there?"

"No problem," said Graham. Rivers had only met Graham in his studio up until now so needed the address. He was not surprised that it was in a fashionable street in Chelsea. He made his way there immediately. It was a private flat in a gated community. All Rivers could do was sit and wait until either Graham returned or Duncan showed up and waited for him outside, too. He didn't know whether Duncan had taken the family car on being booted out of his home. He didn't have long to wait for the answer to that question, though. He soon spotted Duncan Hamilton walking along the street and making his way to the entrance gate. He stepped out of the shadows as Duncan pressed the buzzer for Graham's apartment. "You looking for Graham Hands?" he said to Duncan whose back was turned to him. Duncan froze on hearing the voice. "Philip Rivers, private detective," he said when Duncan had turned round and plucked up courage to face his questioner.

"I might have guessed you'd find me," he said.

"Obvious, really," said Rivers. "I didn't know anyone else you knew who would be prepared to put you up at a moment's notice." Duncan glanced furtively from side to side – trying to weigh up if there was any merit in making a run for it. "I wouldn't try it," Rivers cautioned, "We'll end up in a hell of a mess scrabbling on the floor. Besides, we need to talk. Come and sit in my car." Reluctantly Duncan did as he had been bid. "Now," said Rivers. "What's happened? I've had an excited call from Anne Welsh saying you have confessed to the murder of Jennifer."

"Diane came back home and overheard me talking to Arthur Welsh, I was telling him I loved his daughter and would never harm her. She also overheard me saying I didn't love her in the same way. he went ballistic. Threw me out and said I had confessed to the murder of Jennifer in my sleep."

"And had you?"

"I can't control what I do in my sleep but I didn't kill Jennifer Welsh. I swear."

Rivers nodded. "Did anyone see you at the section house on the night of the murder? There must have been one or two late night pool players around, surely?"

"I didn't realise I'd be needing an alibi, so I didn't take any notice."

"And Diane's alibi?"

"Withdrawn."

"That figures."

"I couldn't understand why she came forward to give it to me. It wasn't as if I needed it. There was no other evidence linking me to the crime."

"Maybe," said Rivers.

"What were you going to say?"

"I was going to say maybe it killed two birds with one stone – and gave her an alibi. She does seem quite a volatile character."

"She is – but murder? No."

Rivers could see a car approaching the gates. "That might be Graham," he said. He got out of the car and checked that it was. "He's here," Rivers told the disc jockey.

"Come inside," said Graham. "I can find you a parking space." Once they were inside Graham's flat, the disc jockey turned to his two companions. "It's late," he said. "I'd like to go to bed. We can settle all this in the morning. Would you like to stay, Philip?"

"Yes."

"Don't worry, Duncan," said Graham. "It'll all look better in the cold light of day."

Except when morning arrived Duncan Hamilton wasn't around to communicate whether things did look better, He had disappeared from the flat.

• • ● • •

A nagging doubt had persisted in troubling Jo for the past 24 hours – that, if Rick had been as friendly with Jennifer as everyone seemed to suggest, he must have known her address. That was why he found himself outside Rivers' client's home that morning. Rick's mother answered the door. "Yes?" she said sharply.

"I'm Jo – Philip Rivers' assistant," he said. "I wanted to have a word with Rick."

"Oh," she said – her frostiness vanishing. Jo couldn't help thinking her initial response had been in part racist having been confronted by a black man at the door in sleepy, rural Hertford.

He shrugged his shoulders, though. There was no way of telling. "You'd better come in," she added.

Rick was tapping away at a laptop in the living room. "Job applications," he said as he looked up and saw Jo. "I have to remember I have to contribute to the cost of hiring you. I can't rely on the bank of mum and dad for everything."

Rick's mother retired from the room and went into the kitchen where she busied herself making bread. There was a hatch between the two rooms which she kept open. She could obviously hear any conversation between the two men in the living room.

"Does that disconcert you?" asked Jo, pointing to the open hatch.

"No, I've got nothing to hide," said Rick.

"Good. There was something I wanted to ask you."

"Go ahead."

"You had a very close relationship with Jennifer Welsh before the night of her murder?"

"I wouldn't put it that highly. We had a relationship snogging with each other at a couple of dances. That's all."

"I find it difficult to comprehend that you didn't know where she lived."

"What?"

"Well, you said you gave up on the idea of going round to her place when you found yourself standing in The Close by her home and you couldn't remember her number. Surely you would have been invited round for coffee beforehand or sent her a Christmas card?"

"Surprising as it may seem, no. Does that answer your question?"

"It'll have to. It's just something that's been bugging me."

"Ours was a very casual friendship."

"Obviously."

At this point Rick's mother returned to the living room. "How near are you to completing your investigation?"

"Things are coming together – but I wouldn't like to put a time scale on it."

"Yet you're still questioning my son as if you think he's guilty."

"I'm questioning everyone as if I think they're guilty," said Jo.

"Our pockets are not a bottomless pit, Mr....?"

"Jo."

"Jo. If you really are not making progress beyond re-examining whether my son is guilty or not, maybe it's time to call a halt to all this."

"Mother," protested Rick.

"I can assure you that there are suspects who have a stronger motive for killing the two girls than your son. We have to cross all the t's and dot all the i's. It's Mr River's way."

"Just bear in mind what I've just said."

Jo nodded. "I will," he said. He turned to go but Rick followed him to the door. "Don't worry," he said, "I'll find some way of funding you if it becomes necessary."

Jo smiled and departed. As soon as he was out of earshot of the house, he telephoned Rivers. "I've cleared up that nagging doubt I had about the Christmas cards," he said, "but I seem to have unleashed a nagging doubt about Rick's parents' willingness to continue funding our operation."

"That would be a shame," said Rivers. "Duncan Hamilton's wife accused him of confessing to the murders last night and now he's gone on the run – so we're definitely getting somewhere." I'm going to see if I can find him. It seems to me we're getting close to the moment where we hand everything we've got over to the police."

"Great."

Rivers turned to Graham Hands – whose home he was still in – after talking to Jo. "So," he said, "where do you think he's gone?"

"'Where Do You Go To My Lovely', you mean?" said Hands. Rivers nodded. If the truth be known, he was now beginning to get a little bit irritated by Hands' attempts to turn everything into a song. Hands began to sense this, too. "Sorry," he said, "but follow the words of the song. Where did he think she went to in her darkest hours? Back to her roots. I would think that Duncan Hamilton would have one more attempt at trying to patch things up with his wife before he tried anything else."

"You may be right," said Rivers. "I'll be on my way. If you hear anything from him, tell him he would be best getting in touch with me – otherwise I'll just hand everything I know over to the police. I will listen to what he has to say. Otherwise, if he won't get in touch with me, find out where he is and let me know."

"I will," said Hands, "but I think he probably thinks I'm in cahoots with you after last night."

• • ● • •

Rivers drove over to the Hamilton home immediately after leaving Graham Hands' flat. Once in his car, his mobile rang. It was Nikki. Damn, he thought, I never called her to say I was stopping over at Hands' home last night. "Sorry, darling," he said. "I meant to call you."

"So you're still alive?" she said. "I suppose that's something."

"We had a really dramatic development in the case last night. It went on late into the night."

"And how long would it have taken to call me?"

"Not very long," he admitted. And I wouldn't be facing this grief in the morning, he thought to himself.

"Oh well," she said. "At least you weren't with another woman. What are you doing now?"

"Trying to track down the guy who's allegedly confessed to the murder."

"Who's that?"

"Duncan Hamilton. His wife threw him out last night."

"You might find you've got something in common with him when you finally deign to come home then."

Rivers sighed. He was in the wrong, he knew. "I'll see you tonight," he said.

"I hope so." She paused. "And good luck with the case."

He smiled. It was her way of letting him know things weren't irretrievably lost between the two of them. He put his failings to the back of his mind as he drew up outside the Hamilton's home. It looked deserted. Diane must have been taking the children to the nursery. He thought for a moment. Duncan would have realised that. Was it beyond the realms of possibility that he was treating today like a normal day and had gone off to work? If he had, there was little Rivers could do about it. He didn't know where Duncan worked and had no means of finding out – other than, he supposed, through Diane. As these thoughts circled round his mind, he noticed Diane returning from dropping Chloe and the twins off at the nursery. He gave her a few minutes to settle in at home and then decided to confront her.

"I'd like to speak to your husband," he said when she came to the door.

"Well, you're on your own there," she said. "I wouldn't."

"Have you any idea where he might be?"

"I don't know and I don't care."

"I heard about what happened last night. He shacked up with Graham Hands for the evening but had disappeared by the morning. If what you say about him is correct, then we have a case of a self-confessed murderer on the loose."

"Are you doubting me?"

Rivers decided this was not the moment to be truthful and say yes. "I just want to ask him about what you said."

"Why don't you call the police? If you don't, I will."

"All right," said Rivers. "I will call the police after I've had a word with him. Could he be at work?"

"I don't know."

"Could you check?"

"I've already told you I don't want to have anything to do with him."

"All right," said Rivers – trying not to sound exasperated. "Can you give me his number so I can check?" At this she relented. A few minutes' later Rivers had ascertained that his company hadn't heard from him that morning. "Is there anybody else he could have gone to?"

"I don't know. He doesn't have many close friends. That's why he went to Graham Hands last night – somebody he probably hasn't seen in two years."

"Could you ring me if you see him?"

"Why should I want to?"

"Because, if what I've heard about what happened last night, you want to see him put away for murder." He handed her his card. She took it without giving any commitment as to whether she would contact him if Duncan turned up. "I might come back later on in the day," he said.

"Suit yourself."

Rivers thought he would be best served trying to close other loose ends in the case rather than hang around Diane's home all day. He got back in the car and decided to head off for Stan Wightman's allotments. "I've been expecting you," said Stan.

"Got caught up on other aspects of the case yesterday."

"No matter. At least it gave me more time to think."

"And?"

"I don't think I can help you anymore."

"You know Thomas' mother believes you committed the murder – and that Thomas believed that, too."

"I'm sure that's the impression he gave to her."

"And?"

"And?" repeated Stan.

"Did you?"

"You think I'm going to confess to you?"

Possibly not, thought Rivers. It would be too much of a good thing to hear about two confessions to the murders in twenty-four hours after four years of silence. "You might prefer to talk to me rather than the police," was all he said.

"Look, we both wound each other up about Rick that night in the allotments and drank quite heavily. I have no knowledge of what Thomas did afterwards but I went home. That's all I'm prepared to say."

"You at two in the morning and Thomas at four."

"Me at two. I don't know about Thomas but I'm not prepared to discuss it any further."

● ● ● ● ●

Jimmy Atherton came out of the studio with the intention of crossing the road and buying himself a croissant at the delicatessen opposite. He had just put his foot on the zebra crossing when a car, driven fast, headed straight for him and knocked him sideways into the road. It sped off down the street leaving Jimmy lying unconscious on the ground. A passer-by came over to him and, on ascertaining he was still breathing rang for an ambulance on his mobile. "Did you see that?" he said to another man standing by the side of the road. "That was deliberate." He turned his attentions back to the singer and recognised him for the first time. "Wow," he said. "You're Jimmy Atherton."

Jimmy, who was gradually coming round, smiled and winced with pain as he did so. The impact of the accident had been on his right side. "The speed he was going he could have killed you." Jimmy nodded but did not feel he had the strength to speak or even sit up. The passer-by held his hand while they waited for the ambulance. "You wait until I tell the missus that I held Jimmy Atherton's hand." Jimmy smiled again – once more sparking off a pain in his right side. A few minutes later the ambulance arrived and Jimmy was bundled on a stretcher.

"Does anyone want to come with him?" asked one of the para medics.

"I'll go," said the passer-by. He sat next to him in the ambulance. "I'm sorry," he said. "You don't know me but I'm a big fan of yours."

"I rather gathered that," Jimmy said weakly.

"Do you want me to contact anyone for you? Relatives? Girlfriend?"

Jimmy nodded. He brought a mobile phone out of his pocket. He pointed to the numbers he wanted dialled. "That's my manager," he said. "You must tell him I can't make my show this afternoon."

The passer-by nodded and dialled the number of Peter Aymes. "You won't know me," the man said. "I'm a fan of Jimmy Atherton's. I'm taking him to hospital because someone's knocked him down on a zebra crossing. No, I think he's going to be okay. He's conscious and he's talking – although he's in pain. What's that? What hospital are they taking us to?" He looked at the para-medic. "It's St Hugh's in Croydon. Near where he was supposed to be performing this afternoon. What's that? You'll come and see him as soon as you can? I'll pass the message on."

"Thanks," said Jimmy. He jabbed his finger down on another number. "Ring that one as well – and tell him what's happened."

The man nodded. "Mr Rivers?" he asked when someone answered the call. "I'm ringing on behalf of Jimmy Atherton. He's been knocked down on a zebra crossing. He wanted me to tell you. He's been taken to St Hugh's hospital in Croydon. What's that? You'll be over as soon as you can but you're in Hertford. Okay." He handed the mobile back to Jimmy. "He's coming too," he said. "No girlfriend you want to ring?"

"I don't have time for that sort of thing," said Jimmy smiling.

"The police will be coming to take a statement from you, too," said the paramedic.

"I'm not surprised," said Jimmy's fan. "It was a nasty business."

They were soon at the hospital where Jimmy was checked out by a doctor. There was severe bruising to his right-hand side and a large bump on his left temple which the medics said they wanted to monitor in case of concussion. "Otherwise, you've been extremely lucky," said the doctor.

"That's what I told him," said Jimmy's fan. "Well," he added, "you're in safe hands now. I'd best leave you. Thanks for the memory."

"I would have preferred to have met you in better circumstances," said Jimmy, "but thanks for keeping me company." He lay back in the bed and fell into a half sleep – only to be woken when Rivers arrived.

"Hallo," said the private detective. "What's happened to you?"

"I think someone tried to kill me."

"Why?"

"I think you know." Rivers racked his brains. "Your report is going to the police soon. What will it say?"

A look of recognition dawned on Rivers' face. "That your manager was stoned on cocaine on the night of the murder?"

"Yes."

"So you think he's tried to bump you off?"

"It may not have been him. Who supplied him?"

"Renee?"

Jimmy nodded. "My old flatmate," he said. "Not a clever thing to do. Your report probably won't go into who supplied the cocaine."

"It wasn't part of my remit," said Rivers.

"So why not eliminate anyone who can give evidence as to who did? Me?"

"But then there's still Peter Aymes?"

"He won't tell. Especially if he knows what happened to me."

"So you want me to investigate this?"

"Yes," he said. "Don't worry. I'll pay."

"I wasn't worried about that and it'll ease Rick's mind if he thinks someone else is contributing to my upkeep. Well, much as I enjoy hospital visiting, I've got a job to do. Remind me where Renee lives." Jimmy wrote the address down on a piece of paper. "Great, I'll be off. Tell the police where to get hold of me when they come to interview you."

Jimmy nodded and settled back to rest again once Rivers had gone. He did not enjoy the rest for long – he became aware of Peter Aymes sidling up to the edge of the bed. "Jimmy," he said. "I'm so sorry."

"So you should be. I'm here because of your cocaine habit."

"What? It wasn't me that drove that car at you."

"Who said it was deliberate?"

"Well, I think the guy that rang me."

"No," said Jimmy. "He just said I was being taken to hospital."

"I'm sorry, Jimmy. I didn't think he was serious."

"He being Renee?"

"Yes. He said we'd both go scot-free if there was nobody to give evidence about the cocaine."

"Why didn't you tell the police? Or at least warn me?"

"I didn't want to get involved."

"Well, you are now." Jimmy winced from pain. The intensity of the conversation was taking its toll on him. "You tell the police about your conversation with Renee. You tell them about your cocaine habit." Aymes moved to interrupt him but Jimmy waved him away. "You tell them that Renee was your supplier. They'll probably go easy on you if you co-operate. After all, you're not pushing the drugs. You're just another middle-class consumer.

It won't even damage your reputation in the pop world. After all, everyone's into it."

"I'll do what you say," said Aymes. Jimmy looked at him. For the first time since they had met, Aymes seemed to be really contrite about what had happened.

CHAPTER TEN

Rivers drove as quickly as he could to the house Jimmy Atherton used to share with Renee Hick. Would the organist be in at this time of day? It was 5.30 in the evening – well before any gig Renee was involved in would start. He could not be sure as he approached the block of flats but decided to take a gamble and attempt an entry He managed to pick the lock – something he hadn't tried to do for some years – and smiled with pride at how easily it came back to him.

"Renee Hick," he shouted. There was no reply. Having got inside the flat, he could not work out quite what he was looking for. Renee would be anxious to cover up any remaining damage to the car from the hit and run on Jimmy Atherton. Therefore, he determined, he should be looking for any evidence of the car – particularly any evidence that showed which garage he used for repairs, MOT tests, that sort of thing. He opened one or two drawers. He noticed one drawer marked "car" and took it out to look at. It mentioned a garage which had given the car its last MOT test. Rivers decided to try the number.

"Good evening," he said when his call was answered. "It's the police here – I wonder if I could ask you if you're currently servicing a car belonging to a Renee Hick?"

"Could I have your name?" asked the person on the other end of the line.

"Inspector Philip Rivers from Croydon police. We believe the car was involved in an accident in our area." Might as well be in for lion as well as a lamb, thought Rivers.

The man on the other end of the line obviously looked through his bookings. "No, sir, no-one of that name here," he said.

Ah well, thought Rivers. "Thanks for looking," he said. He scratched his head. Where to next, he thought? It was then that he glanced down by the side of the telephone. There was a number scribbled on a scrap of paper there – probably recently. Perhaps this was it. He rang it. It was a garage. "Good evening, Inspector Philip Rivers from Croydon police here," he said – warming to his role. "I wonder if you've had a car brought in for you to work on by a Renee Hick?"

"Oh, you mean the one in the accident?"

"That would be it."

"Yes."

"Have you started on it yet?"

"Give us a break. He only brought it in half an hour ago."

"No, I'm not going to ask you to start on it – I'm going to ask you not to work on it. We believe it may have been involved in as serious road traffic accident and we'd like to impound it. When were you going to start work on it?"

"Tomorrow morning."

"Good, we'll have somebody round by nine o'clock tomorrow to have a look at the vehicle. Will you make sure no-one touches it until then?"

"Yes."

"Oh, and don't tell Mr Hick what's happened." He took the garage's address from the man as it had not been written on the scrap of paper. He ran his fingers through his hair. The subterfuge had come easily. Now came the hard part – ensuring a police officer went round to the garage at nine o'clock. There would be little chance of him managing to get an officer from the Croydon force round the next day. He did not know anyone there. Francesca, he decided, would be his best hope of getting things done. He rang her. "Francesca?" he said. "I've got a confession to make: I'm guilty of a crime. Impersonating a police officer."

"What?"

"It's a long story." He told her of the hit and run and the injuries to Jimmy Atherton, of his suspicion that Renee Hick had been behind it to avoid him giving evidence about his drug dealing. He told her he had tracked the garage down which Renee had chosen to repair it. "Unfortunately, I told them the police would be round to impound it tomorrow morning," he said. "If they don't go round, they might start working on it and we'll lose all the evidence. It was the only thing I could think of in the circumstances."

"I'll see what I can do," said Francesca.

"Thank you."

"Will you be there tomorrow morning?"

"No, I wasn't planning to be. Wouldn't it complicate matters if I was? After all, they'll realise I'm Philip Rivers and I'm not a police officer."

"The officer who takes this on will need to know the details of the case. I'll arrange for you two to meet somewhere near the garage at 8.45am. You could then fade into the background when he goes to see the car."

"Okay." He looked out into the street and remembered he was still in Renee's flat. He thought he could see the organist walking down the street and thought he had better return immediately to his car. As he walked towards the front door, he could hear Renee walking up the stairs to the second storey flat. He quickly walked up a flight and waited until Renee was safely inside his flat before descending.

Francesca was as good as her word. Within minutes, she was back in touch with Rivers. "I've found the officer who's in charge of investigating the hit and run. It's an Inspector Paul Saddler from Croydon police. I've told him that the hit and run dovetails with an investigation we're dealing with which involves drug taking. He's happy for us to be present tomorrow morning and when they interview Renee. He wants to meet at the Hearty Café just along the street from the garage tomorrow morning at 8.30am."

"Fine," said Rivers.

They were there, then. All three of them at 8.30am when Rivers outlined the case against Renee Hick – that he had been dealing drugs to the manager of a famous pop star, Jimmy Atherton. He had come across that fact while investigating a murder. The manager, Peter Aymes, had been present near the scene of the murder – although he did not think he had played any part in the murder.

"What about Jimmy Atherton?"

"No, he played no part in the murder."

"Pity," said Saddler. He had been contemplating being involved in a nice high profile case. "And the drugs?"

"No again."

The waitress brought Saddler some scrambled egg and bacon at this juncture. He smiled as he tucked in. Rivers ordered a cup of tea and a slice of toast. When they had finished, they marched off to the garage to inspect the car.

"What do you think?" Saddler asked his two companions. "Is it compatible with a hit and run?"

Francesca and Rivers looked knowingly at the car but it was the mechanic who spoke first. "Very much so," he said. "That's what I thought when it was first brought in."

"Right," said Saddler. "Here's what we do. I'll get a couple of police officers to tow it back to the station." He turned to the mechanic. "When did you say it would be ready for Mr Hick to collect?"

"Five o'clock this evening."

"Stick to that timetable. Don't let him know anything out of the ordinary has happened. We'll arrest him when he turns up to collect it. In the meantime we should seek to interview Mr Aymes about the drugs. Do you want to be in on that?" he asked Francesca.

"No," she said. "I'm afraid we've got another appointment." She looked at Rivers. "Thomas Saunders' funeral."

"Good grief, I'd forgotten," said Rivers.

"We should be there. I'm sure you'll be able to interview Peter Aymes adequately," she said to Saddler.

"Yes, but let's go back to the Hearty Café for another mug of their excellent tea while I write down some details."

• • ● • •

"Come on Arthur, sit down," said Sylvia Welsh. "You're tired. You should rest."

"Yes," he said. "I think you're right."

"It's been a success. Someone's finally confessed to Jennifer's murder."

314

"Well, I'm not sure whether they have," Arthur added. "I seemed just to be getting myself into the middle of a matrimonial row between Duncan Hamilton and his wife. He didn't accept that he had confessed to the murder."

"Well, you can't sort that out," Sylvia added. "You have to leave that to the police."

"Or Mr Rivers – who seems to be acting as the police nowadays."

"They're good at sorting things out," Sylvia continued. "Leave it to them."

"Yes," he said. "There was just one stone I'd left unturned, though. It's Thomas Saunders' funeral today. I thought I ought to go."

"Why?" said Sylvia. "What good would that do? He wasn't a friend of Jennifer's."

"No," said Arthur, "but he's the missing piece of the jigsaw. He died running away from the police. He must have known something that he didn't want to let out. Maybe he knew who killed Jennifer. Maybe he killed her himself."

"That's a far cry from the original mission you set yourself. You said you wanted to mix with some of Jennifer's friends and remind yourself there were some good ones despite the bad that befell her."

"There were two that I found who I got on well with." He paused and then allowed himself an ironic chuckle. "Rick," he said. "To think of all the times I've spent cursing him and blaming him for Jennifer's death. Then there's Jimmy Atherton."

"You told me he discovered the bodies and didn't tell anyone. That's not exactly an act of friendship."

"He explained that. He had his manager with him – who was high on cocaine."

"How can we be sure they – or the manager – didn't kill her? Have you read the papers today?"

"No," said Arthur.

Sylvia picked up a copy of the Daily Mail from the coffee table in front of her. "It's all over the news. Jimmy was badly injured in a hit and run accident."

Arthur grabbed the paper. He furiously read the story. "No," he said. "He was a nice guy."

"They say he'll pull through but who would do a thing like that?" She fixed a steely glaze upon him.

"You don't think I could?" Arthur was astonished. "Apart from the fact that I didn't know where he was recording and that I didn't have time to go to Croydon with all the events unfolding at the Hamilton household. You know me, Sylvia," he said beseechingly. "Am I the type to try and kill someone? Do I believe in an eye for an eye and all that? Anyhow, I was convinced Jimmy hadn't killed Jennifer."

"I didn't really think you were thirsting for revenge but I felt I had to check. So – are we going to this funeral or not?"

"Not," said Arthur. "You're right. There's no-one that was a friend of Jennifer's involved in it."

• • ● • •

The church in Hertford was not exactly packed for Thomas Saunders' funeral. It seemed to be an accurate reflection of Thomas' life, thought Rivers. A young man with few friends. A family who had probably stinted on a social life to take care of their son.

He and Francesca tried to slip in incognito into the back row but – when Professor Saunders turned round and saw them – he got up and made his way over to where they were sitting. He shook them both by the hand. "Thanks for coming," he said.

Francesca was surprised by his reaction but tried not to show it. "We felt we owed it to his memory," she said.

"I'm glad they didn't suspend you after my complaint," he said. "I'm beginning to realise you had to do what you did – and that you've been more thorough than your predecessor."

The man you had in your pocket, thought Francesca. "My colleague Detective Constable Clarke would have liked to have come but he thought maybe it was not appropriate," she said. "He sends his condolences."

"Thank you," said Professor Saunders. "He may be right." His hunched shoulders eased as he relaxed talking to Rivers and Francesca.

316

"Don't feel you have to stay with us if there are other people you wish to greet," said Francesca.

"No," he said looking beyond them to the church door. "I've just seen someone I don't want to greet. Rick Harper."

"Do you want me to go and have a word with him?" said Rivers. "He is my client."

"Thank you," said Saunders. He went back to where his wife was sitting. "Well," he said, "I made the effort to befriend them."

"Sounds as if you didn't want to?"

"No, I think they're good detectives."

Rivers moved over to where Rick was sitting. Rick smiled on seeing his employee. "Do you think this was a good idea?" Rivers asked him.

"I just want to pay my last respects to Thomas. We had been close."

"That's part of the problem," said Rivers.

"We still spoke with each other until a few days before his death."

"I strongly advise you to go. You're upsetting Professor Saunders. Normally, I wouldn't mind someone upsetting Professor Saunders but this is his son's funeral and he's entitled to a bit of consideration here today."

"Very well," said Rick. He got up from his seat and made his way to the door where his departure coincided with Stan Wightman's arrival at the funeral service.

"You here?" said Stan.

"Yes."

"I haven't set eyes on you since the night of the dance. I didn't expect to see you here today."

"Funny who you bump into at funerals," said Rick sarcastically.

"You should leave. You caused Thomas enough grief while he was alive. You've caused me grief, too."

"What grief?"

"The way you treated Mary. That was shabby."

"I agree. I wouldn't do that sort of thing again today – but today isn't about spats we've had in the past. It's about Thomas. I've taken on board the fact that Professor Saunders doesn't want

317

me here – probably because he's homophobic. Ironic, since I'm not gay."

"You were once."

"No. Let me tell you – although, I don't like your tone. It sounds like you think – if I was gay – it would be something to be ashamed of. It would not be."

"Don't try and baffle me with words."

"No-one would have to try very hard to do that."

At this Stan raised his fist – only to have it caught by Rivers who told the two of them: "If you're going to have a fight, please have it outside. There is a funeral about to start inside this church."

"I think you'll see by my direction of travel that I was leaving," said Rick. "You were arriving, Stan. Let's continue on our respective journeys." At that Rick left the building while Stan stumbled on his way to taking up a seat inside the church. He sat by himself at the back of the church. Professor Saunders turned round to greet him. The service began with only ten mourners in the church. One of the last arrivals was Rory Gleeson. He sat on the same pew as Francesca and Rivers.

"Stan," said Professor Saunders moving to greet him, "you're the only representative of the younger generation her. Would you be prepared to say a few words about Thomas?"

"I don't know," said Stan. "I've never done any public speaking."

"It won't be too daunting. There aren't too many people here. It would mean a great deal to me."

"All right," said Stan reluctantly.

"Thanks."

Professor Saunders gave a tribute to Thomas during the early part of the service – saying he was a promising youth who maybe could have made something of his talents if he had lived longer. He stressed how much he had been loved by him and his wife. He then called on Stan to speak.

"I'm not good at this," he began, "but somebody needed to say something on his behalf from the younger generation. Thomas' father is right – he might have made something more of himself if his life hadn't been totally messed up by one Rick Harper who had the gall and insensitivity to come here today for the funeral but then Thomas isn't the only one who had his life messed up by that man." He could sense Professor Saunders was squirming in his seat so decided to change tack. "Thomas, though, was a good friend to me. He would listen to me and I would listen to him. That's what good friends do and I shall miss him because of that. That's all I wanted to say."

"Thank you for that," said the vicar as Stan left the pulpit from where he had given his speech. The vicar drew the service to a close with the blessing and a hymn. The ten people then filed out of the church and congregated in the graveyard outside.

"Mr Rivers," said Gleeson once they were outside. Keep up the good work. I'll just say goodbye to the professor and then be on my way."

Professor Saunders came over to them. "I was going to offer you a drink in the Dog and Partridge to say goodbye to Thomas," he said.

"No, I must be on my way," said Rivers. "Why don't you take Stan Wightman out to lunch? He could probably do with something after making the first speech of his life. Besides, I suspect he is the only one here who really knew Thomas."

Professor Saunders smiled. "You're right, of course," he said. With that, he thanked them for coming again and made his way over to where Stan was standing.

• • ● • •

Inspector Saddler turned up unannounced at Peter Aymes' London offices that afternoon accompanied by a woman police officer. "Is Mr Aymes in?" he asked the receptionist.

"I'll see," she said. "Who shall I say is calling?"

"Just tell him it's the police."

The receptionist rang through to Aymes' office and was told someone would come down to the reception area and escort the officers upstairs. When they arrived, they found Aymes pacing up and down his office. Probably needs a snort of cocaine to steady himself, thought Saddler.

"I'm investigating a hit and run crime yesterday afternoon."

"Yes, I know," said Aymes. "Jimmy Atherton. Tragic."

"Happily it won't be because we understand he's likely to make a complete recovery but it is a serious crime. Attempted murder."

Aymes looked up – fear showing in his eyes. "Do I need a solicitor?" he asked.

"That's a question only you can answer."

"I mean, do you suspect me? I mean I wouldn't." He's far too much of a cash cow for me to want to do away with him, thought Aymes. Saddler was having the same thoughts.

"We don't suspect you of the attempted murder. However, in the process of gathering evidence, we believe it is possible you may have been guilty of a crime."

"Possession of an illegal drug," said Aymes.

"You admit it?"

"Why not? If it's what I need to do to regain Jimmy's trust, I will do it."

"I need to read you your rights. I should ask you to accompany me to the police station."

"Can we not do it here? I'm expecting an important call from Montreal booking Jimmy for a concert tour."

"I can interview you here. We will then pass the file to the Crown Prosecution Service. If they recommend proceeding with a criminal charge, you will be called in to the station."

"That's fine. I'll help all I can."

Saddler read him his rights. Aymes indicated he did not wish to be represented by a solicitor. "We've spoken to Jimmy Atherton," said the inspector. "He advises us that on the night of" – he pulled a sheet of paper from his brief case – "June 4 four years ago you, he and a Renee Hick were at a night club in Hertford when Mr Hick supplied you with an illegal substance – namely cocaine. Mr Atherton advises us you paid for it and snorted the drug in the night club's toilets a few minutes later."

"Yes." Aymes was sitting down now – a hunched figure who was doing a passing imitation of someone who was ashamed of what he had done. It could have been for real, thought Saddler.

"Subsequent to that you went to the home of Jennifer Welsh –

where two murders were committed that night. Mr Atherton noted that your functioning had been impaired by the drug and took over driving the car and led you away from the scene of the crime. At no stage has there been any suggestion that you had any connection with the murders. We merely mention this incident as proof of the fact that you had taken the cocaine."

"I paid Renee Hick for cocaine – something I had done on several occasions."

"Do you know if he supplied anybody else?"

"I don't but I wouldn't be surprised."

"Right, sir, I think that will be all." Saddler and his accompanying officer got up to go. "We will be in touch. Oh, by the way, if you get that call from Montreal, I have to advise you not to leave the country while this investigation is ongoing."

"How long is it likely to take?"

"It'll come to court soon. We are at an end to our enquiries. I can't say how long any ensuing court proceedings will last."

"Do I face a prison sentence?"

"That will be a matter for the courts, too. You would do well to seek advice from a solicitor on that." Saddler saw no reason to be officious and hard-nosed in his questioning of Aymes. The man was obviously trying to be as helpful as possible.

"I can't see how it escalated from supplying that evening to attempted murder four years later."

"Evidence of your behaviour on the night of the murders was going to be passed on to the police by the private investigator looking into the case. If the police decided to question Jimmy Atherton about it, he may well have mentioned the cocaine – even if it wasn't in the original investigation."

"But Renee, he seemed so cool. I can't imagine him thinking he had to commit murder. I liked him."

"I have to say that's irrelevant. Being a drug pusher and trying to protect yourself does sometimes colour your judgement as to how you behave when under threat. Well, Mr Aymes, thank you for your assistance." As he got up to go, the telephone rang. Aymes answered it. "It's your call from Montreal," said the receptionist.

"Thanks," said Aymes. "Hello," he said – his brash confident voice re-emerging again, "how are things in Montreal?"

On being told it was well below freezing in temperature, Aymes replied: "Wow." "Look," he added reverting to business type, "we have a hiccough. Jimmy's been involved in an accident. No touring for the foreseeable future." There was a pause while the person on the other person reacted to the news. "No, it won't affect his voice – either in the long term or the short term." Another pause. "Six concerts in the spring?" He looked at Saddler who had delayed his departure from Aymes' office. The inspector was inscrutable – giving no clue as to his reaction. "I think that will be all right," said Aymes. There was a note of hesitation in his voice. In his mind's eye, he could picture the prospect of a prison cell while Jimmy Atherton and Aymes' deputy were enjoying a lakeside pizza in some Montreal café. "Look," he said, "send me an itinerary and some idea of the fee you will be paying and I'm sure we can negotiate a deal." The conversation ended to the mutual satisfaction of both parties. "I'm sorry about that," Aymes said to Saddler.

"Didn't sound as if you were," said the inspector.

"Sorry – but life must go on."

"You don't necessarily think that if you're Renee Hick."

"No. Apparently not," said Aymes. His two visitors left him now. When they had gone, he opened his desk drawer. There was some powder in a plastic container there – cocaine in fact. He fingered it. At times of stress in the office he had been known to snort some. This time, though, he shut the desk drawer firmly. It would have been too risky. What if Saddler had popped back – having forgotten something? Also, he thought, did he really need it? He walked to a filing cabinet on the other side of the office and brought out a bottle of scotch. He poured a large measure into a glass – also filed in the same cabinet. At least that's not illegal, he thought to himself.

• • ● • •

322

"I don't like it," said Mrs Saunders to her husband when Stan was safely out of earshot – having gone to the toilet.

"What?" said the professor.

"Well, you're treating him like a surrogate son. Paying for his college, giving him a meal after the funeral. Yet he's the one who Thomas said was responsible for the murder of Jennifer Welsh and Lesley Peters. We should be steering well clear of him – or giving the information we have on him to the police."

"We have no information on him and what we know Rivers knows – yet I don't see him hurrying to get Detective Chief Inspector Manners to arrest him. Did Thomas actually say in so many words; 'Stan Wightman murdered Jennifer Welsh and Lesley Peters'?"

"No," she admitted. "He intimated that he had."

"Well, there you are then. Innocent until proven guilty."

"You didn't exactly apply that principle to Rick Harper."

"That's easy. I thought he was guilty."

"And you don't think Stan Wightman is guilty?"

"No."

"So who do you think is guilty?"

Professor Saunders remained quiet for a moment. "It's not our business to find the killer," he said. "That's for the detectives. Anyway, Stan was the only one from Thomas' generation to come to the funeral today. We ought to thank him for that."

"Rick came, too."

"And I'm supposed to be thankful for that? A constant reminder that the only relationship Thomas had was a gay relationship. At least Stan is not gay."

"He's not a lot of things – like good company or interesting to talk to. I could go on. I really hate the way you decry your son because he once had a gay relationship. Move into the twenty-first century."

"Don't say anything," said Professor Saunders laying a restraining arm on her shoulder. "He's coming back."

"I'll just say this. Stan has a couple of parents. A decent couple. How do you think they'll feel if you start lauding yourself and acting all benevolent towards him? They probably think they're doing the best they can to bring him up."

"They'll welcome the interest. Well, the cash certainly. Now shut up and be nice to him."

Stan re-joined them at the table. The waitress took their lunch order. "Thanks for this," said Stan. "I haven't been out for a meal like this for ages."

"Well, you should get out more."

"You could have taken Thomas out a bit more," said the professor. "He'd have loved it. You didn't see much of each other after the murders, did you?"

"No."

"Why?" asked Mrs Saunders.

"I guess we were a bit embarrassed – about our drunken night in the allotments."

Professor Saunders looked at his wife sternly as if to communicate to her not to go down this path – but she was determined to pursue her goal. "He thought you'd done them. The murders, you know."

"Did he?" A look of astonishment came over Stan.

"That, I think, was what he was trying to tell me."

"Was he?"

"Darling," interjected the professor. "Not at the restaurant table."

"It's a fair question," said Stan.

"And one which you're not going to answer?"

"What good would an answer be? If I said 'no', would you believe me? And if I said 'yes'. you'd have to call the police. Besides, if you don't mind, I don't really want to get into that."

"So we should assume you did it?"

Stan rose to his feet. "This was a nice idea," he said. "Thank you, Professor Saunders. I'm afraid I don't like the direction the conversation is taking. I'd like to take my leave of you." He stopped on his way to the exit and turned round. "Have you ever thought that I may think Thomas was the murderer?"

"Do you?" asked the professor. It was his turn to look astonished. Mrs Saunders looked shocked, too.

"It is a legitimate conclusion to make. Look at the facts. The two of us wind ourselves up about Rick Harper with the help

324

of some vodka until the early hours of the morning. My mother confirms that I got home at two o'clock in the morning. You know Thomas didn't get home until four. Which one of us, I ask you, had the most opportunity and time to murder Jennifer Welsh and Lesley Peters?"

Professor Saunders nodded. "I can see that," he said, "so are you saying that Thomas killed them?"

"I'm not, no. I'll leave that to the police or whoever. I'm merely making sure you address the facts. Now, if you don't mind, this wasn't the conversation I wanted to have this lunchtime so I'm going." He turned to face the professor. "I would return the £400 to you but I have to admit the money will come in handy."

Mrs Saunders turned to her husband once he had gone. "What do you make of that?" she said.

"He's right. It logically makes more sense that Thomas did it."

"You sound as if you haven't just come to that conclusion."

"I've known all along that Thomas wanted to say something to us – that he was holding something back. I always thought it might be that he had killed the girls but I was too afraid to ask him outright and he, I think, was too frightened to tell me. That's why I went in hard with trying to persuade the police – the gullible Detective Chief Inspector Brett – that Rick Harper was the guilty party. It was why I complained so vociferously about police harassment of Thomas in the hope that they'd lay off."

"So what do we do now?"

"Forget this conversation took place and get on with our lives."

• • **•** • •

It was four o'clock when Inspector Saddler got a mobile call from the mechanic who was supposed to be repairing Renee Hick's car. "I've arranged for him to come in and collect it at five," he said. "He doesn't suspect there's anything wrong."

Saddler immediately rang Francesca who alerted Rivers. All three made their way down to the garage to await Renee's arrival. He came promptly at five o'clock. "Just come into the office and sign some papers," said the mechanic. The first face Renee saw on approaching the office was Rivers. "What are you doing here?" Renee asked as if genuinely unable to work out why the private detective might be there.

"I've come to witness your arrest."

"Oh no, you haven't," said Renee. He turned on his heels only to find the bulky form of Inspector Saddler blocking the door. Renee made a futile attempt to barge the sixteen-stone copper out of the way but only ended up getting handcuffed with Inspector Saddler then formally arresting him on suspicion of the attempted murder of Jimmy Atherton. "Let's take him down to the police station," said Saddler. "Do you want to accompany us, Mr Rivers?"

"No, I don't think so. You wouldn't allow me in on the formal interview and – besides – there's somebody in the local hospital I'd like to visit."

Saddler nodded and he and Francesca bundled Renee into a police car which Saddler had ordered to attend the garage.

"Now then," he said when they were ensconced in an interview room at Croydon police station. "What went wrong lad? I understand you used to be good friends with Jimmy Atherton."

"Still am."

"Have you talked to him since you tried to run him down? I think you'll find it's a different story now. Don't bother denying it, Renee. We have traces of Jimmy Atherton's blood on the bumper and the front right hand side."

"The car was stolen yesterday."

"And you didn't report it?"

"Didn't have time, man. I had a gig last night."

"And you miraculously had it returned to you within half an hour of the hit and run – because that was the time you took it into the garage to be repaired."

"They must have panicked after the accident and dumped it in the high street. That's where I found it."

"Which high street did you find it in?"

"Near my home in West Hampstead."

"So they stole it, drove it to Croydon where Jimmy was recording, accidentally knocked him down and then drove it back to West Hampstead where you immediately found it?"

"I want a lawyer."

"I'm not surprised. You need one."

"Why would I want to kill Jimmy? He was my main man when we were on the road not four years ago?"

"He was expected to give evidence to the police that you were involved in pushing drugs. Do you remember the night of June 4th four years ago?"

"That's a long time, man."

"It was a memorable night. Two young girls were murdered."

"And that night you were in a night club with Jimmy and his new manager Peter Aymes celebrating the new contract your 'main man' as you put it had been offered. There was a lot of coke about. Jimmy had the diet type." Saddler smiled at his own pun." You offered Peter Aymes something a bit more sinister."

"Who says so?"

"Jimmy, Peter Aymes."

"And the owner of the night club if we need him," said Francesca, "although he says he didn't see the transaction taking place on the premises, only afterwards by Peter Aymes next to his stretch limo."

"Typical. Making sure he's clean."

"So the cocaine was on the premises? You're admitting that?"

"I'm not admitting anything. You can do your best but I'm not saying anything more until my brief gets here."

"Well," said Saddler. "Rather than sit here and admire each other's ugly faces, I shall be returning you to a cell until your brief arrives. You'd better get used to it. I doubt you'll be spending any nights outside of a cell for some time to come."

"But I've got a gig tonight."

"They'll have to make do without their organist, I'm afraid." With that, he summoned a police constable to take Renee to a cell and then turned to Francesca. "I think us humble Croydon plods can cope from here on in," he said.

"I'm sure you can and I wouldn't mind going by the hospital, too." She found Rivers was still there when she arrived at Jimmy's bedside. "We haven't met," she said to Jimmy. "I'm Detective Chief Inspector Manners."

"Ah," said Jimmy. "Rivers has been singing your praises."

"And the whole world has been singing yours," she said pointing to the masses of cards and telegrams by the bedside.

"Do you know Graham Hands?" said Rivers, changing the subject.

"The disc jockey?"

"Yes, I was talking to him earlier in the investigation. I was talking to him at a time when I thought your visit to Jennifer's house may have been linked to the murder and I think we must have spoken about your involvement with Renee. I asked him who he thought had done the murder. He didn't enlighten me about that but the two of the three of you he'd like to see go down for something would be Renee and Peter Aymes. Looks like he's got his wish on that score."

"I appeared on his show once," said Jimmy. "He's always got a song to sum up every occasion. I wonder what he'd chose today?"

"I know what it wouldn't be."

"What?"

"'Walk Away Renee'. Renee can't anymore."

"Reminds me," said Rivers. "I should be in touch with him to see if he's heard anything from Duncan Hamilton."

"Why should he have?" Rivers explained how Hamilton's wife had said the previous evening that her husband had confessed to the murders in his sleep. "He's done a runner," he said. "We must find him."

"When are you going to call for police help in the investigation?" asked Francesca.

"Soon," said Rivers. "I wanted to present you with the killer on a plate. I'm not quite there yet. First there's something I need to test out with Professor Saint, who did the autopsy on the two girls So, if you'll excuse me?"

"Go to it. Nail the bastard."

"I will." Rivers sounded confident.

• • ● • •

The knock on the door sounded as it had been done by someone with a great deal of patience. No frantic staccato knocking just a couple of short raps. Therefore Diane Hamilton was surprised to find her husband standing outside upon opening the door.

"No, Duncan, go away," she said. "I don't want to talk to you."

"Just a few minutes."

"You can say what you've come to say on the doorstep – or I'm calling the police." Or Mr Rivers, she thought to herself. The police had not exactly been active in pursuing the murder enquiry.

"All right," he said. "Take back what you said about the murder confession. Until you do, I'm forced to stay on the run."

"I can't take it back. It's true."

"You know it isn't," he said.

"It's in your dreams. Or nightmares. You say things like 'is she dead?' or 'have I killed her?' Maybe you don't know what you're doing."

"How could I when I didn't do it?"

"I'm not going to argue with you, Duncan. Anyhow, even if you didn't kill the girls, you've acknowledged that you don't love me. Why would you want to come back and live with me, then?"

"I've said that Jennifer was the love of my life. I've said that I don't love you in the same way as I loved Jennifer. All of that is true but – over the past four years – we've built up a bond between each other. Sometimes relationships survive better if they weren't driven by a great passion to begin with."

"That's a great way to woo me back. Let me come back and live with you because I don't love you."

"You're just twisting my words. Can't we go back twenty-four hours to before I made that awful confession to Arthur Welsh?" he said. "You know, I was partly trying to make him feel happy that his daughter was loved by someone."

"Instead you sent him home thinking his daughter had been killed by someone who loved her. It's enough to put him off relationships for life."

Duncan moved a stride forwards towards the door. Diane instinctively edged backwards and closed the door a little. "You're not coming in here," she said.

"I'd like to see the kids."

"Great," said Diane. "The last thing they want – and I want – is for them to witness the kind of row that we had in front of them last night. Give up, Duncan. Just go."

"Let me think for a moment," said Duncan. "I've got no alibi for the night of the murder but I never should have let you get away with putting up that false alibi. It makes me look dishonest – but it also makes you look dishonest. Where were you on the night of the murders?"

"That's easy. With Alison Palmer."

"But I gather Alison is now saying that she only saw you in the morning – that the two of you didn't leave the dance together."

"She's only saying that because I asked her to."

"More fool you," said Duncan. "You've destroyed your own alibi."

"Well, I'll ask her to go back to her original alibi."

"She won't do that. There's a question of witness credibility. If she keeps on changing her alibi nobody will believe her." He noticed Diane becoming a little bit startled at this. "I see," he said. "You've already tried to get her to change her alibi and she's refused. Well, bully for her." He smiled. "You've cooked your own goose," he said. "I've a good mind to go to the police and tell them you made up this story of my confession to deflect attention from yourself."

Diane did not respond. "Have you quite finished?" she asked. "If so, would you go?"

"I'll go all right," he said. He turned to head off back to his car – but stopped to speak to her once again when halfway down the pathway. "I'll see you at the police station," he said.

Diane shut the door firmly and lay back against it to try and relieve her stress. She went back into the living room, saw that the twins were still fast asleep in their cots and thought for a minute. She had Rivers' mobile telephone number. Should she contact him about the visit from Duncan? If she didn't and Duncan carried out his threat to go to the police, she would look as if she was on the back foot. Best to carry on in the vein she had established the previous day – on the front foot. She rang Rivers. "Oh,

Mr Rivers," she said when he replied. "Diane Hamilton here. I've just had a visit from Duncan."

"Right. Is he still with you?"

"No, he's gone."

"You should have rung me while he was there and tried to keep him occupied until I got there."

"Sounds like a great strategy but it wasn't an option. Remember, I was dealing with a one-time murderer who's becoming more desperate by the minute."

"So where's he gone?"

"He was talking of handing himself in."

"To the police?"

"Or you. I don't know whether the police are looking for him yet."

"No, they're not."

"I'm not sure whether it was bravado."

"Bravado?"

"You know, I'm innocent so it'll all be sorted out if I just play it straight."

"In which case, he's changed his tune since last night."

"If I were a betting woman," Diane began, "I'd say he might want to talk it over with a friend before taking such a drastic step as going to the police."

"And the only friend he has is Graham Hands."

"He thinks Graham is his friend."

"I'll get over there as soon as I can," said Rivers. "I've got a little something to sort out first." He paused. "Thanks for calling me," he eventually said.

"Pleasure." So saying she lay back against the front door again and heaved a sigh of relief – believing she still held the ace cards over her husband.

• • • • •

The one thing Rivers had to do before going to see if he could catch Duncan Hamilton was to visit Professor Saint, the pathologist who had carried out the autopsies on Jennifer Welsh and Lesley Peters. He was in his office when Rivers called round.

"Something's puzzling me," he confessed to the professor. "On the night of the murder, two people – Stan Wightman and Thomas Saunders – were working themselves into a lather whipping up hatred of Rick Harper, the lad who had been invited back to Jennifer Welsh's home. They were getting drunk on vodka."

"I'm not here to do the detective work," said Saint.

"Just hear me out. I'm putting things into context with your timetable of events. I don't need a judgement from you as to who's guilty or who's innocent."

"Okay."

"They were in an allotment which was 20 to 30 minutes' walk away from Jennifer's house. They knew Rick had been invited round there, that's a given. Now I've set great store by the fact that – whereas Stan Wightman was clocked by his mother as coming home at 2am – Thomas Saunders didn't arrive home until 4am. That, I thought, gave Thomas more opportunity to carry out the murders."

"Not necessarily," said Professor Saint. "I put the time of death as between 12.30am and 2.30am."

"And Jimmy Atherton's evidence indicated that he saw the girls' dead bodies when he rolled up at their house between one and two in the morning. He, I am convinced, was telling the truth. So what does this mean?"

"You tell me."

"Stan Wightman believes he is protecting Thomas Saunders by being a bit equivocal and uncooperative about what happened that night. He believes, as I did, that Thomas' arrival back home at 4am gave him more scope to kill the girls. He believes Thomas was guilty on that basis – so I should go back to Stan and tell him Thomas couldn't possibly have killed the girl between 2am and 4am if Jimmy Atherton's evidence is correct. And Jimmy's evidence also fits in with your timetable."

"Right."

"It still doesn't absolve either of them," said Rivers, shaking his head. "They could have carried the murders out as a joint enterprise before 2am – or acted individually before 2am."

"Could I put another idea into the melting pot?"

"I wish you would."

"You say the pair of them were drunk?"

"Yes," said Rivers. "The one thing that they both have been frank about is that they discussed their hatred of Rick Harper while consuming more and more vodka. They wouldn't have admitted that if it wasn't true."

"I have to tell you, Mr Rivers, that I don't think these murders were the act of someone who was drunk. The meticulous way in which they eradicated all evidence that they had been there speaks to me of someone who has a very clear head about what they were doing. These two bumbling drunkards should not be your prime suspects."

"You'd have made a great detective," said Rivers.

"I am a great detective," said Saint, "but of a different kind to you."

"Very possibly," Rivers replied. "Right," he said, "I have work to do." Once back at his car, he gave Graham Hands a ring. "Is Duncan Hamilton with you?" he asked.

"No."

"I think you should expect him. He's just left his house – and I think he needs to mull things over with a friend." He paused. "That's you," he added.

"Okay," said the disc jockey.

"Can you hold on to him until I get there this time?"

"I'll try my best. By the way, congratulations."

"On what?" Rivers sounded surprised.

"On stitching up my two favourite people. I gather Peter Aymes and Renee Hick are facing charges over drugs offences."

"As a result of Renee Hick reacting very stupidly to the threat of being exposed as a drug dealer."

"Never mind. I told you they were the two that I would like to see punished at the end of the day as a result of your investigations."

"You did," Rivers said. "Look, I've got to be moving on now but I can be with you in a couple of hours if Duncan Hamilton turns up. Text me."

"Will do."

Rivers decided to drive to the allotments to tell Stan Wightman about his conversation with Professor Saint. Was there any day that he would not be able to find him at the allotments, he wondered, as he drew up and saw that the young man was pottering around planting some geraniums. He got out of his car and walked slowly over to where Stan Wightman was gardening.

"I want a word with you," said Rivers.

"And I don't want a word with you. I've said everything I have to say."

"You haven't said anything. You haven't denied you murdered the girls. You haven't admitted murdering the girls. You haven't explicitly said Thomas Saunders murdered the girls. You haven't cleared him of the murders. You think you're being very clever by muddying the waters. You think – in your heart of hearts – that Thomas is the murderer, which means you aren't, but by not coming out and saying what you feel you think we'll eventually throw our hands in the air and say it's too difficult to unravel. "

"You sound exasperated. You sound as if it is becoming too difficult to unravel for you."

"No," said Rivers firmly. "Let me ask you one thing. Do you think that – by staying out until 4am – Thomas is more likely to have been the culprit, more likely to have had time to commit the murders?"

"I have said that is a legitimate conclusion to make."

"Except that it isn't. The girls were dead by 2am at the latest – probably by 1am. I thought originally that if I found out who stayed out the longest I would be half way to finding the identity of the murderer. I was wrong."

"He could have stayed out in shock at what he had done."

"There you go again. Trying to make me think it was Thomas. Can't you get it into your thick skull that it wasn't? And, if it wasn't, you can tell me the truth about what you and he were doing?"

"You think insulting me is going to make you help you?"

"I don't want you to help me. I want you to help yourself. There's another reason why it couldn't be Thomas."

"What's that?"

"What kind of state was Thomas in that night?"

"We were both wound up. Wound up about Rick Harper."

"Why were you wound up?"

"We'd been drinking. You know that."

"Yes and the pathologist who examined the bodies said the murders couldn't have been committed by a drunk. The evidence was too meticulously cleared away. Someone had very carefully worked out how they should clear the place up so – putting two and two together – it's unlikely that it was Thomas who committed the murders."

"Killing somebody must be a sobering experience."

"Why are you so desperate to make us cling on to the thought that it must have been one of you two who committed the murders?"

Stan looked Rivers hard in the eye. "Guilt," he said. "I suppose it's guilt. Guilt at feeling the way we did about Rick. Guilt that we were probably the only people to harbour such feelings that night."

"It wasn't Rick who was killed, though. It was Jennifer and Lesley. Oh, yes, I know you had your issues with Lesley. But you didn't set out to wind yourself up with hatred of Lesley that night."

"I never hated Lesley. I was disappointed that she'd ditched me and – okay – I hadn't moved on but I didn't hate her."

"No – so that night…"

"I did go straight home after drinking here with Thomas. It was about two o'clock in the morning that I got home."

"So you were here with Thomas until after 1.30am?"

"Yes."

"So if you're telling me the truth now neither you nor Thomas could have killed Jennifer and Lesley?"

Stan thought for a moment. He sighed. "No, I suppose not," he said eventually.

"That should be a great relief to you."

"Yes," said Stan. "It's taking a bit of time to sink in – and I can't quite understand why you believe what I'm saying now."

"Because you've never lied Stan. Oh, you've equivocated and muddied the waters. You couldn't even say your friend Thomas had nothing to do with it because you thought that might be a lie."

Stan heaved a sigh of relief and sat down on a bench behind him. "You don't have to keep things hidden anymore," said Rivers. "If I were you, I'd contact Professor Saunders and tell him you now know his son had nothing to do with the murders. Tell him the fact Thomas was out until 4am is a red herring. He had an alibi – albeit a drunken one – until the latest time that the girls could have been killed. Take his money. Go to college. Start a new life for yourself." Stan looked at Rivers as if he didn't understand the concept. "All right," said Rivers, "just dig your weeds." He left Stan just gawping at him and made his way back to his car. As he did so, his mobile telephone went off. "Yes?" he said.

"It's Graham Hands here. Duncan Hamilton has arrived."

"Great. I'm free now. I'll be over in an hour. Will he still be there?"

"He says he wants to talk to you so I guess he will be."

"Good. See you in an hour." Immediately he had come off the Graham Hands' call, he dialled Francesca's number. "We're close to finding out who did it," he said. "It's down to two people. Could you come to…. " He got a scrap of paper out of his pocket on which he had written Graham Hands' address the previous day and read it out to Francesca… "in about a couple of hours? Hopefully I'll have sorted it all out by then. You should be able to make an arrest."

"I'll organise for a police car to join me there."

"Good. Can you arrange for another one to be on standby – with a social worker? There may be two arrests that you have to make."

"I'm intrigued."

"It's Duncan and Diane Hamilton."

"Diane?" said Francesca shocked.

"Yes, I haven't found out which one did it yet. Professor Saint made it clear my other suspects couldn't have done it."

"Oh, why?"

"The fact the murders could never have been committed by a drunk. The cleaning up at the scene was far too clinically organised. Then there's Jimmy Atherton's evidence that he saw the bodies when he was there between 1am and 2am. My other two suspects had only just stopped winding each other up in the allotment by then. Anyway, I'll see you at Graham Hands' place in a couple of hours."

"I'll bring Gary with me as well."

"Tell him to bring his own car. We might have to divert him to Diane's home."

• • ● • •

"Duncan, I'm surprised to see you," said Graham. "I thought you were on the run."

"I've decided I don't have to be," the former police trainee said as he eased himself into Graham's sofa. "I should stay and fight Diane's allegations. Otherwise, I'll just be running and running. I've thought it through. There's just as much evidence against her as there is against me. By withdrawing my alibi, she's withdrawn her own – and Alison Palmer says she only saw her at her home the following morning. She had a key. She could have let herself in after killing Jennifer. She had the motive, after all. She was getting rid of the woman I loved who stood between her and getting me – or so she thought." He shook his head. "Jennifer would never have come back to me."

"Do you believe she did it?"

"That's not the point. She could have. She didn't confess to me, if that's what you mean. But then I'm damned certain I didn't confess to her."

Graham poured them both a generous measure of whisky. He felt the spirit was the appropriate drink in the circumstances. He handed Duncan his drink. "So that's what you're going to tell the police."

"The police? I thought it was just Rivers coming round."

"You've confessed to a murder – or are alleged to have confessed to a murder. The police are bound to get involved. I wouldn't be surprised if Rivers hasn't arranged for them to come round tonight. Did you kill Jennifer and Lesley?"

"Oh, come off it, Graham, do you have to ask me that?"

"Yes. Did you kill Jennifer and Lesley?"

"No," he said loudly. "Satisfied?"

"And, of course, there's no evidence to the contrary – except in your dreams."

At that stage there was a ring at the doorbell. It was Rivers. "Have you still got him here?" he asked Graham.

"Yes. He's going on about how his wife had an opportunity to commit the murder."

"I thought he would. Would you excuse me for a moment?" He went out into the hallway and rang Francesca.

"He's claimed his wife could have done it," he said. "And she is claiming he has confessed to the murder.

"There's only one way to solve this – get them both down to the police station as soon as possible and sort it out. I'm only a few minutes away from Graham Hands' house. I'll come and arrest Duncan. I'll send Gary to Diane's – with a social worker to look after the kids."

"Great," said Rivers. "I'll make sure he's still here when you get here." He put his mobile phone back in his pocket and walked into the living room. "Duncan," he said, "I'm afraid you're both going to be arrested while the police sort out which one of you did it."

"Which one?"

"Yes. We've narrowed the suspects down to just two. In case you thought so, this is not a game where you can scatter confessions around like confetti. Police are already on their way to Diane's to arrest her. A social worker has been sent with them to make sure the children are okay."

"A social worker?"

"We can't just leave them on their own."

"But I'm sure we'll be able to find someone to take care of them."

"And until you do they'll be looked after by social services."

"But I could look after them."

"No, you couldn't. You're about to be taken to a police station and questioned over the murders, too."

Francesca strode over to Duncan at this point and read him his rights. "There's a police car outside," she said. "I'll take you to it."

CHAPTER ELEVEN

Diane Hamilton was greeted by Gary Clarke on the doorstep – accompanied by a woman and two police officers. "Yes?" she said in an irritated fashion.

"Diane Hamilton?"

"Yes," she said. "Can you make it snappy? I'm trying to put three children to bed."

"This will not be a snappy process," said Gary. "We are here to take you down to the police station to answer questions about the murders of Jennifer Welsh and Lesley Peters."

"Are you arresting me?"

"Yes – on suspicion of murder."

"You can't. I've got three kids to look after."

The woman came forwards and moved out of the shadows. "I'll make sure they're looked after," she said.

"And you are?"

"Brenda Howarth from Hertfordshire County Council social services department. We will look after them until a suitable placement can be found."

"Suitable placement? I am a suitable placement."

"Not while you are being questioned by the police for murder. Your husband, by the way, is also being taken in for questioning over the two murders so cannot look after them."

"We need to get you down to the police station," said Gary. He moved forward and held out a pair of handcuffs as he started reading Diane her rights.

"Handcuffs?" she said. "Surely that's not necessary?"

Gary looked at the two accompanying police officers. One of them shook his head. "Probably not," said Gary. "Will you accompany the police constables?"

"Could I not contact someone to look after the children?" She reached into a jacket pocket and brought out a mobile phone.

"All right," said Gary.

She called her mother's number but eventually gave up as she was presented with an answerphone. "If you make a list of who could look after them we'll contact them and they can come to the police station to collect them," said the woman from social services.

"Is that where they will be held?"

"Until a suitable place can be found. They won't be there all night. A place of safety has been arranged for them."

"A place of safety? This was a place of safety until fifteen minutes ago."

"Would you accompany the police officers?" said Gary. "Ms Howarth will take the children in her car."

At this juncture the oldest child cried out: "I want to be with Mummy," she said reaching out to hold Diane by the hand. Diane clung to her firmly. Ms Howarth motioned to Diane to let her go. "Making a scene won't make it any better," she said.

"I'm not the one making a scene," she said. She accompanied the two police officers to their car – passing Gary on the way. "It's my husband," she said. "He's the guilty party. He's the one you should be charging."

"All in good time," said Gary, "when we get to the bottom of it. On the other hand, if you are guilty, a quick confession could end this agony for your children. We could release him and the children to his care." The children were being bundled into Ms Howarth's van. She had come with a vehicle equipped to cater for three children. "I'll see you at the police station, Ms Howarth," said Gary. He watched as the social worker's car and the police car transporting Diane Hamilton left the scene. He immediately rang Francesca. "Well, I've arrested her," he said. "She's in the back of a police car being taken to the station. Rather upsetting scenes, ma'am." He returned to a form of address that Francesca had many times made it clear annoyed her.

"She had the motive and the opportunity," said Francesca. "As did her husband. Hopefully we won't be keeping them both under lock and key for more than one night and their children can be transferred to whichever of them is the innocent party."

"It occurs to me that we're using the children as pawns in an emotional game to put pressure on one of them to confess," said Gary.

"I think that's exactly what we're doing. At least it's the result of what we're doing even if we didn't necessarily intend it in the first place."

"I'm not sure I like it," said Gary.

"They shouldn't have accused each other of murder if they wanted to continue looking after the kids."

• • ● • •

Duncan Hamilton was sitting in a police interview room by himself when Francesca and a detective constable arrived to question him.

"You have, I believe, waived your right to have a solicitor present?" said Francesca after reminding him he had been arrested on suspicion of murder.

"Yes. I have nothing to hide."

Francesca nodded. "Your wife has alleged you confessed to the murders of Jennifer Welsh and Lesley Peters," she said.

"In my dreams, apparently," said Duncan. "I didn't know the police took dreams as evidence these days."

"You have no alibi for that night?"

"I was in the police section house. By myself. Without my wife present."

"Yet she saw fit to give you an alibi for that night – saying she was with you."

"She gave herself an alibi as well. I didn't know why suddenly – after four years – she came forward with this made up alibi about having slept with me that night. Now I do."

"You were upset – on the night of the dance – when you heard Jennifer had invited Rick Harper round to her house after the dance was over."

"Yes," said Duncan, "I'll admit to that but if that's all the evidence you've got it's a bit flimsy."

"I put it to you that you were a little bit more than upset. You decided to go round to Jennifer's house and have it out with her and tell her exactly what you thought of her."

"And Rick. Don't forget I would have expected him to be there, too and Tim and Lesley. They would have been innocent bystanders but I doubt if they would have just sat there watching me if I had gone berserk and started trying to kill Jennifer."

"In fact, Rick and Tim weren't there. You were confronted by Jennifer. You decided to tell her what you thought of her but things got a bit out of hand and you struck her. She hit her head while reeling from the force of the blow."

"Have you finished, chief inspector? I mean, I'm enjoying this fantasising just as much as you. But that's all it is. Pure fantasy."

"You're quite cool under pressure, aren't you?"

"I'm not under pressure."

"So cool that – after you had dealt with Jennifer – Lesley heard what was going on and ran out to help her. A fight ensued and you killed her, too. You then had the presence of mind to wipe out any trace of your presence. Finger prints, etcetera."

"Did I? How remarkably calm, as you so rightly put it, of me."

"But you're not calm now."

"Oh. Am I not?"

"Because you realise that – as a result of your counter accusation against your wife – she is being questioned just down the corridor from here and, as a result of both of you being questioned, your children have no-one to look after them and are currently being put in the care of social services. If you were to tell the truth and admit you killed the girls, they could be released into your wife's care and start enjoying life and feel safe again."

"The same goes for her, Inspector." She detected, though, that her words had got through to him. He seemed a little less sure of himself after the mention of his children's fate. She glanced at her watch. "I think we will be ending the interview there," she said. "We shall be keeping you in overnight. We need to check out any information that your wife comes up with and resume your interview tomorrow morning. I'm asking the detective constable here to arrange for you to be escorted to a cell."

With that she closed her folder of notes and left the room. She headed for the station entrance to get some fresh air. The desk sergeant interrupted her journey. "Mr Rivers told me to tell you he's gone. He remembered something he had to do. He said he'd be back when he's done it."

"Thank you," said Francesca wondering what it was that Rivers had remembered and how important it would be for the future of the case.

• • ● • •

Diane Hamilton scribbled some names and numbers down on a piece of paper and then handed it to Gary Clarke. "These are friends who could look after my kids," she said.

"Thank you," said Gary. He handed the piece of paper to the police officer sitting next to him. "I'll make sure Brenda Howarth gets them and starts trying to contact them." He turned to the officer. "She's in the canteen with the three children. Make sure she gets them." The officer nodded and left the room. "We'll wait until he returns before we start," he said. "You, I believe, have also waived your right to a solicitor."

"Also?"

"I believe your husband has, too."

The officer returned and resumed his seat next to Gary. "Right," said Gary, "we can start." He reminded her of her rights and then began the questioning. "What did you do on the night of the dance after it was over?"

"I went home with Alison Palmer and stayed the night with her. She will verify this."

"She has said she gave you your own key to her apartment and that she didn't actually see you until the morning – thereby leaving you unaccounted for until the following morning."

"She did amend her statement to that because I asked her to because I stupidly invented an alibi for my husband for the night – I thought he had carried out the murders."

"That was a false alibi?"

"Yes."

"Meaning the two of you were unaccounted for on the night of the murder?"

"Yes. Well, no. I was with Alison Palmer."

"Although she at present is not backing you up on that."

"No, well, she thought the police would cease to see her as a reliable witness if she kept changing her story."

"She was right," said Gary. "We also ceased to see you as a reliable witness. It tends to happen when people continually change their stories. Did anyone else see you leaving the dance?"

"It was four years ago. You're asking me to remember that far back?"

Gary fixed her with a stare. "Yes," he said. "It's the stuff of what murder investigations are made of. If they had, it could help confirm your story that you left with Alison Palmer."

"I'm sorry, I can't think of anyone."

Gary shuffled his papers. "What were your feelings towards Jennifer Welsh?"

"Feelings? I didn't have any strong feelings towards her."

"She was the former lover of the man you married. You felt no jealousy towards her?"

"Not then."

"Not then? What do you mean by that?"

"I shouldn't have said it."

"But you did."

"I overheard Duncan telling someone that Jennifer Welsh was the love of his life a couple of days ago. It was what caused me to cancel my alibi for him and – inadvertently – led to me being here tonight."

"Hell hath no more fury than a woman scorned."

"What do you mean by that?"

"I think you know. That, if anything, proves that you could be roused to great passions of jealousy by the mere mention of her name. He didn't dance with her on that night, then?"

"Not so far as I was aware."

"He didn't flirt with her?"

"No."

"He did nothing, then, to raise the kind of jealousies he so obviously rekindled a couple of nights ago?"

"No."

"Thank you, Mrs Hamilton, that will be all."

"Can I go now?"

"No, we have to await the feedback from the interview with your husband. We will want to resume this interview tomorrow morning."

"That means?"

"You will be kept in a police cell overnight. Yes."

"But my children?"

"Yes," said Gary. He turned to the officer sitting next to him. "Go and find out what's happened to them, would you?" The officer nodded and departed. "They'll be quite safe," he said, trying to reassure her.

"But traumatised and unsure what's happening to them," she said. "God, that's what comes of having such crap parents."

"I'm sorry?"

"We've got to be. Arguing over which one of us killed two innocent girls."

The officer returned at this juncture and whispered something to Gary. "I'm sorry, Mrs Hamilton, Ms Howarth couldn't contact any of the people on your list," said Gary. "Or at least she was able to contact one couple but they couldn't get here."

"Where are they, then?"

"They've been taken to a place of safety. I can't tell you where."

At this Diane burst into tears. "My babies, my babies," she repeated.

Gary maintained a respectful silence for a moment. "I'm sorry, I'm going to have to have you transferred to a cell," he said. "Would you take care of that?" he said to the officer who had been accompanying him. He ushered Diane out of the room. As they left, they could see another prisoner being escorted to a cell a couple of hundred yards ahead of them. It was Duncan.

"Duncan," shouted Diane. "For goodness sake, tell them the truth. You're playing with our children's emotions. Be a man. Tell the police you did it."

He turned round to face her and fixed her with a smile. "Maybe it's you who should tell the truth," he said before he was ushered on his way to a cell again.

• • • • •

"Come on, Jo, we've got urgent business to attend to," said Rivers as he arrived unannounced at the house Francesca and Jo shared.

"At this time of night?" Jo looked at his watch. It was 10 o'clock in the evening.

"Yes," said Rivers. "Duncan and Diane Hamilton have been taken into custody and are being questioned about the girls' murders. We've got to find out which one is responsible."

"Well, my money is on...."

"It doesn't matter who your money is on. We've got to prove it. I want to go round to Alison Palmer's flat and find out just exactly how much of an alibi she is prepared to offer Diane."

"We won't be able to get there until 11 o'clock."

"Then we'd better get our skates on."

Jo shook his head. "She won't respond to pressure," he said. "She's a together lady."

"Then she may suss the seriousness of the situation if the two of us arrive breathless at her door at eleven o'clock at night. Anyhow what's with this reluctance to work late at night? I've never noticed this before."

The two of them – by this stage – were back at Rivers' car and ready to start the journey to Alison's home. Jo responded to Rivers' question after thinking carefully about what to say. "I've been thinking," he began.

"Oh, God, no," said Rivers as he started up the engine. Jo looked at him in askance. "Sorry," said Rivers, "I was trying to be funny. And not succeeding."

"I've been thinking about returning to Calicos. I haven't talked to Francesca again about it but it seems an attractive proposition to me. Escaping from the racism here."

"And doing what? Oh, I guess you could go back to looking after boats but what would Francesca do?"

"I haven't really discussed it with her."

"Exactly. You don't know what she would do," said Rivers. "I do. She wouldn't go with you. She does far too valuable a job over here." Jo remained silent. "Anyhow, can I suggest we delay this discussion until later We are on a really crucial mission here. As I said, we need to know the true value of Alison's alibi for Diane.

Was she at Alison's place all night as per her original alibi or did she only see her in the morning – which means she has no alibi for the time of the killings."

They arrived at Alison's house at precisely 11 o'clock and pressed the intercom buzzer. There was no response. "She's not in," said Jo.

"Damn. She's probably at some fashion event."

"Then she could be snorting cocaine until four in the morning."

"We wait."

"Why is it crucial we speak to her tonight?"

"Because we only have the opportunity to put maximum pressure on either of the Hamiltons to confess tonight or tomorrow morning. They could be released due to lack of evidence tomorrow and then we'd be back to square one,"

"So we sit here all night?"

"If we have to," said Rivers. He glanced at the driveway. "But I don't think we will," he said. "Isn't that Alison Palmer making her way up from the garage?"

Jo focussed on where Rivers was pointing. "Yes," he said.

Alison Palmer had her keys in her hand as she approached her door. She caught sight of Jo – whom she recognised – first. "What are you doing here at this time of night?" she asked.

"It's urgent," said Jo. "Diane Hamilton has been arrested and is being questioned over the murders."

Rivers moved out of the shadows. "We need to clear some things up with you," he said.

"You'd better come in." Once inside, she took her fur coat off to reveal a sleek black dress with a diamond brooch pinned to it. "Partying," she said apologetically.

"I'm afraid the party's over for a while," said Rivers. "Now you said in your last alibi that you saw Diane Hamilton in the morning and that she had been staying with you that night – but you hadn't come home from the dance with her. You'd given her a key and she'd made her own way home."

"That's what I said, yes."

"Is it true?"

"It's what I said in my statement."

"Now is not the time for clever words. You must tell the truth."

"I did see her in the morning."

"And before that? In your original statement you said you'd gone home with her from the dance. How did you go home? By bus, walk or taxi?"

"By taxi." She bit her tongue. "Hey, wait a minute" she began.

"According to my belief, you have just said you went home with Diane in a taxi after the dance – thus confirming what you said in your original statement to the police."

"Wait a minute. I never meant…."

"You never meant to let slip you and Diane went home together by taxi because she asked you to withdraw your original statement to give Duncan an alibi? Is that what you're now saying?"

"You're twisting my words."

"No, I'm only trying to get at the truth. Lie now and you could send the wrong person away to jail for life."

"It is important you tell us the truth," emphasised Jo.

Alison looked at the pair of them. They weren't threatening, she thought to herself. They just looked determined. "You know, she wanted me to change back to my original statement so she could withdraw the alibi for Duncan. I refused to do it. I thought it made me less reliable as a witness."

"Don't worry about that," said Rivers. "Just tell me the truth."

Alison thought for a moment. "You are right. Diane and I did share a taxi home that night."

"What time did you get back?"

"Is there any chance Diane could have set you up and organised another taxi to take her over to Jennifer Welsh's place soon after your arrival at your home?"

"No."

"You're sure?"

"We sat up talking for an hour before we went to bed. She wanted to tell me how much she loved Duncan."

"And that would have taken you to – what time?"

"I went to bed soon after one o'clock. Same for Diane."

Rivers shook his head. "Never lie in a murder investigation," he said. "You never know what the consequences will be.

348

The consequences here are your change of alibi made it look possible that Diane could have committed the murders and then come on to you. It did not help her."

"I'm telling the truth now."

"I believe you. Now we have to make sure that Detective Chief Inspector Manners does. You'll have to come with us to the police station and tell her what you've told me."

"But won't I be in trouble for changing my statement?"

Rivers smiled. "I wish I could say yes," he said, "but the truth is you only changed your statement to us and Jo and I have no powers to punish you. In effect, you're now sticking with the original statement you gave to the police. So let's go."

"Could I change before we go to the police station?" Alison asked. "I feel I'm rather overdressed for it."

"There is no correct dress code for the police station," said Rivers. "Let's go."

● ● ● ● ●

Diane Hamilton was finding it difficult to get to sleep that night. She wasn't surprised at this but thought she might give up the unequal struggle. She banged on the door of the cell. The custody sergeant came down the corridor.

"What do you want?" he asked gruffly.

"Could I have a cup of tea? I can't sleep."

"This isn't a hotel. You'll get breakfast when breakfast is due."

"Thank you," she said sarcastically. The custody sergeant shuffled off down the corridor. "Duncan," she suddenly shouted. "Duncan, can you hear me?"

The custody sergeant turned round again. "Stop that shouting," he said. "You're not the only person in a cell. You'll wake the others."

"I want to wake Duncan," she said. "Duncan," she shouted. "Can you hear me? Duncan, you know I'm innocent. Tell them. Tell them. Then your children can have a parent back. No, your children can have their mother back. Think of them, Duncan. Just what do you suppose they're going through? All alone. Wondering what's happened to us. Tell the police I'm innocent." She started sobbing. "Do one decent thing for our family."

Duncan could hear her in his cell down the corridor but chose not to respond. She's rattled, he thought to himself. She'll confess. Even if it's just to return the children to one of their parents – she'll confess thus ruling out any idea that I did the murders.

"He's not listening," said the custody sergeant. "Please keep quiet so we can all get some rest."

• • ● • •

It was two o'clock in the morning when Rivers arrived at the police station with Jo and Alison Palmer in tow. "I don't know what you expect me to do," said the sergeant on the front desk. "They've all gone home long ago."

As he spoke, Francesca Manners walked through the front door of the station. Rivers had alerted her to the fact that he was bringing Alison Palmer in to make a statement. "That's what I expected to happen," he said triumphantly to the desk sergeant.

"Come into my office," said Francesca. "All of you."

"Alison wants to make a statement in view of the latest developments in the case," said Rivers.

"Good. We would have got round to coming to interview you," Francesca said to Alison.

"In her statement, she will say Diane Hamilton was with her all night on the night of the murders. They didn't go to bed until past one o'clock – by which time Jennifer and Lesley were probably dead. It confirms her original statement rather than the altered one she made to me at the request of Diane Hamilton."

"Right," said Francesca. "I'll take your statement."

"Could I have a word with you in private first?" Rivers asked.

"Yes."

They withdrew from the office and stood by the coffee machine in the outer office area. "This proves without a doubt that Diane Hamilton had nothing to do with the murders."

"So I should release her?"

Rivers smiled. "Not yet," he said. "The statement means that she's innocent and Duncan is guilty. It still leaves you with the problem of proving that. I still think we can exert some leverage on him. If we hold back on telling him we've got the statement and tell him we'll just have to continue to treat both of them as suspects – with the consequence that their children are kept away from them, I think he may crack. It's worth a try."

"Okay," said Francesca.

"One more thing," said Rivers. "Could I have a word with him before you interview him tomorrow morning?"

"Why?"

"To put the consequences of still maintaining his innocence to him. I feel like a sort of sportsman on a roll at the moment. I've managed to prove Stan Wightman and Thomas Saunders had nothing to do with it. I've managed to prove Diane Hamilton had nothing to do with it. I think I can persuade Duncan Hamilton that it's in his best interests to plead guilty."

"All right," said Francesca. "I'll take Alison's statement and hold on to it."

"Best to do that as I've dragged her in here at two o'clock in the morning. It would back me up in telling her how important I thought it was to act quickly."

"You can only see Duncan Hamilton if he agrees to see you. I can't force him to see you."

"I know."

• • ● • •

"He will see you," Francesca said to Rivers when he arrived back at the police station at nine o'clock the following morning. "We'll let you have an interview room with a police constable in attendance."

"No," said Rivers. "I need to see him on his own."

Francesca grimaced. The chief constable wouldn't like it. But, then, he probably wouldn't have liked the idea of Rivers being allowed to see Hamilton in the first place. These were special circumstances, she thought, and she was prepared to take responsibility for anything that went wrong. "Okay," she said finally, "but remember there's a buzzer under the desk on your side of the table which you can press to summon assistance if anything goes wrong."

"Fine," said Rivers. Good old police force, he thought. I'll bet there isn't one on the suspect's side of the table if he or she believes something has gone wrong.

"Don't be afraid to summon help," said Francesca, "and remember – I'll carry the can if anything goes wrong."

Rivers took up his seat in the interview room. Within minutes, Duncan Hamilton was brought in to join him. "I gather you're going to be on your own for this interview," said the constable who was accompanying Hamilton.

"Yes," said Rivers. The constable left the room.

"So what do you want?" asked Hamilton sullenly.

"I know you killed Jennifer Welsh and Lesley Peters."

"Oh, yes? So why haven't they charged me?"

"I know you killed Jennifer Welsh and Lesley Peters. Your wife knows you killed Jennifer Welsh and Lesley Peters. Soon a whole lot of other people are going to know you killed Jennifer Welsh and Lesley Peters."

"How? Are the police going to charge me?"

"The report of my investigation. I've nearly finished it. The conclusion I've come to is that you are the murderer."

"And you'll pass it on to the police. And we'll still be in the same situation – that the police won't know whether it was me or my wife who killed the girls."

"We'll get into that later. You're right. Of course, I will hand it over to the police. – but I'll hand it over to a lot of other people as well. The local newspaper for a start."

"They won't print it. The laws of libel will stop them."

"I don't know. They may risk it. Are you – a guilty man – going to sue?"

"If I have to."

"I'll give individual copies to all your acquaintances. Your employer, the people you work with, Rick Harper, all the folk around here that know you, Graham Hands – the friend you run to in an emergency, the Welsh family, the Peters. You'll be branded as a murderer. The consequences will be much more severe for you than they were for Rick Harper when he was thought of as prime suspect. You'll probably have to move, I shouldn't wonder. Diane won't have you back. Not after what you've done to her."

"How do you know I killed them?"

"Process of elimination. Working out where everybody was that night. You did kill them, didn't you?" There was silence from the other side of the table. "I'll take that as a yes, then. You see, I think Diane's original alibi holds. She went home with Alison Palmer and stayed there all night."

"That's not what she's currently saying."

"No," said Rivers, "and there's the dilemma. If we leave this situation in the muddy waters we are now in, you and Diane remain suspects. Your children are unlikely to be handed back to you. If one of you is cleared, they could be handed back immediately to the other. That person is not going to be you, though, is it?" Hamilton shrugged his shoulders. "Think of them without either parent," Rivers said. "You could make sure that doesn't happen. Clear Diane. Admit what you've done." Hamilton appeared to be a loss to know what to say. "In some ways," Rivers continued, "you're not a bad person. I would lay odds you never meant to kill Jennifer Welsh. Did she say something that caused you to lose your temper? Did she taunt you with Rick Harper? You lost it and lashed out and probably killed her accidentally. Then Lesley came in – and you lost it again. She lost her temper with you because of what you'd done to her friend, Jennifer. She dragged you away from Jennifer's body, I'll bet. You hit her and went on hitting her until she was dead, too. You never set out to be a murderer, I'll bet. And if you didn't, you must at times feel remorse for what you've done." Rivers detected a tear welling in Hamilton's eye. He was getting through to him. "Get it off your chest," he continued, "you'll feel better – I promise you. And you'll be bringing joy back into the lives of three small children who don't deserve to lose their mother."

"I'm sorry, Mr Rivers. " He appeared to be fighting back tears.

"Sorry? What for?"

"For killing Jennifer Welsh and Lesley Peters." With that, he broke down and started crying uncontrollably.

"Well done," said Rivers. He even put a hand on Hamilton's shoulder.

"I think you should now tell the police what you've told me." Hamilton, still weeping, nodded. "Right, I'll go and get Detective Chief Inspector Manners." He opened the door to the interview room. There was a police constable standing outside the door.

"Would you mind looking after Mr Hamilton while I fetch Detective Chief Inspector Manners?"

"No, sir."

Rivers wandered to Francesca's office, thinking to himself as he went: but I still don't know how you had the presence of mind to wipe away all trace of your having been there before you left the murder scene, you bastard.

He put those thoughts to the back of his mind as he entered Francesca's office. "He's confessed," he said. "He's ready to talk to you."

"Well done," said Francesca.

"I'm not sure I deserve that much praise. I did spin him a lie. Well, not so much a lie as an omission of the truth."

"So we can free Diane Hamilton?" asked Gary."

"Not yet," said Francesca. "We need to get Duncan's confession down on paper first just to be on the safe side. We want Duncan still to think the consequence of him not confessing is that his children remain in care."

• • ● • •

Duncan's head was still in his hands when the police constable charged with looking after him sat down opposite him. "Can I get you a drink of water?" he asked.

"No, let's just get this all over with," said Duncan. The constable nodded and was soon replaced by Francesca and Gary.

"I gather from Mr Rivers that you've got something to say to us," Francesca began.

"Yes," he said. "I would like to confess to the murders of Jennifer Welsh and Lesley Peters."

"Go on."

"On the night of the dance in June four years ago, I overheard a conversation between Jennifer Walsh and Rick Harper. She was inviting Rick and his friend, Tim, round to her house to join her and her friend Lesley. I had been in a relationship with Jennifer until just before that dance and I felt jealous. I decided I would go round and have it out with them. At that stage I had no thoughts of harming anyone – just telling them what I thought of them. I thought I would be outnumbered by four to one in the case of any aggravation. I arrived there to find Rick and Tim were not there. Jennifer was getting undressed to go to bed and had just a dressing gown on. I didn't see Lesley. I barged my way in and told Jennifer exactly what I thought of her for inviting Rick round. She started taunting me with Rick – how he was much better looking than me, he was more intelligent and how could I think there was any contest when it came to choosing between him and me. I felt provoked. I hit her hard on the chin and she fell back hitting her head on the chest of drawers in the bedroom. It knocked her out. I then – still in a rage – put my hands around her neck and strangled her. At this stage Lesley entered the room. She went over to Jennifer and I think she must have realised she was dead. She turned on me and started raining punches on me. I fought back hitting her repeatedly until she was unconscious. I then smothered her with a sheet from the bed. I suppose I wanted to make sure that she was no longer able to tell anyone what had happened. I tried to remove any trace of me having been in the house, cleaning areas which I had earlier touched. I realised this may have been superfluous as my DNA is not on file. However, due to my police training, I could foresee a situation where everybody who had been at the dance could have been asked to take a DNA test. I left the scene when I thought I had cleared up adequately."

"Thank you, Duncan. Is there anything else that you want to say?"

"No, I don't think so. Except that I'm extremely sorry for the pain I've caused people – and I hope my confession will clear my wife's name and allow for her to be reunited with our children.""

"Thank you. I'll bring the statement in for you to sign. We'll just get it printed up from the recording for you to sign."

"My children?"

Francesca was conscious of wanting to avoid giving an answer to this until after he had signed his confession. "Don't worry," she said. "I'm sure it will be okay." It only took about ten minutes for a copy of the statement to emerge ready for Duncan's signature."

Duncan duly signed it. "Now will you tell me about my children?" he pleaded.

"Oh, yes, they have been reunited with their mother. We have a statement from Alison Palmer which effectively clears her of any involvement in the crime."

"So it wasn't my confession that reunited them with their mother?"

"It will have helped," said Francesca soothingly.

"So Mr Rivers tricked me?"

"I'm afraid your conversation with Mr Rivers was an entirely private affair. He is a civilian. There is no record of it."

Duncan shook his head in disbelief. He kicked the table leg. Francesca summoned a police constable. "You will be returned to your cell now and brought before a magistrate's court this afternoon when we will ask for you to be remanded in custody."

• • ● • •

Rivers drove straight to his office from the police station that morning. As he was parking his car, he heard an item on the local radio news channel saying that a 24-year-old man had been arrested in connection with the murders of Jennifer Walsh and Lesley Peters and would be appearing in court that afternoon. He heaved a sigh of relief. In truth, he had found the interview with Duncan Hamilton draining that morning and – following on as it did from a late night – he would have preferred to have gone home for some kip. The adrenalin was buzzing, though, and he wanted to tell Jo what they had achieved as a result of their efforts during the night.

He walked into the office to be greeted by Debra. She clapped as he made his way past her reception station. "Well done," she said.

"Thanks," he said. By this time Jo had emerged from his office. He gave him a high five salute. "Not a bad night's work," he said.

"No," said Jo. "Sorry I was such a wet blanket at the start of proceedings."

"Don't worry about that," said Rivers. The telephone rang and Debra answered it. "It's for you," she said to Rivers. "A Mrs Peters?"

Rivers nodded. "Lesley's mum," he said.

"Mr Rivers?" said the woman on the other end of the line. "I want to thank you for not giving up on my Lesley. During the first police investigation, I got the feeling the officer concerned had forgotten that Lesley had also been murdered. You never lost sight of the fact that there had been two deaths that night. I heard on the radio that someone was appearing in court this afternoon – a 24-year-old, I believe?"

"Yes," said Rivers.

"It's not Stan Wightman, is it? He would be about that age."

"No, it's not Stan Wightman. It's a former lover of Jennifer Welsh's. Lesley went to Jennifer's rescue when she thought he was trying to kill her."

"That's just like my Lesley," she said. He thought he could hear sniffles on the other end of the line. "Thank you, Mr Rivers," she said again. "I feel I can start." Her voice was drowned out by sobs "to have some closure now." She sniffed again. "I take it all this was as a result of your investigation?"

"I don't think it would have happened without it," he said modestly.

"My husband and I were talking about having some kind of service in honour of Lesley now we know what's happened. Would you come to it?"

"I'd be honoured to, Mrs Peters."

"Good. Well, I'll let you know what we arrange."

"Thank you," he said. She put the receiver down and he handed his end back to Debra.

"Do I detect a moistening of the eyes?" asked Jo as Rivers shook his head to clear it.

"It's nice when you can do something that means something to people," he said wiping away a definite tear. "Treasure the moment. There are many times when we'll be doing something to annoy people. Remember, you played a part in bringing closure on this case to so many people." And let's hear no nonsense about going back to Calicos Island, he wanted to say but could not bring himself to. You're doing far too valuable a job here.

Jo did take up the ball on this issue. "I've been thinking again," he said tentatively.

"Dangerous," said Rivers.

"About Calicos."

"Yes?" said Rivers. "Weigh it up against what we achieved last night. Closure on a four-year murder hunt and the bringing forward of evidence that allowed three innocent little children to be reunited with their mother."

"True," said Jo, "but I was looking at it from another perspective."

"Yes?"

"Francesca's. She wouldn't want to give up a good job just to sun herself in the beach. And I reckon maintaining our relationship and retaining our love is worth more than being freed from putting up with a few insults from racists."

"Besides," said Rivers, "I seem to remember the white community in Calicos were not exactly pure as the driven snow when it came to racist behaviour."

"So I'm staying."

"Good," said Rivers, "you can always go to Calicos for a holiday some time. Maybe Nikki and I could come too."

• • ● • •

Duncan Hamilton pleaded not guilty when his case came to court. He claimed his confession had been coerced out of him as a result of Rivers' pretence that it was the only way that he could ensure his kids were taken out of care and reunited with one of their parents. He had, his barrister insisted, only confessed to free his children and – in actual fact – had not committed the murders. His legal team realised they could not cast suspicion on his wife again now the police had a statement from Alison Palmer saying that she and Diane had sat up chatting at her home until the early hours of the morning. Rivers was not called upon to give evidence – it was thought it would have been too risky and that he would have cited information from the written evidence of his report on the murders casting suspicion on Duncan. The prosecution referred to Diane's claim that he had confessed to the murders in his sleep as part of the evidence but declined to put her on the stand either. She was not present at the trial, having left her home and started a new life well away from the place and having reverted to her maiden name – which her children also took.

The jury took three hours and 45 minutes to deliver a guilty verdict. Rivers, who had been in court, joined Arthur Welsh, his wife and daughter and Rick Harper for a coffee after the trial was over. "Thank you, Mr Rivers, for bringing Jennifer's murderer to justice," said Arthur.

"I didn't," said Rivers. "You did."

"Me?" queried Arthur.

"Yes, if you hadn't gone round to visit him and he hadn't confessed that Jennifer was the love of his life and he had never loved Diane in the same way as her, she would never have withdrawn her alibi for him and we would have been no nearer nailing the killer."

Arthur reflected on what Rivers had said. "In a funny way, I suppose you're right," he said. "Look, would you come back with us to the house after we've finished our coffees? I feel we should raise a glass to Jennifer's memory."

Rick sat forward in his chair. "I think I've got another reason why we should raise a glass today," he said. He took Anne Welsh's hand in his. "We have decided to get married. We thought we couldn't tell you until all this was over. We could also celebrate the fact that nobody will be spitting at me in supermarkets."

"Maybe I should invite our next door neighbour round for the celebration, too?" said Arthur. "May I say how happy I am for the two of you?"

"I think it would be a step too far to invite her round – but maybe we should tell her to sharpen up her act as a nosey parker. If she had been a bit more vigilant that night she might have spotted Duncan Hamilton going into the house and Peter Aymes' stretch limo – and not just me."

"In a way," said Rivers wryly, "we should be raising a glass to her as well. You'd never have called me in, Rick, if she hadn't spat at you."

POSTSCRIPT

On the same day as Duncan Hamilton was jailed for life for the murders of Jennifer Welsh and Lesley Peters, Renee Hick and Peter Aymes appeared in court over drugs offence. Hick was jailed for seven years for trafficking drugs – while Peter Aymes received a six month suspended sentence for the possession of cocaine. The court had heard how Peter Aymes had helped the police investigation into the offence and – in effect – was responsible for the fact that police were able to charge Hick. Jimmy Atherton was in court – a fact that most of the following day's papers concentrated upon. Peter Aymes was referred to as "the pop idol's manager" while Renee Hick was "a fellow musician who had played in the band Atherton had fronted in his early days as a singer". Two months later Jimmy Atherton ditched his manager. There was no shortage of applicants to take over from Peter Aymes.

• • ● • •

PCs Ray Enderby and Luke Boatman appeared in court in London a week later charged with conspiracy to pervert the course of justice stemming from Jo's arrest. Ray Enderby was jailed for three years as the ringleader while Boatman was given a suspended sentence – the judge accepting he was under pressure from Enderby's bullying character. Both were dismissed from the force.

• • ● • •

Winston Samuel, whose evidence had freed Jo, received a request from the Metropolitan Police Commissioner to re-join the force – a request he declined.

• • ● • •

Rick Harper and Anne Welsh married six months after the trial of Duncan Hamilton was over. Rivers turned down a request from Rick to be an usher but did attend the wedding. He also attended the memorial service for Lesley Peters. His behind the scenes canvassing ensured a large turnout for the event. Lesley's mother never forgot the role he had played in bringing her daughter's killer to justice. Stan Wightman put in an appearance and managed not to grumble about anything. He was now on a college course with the expectation that – if he qualified – he could become the head gardener at a nursery. Professor Saunders had now volunteered to pay him £400 a year to help him through college – a fact which made Stan's mother and father slightly uncomfortable. They were overjoyed, though, when he started dating a fellow gardener he met on the course.

• • • • •

Jo never raised the question of going back to Calicos again.

Also by Richard Garner

RICHARD GARNER

BEST SERVED
COLD

A thriller of revenge and corruption

Journalist Roy Faulkner is the prime suspect in a murder inquiry
when Kate Williams, the fellow journalist he accompanied to
a night club appeared to disappear from the face of the earth.
Worse still, he finds the detective who is investigating the case
harbours a long-standing grudge against him dating back to
their teenage years in a rock band. As evidence piles up against
Roy, he is charged with the murder of Kate. Private investigator
Philip Rivers faces a battle against time to find out what really
happened before Roy is found guilty.

£8.99   ISBN: 978 1 910074 13 8

Also by Richard Garner

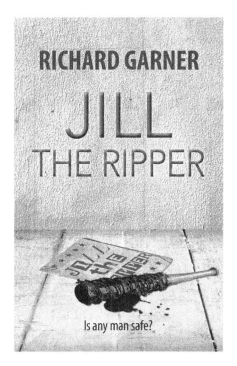

A small revolutionary feminist group publishes a leaflet urging revenge attacks against men for what its author perceives to be the glorification of Jack the Ripper. Soon afterwards, the bodies of two men are found mutilated on derelict waste ground. The police begin to investigate whether there is a connection between the members of the group and the murders, but find few leads.

Private investigator Philip Rivers is called in to help by the parents of their son, who they believe could be the killer's next victim, as he shares a flat with a member of the group. Rivers decides the best way to protect him is to find the killer

£8.99   ISBN: 978 1 910074 19 0

Also by Richard Garner

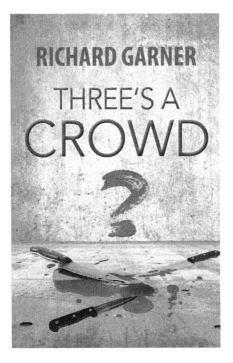

It was supposed to be a quiet night out in a restaurant for private detective Philip Rivers with his friend and colleague Jo – but he could not take his eyes off the alleyway opposite where a man became embroiled in three separate arguments with different women. It transpired that the man, Rob Corcoran was romantically linked with the three women. Three days later he was dead and Rivers was asked by his parents to investigate their son's murder.

Rivers has the help of his partner, Jo and Chief Inspector Manners with whom he had worked before. Can they find Rob's killer before more lives are lost?

£8.99   ISBN: 978 1 910074 26 8